Abbie Eaton lives in Derbyshire
fantasy author who writes stori
ons. When not writing or readin
found with her horses (who often resemble dragons
themselves!).

instagram.com/abbieeatonauthor

tiktok.com/@abbieeaton

DRAGONHART

ABBIE EATON

One More Chapter
a division of HarperCollins*Publishers* Ltd
1 London Bridge Street
London SE1 9GF
www.harpercollins.co.uk
HarperCollins*Publishers*
Macken House, 39/40 Mayor Street Upper,
Dublin 1, D01 C9W8
This paperback edition 2025

1

First published in Great Britain in ebook format
by HarperCollins*Publishers* 2025
Copyright © Abbie Eaton 2025
Map illustration © Laura Hall

Abbie Eaton asserts the moral right to be identified
as the author of this work

A catalogue record of this book is available from the British Library
ISBN: 978-0-00-871014-9

Printed and bound in the UK using 100% Renewable Electricity
by CPI Group (UK) Ltd

To those chasing dreams that feel out of reach, don't you dare give up.
You can do anything.
And to Harry, who always encourages me to chase mine.

NORTHERN BORDER

IRELLIAD

Larkira

Castle Grey

Halos' shop

KINGDOM
of
HADALYN

Dragonhart

CANUS RI

CHAPTER 1

Beneath Castle Grey, there are dragons in a slumber so deep, not even the gods can wake them.

This is what Arla had been told when she was a little girl. But now, at eighteen, she was vicious, and angry, and did not believe in the dragons that had once served the gods.

Did she even believe in the gods anymore? If they were real, they hadn't deemed her worthy of saving.

'The king wishes to see you,' a familiar, tired voice echoed from the stone arch of the doorway, barely audible over the sound of swords clashing. Arla bit her lip against the noise, grateful that she had managed to bully a soldier into practising with her. Not that she could call this practice. If she wanted a challenge, she should have asked one of the King's Guard to engage in her deadly routine rather than a soldier used to guarding doorways.

'Tell the king I'm busy,' Arla ground out between her teeth, frustrated with the lack of skill her partner offered. Or was it lack of food that had put her in this dreadful mood? The smell of roasted pheasant had been teasing her from the kitchens already, and her stomach gnawed at her with the ferocity of a mountain cat.

'Now, Arla.'

'For the gods' *sake*!' she snapped, flexing her fingers as her blade struck the wooden plinth no less than a hair's width from the advisor's face.

As Arla stalked towards him to retrieve her blade, he drawled, 'You don't scare me, Lady Reinhart.'

'I am no lady, Perry,' she said, rolling her shoulders against the stiffness that often came with wielding a blade.

'Quite. I don't know many ladies who would run a man through with a sword just because he threatened to steal her horse.'

Perry's eyes glittered with unreleased laughter and Arla had to hide her smirk as she crossed the room towards him.

'He was a thief and a pig. He deserved it.' She scowled, brushing against the king's advisor, and beginning the long walk from the training hall to the throne room. She hated the long corridors and their sinister whispers; hated that no one save her ever seemed to think there was something odd about Castle Grey, and why she always felt *watched* within its walls.

The palace was quiet today. Arla was used to seeing a hundred maids scurrying in the shadows and disappearing into alcoves concealing hidden doors and servants' corridors. This morning, however, there was only silence and deserted passageways. Not even the soldiers, usually standing so solidly at regular intervals, were at their posts. Something was afoot, and the thought sent a ripple of anticipation through Arla. She curled her palm around the pommel of the blade sheathed at her hip.

She had wanted to practise today because for the last fortnight the king had had her running all sorts of errands – from disposing of common thieves to delivering a letter across town that could have been sent by messenger rather than bothering *her* with the task. But her irritation eased as she took in the silver-framed windows and the thick, red yarn of the carpet on which her boots were certainly too dirty to be walking.

Castle Grey did not have to work hard to live up to its name. The whole place was just that – grey. Even the silver adorning everything in sight went unpolished, only adding to the miserable dullness of it all. But its occasional beauty was not lost on Arla, especially now it was so quiet. Sunlight bled through the windows and, unlike the silver, glass was polished until it sparkled so that the hallways were cast in a soft light that brought out the red of the carpet – the one vein of colour that ran through the palace – and even softened the sharp blonde of Arla's curls into delicate golden waves.

It needs cutting, she thought as her feet arrived in front of the huge oak doors concealing the throne room from the rest of the palace.

It was true, she had not been to see Halos in months, her schedule not allowing a free afternoon. Her friend would laugh at her and the hours it would take to neaten Arla's appearance, but the young woman would still refuse the extra coin Arla offered her. Arla didn't know why Halos didn't take the money; the girl was only in her twenties, and she had twins that crawled about in her skirts as she tended to the patrons of her ragged shop on the main street. Perhaps it paid to be kind to those who had nothing but still tried their best? Perhaps there was something that united the two women who had lost families in the battle of Grey Hill all those years ago?

The sharp rap of Perry's knuckles on the wooden doors drew Arla's mind from war-ravaged families and the memory of mourning bells.

'Enter.'

Arla rolled her eyes. She had grown accustomed to the king's thunderous voice in the last nine years and it did not scare her anymore. She was the King's Assassin, there wasn't much at all that scared her.

Breathing deeply – if only to settle the agitation that came from being summoned so unexpectedly – Arla rolled her shoulders back and tossed her hair over her shoulder since it had mostly unravelled from the braid into which she had woven it into this morning. Then she strode through the doors with a swagger called up from deep within, something she had had to coax and nurture into life in order to make it through training and selection into the King's Guard. Whatever task Cyrus had for her today, she hoped it would include a sword.

'I believe I signed a contract entitling me to one day a week to do with as I wish. I'm now owed two,' Arla called across the hall to the man sitting upon a silver throne. The king arched a grey brow at his assassin, a smirk teasing the corner of his mouth.

'I believe I signed a contract with a fifteen-year-old. You weren't actually of legal age to enter into such an agreement,' he replied, eyes tracking the blonde-haired whirlwind as she marched across the room before bowing carelessly in front of him.

'Then it seems we were both stupid,' Arla mused. 'Your Majesty.'

King Cyrus of Hadalyn curled his lips in amusement. Arla knew he had grown used to her behaviour – mainly her continual disregard of traditional modes of respect for those in authority. The King's Assassin had to be somebody who was quick on their feet as well as with their mind, and Arla had proven she was both before she turned sixteen.

'Well, Reinhart, I see you're ready to play,' Cyrus said, rising from his seat and beginning the descent from the dais towards Arla. He was a large man, with a round, ruddy face and hair that was greying and thin. Arla often wondered how he held any influence at all, given his appearance, but he did, and he knew it. When Kastonia had sent their best soldiers to storm Castle Grey, Cyrus had crushed that army, and the armies that came after. None of the other kingdoms had dared to question his rule in the aftermath.

Not that any other kingdom than Kastonia could reach them.

Hadalyn was a sprawling kingdom and a shared border stretched between it and Kastonia. Beyond Kastonia was an expansive mountain range that no one had ever been successful in exploring, its harsh winters and deadly terrain too difficult to fathom conquering.

Vast ocean surrounded Kastonia and Hadalyn, cutting them off from the neighbouring continent of six kingdoms. Hadalyn was well-respected and held a level of power and influence that Arla had always struggled to understand. Perhaps it was Cyrus's willingness to cut down any who attempted to invade, or perhaps his ability to negotiate favourable treaties with the continental kingdoms, such as importing silk from Gravidum or exporting grain to Malarye. Had they lived in the ancient times when it was rumoured there had only been one king to rule the world, Cyrus would have fit the role perfectly. And he knew it.

Consequently, Hadalyn's relationship with the continent

remained cordial. No one expected the continental kingdoms would come to Hadalyn's aid should Kastonia ever invade again, but they were even less likely to help Kastonia, so the region maintained a stable détente.

'I believe Perry referred to me as *Lady* Reinhart this morning,' Arla chirped, spinning suddenly when another voice scoffed and immediately found its way under her skin. 'Why is *he* here?' she growled, her muscles tensing as she took in Hark Stappen, Ambassador for Kastonia and general pain in her ass. Something was indeed happening if Cyrus had asked Hark to be present, too. She curled her fingers tightly in her fists.

Hark and Arla had despised each other from the moment Hark had come to court two years before – in good faith from the King of Kastonia – and an immediate mutual dislike had formed, from the roots of blood that ran different colours, and kingdoms that did not see eye to eye. Arla didn't know who she liked least, Hark, or Hadalyn's own ambassador, Orson, who they had sent to reside in Larkire Palace with the Kastonian royals. Orson was cruel, and had a personal hatred for Arla after she had become King's Assassin when he had been trained to just as high a standard. Hark was just an arrogant prick.

'Always a pleasure, *Lady* Reinhart,' Hark cooed, bowing exaggeratedly.

Arla could see it for the insult it was, disguised in courteous politeness though it may have been. She marched heavily across the carpeted floor, letting the thick fibres absorb her malice and anger for the dark-haired, pretty-faced diplomat.

'I did not give you permission to speak to me,' she snapped, ignoring the cloud of whisky and leather that attached itself to him.

'I don't need permission to speak to you. Despite what you

might think, you are a solider, not a courtier, and you hold no influence at court.'

Her hand was around the pommel of her blade before Hark had finished speaking.

'Arla!' the king growled. 'I did not summon you both here to fight like dogs, though I am beginning to think dogs might be more useful to me than you are.'

Backing away from the Kastonian, Arla took a seat on the stone steps of the dais, her eyes following the king as he paced the length of the hall. Despite his untidy appearance and the harsh way he often spoke to her, Arla liked Cyrus. He was never unfair to his staff or soldiers, and he'd had the good grace to let a gangly, nine-year-old orphan into his barracks and let her watch his private guard train. Arla smiled at the fond memory. She sometimes wondered what would have happened to her if she had been left starving and alone after the war. Those two months had been the hardest of her life, and it had seemed like a gift from the gods when Cyrus had seen her fall beneath the legs of his horse and brought her to his palace. Even at nine years old she'd been aware of the whispers, of the distaste amongst palace staff that the king had brought home an orphan. How strange and unbecoming it was. She wondered if Cyrus had known then that he would eventually select her to be his personal assassin. Would he have felt differently if he had known the only reason she had been beneath his horse that day in the marketplace was because she was trying to steal the gold buckles from his horse's girth? The King did not employ thieves, but even he couldn't deny that her talents made her perfect for the role.

'Whilst I have my reservations about directing the two of you to work together—'

'Absolutely not,' Arla interjected.

'Arla! You will be silent!' The king glowered at her, and she flopped back onto the steps from which she had so quickly risen.

'Whilst I have my reservations about sending the pair of you on this mission,' Cyrus continued, 'the need for discretion is more important than your distaste for one another.' Arla's interest pricked at the king's words. It was rare he ever requested discretion, and he had *never* set her to work with Hark. He had never asked Hark to work for him at all.

'Shipments of iron are going missing in the north before they can reach Kastonia. I would not normally involve our kingdom in another's affairs, but King Elrod of Kastonia asked for our help, Hark, and it is in everyone's interest to root out troublemakers before it starts to affect us, too.' Cyrus turned to face the pair of them, his pale grey eyes fixed on Arla. Hark did not react, and Arla had no doubt the request for aid had been passed through Hark before it was even whispered about within the halls of Castle Grey. The iron trade was not Hadalyn's usual focus, though Arla supposed Cyrus's interest lay in its role in forging weapons. He would not want to be without it, and he certainly would not want Kastonia to gain an advantage that could tip the balance of a future invasion.

Because if Kastonia were hoarding iron, too...

No. Everything was fine. Hadalyn's army was growing and it made sense that Kastonia's must be, too. It was perfectly reasonable for them to be buying in shipments of the metal.

'I don't need *him*,' Arla said coldly. 'I'm perfectly capable of tracing missing supplies on my own.' Arla rose from the steps again. It was true that she had been north many times, with instructions to kill. Discovering the whereabouts of missing cargo would be a breeze in comparison.

'That may be, but it is not only our kingdom that suffers, Arla; it is Kastonia, too, and Hark will be joining you. This is non-negotiable.' There was no room for argument in the king's voice, but Arla could feel anger burning a hole straight through her.

'Since when have we cared about *them?*' she growled, throwing her arms in Hark's direction. He looked back at her with a sort of amusement that called to the anger simmering in Arla's blood. 'They stormed this very castle to find dragons that *do not exist,* and then waged war on our city because they didn't like what they found!'

A muscle in Hark's jaw feathered, and Arla enjoyed the feeling of satisfaction that came from tapping a nerve.

'We are well rehearsed in the actions of nine years ago, Reinhart.' Cyrus's eyes darkened to the colour of steel. Arla had been toeing the line of disrespect too long not to know when she found herself on the wrong side of it, and that it would not be tolerated.

'When do we leave?' she asked, spine straightening as her mask of obedience slid into place once more. She was the King's Assassin, and if she had learnt one thing in nine years of service, it was when to back off.

'In the morning,' Cyrus stated, his tone almost ... far away, as though the imminent departure of both his assassin and the ambassador was the least of his concerns. Arla didn't care much for what had preoccupied his mind, and with a sigh of resignation, made her way back towards the oak doors through which she had waltzed only moments ago.

The king's voice halted Arla before her shoulders could pass through the doorway.

'I am trusting you, assassin.' A slimy, oily thing turned in Arla's stomach at the statement. It was rare Cyrus ever spoke to her with anything other than warm fondness. It felt wrong to hear him demote her to her role. 'Find out who is disrupting the supply chain, dispose of them, and leave Hark alive.'

A wry smile twisted its way across Arla's lips, and she was glad that her back was to the king. He knew her too well – he'd obviously felt the need to give her a *direct* order not to kill Hark – and he knew the violent, angry streak that raged in her, like a caged wolf who was already plotting ways to dispose of the Kastonian ambassador.

'Of course, Your Majesty,' she said sweetly without turning around. She palmed the pommel of her blade and swept out of the chamber.

She headed towards town. It would be cold in the north, and it had been a long few months since she had left Hadalyn. She wanted to look her best.

She wanted to visit Halos.

CHAPTER 2

Hadalyn was a busy kingdom, and growing steadily by the day as more travellers and refugees abandoned poorer places to seek some sort of security. Not that Hadalyn offered much of a reprieve from the poverty that plagued Kastonia and the continental kingdoms – especially as it grew larger – but its reputation gave people hope. The people still believed that dragons slept beneath Castle Grey and that, one day, they would ask the gods to stop punishing the world and bless them with food, and goods, and *easy* lives.

Arla knew it was stupid. The gods didn't exist. How could they when the world was going to shit?

And the dragons that had once served them? They were just children's stories to scare them into obedience.

She had heard the tales – everyone had. How the dragons had gone to sleep almost a century ago. How the gods had stopped being so prominent, too. And then there were the stories of magic-wielders and how not long after the dragons went to sleep, those with magic in their blood became fewer and fewer until there were none left. Something had changed then, apparently. Where magic had once been openly accepted and seen as a blessing, it was condemned. People had been killed for what their blood represented. Killed for the potential power they could wield over kings and queens.

But Arla had never once seen even a whisper of magic, and the gods had never made themselves known to her, either.

It was nonsense. All of it.

The streets of Hadalyn were busy that morning, and Arla scoffed at a ragged old lady, her back stooped with age, wearing a gold brooch that was probably worth more than the entire wooden shack out of which she had shuffled. It wasn't the gold that bothered her, though, it was the symbol forged from the metal: a flame encased in a heart. A dragonhart. It seemed the old religions were as alive as ever.

Too many people were in the streets – too many since the last time Arla had walked them in the daylight. She knew these streets as if their secrets were inked on her skin; had spent hours lurking in the shadows and dragging unsuspecting thieves into the darkness. It was ironic, really, that she would be the one to rid Hadalyn of thieves, when she had spent the first few years in the king's service stealing from folk just to be able to afford the silk for the dresses she would wear to court. Though Arla was paid handsomely now as King's Assassin, she was no stranger to the ache of a hungry stomach or the bite of cold hands. The money had only begun to suit her well once she had made it into the King's Guard, and now as his assassin, it served her very well indeed.

Arla knew the ladies in the royal court were often jealous of the new silk dresses she would be seen in each week, or the hordes of books that would be delivered in her name, under the pretence they were for the royal library. But she didn't care. She had killed and clawed and fought her way to where she was now. If she wanted lavender oil in her bath after a day of swinging blades and firing arrows, she deserved it. Just as she deserved to have her hair cut and her nails shaped by Halos.

Arla smiled as she reached her friend's door, ignoring the urge to pocket the leather pouch dangling temptingly from a man's belt as he passed by her a little too close. It would be his own fault, really; he had made it easy for her. But Arla knew how desperate people were for money, and even she could not steal from the citizens of Hadalyn, not anymore, and no matter how stupid they were.

Halos had placed a bell above the door since Arla's last visit, and she wondered if that meant there had been trouble with thieves. The thought left a bitter taste in her mouth.

The bell had done its job, though, and as a teetering toddler crossed the floor of the busy shop at a speed that was unnatural for such little legs, Arla's eyes met Halos's amber ones across the heads of two old ladies.

'Arla Reinhart.' Halos grinned, scooping the child, Neb, up in her arms as she made her way towards her friend.

'It has been a while, hasn't it?' Arla laughed, stroking the hair of Neb's twin, Ettie, who had materialised at her feet. Neb and Ettie had grown since Arla had last seen them, and she regretted that she had not visited them in so long that she was shocked they recognised her.

'Look at you,' Halos fussed, with one hand picking up untamed coils of hair that had grown long enough to now end below Arla's breasts. 'Arla, for the gods' sake, you should come by more often.'

Arla chuckled, squeezing Ettie's hand in hers as the little girl pulled her towards the back of the shop behind her mother. Halos placed Neb on the floor and dragged a cushioned chair out, gesturing for Arla to sit. The chair looked new and barely used, and it eased something in Arla's heart to know that Halos could still afford new furniture for her shop despite having to raise the twins by herself.

'I try, but you know how things are. The king's had me running halfway across Hadalyn every evening—'

'Arla,' Halos interrupted, handing the twins a carved wooden horse to keep them occupied. 'I don't pretend to understand what it is that keeps you in the king's employment, but I hope you realise it's not always their fault – the people he sends you after, I mean.'

Arla sighed, running a hand through her tangled hair. *This* was why she hadn't made time to come and see Halos. Her friend didn't understand. She made Arla look at herself the way other people looked at her. Funny, that for an assassin whose identity should have been unknown even to those closest to her, most people in Hadalyn could recognise her if they came face to face. It was something she knew bothered Cyrus, but she didn't care. She enjoyed the look of panic that flashed across the faces of her victims when they realised who had come for them. She hated that she enjoyed the job at all.

'I have nowhere else to go, Hal. The king offered me a chance and I took it.'

'*Didn't*,' Halos said, her voice light and her eyes averted as she prepared the jasmine-scented soap for Arla's hair. 'You *didn't* have anywhere else to go. You do now, Arla. The money you earn would buy you one of those lovely cottages on Grey Hill and you could get a job that doesn't involve killing people.'

Arla sighed. How quickly they had fallen back into this old routine: Halos too good to harm anyone, and Arla too wicked to care.

'I'm good at my job,' Arla muttered, tipping her head back into the basin so Halos could wash the dirt and gods knew what else from her curls.

'It's not a good thing, Arla. People die at your hand.'

'I know.' It was barely a whisper against the argument with which she couldn't help but agree. Arla wished she didn't enjoy hurting people or handing out justice in the name of the crown, but it gave her someone to blame. And when the Kastonians were not readily available, she would take her parents' deaths out on the citizens of Hadalyn. What sort of a person did that make her?

'Horse,' a tiny voice said beside her, pressing the wooden carving into Arla's empty palm. Ettie was a beautiful child, with her mother's amber eyes and dark hair and skin, and an innocence that Arla wished would stay safe within the toddler forever. Her brother wasn't any different; two children born into a world that was crumbling, into a world where they would have to fight to earn a place at the table. All of it was wrong.

'I take it this isn't a social visit. You're off out again, I presume?' Halos asked, wringing the water from Arla's now clean hair.

'I wish it was a social. Cyrus has stuck me with that Kastonian prick from the palace. We're off to the northern border in the morning,' Arla said, forcing the words through her teeth and squeezing the wooden horse tighter as she thought of Hark and his infuriatingly handsome face. In another life, if he hadn't been born with Kastonian blood, she might have learned to like him.

'Oh, Arla, don't pretend to be so miserable. I certainly wouldn't mind being huddled next to a campfire with Hark Stappen.' Halos laughed, scrunching Arla's damp curls before taking her left hand and inspecting her broken nails.

'He's arrogant, and rude, and seems to think that being an ambassador makes him not only more important than me, but untouchable.'

'I'd be careful, if I were you. I've heard he's just as good as you with a sword, if not better, and I wager he'll be a darn sight better at other things than some of the other men you've taken to your bed. The last one wasn't even a noble, I heard!' Halos teased, and Arla couldn't help the snort of laughter that escaped her.

Her friend laughed, too. 'Let's have dinner tonight. It's been so long since I saw you last, and if you're heading out again...'

An ache grew in Arla's chest. She was a terrible friend. When was the last time she had made time to swim with Halos in the Canus River that wound past her old home and by the palace? They had spent hours and hours together in the clear, deep water when they were growing up, learning to swim and dive and forgetting about the world if only for a little while.

Arla swallowed. 'Dinner sounds good.'

'Perfect. Early though, because the twins have to be asleep before the sun goes down or there'll be hell to pay tomorrow,' Halos said, holding Arla's hand flat as she moved to press a blade against the callouses Arla had spent years hardening. Arla snatched her hand back before the blade could bite into the rough ovals.

'I need them,' she stated, leaving no room for argument. 'Besides, if Hark's as good with a blade as you say, I'll have to show him just how useless he is against me, won't I? And I can't do that if I'm crying over new blisters.'

Halos smiled, instead filing the edges of Arla's nails into perfect almonds. 'You really are something, Arla. I presume you'll have a lovely new dress to go along with your sword?'

'Madam Touse is packing my satchel as we speak, though now that I'm being sent north with Stappen, I doubt I'll have the chance to wear it,' Arla said, grinning at the thought of new silk to whisper at her ankles. She couldn't wait to peel the fighting leathers from her skin the moment she returned to the palace. The trousers really did nothing to show off her legs. She immediately regretted the thought when a flicker of emotion passed through Halos's eyes. Halos would never have silk dresses, or leatherbound books to read. Her twins would never have brand-new boots or 'proper' toys. Arla hated the injustice of it, but she knew her friend would never accept the coins or the gifts she wanted to give her. Perhaps it made her a better person than Arla was. Halos had not forgotten her roots, while Arla was flourishing on top of a mountain of death, thievery, and hate.

'Well, at least your hair will look pretty for Hark.'

'I'd rather die.' Arla chuckled, placing two silver coins on the chair for Halos – too much for cutting her hair and filing her nails – and tucked an extra coin into Neb's hand as she bent to kiss each twin on the head. A gift, for a being a gentle person in a wretched world; a gift Halos would never have accepted if Arla had not hidden it in the fist of a little boy.

〜

Stepping out into the heaving street, Arla shaded her eyes from the brightness of the sun and immediately had to jump back out of the way of a trap drawn by a pair of horses with gleaming bay coats. Madam Touse's shop was a few doors down on the opposite side of the street from Halos's shop, and though Arla desperately wished to run the silk of her new dresses through her manicured fingers, there was something she needed to take care of first.

It didn't take long to hoist herself up onto the roof of a brothel, the street shadowy and perfect to conceal an assassin. Arla hissed as her hand dipped into something slimy and wet in the curve of the drainpipe and cursed the gods that she had been stupid enough to leave this little task until *after* she had been to visit Halos.

Soon enough, the vagrant arrived, his grunts filling the alley before Arla could spot him. Brik was a nasty piece of work, and Arla had been in plenty of altercations with the thief. It seemed, however, that Brik was not listening to her previous warnings; Arla had seen him steal a rattle from the fist of a baby only hours ago.

She wouldn't let him take from children.

Settling her head into that calm, still place that was becoming more a comfort than a job, Arla swung herself over the ledge of the roof and landed soundlessly in front of the thief.

'Shitting gods, woman!' Brik yelped, stepping backwards before Arla's hand could twist round the collar of the threadbare rag he wore.

'Oh dear, did I frighten you?' Arla sneered, grabbing the man by the front of his shirt and dragging him into a thin alley between the brothel and a printing shop. 'I won't tell you again, Brik. If I catch you stealing from children, I'll cut off your hands.

Failing that, I'll cut your throat,' she said, shoving him away from her and trying not to retch at the stench rolling off him.

Life on the streets of Hadalyn was not treating Brik well. His hair was matted and long, and the beard of which he had once been so proud had knotted itself in the dampness of the side streets. Arla had warned him plenty, and if she didn't back up her threats soon, she never would, and the fear she had cultivated within Brik would soon begin to fray.

'Go back to the palace and play princesses, Reinhart. You're no more an assassin than I am,' Brik said, beginning to turn away.

It happened so quickly that Arla didn't have time to think between the anger that flared at Brik's words and the tiny dagger she had in her pocket flying through the air and pinning the side of the thief's shirt to the wooden panels of the brothel.

'You want to test that theory?' she said softly, watching the colour leech from Brik's face as she lowered her voice to something dark and deadly. 'I've been more than patient with you Brik. Don't make me lose my temper.'

One cut.

'Bitch,' he spat.

Two cuts.

'I'll kill you!' he seethed, blood mixing in his blackened teeth where it ran down his cheek from the cross Arla had drawn there.

'Threaten me again, thief, and I'll cut something that's worth a lot more to you than your face.'

She smirked as the man's throat bobbed.

'Are we clear?' Arla crooned, digging the handle of the blade against Brik's thigh.

'Crystal.'

She watched as he hurried away, her fingers toying with the silver rattle she had pocketed when he had tried to shove his weight against her. *Stupid fool,* she thought, twisting the rattle in her hands, unsure what to do with it now. There were too many people with too many babies in Hadalyn, so the chances of returning it to its rightful owner were nil. She tucked it into the pocket of her leather trousers and made a promise that when the world was not so miserable, she would find that child and return the toy.

Leaving the alley behind, Arla discovered that Madam Touse had not disappointed. She peeked at the fabric through the folds of paper in which the dresses had been packaged and handed over coins that were likely worth the price of Halos's whole shop. Madam Touse handed the package to the runner boy she often used and instructed him to deliver it to the palace. Arla almost felt bad when she saw the boy struggle under the weight of the fabric and knew his journey up Grey Hill would be long. But at least the child had found a job – a well-paid one at that – and it was more than most had. So Arla simply offered a smile and began her own walk back to the palace.

She had grown accustomed to dark alleys and the slums of Hadalyn; they offered a hundred different places to hide, and they were free of judgement. She didn't need to be King's Assassin here – though she often was; she could be Arla Reinhart, a wicked, stubborn girl who had clawed her way to the top. Halos had reminded Arla of that past, and though her family had never been so poor as to live in these dark, miserable corners of the kingdom, they called to Arla in a way that was familiar and comforting. The illicit affairs that happened in these dingy streets were well practised and Arla didn't acknowledge them. If these people – Hadalyn's vultures, Arla had nicknamed them – wanted to trade powders that made you see things, or transport animals long-since banned from the kingdom, Arla would turn a blind eye. She knew Cyrus would come down hard on her for it if he ever found out, but the trust of the vultures was worth more to Arla than a stripping down from the king.

So no one cared as Cyrus's assassin strolled through the slums, stepping over rats, and piss, and the gods knew what else. They worked with her well enough, both parties content to ignore what the other was doing unless something had gone awry. If Arla was sent here on Crown orders, the vultures would point her in the right direction, on the understanding she would leave the rest of them alone. It was a relationship built strategically over nine years, and one that allowed her to cross Hadalyn in peace.

Or so she thought.

She was experienced enough now to know when she was being followed. And she was skilled enough to know when she was being followed by somebody who knew what they were doing. It was so very slight – barely there at all – but Arla had walked these streets enough times to know that the shadow flickering in the corner of her eye was not caused by the awnings of ramshackle buildings.

It was amusing, really. She twisted the blade in her waistband, the action hidden by the leather fold of her jacket, and purposely turned down a street she knew would be free of vultures and their beady eyes.

Five.

Four.

Three.

Two.

Arla spun as the shadow leapt from the rooftop, her feet working in a well-rehearsed manoeuvre that allowed her to force her weight into the figure that had landed. She pushed hard, revelling in the satisfaction of the body slamming against the wall. Her blade was at his neck before he had time to take a breath.

'Is stalking young girls in the slums how you enjoy spending your time?' she spat into the face of the dark-haired, blue-eyed mass that was Hark Stappen.

He chuckled, kicking a leg out to unbalance her. Arla had read it before he had even moved and deployed her hours of dancing lessons at court to her advantage, stepping over the offending leg. She pressed the blade harder against his skin.

'Wrong move, pretty boy.'

'If you must know, sweetheart, yes, I was stalking you. But had I wanted to stay hidden, you wouldn't have known I was here at all.'

Arla inwardly scoffed. *Unlikely.*

'Then why bother?' She pressed her knife harder against his neck, resisting the urge to pierce the vein that bobbed under her blade.

'I wanted to make sure my partner was well prepared for tomorrow,' Hark challenged, completely unfazed by the bite of silver at this throat.

'*Me?*' Arla laughed in disbelief, sliding the blade away from his neck and sheathing it back at her waist. 'To make sure *I'm* prepared? You may fool yourself into imagining you're part of the king's guard, Stappen, but there's a reason you're an ambassador and not in your own king's army.'

There.

It was the quiver of a muscle in his jaw as she pressed the

nerve she knew would give her the reaction she wanted. Hark Stappen may have a reputation for being accomplished in combat, but he had never once given Arla the proof to back up his lively notoriety.

When he offered not one word to defend himself, Arla knew she had won and turned on her heels with a flick of blonde, jasmine-scented hair.

His hands were on her before she had finished spinning, tightening around her left wrist. She kicked out, sharply, and Hark jumped back, releasing her wrist.

'Touch me again and I don't care what the king said. I'll run you through with a blade so fast you won't have time to pray to the gods.' Venom dripped from Arla's words, and Hark's eyes reflected that deadly poison back at her.

Hatred had blossomed fruitfully between the pair in the two years they had known each other. It would take a gods-blessed miracle for them both to return from this trip alive.

CHAPTER 3

Dinner with Halos was always chaotic.

Arla loved it more than anything in the world.

She had barely made it inside the door of her friend's little house, which was situated not far from where Arla had once lived with her parents, when she was accosted by Neb and Ettie, their hands sticky and grasping, whilst Halos busied herself cooking what looked to be a chicken.

Condensation moistened the windows, their wooden frames rotting and weak, and there was a stack of unwashed pots and a fire almost burnt out in the grate. Parchment littered the kitchen table along with half-sewn dresses for Ettie and odd gloves that were missing their partners. Halos fussed and mumbled under her breath, shouting for Neb to come away from the door as she took from Arla the loaf her friend had collected on her way over.

'Sorry, sorry. Absolute chaos, as usual, but we're nearly there.'

Arla took a seat on a rickety wooden chair, the cushion atop it now so thin it may as well have been a dinner mat.

'We can do chaos, can't we, Ettie?' Arla said, scooping the child onto her lap before she could pull the tablecloth and its contents to the floor.

Halos's cottage felt like home in every sense of the word. Although Arla had an affinity for beautiful, expensive things, she never felt so at peace as when she was sitting in her friend's kitchen surrounded by trinkets and wooden toys and *mess*. The two women had spent long summers in here as children when Halos's mother had been alive, helping her peel potatoes and earning sweet freshly baked pastries as a reward. Arla's parents had frequented this house, too, the two families so ingrained in one another's lives they might as well not have been separate at all. This house had always been busy, so full of life and chaos, just as it was now.

Despite the madness, though, Halos was an excellent cook.

Dinner passed by too quickly and the twins were put to bed with only a little fuss. Halos placed a mug of tea in front of Arla just as the sun began to set. 'So how are you? Actually. No lies.'

Arla's breath hitched, though she didn't know why. Perhaps because her friend cared. Perhaps because her friend had been there through everything. 'I'm good. Dreading going to the border with Stappen but ... I'm good.'

'You can tell me if you're not, you know.'

Arla couldn't meet her friend's eyes. She knew Halos would listen to everything, even the things that kept her up at night, the nightmares and the grief that came in waves even after all these years.

'I passed by my parents' house on the way here. I didn't think it would still hurt.'

Halos reached her hand across the table and rested it atop Arla's. 'I don't think it will ever stop hurting.'

Halos knew that all too well. Her grandmother and her ancestors before that had been kept as slaves by the previous kings of Hadalyn. Halos had grown close to her grandmother after her mother died in the battle of Grey Hill. One result of the war was that the act of slavery was abolished, and those four years before she died, during which Halos's grandmother had been free, had imprinted themselves on Halos's soul. Arla knew her friend still grieved her mother and grandmother deeply.

'We learn to live with it,' Halos said gently.

Arla smiled weakly. Yes, she was learning to live with it. She just wished she didn't have to. She wished she didn't feel the need to tell Halos *again* that some days she had to fight with herself to get out of bed. That some days she disappeared for hours just to walk or train until her head was clear. That sometimes she wished *desperately* that she'd had some other family, some distant relative, even, who could have taken her in and maybe her path would have been different.

'Enough about me,' Arla said, plastering a smile on her face that she was sure Halos wouldn't buy. 'Tell me about you.'

'Well,' Halos began, 'I was thinking of taking the twins down to the Canus this summer and teaching them how to swim like we used to. Ettie will pick it up easily, I just know it, though Neb might need a little persuasion. Oh, and you know the man who works at the blacksmith's? Well he was in the shop the other day helping me fix up one of the chairs...'

Arla let her friend speak until there was nothing left to chew over between them. She left Halos's cottage with a lightness in her heart that she experienced as a kind of relief from her usual shadow and darkness.

~

Arla's new dresses were perfect, and the pages of the latest book she had started reading made her smile as she sat curled beneath a woollen blanket beside the fire in her rooms at Castle Grey.

She wondered what Hark was doing to prepare for tomorrow. Perhaps he was drinking his body weight in whisky at one of those taverns he favoured, or maybe he'd lured a pretty girl back to his rooms.

The thought left a bitter taste in her mouth.

Hark Stappen was a private man, his affairs a mystery even to Arla, who had made it her sole mission to discover everything there was to know about him. He left Castle Grey from time to time to travel back to Kastonia – likely to report to his king on his findings inside Hadalyn, though Arla had made sure there were no secrets Hark could discover that she didn't already know – and a memory sprung to the forefront of her mind.

It had been late one night in the middle of summer. The air was balmy and perfumed with the scent of roses, and the sun had set only a couple of hours before Arla had seen Hark riding out of Castle Grey at breakneck speed.

It had been strange enough for her to saddle her own mare and follow.

He had ridden hard and fast, and Arla was sweating with the strain of keeping up with him. What would be important enough for Hark to ride so hard for Kastonia? Nothing odd had happened in or outside of Castle Grey in recent days, and Hark had been positively relaxed over dinner when he'd declared he was riding for Kastonia in the morning.

He'd said nothing about disappearing in the middle of the night.

Arla's mare, Vetta, was sure-footed and silent, though not even the gods could hide her forever, and the closer they galloped to the border between Kastonia and Hadalyn, the thinner the trees became, until there was nothing to hide Arla from giving chase. Hark turned in his saddle and spotted her immediately.

His face was pinched, and his hair was slick with sweat as he pulled up his horse and waited for Arla to approach. Her own chest heaved with the effort of the gallop, and she was glad Hark didn't give her a second to begin speaking before he tore into her.

'Why the *fuck* are you following me? I told you I was leaving. I don't need an escort, *assassin*,' he sneered, his own chest rising and falling rapidly.

Arla swallowed, straightening in the saddle. 'In a hurry, Stappen? What's so urgent you need to leave in the middle of the night and push your horse to the point of collapse?'

His eyes narrowed, his fingers clenching and unclenching on the reins as his horse pawed the ground. 'None of your business.'

Arla scoffed. 'Wrong, it's *exactly* my business. Where are you going so quickly?'

Something changed in Hark's eyes, something too quick for Arla to place, but she was sure it was too similar to regret. 'It's nothing that concerns you. Believe me.'

His voice was soft, and it was ... strange. It wasn't often that Hark backed down to her, and, given that nothing indeed had happened in Hadalyn that would require him to leave so quickly, Arla's mind jumped to the next possible conclusion.

'You're meeting a girl, aren't you? Does your king hate you so much that he'd send you to live away from your lover?'

She regretted mocking him the second his eyes turned stony, and he tugged his lip between his teeth.

'As I said,' he muttered. 'It's nothing that concerns you.'

Arla was already turning Vetta back towards the town. Fine. If Hark wanted to almost kill himself making it back to his secret lover in the middle of the night, who was she to stop him?

She kicked her horse into a canter and called back over her shoulder. 'I hope she's pretty, Stappen.'

The memory burst when a piece of wax-sealed paper slid beneath her door accompanied by a sharp knock, and she almost screamed in frustration.

Arla had worked too many days in a row to warrant being sent on a job this late at night, and her hair was currently *clean*. But this was what she had signed up for, wasn't it? What she had worked every day for the last nine years to achieve. She wondered – often – if her parents would be proud of her, or if they would be disgusted with what she had done to ensure she could spend her evenings in front of a fire with maids tending to her as if she were royalty.

The crackle of a flame jolted her from her thoughts, and she sighed as she closed the book and placed it lovingly beside the half-drunk tea on the table beside her. Arla didn't bother reading the note before dragging her leather assassin's uniform onto her body, and ritually strapping the array of blades she had come to think of as extra limbs into their correct places.

Only when she was sure she carried enough weapons for whatever assignment Cyrus had for her, did Arla pick up the thick, creamy paper and set off in the direction of the town.

～

Whatever this target had done to piss off Cyrus must have been significant. The man walked with the air of someone used to getting his own way, and the expensive fabric of his jacket informed Arla that he was likely one of the few wealthy enough to live on Grey Hill. He must have done something especially irking to the king to warrant sending Arla after a noble.

Each silent footstep she took behind her victim echoed in her heart. It was the beat of a death drum, a warning that this man meandered through the streets of taverns and bars for the last time. The darkness wrapped around her as it always had, embracing her into its shadows like an old friend as she stalked the man in the direction of the fancy houses and cottages of Grey Hill.

Her focus drifted as irritation hung itself like a mantle across her shoulders, and Arla shifted her blade from one hand to the other and back again. She was tired of these boring, easy jobs Cyrus had taken to sending her on. She thought of travelling alongside Hark Stappen tomorrow and it caused her breathing to become heavier. Red mist began to cloud the edges of her mind. She didn't work with others; she certainly didn't want to be working with *him*.

The thought swirled round and around her head, until she no longer cared that her victim was not yet clear of the town and its keen eyes. She usually waited until her targets were in the dark, deserted paths that led to Grey Hill before she struck. Now, she just wanted him dead before the anger building in her caused her to do something she'd regret – likely involving a knife and Hark whilst he slept.

She was on the man before he could register that death had

swept in, the knife firmly against the skin of his throat as she hauled him behind the back of a building that housed far too many occupants for its size.

She spun him, using his own weight to gain momentum so his back was pressed flush against the shoddy brickwork.

'I should have known he'd send you after me,' the man spat, his voice thick and unfamiliar to Arla. He couldn't have been in the castle often, then.

'Then how careless of you to walk home alone,' she taunted, revelling too much in the trembling of the noble beneath her blade.

'You're a *girl*,' he scoffed. 'Though I shouldn't be surprised that you're the king's favourite. I heard he's easily seduced by *whores*.'

Any level of control Arla had reserved dissipated, ushering in a wave of violence that had her baring her teeth and reaching to her waistband with her free hand for a second blade. She would gut him for his impertinence.

'And that adds treason to the list of crimes you've committed against the Crown,' she said softly.

He made the mistake of kicking out at her – a feeble attempt to swipe her legs from beneath her, Arla thought, and then she was upon him.

She didn't count how many times her blades struck him; didn't count his screams as she plunged her blades into him, again and again, until he didn't scream any more.

She had planned something quick and honourable. A silent slit across the throat would have done, maybe an arrow through the heart if she was feeling particularly adept with her bow. But he had insulted her, and the only way she had fathomed to make him pay was to leave him in a bloodied pulp.

She was sick of being called the king's whore. She had looked up to her king as a father, and had worked her body to the bone to get to become his assassin. She would not let it be taken from her, nor have anyone suggest she did more for him than kill.

As she walked swiftly back to Castle Grey, already sighing at the effort it would take to climb back up her tower, Arla was glad she had kept the hood of her cloak up. Blood really was a nightmare to get out of her hair.

~

By the time the sun had risen over Castle Grey, Arla had jogged two laps of the grounds and scaled the side of the king's tower. She had not made it into the King's Guard through her skills with a sword alone – she had outrun every single soldier she had been pitched against and had hauled twice her body weight up the tower steps. She'd be damned if she lost the level of fitness she had used to hone her body into something this well-tuned and deadly.

Despite the inevitable bad mood that Hark would surely bring out in her on their trip to the northern border, Arla was feeling good as she walked down to the stables in a set of fighting leathers paid for by the king.

It was early – too early for the stable boys to be here – but Arla's grey mare stood outside with a full set of tack tightened and ready to go.

'Hello, beautiful,' she said on a breath, kissing the mare's muzzle with fondness.

'Good morning to you, too, sweetheart.'

Arla whirled at the sound of Hark's voice, which was lower

than usual, as if he had just woken, but yet it was still distinctly Hark: smoky and soft all at once.

'I do hope you can saddle your own horse better than you've done mine,' Arla replied, ignoring his comment, and adjusting the position of the saddle on Vetta's back.

'Oh, no,' Hark chuckled, leaning against the barn door. 'I've picked my pony, princess. You can saddle your own.'

'If you think for one *minute* that you're taking my horse, Stappen—'

'You'll do what? The sun has barely risen, and you're *already* being difficult. The gods know why the king chose someone as pathetic and spoilt as you,' he snarled, pushing off the door-frame and marching towards her.

Arla often forgot how tall he was, how easily he towered over her. And usually she didn't care, she had taken down men just as big – bigger – but today...

Pathetic?

No. She'd been pathetic once. She wasn't anymore. She'd worked hard enough to prove to this kingdom – to this *world* – that she was not pathetic.

But now, with him towering over her whilst she argued about which horse she would be riding, she felt that way again.

Without a word, she shouldered past him into the stables, careful not to knock precious Vetta, and chose the black stallion she knew carried Hark between Kastonia and Hadalyn when he was attending to his ambassadorial duties. With any luck, he would find Vetta too temperamental and swap the mare for the stallion anyway.

Eros was actually a lovely horse, Arla discovered, as they reached their sixth hour of travel out of the centre of Hadalyn towards the border with Kastonia. He was a lot bigger than

Vetta, and Arla felt over-horsed on him. But he was proving to be a sweet soul, and the nickers he whinnied out, either to himself or to Vetta, made her smile.

'Finished sulking?' Hark's voice pulled Arla from her meandering thoughts on dragons and how Eros was definitely descended from them, and the lopsided smirk he had curled his lips into made her want to stab something. Or someone.

'I'm not sulking.'

'You haven't said a word in six hours,' he replied, still turning back to look at her as Vetta picked her way through the forest that lay two hours from the Kastonian border.

'Well done for being able to count to six. Maybe the king will give you a gold coin for being such a clever boy,' Arla sniped back.

'So you *are* sulking?'

'I'm not sulking, *Stappen*. I simply don't like you.'

'Interesting. I was under the impression that you've never liked me and yet it hasn't ever rendered you silent before.'

Gods, he was *infuriating*!

'I was under the impression you knew when to stop talking so I guess we were both wrong,' Arla ground out, her teeth clenching just as tight as her palm was around the handle of the blade resting at her waist.

'Is that a threat, sweetheart?'

Arla's fingers tightened to the point of pain where they lay concealed under the edge of her leather jacket. Eros's withers tensed beneath her and she hoped Hark realised his beast had saved him from the silver shard of metal about to come flying at him. Arla pressed a gentle hand against the stallion's neck to calm him.

'It's okay,' she whispered. To convince herself or the horse, she didn't know.

~

As the sun began to bleed into different shades of red, and gold, and orange, Arla found she was tired and thoroughly sore from riding an unfamiliar horse for so long. They had crossed the border into Kastonia and were still miles away from the closest village, but even so, the ground had never seemed like such a welcome place to sleep.

As she dismounted, wincing at the stiffness in her legs and picking the stallion a handful of grass in gratitude, Arla threw the saddlebags containing her bedroll and food rations onto the floor. Hark had chosen a hillside that was playing host to a crop of trees overlooking the Kingdom of Kastonia, and if she squinted hard enough, Arla could make out lights and the sloping roofs of houses in the distance.

'So is Hadalyn's famed assassin good at making fires, or would Your Highness rather I took on the task?' Hark taunted as he sauntered back from the trees into which he had vanished moments ago.

'What is your problem?' Arla glowered, too tired to even fathom arguing with the pretentious bastard and his maddening smile.

'My problem,' he began, irritation and downright aggression lacing his words as he threw down his own saddle bag, 'is that you are spoilt, and rude, and think the world owes you something.'

Arla's fatigue quickly melted into red-hot fury. Venom dripped from her tongue as she dragged herself off the floor to stand in front of him and declare, 'Perhaps the world does owe me something.' One more step towards him. 'Specifically, *your* world,' she raged, stabbing a finger into his chest and covering her surprise at meeting a solid wall of clearly defined muscle lurking beneath his shirt.

'Oh, we're still on that?' Hark snapped back, pushing her away from him with such force it was bound to leave bruises on her collarbones. 'Because my kingdom killed your parents, is that it? You get to blame me because my blood runs the same colour as the rest of Kastonia?'

'Don't you *dare*!' Arla seethed, a day's worth of anger simmering underneath her skin, just dying to bubble over. 'Kastonia *ruined* my life when their soldiers stormed the city that day. It was not our fault your kingdom had no food. It was not our fault they had no money! But they killed my parents, and I was left with *nothing*! I worked so *fucking* hard to get into royal service. Not everybody gets promoted from soldier to one of the King's Guard, Stappen, and *nobody* ever got selected as King's Assassin. *I* worked the hardest, *I* nearly killed myself to get to where I am, *I* gave up my whole life for the Crown, so if I want to be spoilt, if I want to do as I please, then I will, because I deserve it and you don't get to say a gods-damned word about it when it was *your* kingdom that made me the way I am.'

He was staring at her, as if she had gone mad. Perhaps she had, because she couldn't remember a time when she had felt this angry – certainly not recently, anyway. Maybe it was seeing Halos caring for her twins and calling Arla out for murdering and thieving her way through life, or perhaps it was because Hark had accused her of being spoilt and difficult. All of those things were true, and she didn't feel bad about it. She *wouldn't* feel bad about it.

Because look how far she had come.

'I'll make the fire,' Hark said, turning and strolling back towards the trees. Arla didn't care. She'd slept outside on cooler nights, and on much more dangerous jobs. Alone.

When she returned from checking on the horses, he was placing more wood on the fire, his own saddle bags open and revealing the wax sheets in which he had wrapped his supplies. Good. At least he wouldn't slow her down through lack of food or poor planning. The mission would be quick and simple: dispose of those responsible for stealing the supplies, return to Hadalyn, and place a formal request for the ambassador for Kastonia to be sent home and a new one dispatched in his place.

She had thought it would be easy, being alone with him; it wouldn't matter that his blood was Kastonian. It wasn't Hark who had killed her parents; it was the Kastonian king who had sent his army to raid the city after his troops had been slaughtered trying to retrieve non-existent dragons from beneath Castle Grey. But, gods, it was harder than she had thought. He was proving to be exactly what she had always believed the Kastonians to be: arrogant, and host to a sense of entitlement that made Arla's jaw ache with the strain of clenching it.

'Why didn't you kill him?' Hark demanded, his voice suddenly loud against the silence they had preserved over a crackling fire.

'What?'

'You didn't kill the thief in the alley in Hadalyn. Why?'

'I...' Arla trailed off, whatever explanation she had intended having failed to come to her tongue. Because it wasn't that simple, was it? She didn't know why she hadn't killed Brik – gods, she'd had plenty of opportunities. But she ... hadn't. She settled on, 'He's not a bad person,' hoping it would be enough to staunch the line of questions.

'Liar. I saw him take that rattle, and he pocketed at least six coins from people outside stalls at the market.'

Arla stifled her annoyance at the revelation that he had been following her all yesterday afternoon. She didn't know who she was angrier with, him for his disregard for her privacy, or herself for not realising he was there for so long.

She was slacking. These mindless jobs were making her sloppy.

'It's complicated,' she offered, unable to explain her own actions.

'In what way? He bedded you or—'

'Oh, gods, no!' Arla interrupted, almost choking on a mouthful of cheese. 'Have you seen the state of him? Brik, he, I ... I don't know. He's been there since ... since the war. I was nine and had been sleeping on the streets for about five weeks. I was starving. Brik was much older – seventeen maybe – and he stole me an apple one day. I suppose there must be some good in him. I guess I think he's savable.' The words had come from somewhere buried and long forgotten, but they were there all the same and Arla immediately regretted being so vulnerable in front of Hark – for revealing, not a weakness, no, because Brik wasn't a weakness, but for sharing something that could be used against her. *Gods.* She'd have to kill Brik now.

But Hark wasn't looking at her with revulsion or shock. He appeared deep in thought, and it occurred to her for a fleeting moment that he looked as though she'd put him under a spell. But that was silly nonsense because the magic had disappeared with the imaginary dragons.

'Some people don't deserve to be saved, you know,' Hark said, the softness of his voice foreign to Arla's ears.

'You would say that.' The words were out of her mouth before she could stop them. He had been ... not kind, no, but he had spoken to her gently; he hadn't meant to cause offence.

The hardness was back in his voice in a heartbeat.

'Meaning what, exactly?'

'That your kingdom saw fit to raze ours to the ground because you thought we were keeping dragons from you. You didn't think *us* worth saving at all, did you?'

Gods, could she not control herself?

Hark's face became sharp and pinched, the keen edge of his jaw now more deadly than handsome.

'You're impossible,' he condemned, turning away from the fire and untying his bed roll.

'It's Kastonia's fau—'

'I don't want to hear it. Blame everyone else but yourself, Reinhart; it's all you know how to do.'

She tried to ignore the aching feeling in her stomach and in her heart. No, not everyone was worth saving.

Especially her.

CHAPTER 4

Crossing Kastonia would not be as easy as she hoped.
It never was.

It had been months since she had been sent out
of Hadalyn on a job, and with the shipments going missing,
Kastonia had introduced new laws regarding travel through the
kingdom.

All citizens – whether native or not – were to be presented at
court if they wished to move between the borders either side of
the kingdom. Arla had never heard something so ridiculous, and
had she been sent on this assignment by herself, as she had
requested, she would have taken no heed of the strange new
laws and their infringement on her anonymity. Even Hark
looked reluctant to be riding into the centre of the kingdom, his
fingers twisting in Vetta's mane when he thought Arla wasn't
looking.

She was. It was her job to know weakness and what it
looked like.

Hark didn't want to be here.

Kastonia, despite its reputation for being poor and close to collapse, was a pretty kingdom. They had travelled through miles of meadow and countryside, and Arla wondered how the country had managed to become so poor when it had acres and acres of land suitable for farming. The only answer she could conceive was that the Kastonians were lazy. It only worsened her mood and led her to her thoughts of the people who had butchered her town.

Now, the pair coaxed their weary horses down a cobbled road and into the town of Larkire.

At least we can rest tonight.

The palace loomed up ahead, too beautiful for such a wicked kingdom. Its spires reached high into the sky, gold blinking wildly at their peaks which shone stupidly bright against the grey stone. A balcony overhung the front of the palace, a red and gold banner strung tightly against it. For a kingdom that claimed such dreadful poverty, they had not let the palace lose an ounce of its splendour. Arla loved it immediately.

There were gates ahead, huge iron structures that seemed impenetrable. The cobbled road they travelled would lead them right to the foot of those gates, winding through the stone buildings that made up Larkire. Where there had been an abundance of green and trees in the meadows close to the border with Hadalyn, there was not a whisper of it in the centre of the town. The buildings were harsh stone structures and the rock was crumbling in places. People huddled on the corners of streets that branched out like lungs – too many people for these decrepit buildings – and the air was thick with lingering smoke and the stench of slums. It reminded her of the back alleys of Hadalyn; places where the vultures lurked, waiting to pounce on anything that had carelessly wandered into their piece of town to die. But those were the edges of Hadalyn's town – the back alleys and side streets that were reserved for the poor. The people here, downcast and wary of the two visitors on horseback, huddled in plain view of the palace, in the centre of the city.

Good. They deserve it.

She couldn't bring herself to regret thinking it. Was this what would have become of Hadalyn had the Kastonians succeeded in bringing it to its knees? Even with the jobs Cyrus sent her on, Arla had never entered Larkire, especially in daylight, so the state of it ... it came as a shock. She had expected poverty, but not ... *this*.

She kept her eyes forwards, wringing her fingers in Eros's mane as she had watched Hark do. But she wasn't nervous. No, she welcomed the chance to challenge any of them who dared cross her path. She *wanted* to show them the might of Hadalyn's Royal Assassin. It was they who had made her this way.

Being in Kastonia had never bothered her this much in the past, but then again, she hadn't had to conform to ridiculous rules such as checking in with the royal court on her previous assignments. It was an insult, really, that she would have to declare herself when the Kastonian king had requested Cyrus's help and asked for Arla to be sent. Why should she disclose her movements when their king had instructed them to begin with? It didn't make sense, but then, she had seen little of Kastonia that *did* make sense – from their lush, fertile land free of crops and farms, to the richly decorated palace that bore enough gold on its spires to feed the country for a year.

The streets were becoming busier as they approached the gates to the palace grounds, and Eros tensed beneath her.

'It's okay. This is your home,' she said under her breath, resting a palm on the horse's neck to settle his unease at the growing crowds.

Before she could understand what was happening, Eros reared, spinning in such a fashion that Arla was forced to grasp his neck just to keep herself atop the stallion. As his hooves reconnected with the cobbles, she saw Hark draw a blade from somewhere – she wasn't sure where since she hadn't seen him carry one – and swing the metal so wildly that she was surprised when the throat its tip now rested against did not shower them in a spray of crimson.

'You touch that horse again and I will drive this blade through your throat and string you up over the gates.'

There he is.

It had taken two years for him to reveal himself, but here he was. The violent, skilled soldier hiding beneath the polite and charming ambassador.

Arla had never seen Hark look so fierce, his ice-blue eyes darker than usual as he held his blade steady against the young man's throat.

'Give me one reason why I shouldn't run you through right now,' he growled.

The haggard male shifted under the tip of the blade presented at his neck, but he didn't look scared. Not as he should do. Arla wondered if the people of Kastonia simply didn't care what happened to them anymore.

'You left us, too,' the man said, staring Hark down as if he could turn the blade on its wielder.

'Excuse me?' Hark glowered, a brow rising in what Arla could see was the beginning of his undoing.

'You left us too, Stappen. You left us like the dragons and the gods before them. You left us for the kingdom that broke us.'

It was ... pitiful. But Arla could feel the tether on her temper beginning to fray. How the man could declare that Hadalyn had broken Kastonia was beyond her. It was them who had attempted to crush Hadalyn! And to believe that Hark had abandoned them? Was one measly ambassador that important to the citizens of a country on its knees?

The oddness of it threw Arla off so greatly that she almost missed the thief – a light-haired, skinny man – tinkering with the gold buckles on Hark's saddlebags.

The dagger was out of her hand before the first buckle could slide free of the leather strap on Vetta's saddle.

It met the thief's sleeve with a thud, pinning it to the leather of the saddle before the pickpocket could gasp. Arla had never been more thankful that Hark had been atop Vetta, and not some other beast that would surely have spooked at the knife embedding itself in the tack.

Hark turned slowly, his blade still levelled at the first man's throat, but his attention flitted between Arla and the thief now clutching his hand to his chest. A twisted, cruel smile spread over Hark's face, turning him into something deadly and wicked.

The crimson arc that Arla had been expecting upon the revelation of Hark's hidden violence, now materialised, not from the man who had accused Hark of abandonment, but from the man who had attempted to steal a gold buckle from a Hadalyn horse.

Life as personal assassin to the crown had hardened Arla against most things, and she was the last person to be squeamish, but even she winced at the spray of blood from the man's neck as Hark slit his throat and dropped him where he stood.

'Let it be a lesson that if any of you attempt to steal from your king – or Hadalyn's – you will be met with appropriate force.'

Every set of eyes in the crowd lowered immediately, no one daring to incur the wrath of Hark and his violent display of strength.

'Reinhart!' Hark called, gesturing with his head for Arla to go ahead.

She squeezed her heels into Eros's sides and the horse carried her through the parting crowd and onwards to the palace gates. Hark's actions had stunned her into silence and complicity, and Arla was surprised at her lack of words in response to something that should have roused a thousand.

The gates began to open immediately, the groan of the metal loud over the murmurings of the crowd. Hark had scared them, but they didn't look surprised in the way that Arla was. Did the Kastonian ambassador demonstrate his deadly skill set often?

'That was ... unexpected,' Arla murmured as Hark halted Vetta beside her, both cautious while their backs were to the crowd as they waited for the gates to open wide enough to squeeze the horses through.

'No, it was *exactly* what was expected. You should have been alert,' Hark muttered back, his eyes fixed ahead on the looming palace. Arla clenched the reins tighter.

He was right, and that was worse. She should have been paying attention. The men atop horses believed themselves too important and too invincible to be targeted in broad daylight. How the tables had turned.

'You know I could slide this blade between your scapulars before you finish blinking,' Arla shot back, earning her an arched brow from the ambassador, soldier, guard – whatever Hark Stappen was.

'Perhaps. I could have slit your throat before you finished that sentence and yet I haven't. So I ask, Reinhart, what would be your point?'

He was infuriating. And before today she would have laughed it off and told him that not in a million years could she ever believe him doing so. But now she had seen that wicked side of him, and it had excited her far more than it should. Arla enjoyed violence – revelled in it – and how exciting that it should come from somewhere she least expected. Of course, there had been a lot of talk about Hark's reputation, about how he was skilled enough with a blade that he could rival the King's Assassin. But she had believed it to be no more than just that – talk.

Still, just because he had proven he could threaten a civilian, did not mean he was any good at fighting. And he certainly would be no match for *her*.

The second they were inside the palace gates and through a stone arch that opened out into a courtyard, everything seemed to move incredibly fast, even for Arla who was used to the bustle and chaos of court life.

Stable hands were beside Hark and Arla before the horses' feet had halted.

'Good afternoon, sir, and...?' A short, hunchbacked groom greeted them, taking both sets of reins.

'Lady Reinhart,' Hark supplied, and Arla lifted a brow ever so slightly. It was better than *assassin*, she supposed.

Was it?

Not that the use of such a name had done anything to shield the identity of the blonde-haired girl, her reputation far too widespread to be masked by something as trivial as a name.

Arla Reinhart. The King's Assassin. Cyrus's whore. Lady Death.

No, there wasn't any title that would disguise the assassin in her, and the way she stood with her arms crossed over her chest, eyes already alert and aware of everything within two hundred yards.

The groom knew it, too, his pale grey eyes widening at the bow and quiver of arrows on her back. Arla didn't imagine the step back he took.

'Are we going to stand here all day?' she grumbled, not inclined to show off the superficial niceties or politeness that court life had hammered into her. She didn't like these people. She wanted them to be scared of her, and there would be no end to the scenarios she could dream up about what she would love to do to each and every one of them.

'What she means is, "Fallon, would you be ever so kind and take care of our weary horses and inform the King we have arrived?"' Hark declared, side-eyeing her as he loosened the girths of both horses.

'Of course, your—'

'Thank you, Fallon!' Hark interrupted, reaching to take Arla by the elbow before she saw him think better of it.

Good. It would be a shame to have to stab him in front of his own people.

Rolling her eyes and closing her hand reassuringly around the hilt of her blade, Arla followed Hark into the palace of Kastonia.

Unlike Castle Grey, Larkire Palace was blooming with colour. From the carpets to the drapes, to the gold covering everything in sight, it was magnificent. Again, Arla could not work it out. For a country so obviously poor, the poverty plaguing its citizens was nowhere to be seen inside the royal residence.

Soldiers stood in the doorways, their scarlet tunics sparking a wariness in Arla that had had its origins nine years before, in a house bathed in blood. But none of the soldiers caused either Hark or Arla any bother and were content to let them make their way through winding corridors and small passages until they reached a door painted in gold, guarded by no fewer than six soldiers. She could take on four with no problem – if they were as useless as Cyrus's soldiers – but she would have a hard time with six.

Enough, she told herself. She was on a job and if she were to start gutting the Kastonian palace from the inside out, she'd surely lose the position – if not her head – for which she had worked so hard.

'I do hope you're going to behave in front of the king and queen, Reinhart,' Hark said, on a firm exhale, his fingers toying with the cuff of his shirt rather like they had done with Vetta's mane.

'I wouldn't dream of anything else,' Arla said sweetly.

'Gods, you make me want to cut my own throat.'

'And you make me want to use that blade to stab you through the heart,' she replied, a forced smile fixed on her face.

He's nervous.

Hark hated her, and she hated Hark, but it was rare for him to be so open as to *tell* her how much her presence infuriated him. If he was insisting on goading her into an argument, Hark was uncomfortable and needed the distraction. She'd known him for two short years, but she had made it her sole occupation to investigate the handsome Kastonian ambassador when he had first arrived, and she had been reprimanded by Cyrus more than once for her absence from court when she had spent her evenings tailing the ambassador or eavesdropping on his conversations. If there was anything she did not know or hadn't observed about Hark, it wasn't worth knowing, and if they were going to house a Kastonian in the palace – the very palace they had tried to storm – she would make sure he wasn't a threat. And it had turned out he wasn't.

Movement on the other side of the doors caught her attention, and she was disappointed when a slight man wearing a white tunic and glasses slipped through the gap in the door, obstructing her view of the throne room beyond.

'His Majesty requests you are stripped of all weapons before entry,' the man stuttered, careful to speak over Arla's shoulder rather than look her dead in the eyes.

'Oh, for fuck's sake,' Arla complained, undoing the scabbard at her waist, and dropping it to the floor with a clang that made the man wince.

The doors then began to swing open, and Arla was almost blinded by the bright light that streamed out of the throne room.

'Behave,' Hark growled, before ushering her through the doorway.

CHAPTER 5

Something was stopping her from moving.

Arla had marched beside Hark to halt at the bottom of a dais, and her eyes had refused to rest on the stationary monarchs until she had scanned each corner and crevice of the room for potential threat – or escape, should this go very south. It was an ordinary room, high windows allowing dazzling sunlight to stream in, and decorated in red and gold – a signature of Kastonia, then.

What had stopped her still, was the face of the King of Kastonia. Staring down at her was the same set of ice-blue eyes that she had spotted through the crack in the side of a dresser. Her heart thundered in her chest, her breath catching in her throat as she replayed the scene over and over again. Arla's hands trembled slightly – a telltale sign that she was coming undone and she was struggling to find her way back.

You can do anything.

She inhaled steadily, her nostrils flaring as she slid the mask of King's Assassin back into place. She tilted her chin down, not allowing herself to look directly at the face that haunted her dreams. If she looked at him now ... she may lose herself entirely. She would not allow herself to give in to that panic here. She had got through it once. She could do it again.

The King of Kastonia smiled.

They were wise to have stripped her of her sword.

'A pleasant journey, I hope?' His haunting, deep voice ran through her, silencing every sense until all she could hear was the thundering of her own heart.

'Uneventful, at least,' Hark replied.

'As I should hope it was. The horses will be well tended, and you both properly fed and rested before your departure tomorrow. I trust this little problem will be eradicated quickly.'

Arla bit back the retort she wanted to voice, the accusation that he had eradicated her parents and those who had slept peacefully whilst her kingdom had been raided. If she spoke, blood would be spilled, and with the number of soldiers in the room, she could guarantee much of it would not be her own.

She wondered, briefly, where Orson, Hadalyn's ambassador to Kastonia, was hiding.

'And the lovely Miss Reinhart. I have heard much about you.'

Arla raised her head slowly to meet the gaze of the King of Kastonia. He was a rather plain man, with short dark hair, greying at the roots, but she could not mistake the watery eyes and cruel smile that had haunted her nightmares for years.

'I have heard much about you too, Your Majesty,' she managed to say, her voice couched in that important tone Cyrus had required her to craft through hours spent at royal balls and hiding in the eaves, listening to meetings that needed an assassin's perspective.

'I do hope our facilities are up to your standards. I'm sure it comes as no surprise that our kingdom is not as well financed as your own,' the king continued, eyes boring into her as if he could see all of those dangerous, wicked thoughts she kept concealed.

'I'm sure they will be more than satisfactory, Your Majesty,' Arla said sweetly, and only Hark, who stiffened beside her, seemed to realise that the sweetness came not from politeness but from a sarcastic mocking of the king, who was forcing his kingdom's poverty down her throat. She had been surprised at how impoverished the kingdom looked – she didn't think anyone in Hadalyn knew just how desperate a situation Kastonia had found itself in – but she wasn't buying it for a moment. The king was too finely dressed; his pristine clothes half-covered by a heavy red-velvet cloak with fox fur stitched around the collar. And the queen, half-hidden by the space the king took up, was dripping in pearls and diamonds.

Arla didn't mind her so much. The queen had kept her eyes trained on her clasped hands and was yet to meet Arla's gaze. She was not a monarch; she was a woman who had been sold into marriage and made to sit pretty.

'The northern border is a two-day ride from here, though if your *assignment*...'

The king's eyes flickered between them and his soldiers, and it was clear that he did not wish for anyone to know of this task that had called Hadalyn's prized hunter from her castle.

Interesting.

'... requires a lengthier stay, the palace staff are aware you have full clearance to come and go.' There was an oddness to the king that set Arla's teeth on edge, and it wasn't because he had killed her family and it was taking everything in her not to gut him with her bare hands, but because of the way he was looking at her, as if he could see into her mind. As if she couldn't hide there.

'Thank you, Your Majesty.'

'Please, call me Elrod.'

Gods, she needed a drink.

∽

Arla was led by a burly red-and-gold-suited guard to a room that rivalled her own back in Castle Grey. Huge arched windows looking out over gardens too-well tended for the struggles of a kingdom such as Kastonia. What was going on?

The bed was calling her, the size of it tempting her to lie down and never rise again, and she should like nothing more than to close the crimson curtains around the four-poster bed and shut herself away from the world.

A bathing chamber was concealed by a heavy wooden door connecting to her room, and the scent of lavender lingered in the air. She was glad, at least, that this kingdom had managed to install water pipes and taps rather than relying on buckets being carted by hand through the palace to fill the bathtub.

Returning to the bedchamber, she saw there were rows upon rows of books displayed on polished wooden shelves. They were perhaps the only thing that won her over to the thought that just one night in the castle may not be so bad. They were leatherbound and included stories about the non-existent dragons as well as more prosaic treatises on tax systems in the kingdom; there were at least three on the ancient rules of magic. That made her scoff, though she was drawn to the symbol of a flame inside a heart which had been embossed in gold on those spines.

Ridiculous.

Arla sighed, undoing the hastily woven braid she favoured for keeping her locks under control while on the road. Hark was staying on the other side of the palace – his usual quarters, he had said – so she guessed that soaking her aching muscles in the bathtub would be the best use of her time before dinner. Besides, if she was going to search this palace from top to bottom for information on how its royal family had managed to stay so wealthy while the rest of the kingdom fell into disrepair, she would need the cover of darkness and the family in question to be so deep into their cups that they would sleep like the dead.

The water was hot, and the lavender strong, and by the time she had scrubbed two days' worth of dirt off her skin and climbed out of the bathtub, Arla's eyelids were heavy and the bed too inviting to resist the call of sleep.

One hour, no more, she thought as her head sank into pillows softer than her own back home.

～

Arla had spent too many hours wandering the hallways and empty rooms in the upper levels of the palace – her only entertainment when Perry was assisting the king, and her maids were too busy in the kitchens. There weren't ever any other children in the palace, and she hated that her friend Halos hadn't been allowed to visit. Arla wondered if Perry thought Halos, a few years older than Arla, would want to be in the company of someone younger than her, but Arla knew Halos didn't mind; they were old friends, and had attended school together back when their parents had been alive. She only hoped her friend wouldn't forget about her now that Perry's rules on who could and couldn't enter Castle Grey prevented them from seeing each other.

Arla had been staring at the paintings for too long again. They were making her think of her family and the people she had lost last year. So she had wandered down to the lower levels of the castle — below even the kitchens. It was dark down here, but it wasn't the dark that scared her; it was the strange tugging sensation she had right behind her navel that kept urging her to walk deeper into the shadowy hidden hallways beneath the palace.

Perry would be angry with her if he found her down here. He didn't like her going missing, especially when he had told Cyrus he would watch her.

It was his own fault for passing her off on the maids, then. She was bored.

She kept walking, her fingers brushing the rough stone walls as she followed that tugging in her core. There was a door ahead of her, a dark, ancient thing that made her hesitate.

A low rumble spread through the corridors, and it was enough to send Arla spinning in the opposite direction. Back towards the kitchens, back towards Perry and his kind smile.

∼

Someone was in the room with her.

Arla snapped upright, hand clenched around a blade she had found in the bathing chamber — presumably for males to shave with — and which she had fallen asleep gripping. However, instead of finding herself under imminent violent attack, she watched as the fireplace in the room was lit by two maids in grey gowns. Neither had turned when she had almost launched herself from the bed, and she cursed herself for being so careless.

She hadn't checked the door was locked.

She hadn't checked the windows.

She hadn't checked the floorboards.

She hadn't checked *anything*.

You're getting complacent, Reinhart. Perry's words were now her own. She'd been finding these jobs too easy and had begun to think herself invincible, almost.

'Excuse me?' She summoned her most regal voice – as if she could pull off the role she so often imagined herself in back home – and the two maids spun immediately to face her.

Twins. So identical it was unsettling.

'So sorry, milady— Uh ... Lady Reinhart,' the one closest to Arla began.

'We apologise milady. We knocked but—'

'Why are you here?' Arla cut the sister off, not eager to listen to her own shortcomings – lack of awareness, lack of precautions – repeated back to her from the maids.

'To light the fire, and to inform you that dinner will be in an hour. His Majesty has requested your attendance,' the maid closest continued.

She had a scar on her jaw, Arla noted.

'What time is it?' Gods, she *hated* not being in control, especially in this kingdom surrounded by these people.

'Seven, milady,' Scar answered.

Gods, she was so stupid. She had slept for hours.

'I can find you a gown, if you'd like?' Scar's sister offered, and for the first time since she had sprung awake, Arla looked down at herself. She had gone to sleep wearing the robe she had found hanging on the back of the door, a lovely peach-coloured silk she wouldn't have minded in her own chambers at Castle Grey.

'A gown would be helpful. Thank you.' She wasn't usually so polite – especially to Kastonians – but she was embarrassed at not having noticed them enter. Arla wished for them to be in her favour if it would save them gossiping to the palace staff about how they had found her.

The maids returned quickly, carrying between them a selection of dresses that were strangely her size. Arla wondered if they had 'borrowed' them from the queen and if she would be punished for it. No matter; they wouldn't get within an inch of her. She wouldn't be caught off-guard again.

Settling on a pine-green coloured dress, Arla pulled the fabric over her skin, surprised to find it soft and expensive. The twins – Lilith and Rheia, they had revealed – began combing through her hair as Arla fastened the hundred metal clasps down the side of the dress. How useful that could be for accessing a dagger strapped to a thigh. The blade she had taken from the bathing chamber would have to do. She missed her own weapons, the feeling of being without them as foreign to her as this place. She wondered where they had been stashed and whether she might find the location when she investigated later.

They were right not to trust her.

By the time she stepped out of the guest quarters, Arla was looking much finer than when she had arrived in Kastonia. As much as she enjoyed the comfort of her tight leather clothes, she was just at home in a lovely dress with her hair pinned back from her face. The pins would be a welcome addition to the stash of weapons she was collecting.

Lilith and Rheia led her through the twists and turns of the palace and eventually Arla recognised the route she had taken earlier. She began making a mental map of every corridor and servant doorway she could see.

The scent of roasted chicken found her nose as she followed the twins towards the dining room. She dreaded having to return to bread and cheese when they set off again.

Arla had expected the maids to halt once they reached the dining room, sparing her at least a few seconds to collect herself before entering the room.

They did nothing of the sort.

Lilith pushed through the double doors, creating a vacuum that smothered Arla's senses in chicken, and gravy, and that spicy scent she had noted earlier. She had expected a large dinner with members of the royal court filling the seats of an extravagantly large table. Instead, only four pairs of eyes greeted her from a table designed to seat eight. King Elrod leaned back in his chair at the sight of her, his eyes roaming the length of her body in a way that made her shudder. The queen sat beside him, her mousy brown hair appearing a shade darker in the low light of the room and almost covering her face entirely. Across from her sat a young man no older than Arla, with the same square jaw as the king and the crystal-blue eyes the queen bore. The heir, then.

Arla's gaze met the ambassador, Orson's, narrowed one at the far end of the table, his sneer and pointed features so rat-like it almost sent a chill down her spine. She could see the hatred churning in his eyes and she did her best to reflect it back at him.

The lack of people had taken her off-guard when she'd entered the room, and it left her feeling exposed when Lilith and Rheia melted into the shadows, leaving her in the company of those who were responsible for the deaths of her family, rendering her an orphan.

It's just a job.

A job that was admittedly more personal than most, but nonetheless a job she had been sent on by her king. She did not wish to disappoint Cyrus.

So Arla did what she had been trained to do: she called forth all of the swagger and self-importance she could muster and forced a disinterested expression onto her face. Immediately she felt better; hiding behind the mask was so much easier than walking in here as Arla Reinhart, and to be honest, she wasn't always sure she could differentiate between the two. Both were spiteful and cruel, with an affinity for expensive things. Or was that only when she was the King's Assassin? Perhaps the real Arla Reinhart didn't exist anymore. Perhaps she had gutted her from the inside out.

'Apologies for my tardiness. I don't usually keep to someone else's clock, I'm afraid.'

Too much? Judging by the unamused look on the king's face and the coy smirk from his heir, she guessed it was just the right amount. Orson scoffed.

'No matter, Miss Reinhart. We have all the time in the world.'

Did they? Judging by the state of his kingdom, it seemed that they were running very low on time indeed. Or did it simply not matter as long as the royal family stayed shrouded in a cloak of luxury?

'I don't believe we've met.' The young man stood, offering a hand to Arla that she was reluctant to take. 'Prince Reuben of Kastonia, at your service.'

'Oh, believe me, Prince Reuben, you don't want to be at the

service of somebody like me,' Arla cooed with the courtly voice of a lady, one who wielded a fan rather than a sword as she took the seat offered beside the prince.

'I'd rather be in your service than someone else's. Walls talk, Lady Reinhart, and you have quite the reputation.' He had heard of her, then.

'Then let's hope there's no situation that should require my ... service,' Arla quipped, drinking deeply from the white wine she had covertly analysed for any hints of hemlock or belladonna.

'Your ... talents are so well known due to your lack of discretion that it's a wonder you still hold the title,' Orson said sneeringly.

Arla smirked. She had missed burrowing beneath Orson's skin and reminding him of all that he'd lost; of how she had worked and trained harder than any before her; of how she had proven her loyalty so thoroughly by stabbing a knife through the centre of her palm, that Cyrus had created the role of King's Assassin specifically for her and sent Orson, her closest competitor, to Kastonia as ambassador. She knew he was equally matched to her in skill. He knew it, too.

'So lovely to see you again, Orson. I do hope you're enjoying your time in Kastonia?'

He bristled beneath her taunt and she thought he might be preparing to leap across the table to strangle her, when the king spoke.

'How are things at home, Miss Reinhart? I hear Hadalyn has been in talks with the royal houses on the continent?' If Cyrus had been in talks with those across the sea, it was the first she was hearing of it, and if he was keeping that sort of information from her, it was concerning. Whatever moves the King of Hadalyn made, Arla was sure to be dragged into it.

'I'm not privy to that sort of information. And you know I couldn't say, even if I knew.'

'Liar,' Reuben replied, smiling into his glass. She couldn't stifle her own grin at the prince, even though it was making her jittery being so close to a family she wished to kill. He was handsome, in a princely way, with perfectly pressed clothing and light brown hair – the same gentle shade as his mother's – that was well groomed and thick.

'Indeed. I find it hard to believe that the king's sharpest weapon would be excluded from such important discussions,' King Elrod pressed, and Arla dug her nails into the top of her thigh under the table. She was in no mood to be questioned, especially concerning something about which she had no knowledge and which therefore irritated her since it suggested Cyrus had deliberately kept her in the dark.

But before she could snap, she was overwhelmed by an airy caress of whisky and leather.

Hark Stappen had entered the dining room like a storm cloud.

'I do hope I'm not interrupting what I suspect was about to be a rather lively conversation?' he said, taking the seat opposite Arla to place himself beside the king. He looked ... regal.

He had been ragged and journey-worn when he had arrived alongside her at the palace, but now he was clean-shaven and dressed immaculately in black, topped with a dark navy doublet detailed in gold.

'Not at all,' Elrod chuckled, clapping Hark on the back as a servant handed him a glass of amber liquid.

'You've been drinking again,' the queen said gently, capturing the attention of the room. Arla watched Elrod's face flash with an emotion she hoped she hadn't interpreted correctly as Hark offered a soft but vulpine smile to the Queen of Kastonia.

'If I can't drink the whisky of my home country, Arabelle, what use is it in staying?'

It was an odd dynamic, and one that Arla didn't want to begin to unpick, despite it being her job to report back on all she had learned. If an ambassador was able to speak to the queen in such a way, what did that say about her? Or the king? She had seen the annoyance cross Elrod's face when Arabelle had addressed Hark, and Arla knew the queen would be on the receiving end of his temper now for having left the safety of the cage in which she was usually kept.

It made her hate Hark more, hate *them all* more.

If Kastonia treated their *queen* this way, it was no wonder the country was falling apart.

CHAPTER 6

Dinner passed uneventfully, much to her surprise. Even Orson had been uncharacteristically silent. Arla hadn't trusted any of the dishes of chicken, or pheasant, or fish, but after watching every person sitting at the table eat the same food from the same silver platters, she decided she was too hungry to dissect each mouthful for traces of poisons or sedatives.

The wine had been plentiful, though Arla had been clever to disguise that she was not drinking half as much as the others did; she needed them tired and well on their way by the time the meal was finished. She was intrigued by them, much to her disappointment. She had only wished to feel hatred and disgust towards the Kastonian royal family but could not help the desire to know more about them and the workings of their kingdom. Especially the prince, who winked at her whenever her eyes strayed his way. It seemed they kept a very small court; only those who were integral to the running of the country were welcome at the palace. How different to Hadalyn, which was often heaving with courtiers, and entertainers, and people who just wished to spend time there.

In a brief moment of silence as each of them lifted their glasses to their lips, Arla took the chance to question the Prince of Kastonia.

'It must be daunting, being the heir to such a large kingdom?'

'I believe it is—' Reuben began before Hark cut him off.

'It's getting late. We have a long journey tomorrow, Reinhart. I suggest our beds would be a better use of our time?'

Reuben snorted at Hark's words, and it only worked to confuse Arla further.

But chairs were being pushed back from the table as each of them rose in unison, breaking the ruse that the royal family of Kastonia were enjoying their evening with the assassin from Hadalyn.

Who would be the first to slit the other's throat?

Hark disappeared as quickly as he had arrived, and Arla was glad when the bubble of anticipation finally popped at his exit. He made her nervous, as though he could cut her at any moment, and she would not have the capacity to stop bleeding. Her mind kept wandering to him and the far-away corridor he was housed in on the other side of the castle. It frustrated her. She of all people should be able to spot a wolf dressed as a lamb – had been one herself.

By the time the clock hit midnight, she had paced the length of her bedchamber so many times that the soles of her feet had begun to memorise the grain of the wood on the floorboards. Finally, she could begin to unravel the mystery and well-kept secret of Larkire palace and the family that called it home. With the practised silence only a thief – or an assassin – could master,

Arla slipped through the door and out into the winding hall-ways of the palace.

There was a ticking somewhere in the labyrinth of corridors, and Arla let her ears adjust to it and then block it out. That would be a constant, and it was not important to her search for ... what? What had possessed her to don a black cloak and move like a wraith through shadowy corners and concealed servants' doors?

Something that would explain how the royal family had stayed so wealthy when their kingdom was at risk of collapse? Or why she had not heard of Prince Reuben in all her years slinking through this kingdom? Perhaps something else entirely? Could she find an answer to the question that had plagued her for years: what had bewitched the Kastonians into storming Hadalyn and killing her parents in search of non-existent dragons and long-extinguished magic?

It was laughable, really. That Kastonia had been so desperate to search for these mythical dragons in the hope of persuading them to ask the gods to end the suffering Kastonia was experiencing. As if the gods cared that Kastonians were too lazy to grow food or help themselves! Arla had seen the fertile land on the way here; Kastonia was more than capable of growing its own food. They'd bought plenty of seeds and tools from Hadalyn in the past – Arla had seen the trade documents on Cyrus's desk – so why weren't they making use of those lush meadows? Clearly they didn't care to help themselves.

They'd blamed Hadalyn of course. Hadalyn, which was thriving and growing stronger each day. Hadalyn, which was supposedly hiding dragons beneath Castle Grey and using the dragons' connection with the gods to bring prosperity to the kingdom.

Kastonia was jealous. Jealous enough to send troops into Hadalyn and slaughter their people.

Gods, she hated this kingdom.

It didn't take her long to find something of interest. Like a shadow, she slipped behind a velvet curtain to watch in secret.

A heavy, wooden door with intricate gold runes carved into the oak stood ajar, allowing Arla's eyes access to an eccentric, wonderfully decorated royal suite. She could see the queen, who had been backed against a green chaise, and even from outside Arla noted her scared eyes and trembling fingers. They should have been long asleep from the amount of alcohol Arla had seen them consume.

'I have given you a home, and a *crown*, and *that* is how you think to conduct yourself?'

Arla ground her teeth together as Elrod's fist gripped Arabelle's arm hard enough that it would be sure to bruise.

'It won't happen again,' the queen whispered, barely loud enough for Arla to hear. Why she had married him, Arla couldn't say. The queen was young, and pretty, and could surely have found a better match with a lord in a wealthier kingdom. Was having a crown worth this? Arla didn't think so.

She wouldn't find the answers she was looking for here, not with them all still awake. The townspeople might be of more use to her. Or perhaps the servants? Cyrus had night servants to respond to his needs; surely someone as self-absorbed as Elrod would have similar expectations and she didn't want to be discovered by any of them while skulking around. She doubted his servants harboured any kind of loyalty to him – they probably weren't even Kastonian – but she couldn't be certain.

As silent and sure-footed as she had ever been, Arla abandoned her position behind the curtain, leaving Arabelle to

Elrod's wrath. She did not have time for guilt. Arranged marriages were common amongst the nobility; if she reacted to every woman crushed beneath the ego of a man, she'd never get anything done.

The servants' quarters were not hard to find because there was an abundance of hidden doors and breathtakingly narrow staircases throughout the palace. She wouldn't take them, though. Arla had almost failed her training in the King's Guard when they had locked her in a tiny cupboard and tasked her with forcing her way out. She hadn't done well with small spaces after that fateful day when Kastonian troops had stormed Hadalyn and her parents had locked her in their dresser to keep her safe. The thought of being trapped in a tight servant's passage caused her breath to catch in her throat.

Not tonight. Not tonight.

It was warmer on the lower levels of the castle. It had been far too easy to descend to this level, down the main staircases of the palace. Not a single soldier lined the walls or alcoves, leaving the perfect hiding spot for an inquisitive assassin. The floors down here were laid with huge stone slabs and torches flickered in the corridors. Someone must be awake if the torches were still burning.

A sorry-looking wooden door hung on one hinge at the end of a passage lit by two sputtering torches. Clearly the beautiful rune-carved oak was reserved for quarters of the castle that were meant to be seen. Creeping slowly on soft feet, Arla approached the door, craning her neck up to squint through a gap in the wood. Two tired servants sat nursing what looked like tea at a wooden table. It would be easy to get them to talk. And if not, there were always other ways.

'Do you always stand on your tiptoes to spy on people?'

She whirled, knife free of her belt and against his throat in an instant.

'That would be a yes, then,' Hark chuckled, not at all concerned by the blade against his neck. This was becoming a regular routine between them.

'Gods, I'd love to stab you,' she whispered angrily, pressing the silver harder against the pulsing vein in his neck.

'I'd like to see you try, sweetheart.'

Astonishingly fast, even for Arla's reflexes, Hark twisted and disarmed her, catching the blade before it could hit the stone and alert the servants to their presence on the other side of the door.

'Now, care to tell me what you're doing down here?'

'I don't have to explain myself to you, Stappen,' she growled, bringing her leg up into the side of his knee and swiping her dagger free of his grip.

'On the contrary, *Reinhart*. I find you sneaking about my home, armed to the teeth with swords and daggers, and that's *exactly* what you're going to do.'

'Your home?' she scoffed, pulling the edge of the cloak tight around her to disguise just how many weapons she currently sported – it had been a lucky little accident that she should stumble across her own blades as well as a few extras she had discovered on her jaunt around the palace. She'd had to leave her bow where it was, its shape was no good for sneaking around. She'd fetch it later.

'Or would you rather explain yourself to the king? I am sure it can be arranged,' Hark said, leaning casually against a stone pillar.

'I don't want to spend another *second* in that bastard's company, and while we're on the topic, I don't wish to spend another *breath* in yours, so if you'll excuse me, I'll be going to bed,' she growled, shoving past him to disappear in the shadows again.

Gods, he was such a thorn in her side!

He had ruined what would likely be her only opportunity to explore and find answers. She could only hope to enjoy a few hours' sleep before setting off to the northern border and discovering who – or what – was stealing supplies.

CHAPTER 7
HARK

He *hated* the way she looked at him. The same level of disgust and resentment she had rendered from the moment they had been introduced two years before was stronger than ever. Like it was *his* fault her parents had died. Perhaps if they had laid down their weapons and stood aside upon the storming of Hadalyn, they would have kept their heads. But no, if Reinhart was anything to go by, her parents would have been just as stubborn and disrespecting of authority.

He didn't know how she'd made it to 'King's Assassin'. Gods, she hadn't even noticed him following her through the slums, and she had been surprised to see him tonight. She was becoming too confident in her own abilities, too sure that there was no one alive who was as skilled as her.

Easily rectified, he thought, in the shadows of the servants' quarters. It hadn't been a shock to find her wandering the hallways; in fact, he'd have been disappointed if she hadn't been. Her king certainly would.

It was obvious – her anger. It was a burning, living thing that flared brighter the more she learned of Kastonia and its royals. He knew she would want answers about why Larkire Palace was so wealthy when the rest of the kingdom wasn't. She'd find out soon enough and the thought made him itch. She would be livid; she would want to hurt every member of Kastonia's royal family and Hark didn't want to be anywhere near her when she did find out.

She would hate him even more. But he couldn't tell her yet; wouldn't tell her *ever*, if he had any sense. Gods, she would be a liability! He would not be able to control her then – and nor would he want to. Arla Reinhart was a whirlwind, a force to be reckoned with.

But his breath had hitched when he had walked into dinner tonight. The sight of her in that dress the colour of pine needles had made him wish he'd swallowed half a bottle more of that rich, smoky whisky he longed for during his time in Hadalyn.

And the way she flirted with the prince? Gods, he'd wanted to throw himself from the top of his tower!

He didn't know what she was doing to him. Was it magic? Had she put him under some sort of spell? One that had manipulated him into not hating the sight of her recently.

Gods, he'd spent too long in Castle Grey.

CHAPTER 8

She hadn't slept so poorly in years. Hark had unnerved her in the passages beneath the main levels of the palace last night, and the way she had seen Elrod treat the queen had angered her to the point that it had taken her hours to fall asleep. She hadn't found answers, and nor would she find any on this job. But there would be other chances to visit Kastonia, other chances to sneak into this palace on her travels – especially now that she had learnt the layout and guard rotation. At least Orson had scurried back to whatever hole he was kept in and she hadn't had to endure *that*.

It was raining. She could hear the heavy spat of water bouncing off the window ledge, and if the grey, miserable light barely peeking through the window drapes was anything to go by, winter was well on its way. It would be cold on the northern border; she had been there before when she'd had little knowledge of the climate in the north, and it had taken her not even an hour to regret not packing sheepskin-lined clothes.

Her muscles twitched, unused to lying in the comfort of a

bed when she would usually have been up early and running laps of the castle boundaries until she was almost sick. She couldn't do that here. Not only did she not know these grounds, but she didn't want to appear weak when she was bent double, trying not to vomit after pushing her body beyond its limits. Not that lying in bed was making her look particularly strong.

If she closed her eyes, she could pretend she was at home in Hadalyn. Not in her rooms at Castle Grey, but at home with her parents in their little white cottage by the river. She missed them. Constantly. She missed the long walks they would go on through the meadows after school had finished and her father was home from his job as a carpenter. She missed the way her mother made sure there was always something sweet for dessert and how she'd always hold Arla's hand a little too tightly when they went to the market.

Pretending was useless, though. It only hurt her, and it didn't disguise the fact that she was deep behind enemy lines and that she would be forced to be amicable with this family despite her urge to gut them. She had thought about it. For long hours when she couldn't sleep. She had imagined killing them in their beds and setting the kingdom ablaze. But she would lose her place as assassin and would be left homeless. And that was *if* Cyrus left her alive.

Sighing, Arla dragged her body from the mattress, not admitting even to herself that it had been beyond comfortable, and she would have liked her bed in Castle Grey to be as lovely as this. Lacing her boots tightly around her calves, Arla made her way down to the stables.

Gods damn her if she was letting Hark Stappen steal her horse again.

～

'It's lame. Pulled a shoe on her way in,' a gruff voice called from the stack of hay in the corner of the barn. Arla had made a beeline for Vetta and was already in the process of saddling the mare, when Fallon – she remembered his name now – called out to her.

'What do you mean she's lame?' Arla snapped, already blaming Hark and thinking of a thousand ways she would make him pay for damaging the mare she had spent years training to be battle ready.

'Pulled a shoe on your journey here, milady. Blacksmith won't be here until tomorrow.'

'She needs to be ready today. We're travelling to the border. King's orders.'

'Sent a message to His Majesty already. Trip's to be delayed.'

She wanted to hit something. Spending another day in this place was going to drive her insane.

'Then I will take another horse.'

'None fit, milady. The horses haven't been sat on in well over five years,' Fallon muttered, moving from Vetta's stall to the one opposite her.

Five years? Had the kingdom really disbanded its mounted cavalry? 'Why not?'

'You try feeding a barn full o' horses when there's no grain. Costs an arm and a leg.'

Was Kastonia so poor they hadn't been able to afford the upkeep of such a prestigious arm of their military? There were only a handful of horses in the barn now, and Arla wondered if the others had been sold ... or used to feed a starving kingdom.

'Good girl, Vee,' Arla breathed, stroking the mare's neck, and inhaling the sweet scent of hay and horse sweat. She had to make the best of it. If she couldn't leave today, that meant another opportunity to find answers, and this time she would make sure she got them.

~

'You look tired, Reinhart. Something keep you awake?'

Arla squinted at Hark over the breakfast table. She was in no mood for games today.

'Nothing at all,' she replied sweetly, noting the king's eyes on her as she curled her lip at Hark.

Hark had dressed well. The navy jacket he wore was well fitted and looked as though it was worth more than some of the houses on Grey Hill. He wasn't wrong, though; despite her eagerness to leave the castle before the sun had fully risen this morning, she was feeling the effects of little sleep and knew her eyes carried dark circles beneath them. *Tough.* She had worked harder missions, and on less sleep. This was nothing.

'Hark suggested you train together this morning, Miss Reinhart. We have heard so much about Cyrus's assassin and her swordsmanship, after all.'

Each and every word the king spoke was a political move. It was perhaps a power play, or an attempt to gain a glimpse into the inner workings of Hadalyn, and Arla didn't like it at all. Yes, she had thought she could use the morning to train, too, but she was loath to reveal just how fatal blades could be when wielded in her hands. And if she was going to kill that man one day – and she would, by the gods she would! – she wanted him to be surprised at just how ruthless she was. She wanted to watch the fear widen his eyes when the time finally came to kill him.

'Of course, Your Majesty. I had hoped to be leaving before breakfast, but it seems my mare has thrown a shoe.'

Gods she almost wanted to laugh for the way she spoke to him. Her years in Cyrus's court had taught her well, and she knew that he too would laugh at how delicately she was handling the King of Kastonia. At least, he *would* have laughed, before he had been consumed by the disappearance of Kastonian supplies, and the talks he was rumoured to be in with the continent.

'Shall we?' Hark gestured, rising from his plush, velvet seat.

Gods help you, Stappen.

'I'd like nothing more,' she chirped, snatching an apple pastry from the table and tearing into it with the viciousness she wished she could unleash onto the royals.

He led her through winding hallways of red and gold, now bathed in the light of day so she could see what had been shadowed and dark for her the previous evening.

'You could smile, you know,' Hark muttered, rolling his eyes as they took another right turn to reveal a circular chamber with pillars that housed glass so perfectly polished it could be mistaken for not being there at all. She spotted blood on the marble floor, though. A tiny rust-coloured smudge in the bottom corner, entirely too small for anybody to see besides a keen-eyed assassin. This would be their training ring, then.

'You might slip and fall on your own blade but we can't all get what we want.'

'Are you always so pleasant?' he drawled, his back to her as they entered the circular chamber.

'Only to those who manage to piss me off before my day has begun.'

She met his blade with the speed and strength of someone

who had fought men twice his size and won. She had been hiding her sword down the column of her spine, concealed nicely by her leather uniform and braided ringlets. The look of surprise on his face was quickly replaced with one of determination and ... amusement.

'First rule of dancing with the devil, Stappen: if you're going to pretend not to carry a weapon, you'll have to do better than that. I saw you swipe that sword on your way into breakfast.'

'You think of yourself as a devil?' he scoffed, sliding his blade against her own before spinning and meeting her again in a flash of silver.

'Better a devil than some made-up gods,' she spat, forcing him backwards with a surge of strength through the metal.

'Come on then, *assassin*, let's see what you've got,' he goaded, feinting left and swinging his blade towards her. *Too easy.*

She tracked his blade with her own, arcing above them and backing him into the wall.

Come on Stappen, where's this talent they speak of?

Block, parry, lunge. All of it came as naturally and easily as breathing. Swords were in her blood – or they been planted there, at least. Nurtured lovingly to bloom in the form of a series of moves so familiar that she was hardly breaking a sweat in the fleece-lined leathers she had chosen this morning in preparation for the iciness of the northern border.

It was becoming an effort to hide the grin threatening to spread over her lips. This sort of exercise made her heart sing. She had done this – had *become* this – to protect her kingdom. Had become lethal and wicked to ensure that nothing would ever threaten Hadalyn's walls again. Her body had been crafted for this, a sword had become an extension of her arm, and she swung it as though she could cleave this kingdom in two. Hark Stappen would be a good place to start.

He had made it too easy for her to back him against the wall, but she saw the danger flicker in his eyes as his back scraped the marble.

He came at her with such force that it reverberated through her elbows as she took the brunt of his attack. *This* was the man whose reputation had preceded him.

He pushed her back, lunging and lunging as she blocked each swing of his blade, gritting her teeth against the strength he had drawn from gods-know-where that was now shuddering through her sword. Fire burned within her, eager for the challenge, grateful for it. It had been too long since she had faced a worthy opponent.

'Come on! This is not the notorious assassin we've heard spoken of in such terms,' he mocked, twisting easily out of the lunge attack she made. She hadn't wanted to truly hurt him in training; holding back was her normal now because it was rare that anybody could ever coax the need for actual *skill* from her.

Tunnelling down into the anger and resentment simmering inside her, she ground her teeth together before launching into a series of moves so quick and deadly that she doubted anybody but her could keep track of where her blade was.

Wrong, though. Hark met every swing of the sword, not even grunting as she threw her weight into the attack.

'There she is.' Hark grinned.

He was a blur, as though the world had melted away around them whilst they danced the deadly steps of combat. She'd had little experience of sparring with somebody as skilled as her – almost better, even – and her arms were straining under the power flowing down her blade.

The blow to her shoulder sent her sword flying and pulled a hiss from between her teeth.

'That's not training, you prick,' she growled through the pain, already preparing herself to move the shoulder back into place. It had been troublesome since it had first been dislocated during the early days of her instruction for the King's Guard. It now had a habit of sliding out of joint at the slightest of knocks, and every one was painful.

'Can't handle a little pain, *sweetheart*?' he jeered at her, twisting the blade in his hand before hanging it up on a wooden rack against the wall.

'I handle pain just fine. It's you I can't stand,' she spat, gritting her teeth as she lined her shoulder up against the doorframe ready to lurch forwards and knock it back in.

'What are you doing?' Hark started towards her, shock rippling his handsome face at the realisation of what she was about to do.

'Squeamish, Stappen?'

'There are healers that live in the hills, Reinhart. Proper healers who can sort that for you.'

'You didn't seem concerned when you shoved the hilt of your blade into it,' she muttered, using her words to conjure up the courage needed to endure the few seconds of pain that would bring immediate relief.

'The women in the mountains are proper healers – the old kind. The ones who use magic to fix you!' he snapped, and Arla could have sworn she saw what looked like worry appear on his face before it was quickly squashed.

'Don't be so bloody stupid,' she scoffed. 'I won't listen to this nonsense about magic, dragons, and gods anymore, Stappen! These ignorant, *ignorant* superstitions are what got my family killed in the first place! Ugh, gods!' she yelped as her body slammed into the doorframe. Blinding white pain stole her breath from her lungs, and it took everything she had not to throw up at the sensation of her shoulder slipping back into place. She rolled the joint a few times, and then, content that it wasn't about to slide out again, she met Hark's eyes.

'I'm not the one who killed them.' His voice had dropped so low that it pricked the hairs on Arla's arms. This was dangerous, dangerous ground.

'No, but your blood still runs Kastonian,' she spat, turning away and stalking from the room.

～

Sneaking out of and into buildings now came as naturally to Arla as breathing, and it didn't take her long to scale the huge stone walls surrounding the palace and slip into the bustle of the townsfolk. She could have disappeared if she'd wanted. She could have left the kingdom through the dozen or so routes she had mapped and used before to sneak through the place. But it wasn't in her blood to run from a fight, and gods would this be a fight if she had any say in it. The Kastonian royals were hiding something, and snooping through the passageways and eaves-dropping on conversations between servants was not going to give her answers.

People would, though. She knew enough about court to know that secrets belonging to castle walls often leeched into the population like a plague. If she could stomach the stench and the revulsion at being near the scum that had tried to burn her home to the ground, she would find answers.

Arla meandered through the puddled streets, stepping over

suspicious liquids that made her nose wrinkle until she found herself passing under a shadowed, half-dilapidated archway with that wretched dragonhart symbol carved into it. Before her eyes had even adjusted to the lack of light in the abandoned building, she could hear a mumbling beneath the ground.

It sounded like ... hundreds of voices beneath her feet.

She descended down a set of worn stone steps that took her beneath the city, holding her breath as damp warmth choked her lungs and slithered over her skin. At the bottom of the stairs she stopped and looked around her in amazement. Dozens of awnings had been assembled into makeshift stalls selling meat, trinkets, and what she assumed was medicine in brown glass vials. A sprawling market stretched before her, an entire city hidden beneath Larkire. There was a distinct smell of sweat and meat and an unfamiliar scented smoke that Arla suspected was the result of whatever herb a group of men were puffing on in the corner. There was fighting somewhere, too – she could hear the chants, the cheers, and the booing; could almost see the exchange of coins between grimy hands. She herself had fought in pit fights against men bigger than her just to work off the waves of anger that often overwhelmed her. She suspected Larkire had the same predisposition to the illicit violence.

Torches were lit and burning at regular intervals between the makeshift stalls, and shafts of light trickled down from cracks in the ground above them. The whole place sang of lawlessness.

It was perfect.

Arla dipped between stalls, biting her lip against the rough elbows that dug into her sides, and the passing of illegal powders into hands that quickly hid them away. Animals were being traded, too – creatures that had been banned in Hadalyn for their viciousness. A particularly feral, mountain cat roared at anyone who got too close as they peered through the bars of its cage. She recognised it as a species that hailed from the Kingdom of Glacit on the continent.

It didn't take her long to identify a dark corner overlooking what appeared to be a gambling ring. She knew more than just coin passed between hands here, and wondered, briefly, why Elrod hadn't sent guards to disperse the underground market.

'Drink, miss?' A young boy appeared at the table she claimed for herself, shifting from one foot to the other as he awaited her response.

'Ale. Please,' she quickly added, pressing a coin into his rough, work-worn hands. It would pay for his silence. She was too odd for him not to speak of when he collected her drink.

Groups of men hasty to gamble their few remaining coins came and went from the tables around her, some decidedly happier than when they sat down, and some she didn't think would make it through the evening as they lost everything to a poorly played hand.

Just as she was despairing of learning anything relevant or juicy – the patrons too engrossed with their games to bother discussing the poor state of the country – a new group arrived to occupy the table closest to her, and there was not a card or coin in sight.

'Died in his sleep I heard.'

'No money for a healer. Couldn't get a message out to those in the hills either.'

That was odd. It was the second time in the space of a day that she had heard of the women in the hills. *Magic healers,* Hark had said.

'Maybe if the king hadn't taken everything for himself, the

apothecary might have had the supplies to help,' a gravelly, hacking voice snapped over the rim of a glass.

'What do you expect? The dragons left. The gods abandoned us. What little there is goes to who can afford it. Don't say you wouldn't have done the same.'

'But there was nothing left to take. Whatever wealth the king has now, it comes from outside. This poverty is a curse from the gods.'

That much she knew. This wealth had not been within Kastonia's walls before the attack on Hadalyn. The gold, and the food, and everything else had to have come from elsewhere. There was nothing left to be taken from a kingdom already suffering.

'The dragons would have fixed this. They'd have asked the gods to stop it all,' one of the women began. 'If those bastards in Hadalyn had just let us in … if they'd let us into the catacombs—'

'But they didn't,' the rough-voiced man from before interrupted. 'They didn't, and we're worse off for it.'

'It's not their fault,' a small voice chimed in. A thin, scarfaced man sat half-hidden from Arla's view at the table, nursing a tankard of ale that looked likely to render him entirely useless tomorrow. 'The dragons were weak after a battle between the gods a century ago. You've read the books. You can't deny it. They couldn't stay here and I doubt they'd have chosen their resting place to be beneath Castle Grey if they'd had a choice about it. They didn't abandon us and neither did the gods. It's not their fault they're too weak to keep serving us. Let them be.'

A battle between gods?

She didn't believe a word but it was the first time she'd

heard of it. No one in Hadalyn had ever spoken of such a battle taking place.

The gravelly voice returned, anger lining his throat that had her rolling her eyes as she sipped nonchalantly from her own drink.

'Of course they're underneath that castle! Where else would they have gone? Hadalyn was where the dragons spent most of their time – the gods, too, back when they walked the earth. If there's anywhere in Hadalyn to hide, it's beneath the palace and Hadalyn's people know it. They deserve to die for keeping them from us.'

Arla's chest was tight, her knuckles turning white where they gripped the tankard.

'The dragons served us all – every kingdom,' the soft-spoken man from before continued. 'Just because they resided in Hadalyn's meadows long ago doesn't mean they only cared for that kingdom. The books and journals from back then say they were always in other kingdoms and aiding anyone who needed them. I don't believe for a minute that Hadalyn's people claimed them for themselves. They wouldn't be suffering from the same poverty that's plaguing our own kingdom if they had the favour and aid of the dragons. Besides, no one can get inside the tunnels. There's no entrance, so how could a beast the size of a dragon get down there?'

She'd heard enough. Since she'd first stepped foot in this kingdom, all she'd heard was rubbish about gods, and dragons, and magic. Utter nonsense. Kastonians were delusional.

But one thing was clear, the people were not happy.

She lurched in her chair as a hand slammed on the table before her, all gnarled knuckles and broken skin. 'Now, what's a pretty thing like you doing in a place like this?'

Arla looked up at the man, his back bent with an unhealed injury and desperation in his eyes that had Arla palming the blade at her waist.

'The same as you. I want to win something.'

'And what have ya to offer?' the man asked.

She was reluctant to reach into her jacket and hold up the silver chain, but it was all she had to bargain with. It had been a present from Cyrus for her fifteenth birthday.

'You win, you take the silver. I win, you answer any questions I have and you never speak of me to anyone again.'

The man blinked at her, perhaps evaluating what would be the best way to take the chain and run. In the end, he decided against it and slumped into the chair opposite.

'I take it ya know your cards, girl?'

Arla smiled.

~

'I don't know where ya learnt to play like that, girl, but a deal's a deal.'

She could have won in the first three moves, but had let it play out to at least give him the sense of a game. She needed to keep him sweet if she wanted answers, and if she made a fool of him then he might not tell her what she wanted to know. Arla pocketed the chain, relieved not to have to part with the gift.

'Thought I had you at first, but you won, fair 'n' square. How's about you start askin' those questions o' yours?'

Worth swallowing her pride, then; she'd known it.

'My first question,' she began, rocking back on her chair and dragging her attention from where it had strayed to a deal over what she was very much afraid was a human heart. 'How come the King is so wealthy whilst the rest of the kingdom has been reduced to running underground markets just to stay alive?'

The man looked at her, all black teeth and wiry hair. He reminded her of Brik. 'Not from round here, are ya?'

'I'm asking the questions,' she said firmly.

His eyes flared slightly, as though he couldn't believe the impertinence being flung at him from a girl young enough to be his daughter. 'Sommat's wrong with tha' castle. You 'ear all sorts down here. Dark magic, sacrifices. Doesn't stop 'em all from trippin' over 'emselves to get a glimpse o' the King though, does it. Or his lad, for that matter. Always 'ated the place, meself. Sure, the gold's nice to look at and we find ourselves drawn to the place as if sommat's possessed us. But nah, sommat off about it.'

Of course. It *always* reverted back to magic, didn't it?

'I don't believe for one minute that you believe magic exists, let alone that there are whisperings of it in the palace. And it doesn't explain the riches, either.'

The man shifted under her gaze, the threat of who she really was ready to blow her cover as she tiptoed along the line of impatience. 'He took everythin' after the war. Had them slaves from Hadalyn for a while, too. Reckon 'alf of 'em never made their way back.'

She was over the table and gripping the front of his ragged shirt before she could consider the consequences of her actions. 'Hadalyn's people were freed. Every single one of them. The treaty was signed. Your King can't have slaves.'

He had the common sense to tremble beneath her grip. 'I ain't saying that. But 'e made good money off 'em back then, I 'eard. Maybe it's pure greed, but none of us folk know why he keeps the gold for 'imself. Mark my words: there's rumours of odd things in that palace, girl. Things none of us ought to be meddlin' in.'

She released his shirt, shoving him backwards into his seat. She hadn't come here for more rumours of magic and the fantastical suspicions of an oppressed people.

The man took a long look at her before bowing his head and disappearing into the throng of the market.

CHAPTER 9
HARK

Dinner had made him want to claw his own eyes out. Arla had swept in like a storm and winked at the prince. Then she had started on Orson about his lack of prowess with a blade, despite him being the only person rumoured to rival her skill at Castle Grey. And then, to top it off, as Elrod had scolded Arabelle for wearing red – as if it were an offence to the gods – Arla had smiled sweetly and told the queen how much she liked the colour.

He'd thought Elrod would kill the girl where she sat.

As it happened, Arla had decided to keep her mouth shut for the rest of the evening, though she would have to try considerably harder for Hark not to notice the way she hung on every word spoken as if they contained centuries' worth of secrets. Perhaps they did, but he failed to see how asking about Kastonia's trading routes with the continent would reveal anything.

Then again, he never had been able to predict the mind of Arla Reinhart.

She had disappeared quickly after that, a train of midnight-blue silk following in her wake that had all but fucking possessed him for some reason he had no desire to untangle. Not tonight, anyway.

But perhaps it was why he had lingered after the rest of the palace had gone to bed. Perhaps it was why he was waiting down the corridor from her room because sleep had been but a distant tease.

She slipped so silently out of her door he'd have missed it if he weren't used to the unique way in which her body moved.

Arla wasn't dressed in her fighting leathers or the stunning dress she had worn earlier. Instead, she looked as if she had been dragged from sleep. Her hair tumbled across her shoulders and down her spine, and she wore a robe that was the colour of rich wine. Her bare feet padded slowly along the hallway – slow, gentle. As if she had all the time in the world.

She hadn't come to spy tonight. She'd come to wander.

He'd heard from the maids at Castle Grey that she did the same there, too, when her dreams forced her from the depths of sleep.

He couldn't stop himself following her – couldn't stop *watching* her – as she trailed her fingers across balustrades and stone walls and around the golden frames of portraits of long-forgotten kings.

What Hark hadn't accounted for was that they weren't the only two people awake in Larkire Palace.

Prince Reuben looked as fresh as ever – as though sleep didn't have the privilege of roughening his appearance. Hark had known him long enough to know he, too, wandered at night – mostly to make sure his father hadn't been entirely too wicked to the queen.

Hark pressed himself closer into the alcove from which he'd

been watching Arla. The girl didn't react as Reuben approached her. Either she'd known he was there longer than Hark had, or she simply didn't care about being snuck up on.

'Enjoyed fighting with my father so much that you must argue with his ancestors, too?' the prince said as he reached Arla's side. She'd been looking up at the portraits for a while.

Arla laughed. It was one of those delicate laughs with which she rarely graced anyone. 'I think Orson felt the worst of my tongue tonight.'

The prince laughed, too. 'Indeed. I bet he's plotting a thousand ways to kill you in your sleep.'

'He'd have to best me first, and we both know he can't.'

Hark's skin prickled with something he couldn't place. He hated how friendly they were. They had met each other only two days ago and already developed an ease of manner which rendered them comfortable being half-dressed together in the corridor in the middle of the night.

'You can't sleep, either?'

Arla sighed, twisting strands of golden hair around her fingers. 'It's not often I do – sleep well, I mean.'

'Nightmares?'

'Sometimes,' she mused, beginning to stroll along the corridor. Reuben lingered at her side like a pet dog. 'Other times I find myself unable to stop thinking. Of what-ifs, and of the most terrifying scenarios that I know in the light of day have no possibility of ever coming true. But—'

'But in the dark it's different,' Reuben finished.

Goosebumps peppered Hark's body. It felt too much like he was eavesdropping on a private, intimate, conversation.

Yet he still couldn't stop his feet from following them.

'You're awake, too, Prince Reuben. Tell me what keeps you out of bed.'

Arla's voice was soft. Too soft. Too vulnerable. Hark found himself wanting the hardness back. The readiness to kill at a moment's notice.

Reuben huffed a laugh that held no amusement. 'My mother, mainly. She struggles here – has done for as long as I remember. It's wrong of me to spy but—'

'But you want to make sure she's safe,' Arla interrupted. 'I get that. Losing my parents tore me in half. I was lost at first, without them.'

Fucking gods!

He wanted to kill her.

For all her talk that needled and goaded about how much she *loathed* Kastonia and its people for what they had done to her parents, and here she was revealing her deepest feelings with its *prince,* of all people!

He should stay and listen to all of it. Should stay and follow them through the corridors and hallways of Larkire all night, listening to them share their feelings and downright *flirt* with one another.

But the thought of it made him want to vomit.

And besides, he had better plans, involving an old friend with silver hair whom he was supposed to have met in his rooms twenty minutes ago.

Damn Arla Reinhart and the prince.

CHAPTER 10

'Get out!' Hark groaned, pulling a shirt from the floor beside the bed as Arla charged through the doors into his room.

She'd seen the prick following her last night. She'd forced herself to go back to her own rooms after Reuben had left her, rather than batter Hark's door down to demand why he continued to *spy* on her.

But she'd been too vulnerable then, dragged out of sleep by images of her parents. Too still. Too dead. She'd tried to go back to sleep, of course. Had tried to distract herself with a book on the history of the kingdoms. How the kingdoms had been *queendoms,* once. How there had been wars fought over the land Hadalyn and Kastonia occupied. How in the Kingdom of Velor, on the continent, there were vast lakes rumoured to be home to mythical creatures – women with fishy tails who sang so beautifully they could lure men to their deaths. It was all nonsense, of course, but she enjoyed the tales of lands beyond the continent, where there were groups of islands with strange names such as Osana and Trapaly, which were home to magic beings with pointed ears.

None of those stories had kept her from wandering the corridors last night. Nor had they kept her from spotting a silver-haired girl disappear into Hark's rooms, or from becoming irrationally furious with him as a result.

She was leaving.

Today.

'Get up!' she snapped again, tossing Hark's saddlebag towards him.

'Hate to break it to you, sweetheart,' he said, stretching his arms high above his head, his voice coarser and smokier than usual and the remnants of sleep lingering within it, which made her heart stutter slightly, 'but the storm doesn't look like it's about to break anytime soon. You might be eager to go but I'm sure your mare won't thank you for it—'

'Vetta would gallop into hell if I asked her—'

'That may be so, but the road will still be blocked, and even if it weren't, the ground is likely to slip away beneath the horses' hooves. You wouldn't want yours to pick up another injury, would you.'

It was true. Every word.

The shingle and mud that made up the path towards the north would be a death trap in this weather. She owed her beloved Vetta more than forcing her out into these conditions.

Arla sighed, collapsing into a cushioned chair so inelegantly she could hear Perry scolding her for it in her head.

'Where's the girl you lured back, Stappen? Got bored of your incessant arrogance or are you really *that* bad in bed she had to escape before you could take her clothes o—'

'Don't you have somewhere to be?' he snapped. 'Or are you

actually incapable of entertaining yourself without resorting to violence that you must sit in my rooms and spout falsities?'

She smothered a smirk. 'When your boredom finally wins out, you let me know. We need to finish that duel.'

Hark barked a laugh. 'I *won* that duel.'

'No,' she said, tossing her braid over her shoulder. 'You cheated. There's a difference.'

'Your shoulder won't be up to it,' he said, striding to the windows. Arla didn't miss the grimace he tried to hide at the state of the weather outside.

'I've kept training through worse.' Her ankle often reminded her of it.

There was a surprising softness in Hark's gaze as he turned to face her. 'I know you have.'

She didn't know why her stomach swooped or why her palms became clammy, but she was out of the door before she could give it a second's thought.

She wandered for a while, running her hands over expensive banners and doorknobs with jewels encrusted into them. Larkire Palace was a thing to be admired, and she couldn't help but be drawn to it. It oozed luxury and treasures and secrets and she hated how much she liked it.

At the sight of a carved oak door protected by no fewer than four guards, Arla's intrigue was piqued beyond thoughts of where Larkire bought the yarn they used to weave their carpets. She strode past the door, noting the way the guards' hands twitched where they rested on the pommels of their swords.

Interesting.

It had to be where Elrod kept the most priceless jewellery and diamonds in his collection.

Arla was almost to the front doors of the palace, when Orson appeared from nowhere.

'Skulking about as usual, I see. Never knew when to keep your nose out of other people's business even when you were a girl.'

Ah. The same argument again.

'Not my fault Cyrus picked me, Orson,' Arla said sweetly, flashing him one of her most vexing smiles. 'Tell me, are you bitter because you didn't get chosen to be the King's Assassin *or* head of the King's Guard, or is it because you were beaten by a girl?'

Violence flashed in his eyes, a promise of all the things he'd like to do to her. He raised his fist in an instant, aiming straight for the spot in between her eyes.

He halted mere millimetres from her face.

'Tsk. You never did learn to control your temper,' Arla cooed, sauntering past him. She hadn't flinched and she knew it made him even angrier.

'I'll fucking kill you one day. Cyrus only sent me here as ambassador because he knew if I stayed in Hadalyn I'd slit your throat whilst you slept and he didn't want his *pet* to bleed out on the carpet.'

He was seething, a thick vein bulging in his forehead as he sneered at her. Orson wasn't much older than her – a couple of years, perhaps – but he had always treated her condescendingly, as if she were a child.

It made it all the sweeter that the role of King's Assassin had been created just for her.

'There's the temper again,' she called back over her shoulder. 'One of these days it'll be the death of you.'

~

'Your spying really has improved if you can read at the same time.'

Gods, she *hated* Hark Stappen.

'Why don't you disappear back to whatever dark hole you've crawled out of,' she said, not lifting her eyes from the page she turned between her fingers. The tavern she'd chosen to hide in for the afternoon was small and relatively quiet. It had been perfect. Until he'd arrived.

Hark huffed a laugh. 'Because, sweetheart, it's better *I* find you than the king, who is currently on his way through the town with an entourage. And you're not supposed to be here.'

Her ears pricked at that. She'd known they wanted her to stay inside the palace, but to send the guards *and* the king into Larkire to look for her?

'I'm surprised your king is so concerned with my where-abouts. It's not as if I'm fomenting rebellion or about to torch the place.'

'Debatable,' Hark mused. 'They're not, of course, out here in the middle of a storm advertising the fact that they're searching for you. Elrod does ride through the town sometimes – though admittedly not in these weather conditions – so it won't be entirely out of the ordinary for the townsfolk. But Orson's been in his ear all day, whispering that you're trying to discover secrets to use against them.'

Not exactly untrue...

But Orson was a traitorous bastard. His loyalty should be to Hadalyn and that included her.

'So they've sent a search party after me? Gods, don't they have anything better to do?'

'I would if I were them.'

'Why are *you* here?' She sighed, fastening her cloak at her throat. She didn't want to return to the palace. Not before everyone had gone to bed at least, and she wouldn't run the risk of seeing Hark with that silver-haired girl again.

The thought of him with her was enough to bring bile to her throat.

'Because you need to come back before Elrod can accuse you of espionage and have you executed.'

Please.

The thought was laughable.

But Arla gathered her things and left the tavern with Hark. They'd almost made it back to the palace gates when they were stopped by the King himself.

He rode a hulking grey beast with red and gold decorative banners stitched to its bridle. Water from the golden crown on the king's head ran in rivulets down his face. Arla could barely hear what he was saying over the wind.

'I do hope you've enjoyed your time in the town, Miss Rein-hart. Perhaps some tea? Something stronger, maybe?'

She felt Hark stiffen beside her and resisted the urge to balk beneath the king's gaze.

'That sounds lovely,' she managed to say through gritted teeth.

～

The king hosted her in his private rooms, sending Hark away to discuss trade deals with Orson. Arla smirked at the expression on the ambassador's face.

Reuben sat beside his father, his easy grin settling her

nerves at being so close to the man responsible for ruining her life.

The King poured the tea himself, a gesture so unexpected and strange for such a man that Arla couldn't work out what game he was playing with her.

'Tell me, Miss Reinhart, why you would venture out into my city when the weather is so atrocious. Is our palace not sufficient for your needs?'

Ah. So Hark was right. Elrod didn't want her loose in his city.

'The palace is a monument to luxury and grandeur, Your Majesty. Only, I am not used to being confined by the weather – a nervous disposition, if you will.'

Reuben raised a brow as he lifted the cup of tea to his lips. Arla didn't think she'd ever be able to get a lie past the prince. He seemed to have a knack for seeing straight through her.

Elrod raised a brow, leaning back in his chair and eyeing her in a way that was almost repulsive.

'I find it hard to believe Cyrus would employ someone with any sort of disposition besides one suited perfectly to disposing of his enemies. So tell me, assassin, what secrets were you hoping to learn in my town?'

Heat prickled at her skin, and for half a moment Arla could almost feel the wrongness of which the man at the market had spoken. There certainly was an oddness to the king, and she'd be a fool to lie so obviously in front of him.

'Secrets of Kastonia's history, mainly. Your kingdom is one I don't know well – even the ones on the continent have hosted me from time to time over the last couple of years.'

'Ah,' the King said. 'It is only natural for you to wish to know more about the closest neighbouring kingdom to your own, especially given our ... strained relationship. But there are no secrets here, Miss Reinhart. Everything you wish to know is in the history books.'

Bullshit.

'So tell me about the magic, then, Your Majesty. Your people speak of it as if it is still real. Tell me why that is.'

If he was playing a game, then she could, too, even if it meant biting her tongue while she heard more superstitious fairy tales about the eccentric beliefs that had this kingdom in a chokehold.

Something flashed in Elrod's eyes. Something that had her questioning if he might actually be about to plunge a dagger through her heart. But then his face cleared, and he spoke as if it were the most normal thing in the world.

'Magic was ... unlike anything we've ever seen, I believe. Long ago, magic was wielded freely in this kingdom, and in yours, too. The dragons were still seen around then, relaying messages from the gods and protecting those with magic in their blood. Those who didn't have magic became jealous, as is the way of things. Those who had magic threatened a greater power, one that reached beyond the mortal will of kings and queens. But over time, magical blood was diluted and eventually ... ran out – or so I've heard.'

His eyes had taken on a faraway look, and...

Oh gods, he fucking believes it, doesn't he?

Every single word. But there was an edge to his tone, one she hadn't heard others exercise when it came to the rumours of the magic-wielders long before.

'Tell me, Miss Reinhart, do you despise my kingdom for what we did to yours?' he asked suddenly.

For a moment, Arla thought her heart had stopped beating.

She blinked slowly, exhaling somehow through a jaw clenched so tightly she was sure it would crack.

'I ... I believe wholeheartedly in the cooperation of our two kingdoms. Whatever happened before is ... in the past.'

It broke her heart to say it.

There was silence. A stillness. She could feel every muscle in her body stretch tight. Tighter. Tighter. Until she was sure something would snap.

She jumped at the barking laugh released from Elrod's throat. 'A political answer, if ever I heard one. Cyrus has trained you well, Miss Reinhart.'

The king slurped the dregs of his tea, banging the cup down onto the saucer resting on the glass table between them.

Arla thought he must be able to hear her heart thundering in her chest.

'Excuse me, I have business to attend to,' Elrod said, rising from his chair and threatening to send everything on the table clattering to the floor. 'I do hope the *inside* of the palace will be sufficient for the rest of your stay.'

She took it as her cue to leave, rising gingerly from the cushioned seat. She didn't dare meet the gaze of the king, but the prince offered her a small smile as she slipped from the room.

CHAPTER II

Arla's heart didn't stop trying to leap out of her chest for long hours after she had left the king. She retired to her rooms, locking the door firmly behind her and pacing until she was sure the soles of her boots were about worn through.

Her breathing came too quickly, her ears filled with a rushing that wouldn't abate.

You're fine. He doesn't know.

But she didn't believe her own lie, because there was no way she could have hidden the blanching of her face or the way her words stumbled off her tongue when he'd asked if she despised them.

Of course she did.

She did, she did, she DID.

But she couldn't breathe a word of it. Not here, not now, not whilst she was still on a job.

The invitation for dinner arrived and she excused herself under the pretence of a headache. Hark would certainly see through the lie. Orson would continue to think her rude. Only the prince might miss her presence.

Arla finally managed to tamp down the fluttering feeling in her chest, but it was hours after dinner would have finished. She took to wandering the hallways again, wondering if she could con the guards into letting her see the palace diamonds. She wouldn't try it, not tonight – too many guards and she didn't have enough patience to do it in a way that would not cause a ruckus.

She found herself heading in the direction of the library, the lure of a book and somewhere far away from prying eyes was too comforting to resist. She didn't pause before slipping inside and closing the doors softly behind her.

It was a beautiful place, all worn, polished wood and creaky floorboards. A fire roared in the hearth of a magnificent fire-place, the mantel so beautifully carved she almost found herself believing in magic.

She ran her fingers over the spines of old books, some of them embossed with those funny symbols, and the dragonhart she'd seen on the books in her room. She breathed in the air, the scent of ink and ancient parchment washing over her in a familiar way. This was better. She could catch her breath here without feeling as though she would come undone.

'We should stop meeting like this, don't you think?'

Arla spun, cursing herself for not checking she was alone.

Reuben's eyes settled on the blade in her hand and he let out a low chuckle.

'My apologies, Lady Reinhart. I didn't mean to startle you.'

She swallowed thickly. Reuben was without his princely perfection tonight. Instead, his hair was ruffled, as though he'd been dragging a hand through it; gone was the doublet and expensive shirt. Tonight, he wore loose black trousers and a shirt that hadn't been pressed free of wrinkles.

'No, you're fine. I ... wasn't expecting anyone to be here. It's late.'

It was. She'd watched the sun set and the moon rise before she finally ventured out of her rooms. It seemed the prince shared her restlessness.

'It is,' Reuben said lightly, turning and stepping closer to the fire where a small wooden table sat between thickly cushioned armchairs. 'I assume someone like you knows the rules of chess?'

Arla couldn't help but follow him. 'And what do you mean by *someone like me*?'

Reuben laughed again and a grin began to split her lips at the sound of it.

'Someone who is far too clever to let a thief beat her at a game of cards in the market.'

A rushing filled her ears and her heart started that erratic rhythm again.

'Relax,' Reuben said. 'My father doesn't know. I doubt he knows the market even exists – or if he does he pretends not to – but walls talk and the guards even more so.'

Reuben moved a black knight. She followed with the white pieces laid out in front of her.

'Why didn't I know about you? Your people don't even speak of you.'

'Because,' Reuben said, moving a piece and knocking out one of her pawns. 'I've always been a secret. My father didn't want Hadalyn to know of my existence in case they should try to kidnap me. My mother was all too keen to keep up the ruse, if it meant she got to keep me close.'

'So, what, the people believe they have no heir? Surely that makes your father look weak?' Arla took the knight he had first moved.

'Oh, they know there's an heir,' he said lightly, his tone too full of secrets she wanted to unpick. 'But the details have always been on a need-to-know basis. I don't know what Hadalyn's been told, or what is generally believed over there.'

As far as she knew, the people of Hadalyn had no knowledge of a Kastonian prince, but perhaps the king's most senior advisors did – they must do, surely – though Cyrus had never spoken of it to her.

Why hadn't *she* thought of it?

'Tell me about your mother,' she said softly, breathing around the lump in her throat that formed at the memory of her own.

Reuben was silent for a moment, and when Arla looked at him there was a pain in his eyes that mirrored her own. 'She deserves more,' he said quietly. 'She has devoted herself to my father, and all she has received in return is a loneliness I think will be incurable.'

Arla almost felt sorry for the queen.

Almost.

Until she remembered who Arabelle was. The queen, too, had been complicit in the attack on Hadalyn.

'At least she has you,' Arla said gently.

'How could that ever be enough?' Reuben was studying her, a frown deepening the lines of his face before he cleared it of all emotion. 'Tell me, what's the deal with you and Hark? Do you really hate each other as much as you make out? I can tell you despise Orson for real, but Hark? I haven't made up my mind yet.'

Ah, now this she could answer honestly.

'Hark Stappen has a unique brand of arrogant self-importance and a penchant for getting on every last one of my nerves.'

Reuben barked out his laughter, accidentally knocking the table so Arla had to intervene to prevent the chess board from tumbling to the floor.

'Yes,' Reuben managed to say, 'he does have that effect on people, doesn't he.'

She felt the corner of her lips tug upwards. So the ambassador had a reputation for his infuriating presence, then. At least it wasn't solely directed at her.

'I don't imagine Orson is much better. It's a miracle that bastard hasn't tried to gut me in my sleep.'

'What went on there?' Reuben asked, swiping another one of her pieces from the board.

'He tried to go up against me for leader of the King's Guard. He lost. I became King's Assassin. Cyrus sent him here as ambassador to stop us fighting. Nothing else to it.'

There *was* more to it. Orson had made her life a living hell when she'd been in training – had revelled in the torture she endured during the six days – and it had taken that knife through her palm to prove just how serious she was. The scar was worth it for the look on his face when Cyrus granted her a title.

'That's why he spends so much time getting close to my father. Wants a job at the top of the army, I bet.'

Arla stilled for half a second. Orson should be no more than civil to Elrod – he was only an ambassador, after all. He should still be loyal to Hadalyn.

Then again, Arla wouldn't put it past him to switch sides. She'd always known him as a slippery bastard.

She was growing tired, her eyelids dropping with the heat of the fire. She was hardly watching the board now.

'Don't you wish sometimes you could escape. Go anywhere in the world where no one can find you?' the prince asked.

It was a dream that often tempted her.

'Why do you say that?' she asked.

'Because, what's the point in staying somewhere you aren't wanted?' Reuben said, his eyes lost in a faraway look. 'My father thinks me weak – not cut out to represent this kingdom. I think if it weren't for Mother I'd have run a long time ago.'

There was a vulnerability to the prince she should be exploring, figuring out, so that she could use it to her advantage. She couldn't bring herself to do it.

She'd never had many friends, always finding relationships too difficult, too complex when she saw others making it look easy. But right there, cosily playing chess by the fire in the library, she thought she might have made one.

'Checkmate,' she uttered softly.

Reuben stared at the board and then at her face, as if he'd only just realised they were still playing. Something flashed in his gaze then, and that vulnerability she had seen seconds ago began to harden over.

'The storm is meant to be worse tomorrow. Another few days before it breaks, the guards were saying.'

Arla couldn't help the sinking feeling in her stomach. She needed to leave. Days ago.

But Reuben was looking at her again, that charming grin finding its way beneath her skin. 'I'll see you tomorrow night?'

A soft smile parted her lips. 'Yes, you'll see me tomorrow.'

It was five days before the storm passed, which made ten since she had left Hadalyn. It was too long. She should be on her way back home by now.

She had spent her evenings with Reuben in the library, laughing over games of chess and discussing books that made her heart sing. She'd grown to like the prince – had somehow separated him in her mind from the atrocities of Kastonia and its king. She hated that there was a part of her that would miss Reuben when the sun finally rose and she could set off for the border.

Hark seemed all too desperate to be leaving, but as she strapped her weapons back in their rightful places, Arla was surprised to find she couldn't summon that same desperation.

CHAPTER 12

'Cold?'

Yes, she was bloody freezing, actually.

'No,' Arla uttered, glad of Vetta's warmth as the mare carried her over the frozen ground. Winter was well on its way, and if it was freezing here in Kastonia, it would be unbearable on the northern border.

'Liar.' Hark smirked from astride Eros, immediately better suited to the black stallion than she had been. Her short legs were no match for such a beast.

They had met each other on the way down to the stables, both hauling their saddle bags packed to the brim with warmer clothes and an excess of bread and cheese. It would be fine. She had worked in the cold before, and for a job as simple as intercepting stolen supplies, she would be back in the warmth in no time. Five days. That's all she would allow herself. Five days to make it to the border, kill a thief, and return to Hadalyn. Easy as blinking.

Perhaps it was the quiet beauty of the morning after the

storm, or maybe she was relieved to be finally on the road again. Either way, she hadn't mustered up the usual level of irritation at seeing Hark Stappen ride beside her this morning and was the first to speak between them.

'It's nice to be outside again, don't you think?'

Hark scoffed, a rough sound that made her turn in the saddle to face him. 'I'd have thought you'd want to stay in Larkire. You certainly looked content enough.'

Ah. So he'd seen her with the prince, then.

'I had to do something to keep me entertained, Stappen. It was that or start killing people.'

She hadn't meant it literally – she didn't think so, at least – but the comment only seemed to feed Hark's irritation.

'I guess I can't say I'm surprised. You have a knack for culti-vating royal favour. Cyrus's whore – isn't that what the courtiers call you? How else could you manage to charm your way into his good graces? It surely can't be for your skill.'

Gods. He had woken up ... cruel.

'At least I've made something of myself. "King's Assassin" has a better ring to it than "Kastonian Ambassador", don't you think?'

'Aren't you just so lovely this morning.'

She *hated* him.

'You're pathetic, and had I not been on specific orders from my king, you'd have been dead before we crossed Hadalyn's border,' she spat back.

'And you think that would work? You have seen the might of Kastonia before – and it didn't end very well for you or your parents, did it?'

She swallowed the bile that rose in her throat. He'd gone too far. Her skin was suddenly hot, and a roaring was beginning in her ears so loudly that she couldn't think straight. Her heart pounded against her chest, and she didn't know if he was still speaking or not; couldn't focus on anything but the burn in her throat and the bitter taste in her mouth.

Was he trying to get himself killed?

Because she could happily do it right now.

CHAPTER 13
HARK

Gods, he was such a prick.

He hadn't meant to *upset* her. At least, that's what he thought was happening. She had shut down completely, her spine had stiffened, and a grim line had replaced the arrogant smirk she so often wore with pride.

He couldn't apologise, though – didn't want to. He couldn't grow to *like* her, and he certainly couldn't care about offending her.

The less he knew about Arla Reinhart the better. She was a conniving, wicked little wretch, and it was as plain as the dragon tattooed on his heart that she didn't plan on letting him return to Hadalyn alive. He'd be lucky to make it back to Kastonia without a blade in the back, especially after this.

For two years they had just about tolerated each other. Two years of nasty retorts and looks that would threaten the gods. But now that he had crossed the line, he regretted it and didn't know why. Perhaps it was seeing the fire leave those coal-black eyes – though they were not black at all when you looked closely, more the colour of coffee beans in the right light—

Enough. He shouldn't be close enough to even tell.

But he still felt relief when she began speaking again.

'Prince Reuben is rather confident, isn't he?'

Hark's shoulders stiffened at her words. He shouldn't have mentioned it before – that he'd seen her getting close with the prince. Now she knew it irritated him, she would prod and poke at that annoyance until she dragged a reaction from him.

'No more confident than other princes,' he said, clenching his jaw against ... what?

He blocked out whatever she said next, the grinding of his teeth the only sound he allowed to penetrate the bubble of nothingness he wove around him. She had got closer to the prince in the span of a few days than Hark had ever seen her be with anyone at Castle Grey. It had angered him beyond words the first night; had rendered him tossing and turning all night for reasons he couldn't explain. She hadn't known the prince existed before this mission. King Elrod kept the boy on a tight leash and he almost never allowed him to leave the four walls of Larkire Palace. Hark presumed Arla's ignorance on the matter was also partly the result of allowing her hatred to blind her to the facts. She'd probably never cared to spend a second of her time researching the kingdom that had stormed hers. He knew she had only travelled through it a dozen times, never lingering a second longer than she had to. Still, he had been surprised.

'He's charming really – for a Kastonian. I'd expected someone bitter and twisted like the rest of your—'

'Enough.' Lethally soft – a warning. Hark didn't know how he'd let her back into his head, only that he didn't wish to hear a second more for fear of what he would do if he heard the prince's name on her lips again.

But Arla Reinhart had never known when to keep her gods-damned mouth shut, and Hark hated that he was glad of it.

CHAPTER 14

Hark's warning stopped her in the middle of the sentence. He had all but growled it at her, and Eros tossed his head against the pressure Hark maintained on the reins, knuckles almost white with the tension.

'Not nice, is it? To hear that—'

'You know you're not the only one who's suffered, Reinhart.' He halted the stallion abruptly, spinning in the saddle to face her. Had she not faced down nastier, more dangerous men, she might have shuddered under the thunder that rolled in those stormy eyes. 'You think it's easy, trying to support a kingdom that doesn't want to help itself? You think it's easy watching your people suffer and starve to death and knowing there's not one damn thing you can do about it?'

He was furious with her; she'd hit a nerve and it was stinging over and over as he tried to defend a kingdom that was inexcusable. Something in her – something cruel and wicked –

delighted in it, and now she had him between her teeth, she wanted to make him bleed.

'Oh, there's quite a lot you could have done for them. But now they're too far gone so you may as well let them die and live in luxury alongside the king and queen in that magnificent castle of theirs.'

Gods, she needed to learn when to stop.

'You moan about how terrible your life has been.' His voice had melted into something deadly soft – a warning, if ever she had heeded one. 'But what's even sadder than the sorry excuse for an assassin that you are, is that no one will ever love you. Or like you. Or want you. You are nasty, and wicked, and you can sit atop that mare and lecture me on *my* kingdom, but is yours any better, Reinhart? I don't see it blooming with wealth and vitality, either.'

He left her there, Vetta pawing the ground as Arla's mind went blank. She deserved it, really. She *was* wicked, and nasty, and cruel, and he was right: no one *would* ever love her.

So why did her heart ache as she urged Vetta into a trot to catch up with him?

'I don't pretend to help my people,' she said softly, trying against her own instincts to patch a bridge between them. She didn't know why, really, because she was planning to kill him before they returned anyway – if she could figure out a way to do so without Cyrus killing *her* – but it would be a long journey if they weren't speaking. And besides, she needed him to at least cooperate with her if they were going to dispose of the raiders that had been following them for the past hour. She wondered if he had noticed them, too.

'Then how can you lecture me on mine?' he replied, somewhat less sharp than he had been before.

'Because it's easy. I see Cyrus trying every day to solve trading issues and famine, to build relationships with other kingdoms and improve the land. I see myself out slitting the throats of thieves and Hadalyn's enemies, but when I look at Kastonia... Well, I see a kingdom that doesn't want to help itself. I see the meadows and acres and acres of rich farmland that no one tends. And *why*? You have far more land than Hadalyn ever had. I guess I find it difficult to understand why no one has the motivation to grow their own food rather than relying on hand-outs from other kingdoms.' Gods, this was the most vulnerable she had been in years, and she hated that it was in front of Hark Stappen, of all people. She'd have to do something extra violent to make up for the sliver of softness in her heart.

'I won't pretend that the king and queen are good people, but don't blame the rest of Kastonia for a decision that two people made. And that land...' Hark was silent for a long minute, his eyes hazy as he relaxed the reins slightly. 'That land may look rich and fertile, but nothing will take there. It hasn't since the dragons went to sleep. They've tried for years to grow their own food; it's not their fault the land is tainted.'

It was an incredible excuse. She didn't believe in dragons or magic or that the land was cursed. But perhaps there *was* something wrong with the soil. She had heard of diseases that spread through the earth, and, honestly, the way Hark's brows pinched together and hearing the raw emotion in his voice persuaded her to his cause. Perhaps Kastonia really was struggling to grow crops and there wasn't anything to be done about it.

'Well, let's hope Prince Reuben uses his charm and skill to rule the kingdom a hell of a lot better than his parents,' she said, trying to steer the conversation back onto safe ground.

'If you don't watch yourself, Reinhart, people will start thinking you're infatuated with him.'

'Oh, don't be so ridiculous.' She laughed, the action foreign to her in present company. It was out of place, really, considering that the shadows in the trees were inching towards their horses despite the brisk pace they kept up.

She reached behind her slowly to feel the reassuring smoothness of the wooden bow at her back.

'Really? You haven't shut up about him since—'

'I'm going to need you to duck,' she interrupted, twisting in her saddle.

'What?'

Too late. The arrow flew with the twang of a bowstring and arced over the top of his head before finding its mark between the eyes of a raider in dirty, ragged clothes. It was perhaps the truest arrow she had ever fired.

'Fucking gods!' Hark exhaled, twisting in his own saddle to face the growing group of outlaws slinking out from the trees behind them.

'I said *duck*.' Gods did he ever listen? The blade she had sheathed at her waist flew past him, narrowly missing a high, sculpted cheekbone as it hit the target with a thump followed by a thud as the body fell from the ash tree and hit the earth.

'A little warning would have been nice,' Hark called as his own blades began flying at the encroaching raiders. Gods they must have been out here for months – if not years. Their skin was thick with dirt, though they were not hard to spot even from the distance she maintained with carefully aimed flicks of her now dwindling stash of blades.

'I'll argue with you later, Stappen. I'm a little preoccupied!' Gods he was a pain in her arse, and it was a constant effort to get a clear aim on their attackers with his horse panicking and turning tight circles. Not Vetta though, never sweet Vetta who had been put through rigorous training to ensure she would stand still as an ox when she was asked to. Eros seemed as unsure as his mount.

Or not.

Hark was hurling blade after blade after blade into the mob, each one hitting its mark in a heart or an eye, even with his stallion spinning as wildly as a beast that had come unbroken from the mountains.

Arla cursed her own stupidity for not strapping an armoury's worth of weapons to her. She was an assassin, and she was currently being assisted by the ambassador of the neighbouring kingdom. Gods, he'd never let her live this down.

She unsheathed an arrow and fired it at the raiders. She loved her bow. It held a certain elegance that had attracted her the very first time she had felt the strings against her fingers, though her first attempts at firing one, at the age of fourteen, had been laughable – her arrows often hit their targets but never quite where she had meant them to.

Still, she was glad she had brought it when her next shot resulted in a raider falling from a tree with an arrow in the gap between his nose and eye socket.

'I'm not one to run from a fight, Reinhart, but as we have horses and they don't, d'you think—'

'I do think, yes.'

It was all that was needed for Hark's heels to dig harshly into Eros's side and send the horse launching into a gallop, Vetta quick on his heels as the raiders hollered and threw their own knives back at them. She had lost two lovely blades today; Cyrus had better pay her extra for the inconvenience.

There had been so many of them. Not that she had been shocked to know they were following her, exactly. Raiders had been living in the wilderness, away from civilisation, for as long as the kingdoms had begun falling. She encountered them almost every time she needed to cross the border into Kastonia, and they had been relatively easily dealt with. But never so many...

Had attacking strangers in the woods become a better life than living in a kingdom protected by walls and kings?

There were a few towns between the centre of Kastonia and its northern border, but she had never spent any time in them. They were small and unwelcoming, and were often comprised of local citizens who stared whenever someone new entered their secluded piece of the world. It was surprising that Kastonia still held any claim over the towns, really. They had managed to negotiate their own trade deals from across the sea, and they were loath to share with the rest of the country. The townsmen were rulers in their own right, and she wondered if Elrod only allowed the towns to continue their existence because the taxes they paid offered much-needed coin to the Crown and its grossly wealthy palace.

'At what point were you going to tell me that they were following us?' Hark asked her as they pulled the horses up beside a stream.

She laughed, swinging her leg over the saddle and stretching her muscles in the few minutes they allowed themselves.

'I did. I told you to duck.'

'When they were already on top of us!' he scolded, dropping down from Eros and splashing his hands in the water.

'Well maybe you should be a little more aware of your surroundings.'

He said nothing, and when she looked up at him, she caught the fleeting smirk he tried to hide. 'Come on, we're only an hour from Irelliad.'

'Irelliad?'

'The town we're staying in.' He hauled himself back onto his stallion and checked the leather straps on his saddlebags, which were slightly lighter now that they had been relieved of some of their provisions. It was strange, having another person with her on a job, and she didn't know if that made her more complacent than she had already started becoming. If she'd been on her own, she would have planned where she was staying and known the entire time. This time she had left it to Hark to dictate to her when and where they would be resting.

It was comical, really, that she didn't plan or plot anymore. She was content to go with the motions, reacting to what she faced rather than preparing extensively for it as she had done in her first couple of months as assassin to the King of Hadalyn. Had she become so good that planning wasn't needed?

Or was it that she no longer cared whether she landed herself in danger; that killing and slaughtering her way out of situations didn't have the same effect on her as it used to?

CHAPTER 15

Trelliad was a dreary place, clearly made bearable only by the alcohol carried on the breath of everyone to whom Arla and Hark begrudgingly spoke. Every wall of every building was cracked, and the roofs sloped and sagged in places that suggested snow had weighed them down considerably in the years they had stood here. The streets ran through the town in a wet, windy route full of sludge and cobbles that were worn smooth. It seemed the only bit of life was imprisoned in the few taverns peppering the landscape.

It was perfect.

Arla had spent many hours hiding in slums and dirty, over-crowded taverns as part of her job, and this sad little border town would not be any different. If she wanted amusement, she could cause a brawl. If she wanted a drink, well, that was obvi-ous. If she wanted a few moments of distraction and wandering hands, there would be no shortage of men she could choose to tumble with – the gods knew it would keep her mind from wandering into darker places for at least a small portion of her evening. She'd started a tally of the nobles she had coerced back to her rooms at Castle Grey. Owain Hendrics – one of the court musicians – had kept her entertained for the longest; he would certainly be welcome back.

Hark, on the other hand, looked appalled.

She stifled a chuckle as they sidled up to a barn that had surely seen better days, the paint so old and peeling she couldn't decide what colour the wood had been. But a barn it was, and the smell of sweet hay rolled out from the entrance as a thin, reedy man approached, taking the horses with nothing more than a grunt and a finger pointed to the front door of the tavern opposite.

'Gods, this place is disgusting,' Hark grumbled as he pulled the door open, scowling where it hung detached from the bottom hinge.

Arla smirked to herself. 'Stop moaning. It's cleaner than the shit-hole that surrounds Kastonia's palace walls. And don't pretend you won't find a nice lady to take back to your bed. Honestly, Stappen, the day you sleep alone is the day those imaginary dragons wake up and fly home.'

He didn't reply, instead shoving past her and striding up to a broken desk and a shaky old woman.

'I need two rooms.'

Good gods, this was going to be hard work. He would have them thrown out before the horses were unsaddled.

'Please, madam, if you don't mind,' Arla said quickly, summoning her courtly charm and sliding in front of Hark. The woman looked her up and down, and Arla prayed to whatever gods there were left that she wouldn't recognise her.

'*Two* rooms?' the woman asked, eyes squinting as her gaze switched between the pair of them.

'Please. My brother really does snore loud enough to wake the dead and we've had a long journey.'

'Say no more,' the woman said, waving a hand and pulling two rusty keys out from the inside of her tunic.

Gods, what sort of a place had Hark brought them to?

'Brother?' he grumbled in her ear as the woman counted the coins Arla had handed over. Too much for the rooms they needed but it would be enough to buy the woman's silence. She hoped.

'Well, you couldn't possibly be my lover, could you? I don't have any intention of sharing a room with you,' she hissed.

'What about *friend*?'

'Hmm, I didn't think of that.' She winked, swiping the keys from the table as the woman nodded once at her, clearly satisfied with the overpayment.

Hark sighed, running a hand through his midnight strands before hauling the saddle bags up the stairs behind her. *Friend.*

Of course she'd thought of it – it had been her first answer, actually. But to piss him off? Yes, *loudly snoring brother* would do nicely.

The room was ... fine. It was missing the silk sheets and the jasmine oils in which she would have liked to bathe, but it would do. If you didn't look too closely, it was possible to ignore the holey bedding and thick layer of dust on the rough floorboards.

Gods it had been too long since Cyrus had sent her on a job so far afield. She had got so comfortable living the luxurious life of a royal, that she had begun to forget that she wasn't one.

The sharp rap on the door was unexpected, and her hand was on the blade concealed beneath her cloak before the door handle had started turning. A door that didn't lock. How convenient.

What appeared on the other side of the door, arms straining under the weight of two steaming bowls, was not a thief or someone sent to kill her, however, but Hark Stappen, freshly washed and bearing hot food.

All thoughts of pissing him off dissolved immediately.

'Is that—?'

'Stew. Pheasant, or rabbit or... Actually, I don't want to know what it is,' Hark said, shouldering through the doorway and handing one of the bowls to her.

Gods, it smelt delicious. Rabbit, vegetable, lamb, fox – she didn't care. Only wine could have made it better.

Hark sat at the foot of the bed, watching her as she shuffled so her back was against the headboard and her knees created a cage for the bowl to sit in. The warmth seeped through the leather uniform she wore and for a split second, she imagined she was at home in Castle Grey.

'Thank you,' she said in between spoonfuls, slightly surprised he had bothered to fetch her anything, let alone chose to eat *with* her.

'I figured being hungry as well as cold would make you entirely unpleasant tomorrow, Reinhart,' he said, the corner of his mouth tugging upwards slightly.

'Add that to the loss of my favourite blades and you'd have been in for a difficult morning.' She grinned back, surprised at how quickly her mood had changed upon the arrival of steaming hot food.

'Don't think I didn't notice how poor those arrows were that you fired today. I nearly lost my head at one point.'

She snorted into her stew. Out of a dozen arrows she had

fired, only two had found their mark. Of course he'd noticed. 'I may not be very accurate with it, but a bow is my favourite.'

Hark barked a laugh. 'Favourite what? Way of getting yourself killed with your own arrows?'

She grinned again, nudging him with her foot. 'I've practised a *lot*—'

'Not enough, by the looks of it,' Hark interrupted.

'Hey, you should have seen me the first time I held one. Nearly sent Perry to the infirmary with an arrow through his shoulder.'

'If you're so bad,' Hark chuckled, 'why on earth would you continue to use one?'

'Because I get better every time I shoot. And I look good with a bow.'

'You are the vainest woman I've ever met,' Hark said, laughing softly and dragging a hand through his hair. 'It's a wonder you passed the King's Guard tests at all.'

'I passed because I don't *need* a bow. There's a difference.' Hark arched a brow. 'I haven't missed a target with my blades in all the years I've been in royal service,' she said proudly. It was a testament to her skill and perseverance that she had transformed, from the gangly child the king had plucked as his ward, to the woman she was today.

'You haven't missed a single shot?'

'Not one.'

'I don't believe you. There's no way you can throw blades half as far as an arrow would fly and still hit your mark,' Hark stated, placing his now empty bowl on the floor and pulling his legs onto the bed.

'I didn't say I could throw as far as an arrow, but I'm not far off. I stand by my first answer; I have never missed a mark.'

'How?'

'Because I never take a shot I can't make.'

'Oh,' was all he said, drinking deeply from the canteen he had brought with him. They settled into an easy silence as she finished her food. She thought he would leave her now, go back to whatever it was Hark Stappen did in his spare time – likely something involving the pretty housemaid they'd passed on the way in – he spoke again.

'Why did you do it?' he asked softly.

'Do what?'

'Almost kill yourself to become King's Assassin?'

Gods, it wasn't an answer she could easily give. She didn't know herself, really. Just that she had been so broken, and so beyond fixing, that the only way she could find to collect those shattered pieces of her heart was to vow never to let it happen again. She would bleed onto the stones of Hadalyn before she let her people be mindlessly slaughtered again.

'Because I won't be weak again. I won't let Ettie and Neb lose their mother the way I lost mine.'

He didn't speak for a moment, and she wondered if she had laid too much of herself open in that one short sentence. She hated this ... vulnerability. She found it difficult to get the words in the right order and force them to leave her tongue. But she was tired, and the warmth of the room was toying with the icy walls she had built around herself.

'I watched you train every day when you were going through King's Guard, you know.'

No, she *hadn't* known.

'Not on purpose. You were just always where I happened to be.'

That had been intentional. Curse her heart if she would let a wolf into the den without knowing everything there was to know about it. Hark had arrived at Hadalyn the very same week Cyrus had finally given her permission to test for the King's Guard – to move from soldier to the elite team tasked with protecting the king.

'I thought you couldn't possibly be serious, even after you went through "the six days".' Gods, that had almost broken her. *The six days* – one of the most brutal parts of training to be in the King's Guard, the trial that separated soldier from guard. Six days of torture. Those who broke maintained their rank as soldier; those who passed were King's Guard. There was a reason there were rarely more than a dozen at a time.

'But then I watched you drive that knife through the palm of your hand over dinner after your first three months in the Guard.' He winced across the bed from her, and she couldn't help but do the same at the painful memory of it. Hark had been at Castle Grey for nine months at that point and she had spent most of those months arguing with him over dinner. Gods, that had been more than a year ago now...

No one had believed that she was good enough to lead the Guard. They said she wouldn't sacrifice enough.

That single act of self-inflicted violence had prompted Cyrus to create the position of King's Assassin for the one person who was loyal enough to kill herself for him if he asked it of her.

'Cyrus was furious with me,' she scoffed, glad now that she could see the amusement in an act that had left her unable to wield a sword for weeks.

'You bled over the tablecloth at a formal dinner. He'd have hanged you, had your loyalty not impressed him so much.'

'Yeah, well, I said I would bleed for the people and I meant it.'

'It won't happen again,' he said softly, almost to himself rather than to her. As if he had any sort of say in it.

It kept her awake at night – the worrying. Kastonia was more desperate now than ever before, and the old beliefs clearly raged so prominently amongst the people that she couldn't help but expect another raid on her kingdom.

'Do you ever feel bad? For what your kingdom did to mine?'

'I hate how it affected yo— Your kingdom. The survivors. I hate how it affects them...' he said solemnly, a faraway look in his eyes, as if he could see back nine years ago to that fateful day. 'Go to sleep, Reinhart. Tomorrow will be a long day.'

He took the empty bowls, then, and slipped out of her room with a fluidity she would have been glad to master herself.

She fell asleep wondering how the two of them had ended up here. He'd watched her train and go from guard to assassin and she had spent the entirety of it hating him. But tonight he had been kind. He had brought her food when he didn't have to. She supposed she could respect him for that. Besides, he wasn't bad to look at, and he appreciated her violence and quick temper. It was more than anyone else had ever done.

A small corner of her heart wondered what could have been, if he hadn't come from that wretched kingdom.

She squashed the thought immediately.

CHAPTER 16
HARK

S leep didn't find him for many hours after he left her. The image of her curls tumbling around her shoulders as she watched him leave was burning a hole straight through him. Those deep, dark eyes he knew had been tracking him across the room like she was preparing to pounce at any moment... She could have easily been a courtesan – could have married well and ruled over kingdoms on the continent.

But she hadn't.

Arla Reinhart had decided a profession of blood and violence was better suited to her fiery heart, and Hark didn't know what sort of damage had to be done to someone for them to decide they were worth nothing more than the king's crest and a leather uniform. He knew she regretted the rare moments she had been honest and open with him, but he had seen something else pass over her face when she finally spoke about her life. Relief.

He had heard of the dark moods that often saw her go missing from the palace. He didn't know where she went. He only ever heard the whispers of the servants saying Arla was affected by the same low moods as her king, by which he often found himself trapped. The first time she disappeared, Hark had found himself walking the streets of Grey Hill in the middle of the night half expecting to find her—

No. He'd stopped himself thinking it then, and he wouldn't now. Arla was sensible; she wouldn't do anything.

He'd known even back then that he couldn't truly hate her, no matter how much vitriol she hurled his way. He'd lain awake every night she went missing after that, unable to let himself fall asleep until he heard the telltale sound of her window latch down the hall.

Gods, what was he getting himself into? Arla was a trained assassin. She had been groomed to be a killer, a discoverer of secrets, a manipulator. And that was exactly what she had done tonight. She was teasing him with glimpses into her life to make him trust her; to make him see her as a person and not a weapon belonging to Hadalyn's king.

She would make him trust her, and then she would drive a knife through his back.

Maybe he'd let her.

It might stop the fucking pounding of his heart that hadn't let up since leaving Hadalyn. He'd known it was coming of course – he couldn't be holed away in Castle Grey forever whilst Kastonia was falling to sickness and poverty. And there was the case of these *shipments* Elrod had got himself involved in that had inevitably snared Hadalyn's king, too. But this journey, this *job* they'd both been sent on...

Well, nothing good could come of it. Arla would curse him all the way to hell and probably fucking beyond it when she found out the sorts of things Kastonia was dealing in. Cyrus was out of his mind if he believed she'd go along with it, though the old king was likely senile, anyway – or heading that way at least. Cyrus was a strong leader, yes, but the edge that had granted him victory in the battle of Grey Hill all those years ago had smoothed with age. He trusted too easily. He'd agreed to work with Elrod on these shipments, for fuck's sake! It was the beginning of the end for Hadalyn's king, and Hark could see it a mile off.

He'd try not to think of it though. He'd keep his focus on the journey to the border. Not that the thought of that filled him with any less dread. Journeying to the border never came without its challenges. Always too cold, too wet, too many towns they needed to stop in at on the way with people that looked at him through narrowed eyes. Kastonia's people weren't happy; they hadn't been for a long time. And with him being so close to the king, he was an easy target – someone on whom they could take out their frustrations.

He hated his position sometimes.

But maybe this would be the last time he'd have to make the journey. Perhaps, if he didn't die at the hand of Hadalyn's assassin, he could go somewhere far away – the continent, maybe. He ignored the voice in the back of his mind telling him there was no way. No way, no way, no way that he could *ever* cross the sea. Too much responsibility here. Too many secrets he'd sworn an oath to protect.

But ... he had dreamed once. Of what it would be like to be a sailor. To captain a ship. The sea had called to him from the moment he was born, as if his blood moved with the tide. What if he ran? What if he left all of this behind and fled on a ship to map the wildest of seas and maybe, if he was lucky, marry the daughter of a fisherman? What a simple, lovely dream.

That he could never fucking have.

He sighed, dragging a hand through his hair, swallowing at the memory of Arla's face in his mind, so soft and open tonight.

He fell asleep to the dream of boats and women that would lure him to his death.

CHAPTER 17

It was still dark outside when she pulled her cloak tightly around her shoulders and met Hark saddling the horses. Their conversation had kept her awake last night; had kept her turning over the pieces of themselves they had laid bare. She wouldn't make the same mistake again. She had been hungry and tired, and ... in need of a friend. But Hark Stappen was not a friend. He could never be a friend. His blood ran scarlet; hers ran grey – they could never, *ever* be mixed.

He too looked tired. Dark circles hung under his eyes and the icy blue of his irises was a steely grey this morning. She wondered if he regretted the olive branch carefully laid between them last night or if he wished to snap it in half like she did?

'I hope you packed warm clothes, Reinhart. The frost is unlikely to thaw today,' he huffed.

'Here,' she said, tossing a pair of leather gloves towards him. They weren't fleece-lined, but they would keep the frost from biting at the bare skin of his hands. Her fingers were already warming in her own pair.

'Where did you get these?' he questioned, and she knew he was already regretting asking.

'I bought them,' she replied.

'Sure you did.' He rolled his eyes, knowing as well as she did that no merchants operated before the sun was up. Nevertheless, he forced his hands into the leather anyway.

'Let's go.'

~

Some days, she regretted becoming the King's Assassin. Today was one of those days.

She'd have much preferred to be clothed in silk and jewels, and to be reading books in front of a fire in the library, away from everyone else. Of course, she enjoyed court life, too; that couldn't be denied. She felt a certain draw to the perfect superficiality of it, and she wondered sometimes if perhaps being a courtier was a deadlier profession than her own. She had seen the way the women fought using batted eyelashes, or an elegant stumble over a non-existent obstacle, to capture the attention of the king or another of the nobility that frequented the palace.

The king would never marry. A distant cousin was next in line for the throne, a man significantly younger than Cyrus who was having what she imagined to be a lot of fun studying on the continent, ready for his ascension to the throne one day. Cyrus hadn't shown any interest in marriage in his fifty or so years, and though he was kind and fell into every single trap the ladies laid for him, his heart belonged to Perry.

She thought of the king's advisor with a special fondness. Perry had raised her on behalf of the king when she'd been brought to the castle, and since hitting her teenage years, she and Perry had squabbled almost every day. There was an enduring love between them that was untouched by the snipes and horrible things they said to one another when Cyrus's moods rubbed off on them both – which was often – and only Perry seemed able to chase them away.

'What are you smiling at?' Hark asked, looking over at her from his seat atop Eros. The sun had risen, finally, but it had done little to chase away the damp fog and the utter misery of the weather. Perhaps it was just too cold for the sun's rays to reach them this far north.

'Nothing. How far away are we?'

She knew exactly how far away they were. She'd been to the northern border enough times to recognise the sharp uprisings of rock and barren landscape that told her exactly where they were.

'Close. I'm hoping whoever is stealing supplies is stupid enough to do so in broad daylight,' Hark replied.

She scoffed. Not likely. Whoever was stealing the shipments was organised enough for Elrod to request the assistance of Hadalyn's assassin and to send this useless ambassador along with her.

Not useless. He nearly bested you, remember?

'What's so important about these shipments to warrant Elrod *and* Cyrus getting involved?'

Hark's shoulders tensed, and Arla wondered what he knew that she didn't.

'Surely Elrod could have used his own soldiers to handle this without requiring me to leave Castle Grey? she continued. 'Or is Kastonia so poor that they don't *have* soldiers anymore?'

Wishful thinking. She knew their army would be fit and ready to march at a moment's notice.

'No idea. Perhaps some kingdoms can't afford to lose even a single crate of food, Reinhart.'

'I thought the shipments were iron?'

Hark paused. It wasn't the first time she'd thought there was something more to these shipments than the raw material for weapons.

'Iron, mainly. But there are crates of grain and food brought in from other kingdoms alongside it. Elrod is most concerned with the iron and the money that both he and Cyrus have invested in getting it here. The food is secondary.'

Right.

'Perhaps, if your king weren't so greedy, then your kingdom wouldn't feel the effects of a single missing crate,' she finally replied, mentally readying herself for the next argument that would form between them. It truly was exhausting being around him.

'That's not the reason the kingdoms are suffering, and you know it.' He didn't look at her, just kept his eyes fixed on a point in the distance.

'Oh, enlighten me, Stappen, as to exactly what you think is making your country so poor, because it's certainly not ours. *We* were coping just fine until we had to start taking in *your* citizens because *your* king was too *greedy* to be able to support them!'

It would all come out, then. Just how frustrated she was at trying to help rebuild her own kingdom and protect its people whilst also keeping track of the hundreds of Kastonian refugees that were arriving in Hadalyn each month. It filled her with a fury that often carried her to the training rooms so she could take that anger out on whoever was available to duel with her.

She hated that Cyrus even entertained the treaty between Kastonia and Hadalyn. How he could stomach allowing Kastonia's refugees into Hadalyn after what their forces had done? She would never understand the political chess game involved in ruling a country.

'Oh, stop it!' he snapped, turning in the saddle to face her. 'The kingdoms are suffering because the gods demand it so. We're being punished. It's clear as day.'

Oh gods, she really was going to start laughing.

'Do you think for one moment I'm going to believe that? The gods disappeared a very, very long time ago – if they ever existed at all – and to think they care enough to *punish* us? Don't be so ridiculous.'

Hark's eyes turned dark as she spoke, and for a minute she contemplated gripping the blade sheathed at her thigh for fear he was going to throw his own at her. The thought sent a thrill through her blood. He truly did believe in the old religion, then.

'The sooner this is dealt with, the sooner you can return to killing people, and thieving off your own citizens, and skulking around with those *vultures*! I've about had enough of—'

'I don't think we're too far off your wish coming true, Stappen,' she interrupted, her gaze focused over his shoulder to where the rock dropped away and revealed a drop so deep, she didn't think they would ever see the bottom of it.

They did, though. Because at the bottom, on the flat plains of some barren, frozen landscape, were the shipments.

~

'Slaves? The shipments are *slaves*?'

She couldn't believe it – wouldn't believe it.

Keeping slaves was forbidden. So to trade them like this, on this scale...

But the man at the market ... the man she'd wagered her necklace to question ... he had mentioned the slaves. He'd told her Elrod was making money from them.

She'd believed it was a lie. Believed he couldn't possibly have any of Hadalyn's people so many years on.

Gods, she had underestimated what her King was capable of. Or did Cyrus even know? She couldn't imagine he did. He had been outraged in the months after the war at the knowledge that groups of his people had been rounded up and dragged to Kastonia as slaves after the raiding of Castle Grey, and he had been furious enough that he had banned anyone, ever, across *any* kingdom in *any* continent, having slaves. He would bring the might of Hadalyn to their doors, he had said.

So to send her on a job to protect the shipments of slaves...

None of it was right. And Halos—

Bile rose in her throat. If her friend knew that this was happening, that people were being kept the same way her grandmother and relatives before her had been...

A roar filled Arla's head, a cacophony in her ears rushing with the force of it. This was *wrong*.

'I— I'm not doing this,' she stammered, digging her hands into the gravel on which they knelt. They had tied the horses far away from the ledge, and they had pressed their bodies flat to the floor to peer over the ledge and watch what was unfolding below them.

This was organised. Protected. *Well-funded.*

Only royal money could afford to create a settlement like this. Brick buildings had been erected – so strange to see that here, far away from ... anything. And there were tents guarded by armed soldiers with more blades than she had ever seen soldiers carry, ever. They wore black uniforms, not the scarlet of Kastonia or the grey of Hadalyn.

And the people... The *slaves*...

Never had she seen people chained together in such a way. Manacles circled their wrists, and long chains ran between them. There was no need for such *security* because they had no chance of ever being powerful enough to overthrow the guards.

And...

Oh gods...

She wasn't sure if she'd made it up in her head but ... but she thought she recognised the face of a man down there. A man who had been a friend of her father's all those years ago. His face was aged and he was thinner, but she never forgot a face, and she knew that face had come from Hadalyn.

There were people from Hadalyn down there – *her* people.

Halos could have been down there...

Arla suddenly understood the fear her friend harboured – that the soldiers would come for her and her children one day and chain them up as they had their ancestors.

Arla couldn't explain the feeling in her chest. Something in her very blood was *roaring*. The way there was a primal urge growing, growing, growing—

She needed to get them out.

Huge transports holding cages with thick iron bars – *iron* – were parked in organised rows, each of them pulled by heavy horses and each playing host to two armed guards. What had the King of Kastonia got going on here?

'I didn't think I could hate your kingdom any more, Stappen,' she breathed. She thought her words must be barely audible over the pounding of her heart. 'But *this,* this makes me want to burn it to the ground.'

She was seething, boiling, *furious* with them – with him. He had to have known. Gods, there was no way he didn't know what his King was up to. He was the ambassador for fuck's sake! And *Orson* – did he know?

She hadn't dared turn to face Hark yet, and he hadn't spoken either, but she could feel him lying next to her, his heavy breathing causing his elbow to brush hers slightly. She wanted to kill him.

'I didn't know...' he whispered, trailing off into a silence that caused her to turn and face him.

He looked ... pained.

'I'm getting them out,' she said, scrambling to her knees and counting the blades she had on her. She wouldn't allow it. She had seen the state of the slaves that had been recovered after the Siege of Grey Hill and she would not rest until every manacle was cut, until every guard, and slave master was killed. She wouldn't rest until she'd brought the Kingdom of Kastonia to its knees.

'You are not,' Hark growled, grabbing her wrist and pulling her back to the ground. Dangerous move.

'You *ever* touch me again—'

'You'll kill me, yes I know. Now shut your fucking mouth and listen.'

It stunned her enough to bite back whatever nasty retort was burning on the tip of her tongue.

'You go down there, and I don't care how good you are, how sparkling your reputation is, you will get yourself killed.'

'I'm not leaving them—'

'I'm not saying we leave them, Reinhart. I'm saying you're

going to get yourself killed and your king will have my head if you do. A storm is coming and we won't succeed if we charge in there blind with rage. We go back and make a plan. Then we get them out.'

He was right. Gods, he was right, but she couldn't stand to watch for a heartbeat longer. She was chilled to the bone. Annoyingly, Hark had been right; the frost hadn't thawed at all. The slaves down there – women, men, *children* – wore less clothes than she did, some of them only rags. How they still stood upright in this biting cold she didn't know.

'Get me as many blades as you can. I can hit the guards from here,' she urged, tugging her wrist against his grip. He only held her tighter.

'You do not have a hundred knives, and you cannot fire them all at once. They'll shoot you down before you can finish the end of the first run.'

'Arrows, then. I'll hit them from here—'

Hark's voice was too soft when he spoke. 'You will die, Reinhart.'

She knew. She knew that to throw a single blade could land her with an arrow through the heart. But she wouldn't leave these people.

'I can't—'

'I'm not asking you to leave them,' Hark urged, eyes burning into hers. 'But you are no good to them right now. We go back and we make a plan.'

He looked desperate, and his eyes pleaded with her. They were a sparkling, distracting blue against the grey of the picture below them. She believed him. He hadn't known Elrod was trading slaves, and she hoped to the gods that Cyrus didn't know, either. She would kill them all if she had to.

'I am *trusting* you, Stappen,' she whispered angrily, though the venom didn't reach her voice. It had shaken her, seeing them there, chained to one another on such a scale. How many of them had come from Hadalyn? How many were still prisoners from nine years ago?

'I'm not asking you to trust me – gods, I doubt all the silk and books in the world could buy your trust – but I'm asking you to be sensible. *Please.*'

Something was hiding beneath Hark Stappen's stony exterior, and for a few, fleeting seconds she saw its form. He cared. And he cared enough not to let her kill herself for them if he could use her to help.

'I'll kill them all,' she whispered, vowing upon gods she didn't believe in, upon the kingdoms, and upon herself that she would not stop until she had burned this entire place to ash. She would be unstoppable when she started. The streets would run red with Kastonian blood, but this time, there would be no survivors.

He was gripping her wrist, still.

'I know. I know.'

It seemed to her that Hark had made a very similar promise.

CHAPTER 18

HARK

She had behaved exactly as he knew she would.

He had seen the fury in her eyes, the vengeance she would rain down upon Kastonia – upon his people.

The worst part was he didn't blame her.

He had been sickened when he had found out, and nothing he had said, or bargained, or promised had persuaded Elrod to release them. Gods, he didn't know how he would *begin* to explain it to her. What was really going on here, and why he couldn't allow her to charge down there like a whirlwind of death and fury and start killing guards. He had bet himself she would kill more than half before the soldiers had even realised what was going on, but it was too dangerous. Too many things could go wrong; too many things that neither of them understood.

No wonder the gods were punishing Kastonia.

She was quiet as he led her back towards somewhere warm – not Irelliad, no. There would be talk if the two strangers turned up there again, and he couldn't count on Arla not to start gutting those who couldn't keep their whispers behind the walls. She was deadly like this, as if the wrongness of the slave traders had slithered inside her and corrupted any thread of good that ran through her heart. She was too dangerous to be around anyone who would spark her irritation.

Vorstrum would work. She would like the crowds there, and if she felt the need to release the violence she wielded, she would meet her match in the brawls he was sure she would incite.

Not that he wanted her out of his sight tonight. Though he was angry with the king and angry with the kingdom, his people didn't deserve her wrath. But it was inevitable. He would have to wait until she was asleep to meet his crew, his *friends* – people who were allies and upon whom he was relying for information and updates on what had been happening in his absence.

There was more than one reason he had chosen Vorstrum to shelter them tonight.

CHAPTER 19

S
he felt sick.

Her anger was a living, throbbing thing as Hark led her into another of Kastonia's independent towns that had sprung up about two hours from the northern border. It was slightly bigger than Irelliad, and the crowds were a moving, heavy presence even as the night pressed in. Music rolled out into the cobbled streets, and the buildings here at least appeared sturdier than their counterparts in Irelliad. There were taverns and bars, and it gave her plenty of reassurance that she would find something – or someone – on whom to take out her frustration.

But she'd have to get past Hark first, and from the grim line set into his face, there was no room for arguments. She would have to wait for him to fall asleep, then.

Hark led the way through the writhing crowds that barely parted for their horses, and halted outside a tavern which had a small barn adjoining it. Pulling their cloaks tightly around them, they ambled through the door to the tavern, careful to avoid the gazes of any who glanced their way.

After handing over too many coins for the value of the rooms, two shiny silver keys were hastily handed over and the hooded companions disappeared into the corridors above the taproom.

'I can see if there's anything to eat?' Hark said, pausing before his door which was at the opposite end of the corridor to hers. She was pleased since it would be easier to sneak out if she didn't have to worry about him being on the other side of the wall. But then she wondered, for a moment, if it was kindness she saw in his eyes and she didn't know what to make of that. It was masked quickly enough with a huff of annoyance that it was taking her too long to answer his question.

'I'm fine. I'm going to go to sleep,' she replied, stifling a yawn that wasn't entirely faked. She wasn't sure it would be enough to convince him. In fact, she would consider it a blessing from the gods if he believed her at all.

But if he didn't buy the feeble excuse, he didn't argue with her, instead bidding her goodnight and letting himself into his room.

Arla's own room was simple but warm – perfect. She would leave it a few hours before venturing out; she needed to make sure Hark was asleep and not about to impede her spying. She didn't know what she was looking for, exactly, but she knew something wasn't right. She wanted *more*. More information on the Kastonian royal family, more information on the slaves – gods, just the thought of them flared a simmering anger in the pit of her stomach.

How dare they—!

Enough.

She needed to clear her head. She would obtain nothing if she was fixating on all the wicked, dangerous things she wanted to do to Kastonia. She couldn't afford to fall asleep, either. Judging by the way her eyes were drooping in the warmth of the room, it was likely she would sleep right through and gather no information at all.

Fighting the languor in her body, she moved to sit by the narrow window, rolling her eyes at the heart-shaped symbol someone had drawn in black ink on the frame. She rested her forehead on the cool glass to watch the dealings of the people in the street below. She observed hands exchanging wrapped items in the shadows, and when she noticed the golden pins some of them wore it made her grit her teeth.

She was fed up with this kingdom and their ridiculous superstitions, their obsession with false magic. But she would watch and, if she was lucky, she might learn something of Kastonia and its odd little towns. It was something they didn't have in Hadalyn. The lands of her kingdom merged into one another, only separated by demarcations between farming and business regions. Grey Hill seemed to house the beating heart of Hadalyn, made busier by the chaos of Castle Grey's revolving door of trade and exchange.

So she would be content to sit here awhile and observe this strange little town in Kastonia. Then she would venture out, and she would find what she needed to bring this kingdom to its knees.

CHAPTER 20

HARK

For a moment, he'd been concerned.

If he was being truthful, she looked exhausted.

His concern had quickly given way to impatience, however, as he waited for the clock to hit eleven so he could finally meet his friends and hear what they had to reveal about the state of the kingdom and what was happening regarding the extraction of the slaves.

Gods, she was going to kill him when she found out. He'd seen the deadly fury bubbling behind those coffee-coloured eyes, and for a moment he'd been worried about what she was capable of. He'd seen her do terrible things, and he had never seen her falter. Ever.

There was a part of him that wished he'd told her. Ages ago. Having someone like that on his team...

But though he'd never seen her falter, the thing about Reinhart was that she was unpredictable. There was no guarantee she wouldn't go charging in and demand an army from her king. She'd blow it all. Every hour he and his friends had spent trying to help ... well, it would all be for nothing if Arla breathed a word of it.

He slipped out of the tavern a few minutes before the bells started ringing, melting into the crowds and disappearing down side streets and alleys to eventually emerge on the fishing docks. They were small, and honestly, he was surprised they had cared to build docks for the number of boats that bothered to land here. The cove was barely a lake, only accessible by a deadly narrow river filtering back to the sea somewhere. It was littered with shipwrecks and jagged rocks – too dangerous for the trading ships or even larger fishing boats. But they were quiet and away from the bustle of the crowds, and full of shadows and dark corners to hide criminals and trade in illicit affairs.

Perfect, then.

'About time, Stappen. We thought you'd lost your way in Reinhart's bed.'

The bastards.

He couldn't hide his grin as they pulled him behind stacks of wooden pallets reeking of fish and damp.

'You should know me well enough, Seb, to know that lying with the Hadalyn girl is the very last thing I would ever do,' he chuckled, pulling his friend close and slapping an arm around him.

'We know you well enough to bet on you being smitten with her already.' Another shadowed figure laughed at this. He couldn't remember the last time he had seen all of them together.

'Where's Kase?' he asked, only making out three figures in the dark.

'Here,' a gentle voice said from behind him, revealing the silver-haired, slim-framed girl he had conned into his service.

Here they were, all four of them. His crew.

'What have we got?' Hark asked, eager to learn what his friends had been up to in his absence. Kase had revealed almost nothing when she'd met him at Larkire, insisting they'd explain once he made it to Vorstrum.

He had missed his friends. The assignments at Castle Grey had kept him for longer than he liked, and he often worried that they might forget he was part of the gang at all. He tried, of course. Those days when he said he was returning to Kastonia to report back to his king had almost killed him when he never, in fact, returned to Larkire and rode through the night to help his friends. It was a wonder Arla hadn't seen straight through the lie. She'd almost caught him once. Had followed him all the way to the border between Kastonia and Hadalyn and it was luck that he'd spotted her before she could ruin everything he'd been working on.

'Not much I'm afraid,' a tall, dark-skinned man admitted, edging closer so the moonlight illuminated one side of his face.

'Don't be so negative, Jaz,' Sebastian snapped. 'We're getting more out each week. It's just ... difficult. They don't want to trust us.'

Hark had thought it might be like this. The slaves most likely wanted them dead, what with them being Kastonian and all; he couldn't expect them to realise that his crew were their rescuers, not their captors.

'Anyone get hurt?' He wasn't sure he wanted to know. He'd put them in danger by asking them to do this, and there wasn't a day that passed that he didn't wonder if his friends were safe.

'Jack had a run-in with one of them. Thought he'd snapped

his spine the way he carried on.' Seb laughed, but Hark found it hard to temper the flare of worry and anger at his friend's misfortune. Jack had stayed quiet, and when he inched closer so that the light washed over him, Hark had to grit his teeth against what he saw in the face of his friend.

Jack had been fit, muscled, and deadly when Hark had last seen him months ago. Now he leant heavily on a cane, and the ramrod-straight spine he had always maintained was hunched over. He looked like a feeble old man. Only his hair, still a sandy-blond abundance, gave any indication that he was in his twenties. Even Jack's eyes looked old and misty, as though he was looking through stained glass and struggling to see them clearly.

He looked ... addled. And given the type of mission Hark had sent them on, there was only one thing that could have done that to him.

'Fuck, Jack. I'm sorry—'

'Oh, stop it,' Jack said with a curse, waving the cane at him. 'I'll find a healer once we're done. they'll draw the magic out, I'm sure.'

Gods, he hoped so.

This was why mortals couldn't have magic. It broke them. It made this whole thing just *pointless,* and Hark didn't know what was possessing the kings to keep going. Unless...

Unless they'd found a way to hold it.

Fuck.

'I've missed a lot, I take it,' Hark said with a sigh, running a hand through his hair and scanning the faces of his friends. Each of them stared back, unblinking, ready to take an arrow for him if he asked. What had he done to deserve such loyalty, such trust? It was indeed a blessing from the gods to have friends such as these.

'I think you'll want a drink, Stappen.'

He thought so, too, and as much as he despised the thought of being seen, especially in a tavern, drinking with these—

Gods, he didn't even know what people thought they were. He'd been away too long, and now the thought of a cold drink in his own kingdom was too good an offer to pass up.

CHAPTER 21

Arla was almost to the door of the tavern she had seen across the street when she heard the telltale sound of booted feet behind her. She had lived inside Castle Grey for too many years not to recognise the sound of Cyrus's soldiers. But for them to follow her to Vorstrum...

She disappeared down a dark alley, waited a moment, and then slammed the body of the soldier against the wall as he rounded the corner. He didn't wear his usual uniform – clever man – but she had recognised his footfalls all the same. He'd been guarding the royal suite for as long as she had been at the castle.

'Explain. Now.'

He had the good sense to look petrified, his blue eyes widening as his fingers shook around a rolled-up scroll of parchment.

Arla tore it from his hands, unrolling it and scanning the familiar handwriting.

Return home.
Change of plan.
C.

She screwed up the parchment in her fist, tightening the grip on the soldier's tunic.

There was no way in fucking hells she was returning to Hadalyn, not now. She wouldn't let herself dwell on the question of whether Cyrus knew about the slaves – he simply couldn't – but she'd be damned if she returned to Castle Grey to demand he summon an army without knowing everything there was to know.

Tomorrow she might think on it. But today, Cyrus wanting to change her orders so late into the job made her suspicious. She could only imagine that Orson, the fucking rat, had lied to Cyrus about her behaviour in Larkire and she was being summoned home as punishment.

'Tell the King I'll return the day after you. Our horses are weary and need rest,' she said, releasing the soldier. The lie had come easily and he bought it, nodding once before retreating back the way he had come.

She didn't know when exactly she would return home. Nearly two weeks had passed already, so what was a few more days? For now she was content to let the palace think she was on the way.

～

Not one person glanced at her as she made her way inside the tavern, and for a moment it felt as though she was still in Hadalyn, moving amongst thieves and fighting in the pits with men twice her size. She very rarely came out with more than a bruise.

But the memory of what she had seen at the border dragged her into the present, bringing forth that unwavering, furious anger she had been caging in all evening. She didn't know what the true purpose of this evening's expedition into town was anymore: to gather information on what had been going on behind Kastonia's doors, or to blow off steam in a bar brawl – or something a little more dangerous? All, she hoped.

She entered the first tavern she found. She was immediately hit with the stench of sweat and ale, and a familiar comfort wrapped its arms around her. She would enjoy tonight's quest because it was all too natural to become someone else and eavesdrop on conversations between patrons at the bar. Even the subtlest of men had a hard time keeping secrets from her when she batted her eyelashes and promised an hour of her time for the price of a secret. She had yet to deliver on any of those promises.

It took all of two minutes to charm a flabby, red-faced man into buying her a drink, and even less time for her to dissolve into the wave of people and find a seat in the back where he could not find her. Spying in taverns was becoming a pattern, apparently, but this bar was proving to be void of anything of interest. Everybody here was too drunk or didn't care enough about the state of the world to bother discussing it.

The lack of information was frustrating her and she wondered why she had not just gone to sleep like Hark had.

She gritted her teeth at the thought of him. Or rather, at the smile that was trying to break through her carefully held restraint.

Ugh. Hark Stappen.

She could never, *ever* be friends with him, and she certainly shouldn't be trying to hide a *smile* at the thought of him.

He had been kind though. No, not kind. It was more like—
Enough!

He hadn't been kind. He had been keeping her on side by promising to help free the slaves. Gods, what was he thinking? If Elrod found out that his ambassador was actively planning to steal *his shipments* out from under him...

She didn't dare entertain the thought that Cyrus might know; that he might have sent her here to see if she would betray him.

No. Cyrus couldn't know. He was a kind man and he would be utterly *livid* when he found out what Elrod had been up to. What his *shipments* had really been.

There would be no aiding Kastonia, then. Cyrus would send an army and make them pay for ever going against that treaty.

Sighing, and with a slight sway to her walk that hadn't been there before the ale she'd swallowed, she made her way to the back door of the tavern. The alley behind the building wasn't much clearer, but as her disgust at the vomiting drunken patrons had her storming through the lingering crowd, one sentence caught her attention and caused her feet to halt abruptly against the cobbles.

'They moved another lot last night. Wagon full of 'em.'

She turned slowly, careful not to catch eyes with the group whose conversation she had been waiting for all night. They were huddled against the wall – two men holding pints of ale and a woman smoking something that made Arla's chest ache. She caught sight of that gods-damned dragonheart symbol tattooed on the inside of the woman's wrist and groaned internally.

'Terrible business. I doubt half of them make it to the border alive.'

'King's not 'appy. I 'eard, another lot went missing this week.'

'Yeah, well he won't be, will he, all that power escaping his greedy hands.'

What?

'The bastard can burn for all I care.'

His people weren't happy, then. It wasn't at all surprising, judging by the wealth he liked to flaunt in his scarlet palace.

'It's only going to get worse for him. I heard the boy is back with his crew.'

What in the gods' names was going on?

'I 'eard more than that. I 'eard he brought that 'ore with 'im.'

'That *whore* could cut your throat right now and you wouldn't even know she was here. You don't get to where she is through bluffing.'

Surely not...?

'You're telling me a *woman* was appointed to be the King's Assassin without him bedding her? The position didn't even *exist* before she whored herself to the king.'

They *were* talking about *her,* then.

But that meant...

She was going to carve the bastard's heart out and feed it to him.

She wrenched open the door of the tavern and slammed it behind her with such force that it could have rattled the stars, unable to escape the rage swelling in her body. She didn't care who, or how, or what, but somebody was going to be on the receiving end of her wrath and likely send it back to her in the form of a fist.

~

Later, Arla stormed the streets back to the inn with the fury of the gods beneath her feet, twisting her blade over and over in her hand. She didn't know who she was angrier with – Hark for lying to her, or herself for not realising what was going on.

She'd promised not to harm the ambassador, but after what she'd learnt tonight, gods help Hark Stappen when she found him.

CHAPTER 22

She was too angry to silently and unobtrusively scale the side of the building and climb back through the window, so she used the normal entrance.

She was just past Hark's door and on the way to her own room, when the creak of hinges halted her in her tracks, and the fury she had spent the walk back convincing herself to bury until morning came rising from that horrid, dark place within her.

'Where have you been?' His voice was husky, like he had burnt his throat on whisky. She stiffened where she stood, barely able to control the trembling coursing through her.

Not now.

If she began this with him now... Gods, the tavern was likely to burn between them.

'That is none of your concern. I suggest you leave me alone, Stappen.' Bitterness dripped from her tongue, and she surprised herself at the power contained in her words.

'Excuse me?'

Oh gods.

She turned, her tangled curls whirling with the force of it. She took him in, eyes raking the length of his body as he stood in the doorway, one arm leaning casually against the doorframe as he watched her. His hair was tousled, and the top of his shirt unbuttoned. He looked...

Gods, she couldn't afford to go there right now.

Pushing off the doorframe, he began to move towards her, his eyes widened, the icy blue of them dark in the low light of the torches.

'What the *fuck* have you been doing?' he growled.

Her feet shifted slightly, ready to intercept the attack that was coming, judging by the ferocity in his body. She wouldn't step backwards; it was simply not in her.

She took his legs from under him as he grabbed her hands, leaving him wide eyed and held up only by the fact that he was pressed against the wall of the narrow corridor.

'I've told you before that if you touch me—'

'Where have you been?' he persisted, his eyes still wide and scanning her. She looked down at herself, wondering what was causing his strange behaviour. It was evident immediately. She was *covered* in blood.

How had she forgotten it? She'd felt the hot splash of scarlet as she'd fought in the tavern, but the thought had fled her mind on the way back to the inn. She'd been fuelled by so much anger and hatred for this wretched kingdom that she hadn't thought to wash the blood from her hands or, if his look of horror was anything to go by, her face.

'It doesn't matter.'

'Reinhart—'

'Don't *Reinhart* me,' she snapped, stamping her foot as she edged closer to him. 'You're a liar, and gods help you, Hark Stappen—'

'What are you talking about?' He grabbed her then, pulling her into his room and shutting the door. Had she not been so overwhelmed with rage and ... and betrayal, she would have fought him.

'The slaves!'

His face betrayed nothing, and that hurt her more. He'd let her believe they were going to get them out. He'd let her believe he was shocked to discover the shipments were actually slaves. But he'd known all along. Worse, he had been *stealing* them himself, if what she'd overheard at the tavern was true.

'You knew! You knew all along what was happening! You knew the shipments were slaves. You let Cyrus send us out here —' She was shouting now, and she didn't care how thin the walls were. Let them hear. Let them know what a bastard he was.

'You don't understand—'

'I don't understand? You're right I don't fucking understand! Your kingdom slaughtered my people, and now I find out that they're trading slaves – which is *illegal*, may I add—'

'Because everything you do is within the law?' he interrupted. It was only now she noticed he still held her wrist.

She snatched her arm away, putting as much distance between them as she could in the cramped room.

'I *help* people! You're stealing slaves from under the king's nose and doing ... what with them? Gods help you—'

'I'm helping them!' he shouted, stepping towards her. 'I'm helping them, you stupid girl! I don't agree with it, either, and if you'd just *waited* for me to explain that to you instead of charging ahead and coming up with the wrong answer, *again,* then you would know that!'

She straightened, and her shoulders brushed the wall. He'd somehow backed her up against it with the force of the anger rolling off him. He looked dishevelled and furious, but *she* was the one who had the right to be angry, not him.

'You don't get it, do you?' she snapped back, forcing herself forwards and squaring her shoulders as he took a step back from her. 'I don't care if you're saving them or not. You let this go on for however long it already has. So why *didn't* you explain it, Hark? Why didn't you tell me the truth? You *know* I would have helped!'

Gods, her voice was breaking, and she was fighting back the knot in her throat. Why was she so upset? He opened his mouth but said nothing.

'I can't talk to you.' She choked back the emotion and shoved past him. 'Don't touch me!' she exclaimed furiously as he reached his hand out to her.

She wanted to wake up from this horrible nightmare in her room at Castle Grey and find it had all been some terrible dream. She'd worked so hard to cut away the darkness from Hadalyn... How many of them were her own people? How many had been killed or suffered worse fates already?

The thought of it exhausted her, and knowing this was about to become a job far larger than anything she had taken on before, she almost buckled where she stood. His hand was suddenly around her wrist, and when she made to yank hers away he tugged her back, his eyes dark and blazing as she met his gaze.

'You're not going anywhere,' he seethed, his voice a growl in his throat. Something swooped low in her stomach – challenge perhaps, or could it be something different? He was looking at her so intently that even her iron will seemed to be on the verge of bending beneath him. 'You're staying here. With me.'

'Like hells I am!'

He pulled her closer, until there was barely an inch between them. She could see the brilliant blue of his eyes now, all ice and danger. 'Do you think for one moment that, after waltzing back in here in the middle of the night looking like you've come from a slaughterhouse, I would consider letting you go? I won't subject my people to the likes of *you*.' His voice was lethally soft. Almost a whisper.

Her heart was fluttering now, the traitorous, wicked thing. It was rare for a man to manage to ignite something within her, and Hark Stappen *certainly* shouldn't be capable of it.

Her chest heaved as she struggled to breathe around the knot inside her. She wouldn't crack before him; she wouldn't allow it. But he was watching her, with that goading look in his eyes that was driving her closer to the edge, where she was afraid she would come undone completely, and then he would see how broken and damaged she was deep within her soul.

She thought he might say something; she watched his lips purse as though he would curse her to the depths of hell. But then ... then his eyes flared and the voice that escaped his lips was filled with something so deadly it sent a shiver down her spine.

'Who hurt you?'

She stilled.

'Reinhart,' he growled between his teeth, 'who was stupid enough to draw blood from you?'

She didn't think she was breathing. He was so close. So close. And there was a cruelty in his eyes that sung of pain. She hadn't known she was bleeding – gods, she was covered in everyone else's blood so why distinguish her own?

But the brawl in the tavern just now had been more violent than usual. She'd taken a blow to the jaw that had sent her reeling backwards. She lifted a hand to her temple where Hark's eyes had rested.

When her fingers came back sticky and warm, she swallowed against the sight of her own blood.

Stupid.

She'd lost control so thoroughly in the bar that she hadn't noticed until now the nausea that accompanied the blow, or how it had been growing steadily since she'd left the tavern.

And Hark ... he looked as if he were capable of setting the world on fire.

'Why do you care?' she managed.

Hark's fingers tightened around her wrist and she resisted the urge to knee him between his legs. Chances were he'd likely hit her back harder.

'I care because they know we travel together. An attack against you is an attack against me and my kingdom, and I won't stand for it. Even if your inability to control yourself is what started the fight in the first place.'

Arrogant, self-righteous bastard.

'Get. Off. Me,' she said, but the fight had gone from her. It wasn't anger burning a hole straight through her now, it was something different. Something hot and twisting and far too tempting.

She saw the challenge in his eyes before he could speak. Felt the tension in his fingers as he closed the gap left between them. His chest pressed against hers, the blood on her clothes swallowed up by the black of his shirt as he held her tight against him. A grin split his lips. He ran his tongue across his teeth as his infernal smirk grew wider.

He was infuriating. Too wolfish and sharp by half, but nothing she knew she couldn't take down if she needed to.

It wouldn't matter, though, would it? Because there would be no taking him down – at least not in the way she had been trained to do.

'Get off me,' she repeated.

He pulled her even closer and purred, 'Make me.'

Whatever was between them pulled taut and then snapped entirely.

And then she surged forwards as he bent down towards her, their lips crashing together as surely as anything else she'd ever known. He tasted of spice and smoke and whisky. Of danger and secrets and broken promises. She could get drunk on just the idea of it.

His hand tangled in her hair, pressing her ever closer as his tongue slipped between her lips and the world around them shattered. Her fingers moved at expert speed, undoing the buttons of his shirt as his arms reached beneath her bottom and he lifted her so she was against him.

'I hate you,' she gasped as he slammed her back into the wall, kissing her again as if she were nectar and his life depended on it. She didn't know how he managed it, but within seconds her shirt was torn and her bare skin was melting beneath his touch.

'Keep telling yourself that, sweetheart,' he groaned, rocking against her and eliciting a noise from her that had him nipping at her lip.

Her own hands tore the shirt from his skin and, gods ... she'd seen her fair share of men when she'd found one intriguing enough to take back to her rooms at Castle Grey, but *Hark...*

She didn't think there was a word to describe this level of perfection. His skin was so tanned, so smooth across the solid planes of muscle that she couldn't resist trailing her hands over his chest, down to his stomach, *lower...*

'So wicked,' he whispered, pinning her against the wall, the hard length of him pressing against her core and teasing her with delicious friction.

She rocked against him, revelling in the moan that spilled from his lips as she reached lower and lower.

He growled and then the room was spinning.

Spinning, spinning, spinning as he laid her on the bed, his hand trailing up the inside of her thigh as he gazed at her as though she were something to be admired. There was a ferocity in his eyes, something burning and raw and, gods, she thought she could watch him forever and never get bored.

All thought ceased when his fingers found the apex of her thighs.

She gasped, rolling her hips for *more, more, more.*

'So impatient,' Hark murmured. His fingers moved higher, sliding along the waistband of her trousers. He was toying with her, like a mountain cat playing with its prey.

She kissed him harder, sliding her hands behind his neck and up to tangle in his hair. The sound that rose from his throat had warmth gathering where she wanted his fingers.

'Please,' she managed to pant between breaths, rocking her hips against the hand that trailed along her waistband.

'And here I was thinking you had no manners,' he murmured.

'Fuck you, Hark,' she gasped.

Later, she might wonder what in the gods-damned world she was doing. Why she was writhing beneath Hark Stappen. How she had allowed something within her heart to grow to *this* without her knowing about it.

Later she might think what a fool she'd been.

Later could get fucked.

His hand slipped beneath the fabric, brushing against her and dragging a moan from her lips. She was almost embarrassed by how desperately she was ready for him; how she arched her spine at his touch as he circled around that sensitive spot, never quite pressing there.

She should touch him back – she wanted to – but then he found that sensitive bundle of nerves and she thought she might have lost all ability to do anything other than exist beneath his touch. She bucked her hips against his fingers. More. She needed *more.*

'Please,' she said again, tightening her fingers in his hair. Hark groaned again, and she felt him grin against her mouth as she kissed him between moans.

'I might get used to you begging me, Reinhart. I think it might be my favourite thing you've ever said.'

'If you don't shut your mouth I'll—'

'You'll what?' And then he slid his fingers inside her and she cried out at the sensation.

She couldn't control the way her hips moved then, desperate for him to give her more.

She couldn't think around the feeling, couldn't do anything but moan and beg and move against him as pressure built higher and higher.

His fingers moved in and out, driving that tightness in her

core further and further until she was sure there was nothing left of her.

'Perfect,' Hark murmured, barely audible over the sound of her moans. And yet it was still enough for her to come undone.

Release shattered through her, sending her plunging off the edge of the *thing* they had built between them. She cried out, only for him to press his lips against hers, quieting the sound with his kiss.

When she finally found herself again, Hark was watching her, his shirt somehow back on as he blinked lazily. Her head pounded and her mouth was dry, and yet she had never felt so exquisite.

'Sleep, Reinhart,' he said, rolling over to lie beside her. 'We've a long day tomorrow and that concussion is bound to render you entirely unpleasant.'

She'd hardly settled her breathing before sleep found her, enveloping her so thoroughly she wondered if Hark had managed to drug her.

She didn't care.

Tomorrow.

Tomorrow she would think of what this meant and why she was so easily persuaded to lie down and close her eyes next to him.

Tomorrow she'd sort through it all.

CHAPTER 23
HARK

Upon finding the space beside him empty, a cold wave of dread doused Hark with the fear that Arla had returned to Hadalyn in the night and told her king what she had found. Or worse, that she regretted what they'd done last night.

His lungs were burning by the time he'd raced through the inn to find both horses still content in their stables and Arla's saddlebags hanging by Vetta's stall. The sun had hardly risen; it was just a blend of pink and oranges bleeding into the sky.

Where could she have gone?

Sighing, he walked out into the empty streets of Vorstrum. It had been beautiful once – not too long ago actually. But the strain of a crumbling kingdom and its punishment at the hands of the gods had hit Vorstrum hard. Now it was dreary and miserable, lacking colour and ... and she was running herself ragged up the hill that sat behind the town.

How she was managing it, he wasn't sure. The muscles in his legs were burning just on the walk to the foot of the hill, the cobbled road looking like a staircase it rose so steeply above him.

She hadn't seen him yet. Or perhaps she had – it wasn't often that something slipped her attention.

He watched her sprint up, up, up. He watched her thighs tense with the strain she placed on them as she hauled herself – as well as a saddle pack he hadn't noticed was missing – back down the road. She looked wild, and sweaty, and *alive* as she pushed her body *hard*.

It wasn't strange for her to be training before the world was awake. He had lived in Castle Grey long enough to have become accustomed to a knot of wild blonde tangles scaling the tower he slept in as his wake-up call, but this was hard work even for her. The pack looked heavy, and he knew if he opened it he would find it filled with rocks and solid objects. He could see her chest heave even from this distance.

How long had she been at this?

He squared his shoulders as she headed towards him, and his jaw ached with the pain of clenching it as she strode straight past without a second glance.

Fuck. Last night had ruined everything.

'Stop it,' he ground out.

He watched her back stiffen and her footsteps halt, and for a moment he wondered if it was wise to have this conversation so early in the day. 'You're pushing yourself too hard. We still have a long day ahead of us.'

Nothing.

'Are we at least going to address what happened last night?' His cheeks heated at the thought of it, but he didn't miss the way her hand reached for the knife he knew she carried on her belt. She didn't follow through with the threat, instead making to stride off again.

His arm was outstretched and tugging the strap of the saddlebag before he knew what he was doing. The weight of it jerked her back, and she spun quickly, if only to avoid falling at his feet.

'Get off me.' Gods, she sounded lethal. Deadly. Dangerous. 'Last night was a mistake. A stupid, reckless mistake that will never happen again and we shall never speak of it.'

He'd known the minute he had woken that she would do this, but it still tore something open in his chest that she could hardly bear to look at him.

And there was still the issue of what had led her to his room in the first place.

'Are you going to let me explain what you heard last night?'

Fire burned in her eyes. 'No, I won't. I don't care what you have to say. You *cannot* justify what you have done.' Her voice was breaking again, and silver lined her narrowed eyes. 'You let Kastonia take them, and sell them, and I know most of them will end up dead and you didn't do *anything*. There are people from *Hadalyn* down there, Stappen. *My* people. Suffering beneath your king. Again. And you *didn't tell me*.'

Gods, is she ... is she crying?

'I won't let you break my kingdom again. I *won't*—'

'Cryus knew.'

Her face paled, her lips parting but releasing no sound. The gentle arch of her eyebrows furrowed so slightly he might have missed it if he hadn't known to look for the subtlest of changes from the expression on Hadalyn's assassin's face.

What have I done?

CHAPTER 24

*C*ryus knew.

Two words that brought her world to a halt.

Cryus knew.

He simply *couldn't*. They were his people – Hadalyn's people. Why would he send her out here to find slaves he already knew about? It didn't make sense... Had he sent her that note to come home because he'd finally realised there was no way she would go along with this? Did he regret sending her out here, now that he'd had time to think on it? Did he hope the note would catch up to her *before* she found out about the slaves?

'Why would he know...? Why would he send us here if he knew?' She was mumbling now, trying to piece each part of it together. What had Cyrus thought she was going to do? He couldn't for a moment think she would be okay with this, that she would actually dispose of whoever it was stealing Kastonia's slaves and then go back to Castle Grey as though nothing had happened? He certainly couldn't know that it was Hark that had been stealing slaves.

Unless...

Unless Cyrus had thought she would kill Hark.

'He thinks I'm so loyal to the crown that I would kill you for this, doesn't he?'

Hark's face revealed nothing, and it only confused her more. She was beginning to think she wouldn't have it in her if it came down to it, and that ... that was something she needed to sort through. That was something she needed to harden her heart against because they were supposed to hate each other.

Forget last night and the slimy regret that now coated her skin, because, in truth, she had begun to feel that hostility between them slipping long before last night, hadn't she?

'Just so we're clear: I did not expect this to happen the way it has,' Hark said.

'What?' She laughed in disbelief. 'You didn't expect that I would find out that you were rescuing slaves from under the noses of *both* kings? Gods, Stappen, were you planning on telling me at all?'

She couldn't think; this was too much too fast. Her own king was in all likelihood counting on her to kill the Kastonian ambassador for rescuing slaves that were part of an illegal trade. Who did Cyrus think she was? Who did *Hark* think she was?

Inhaling deeply, she stared into his now icy blue eyes and willed her own to clear of the angry tears she wouldn't let fall.

'I sincerely hope you have a plan.' She certainly didn't and, truthfully, her head was spinning with the betrayal of her king. She'd trusted Cyrus; had grown to love him as a father, almost. But in the end it wasn't enough. He'd broken every ounce of trust she had in him and now she was stuck behind enemy borders about to betray both kingdoms. She didn't believe in the gods, but she wanted to pray to them anyway.

'Come on,' Hark said. 'It's time to meet my crew.'

⁓

She could barely keep her hands still as Hark led her through the winding cobbled streets.

Pull yourself together.

She couldn't very well walk into a den of Hark's so-called crew whilst shaking with rage and on the verge of angry tears. Taking a deep breath of cold air, she rolled her shoulders back and blinked away the tears.

She hadn't taken notice of where Hark was leading her, only that she could see water and fishing docks. She followed him down a narrow alley beside what she could only conclude were the dockmaster's offices. It was a filthy, miserable place, and for the first time in nine years, she hesitated.

Hark was lifting an iron handle from where it appeared to be secured in the ground, and beneath it was a thick, solid wooden door. A trapdoor, in the docks. Wherever he was taking her wasn't somewhere she was comfortable with, but she couldn't seem to force the objection through her lips. She watched as he lowered himself into an unfathomable darkness, and her fingers began to tremble again.

Enough, Arla.

He hadn't said a word to her, and for that she was grateful. She might be able to trick herself into some semblance of calm if he kept his mouth shut.

This was different to the underground market in Larkire.

There, she'd heard the voices long before she'd descended the steps and had known she couldn't be trapped down there.

She didn't look as she followed Hark into the oblivion, breathing hard through her nose as she descended into a warm, murky hole. At least it was dry.

'Watch your step. The floor is uneven,' Hark mumbled, jolting her in the darkness. Even his whisper seemed loud beneath the docks, and she could smell the whisky and leather scent of him as she inched closer to his back. The walls were close down here, and she didn't want to know what this tunnel was or what it had been used for. Her fingers brushed the cool stone either side of her, and she bit her lip against the pressing fear that accompanied the tight space.

This was what had almost broken her in training.

It was the worst kind of torture – small spaces. They whispered to her in her darkest hours and dragged her back to the nine-year-old girl locked in a dresser, covering her ears against the sound of swords clanging and the sickening thud as her parents' bodies hit the floor one after the other.

They had locked her in there to keep her safe, she knew. But it had been hours in the cramped darkness of the dresser, smothered by her mother's rose perfume that was embedded in the clothes draped over Arla's tiny body. It had been hours before someone had found her, hours of hiding in the dark and peering at her fallen parents through the narrow crack in the dresser. It had taken two years before she could lock a door behind her.

'Reinhart?'

'Hmm?' She hadn't realised he was speaking.

'You okay?'

'I'm fine,' she ground out, tightening the mask of King's

Assassin around her heart. She would not falter. She would not fall.

'It's not far now.'

She knew that. The air was getting warmer and there was a low rumble signalling voices perhaps two hundred yards ahead. Still no light, though, and for a moment she cursed herself for being so trusting. She was trusting him not to lead her into a trap. Stupid, stupid trusting heart! She was becoming too soft; she needed a stern reminder – perhaps blunt force to the head or a light poisoning would do it.

'There are tunnels all over Kastonia, you know,' Hark said, his voice echoing against the stone. 'The ones in the capital are closed up now; they were exploded to stop smugglers from getting into the city.'

She knew what he was doing, and in another life, she might have reached for his hand – something in her wanted to, actually. She had felt the softness of his hands, had experienced how gentle and exquisite his touch was on that night they'd spent together. Perhaps that other life wasn't such an absurd notion—

Arla shook her head clear of the thought. None of that could ever happen again.

'The other tunnels still operate?' she asked, aware of how quick her breathing had become.

'Some. Most collapsed over time, but the ones in Vorstrum are well maintained. They've been integral to the slave extraction process.'

She didn't know what to say. She'd been caught off-guard with the revelation of the slaves and Hark's involvement in their liberation. She didn't know how she felt about his clearly extensive involvement and his unwillingness to tell her before. How had he been running such an operation from all the way in Hadalyn? Was this what he'd been doing when he told Cyrus he was returning to Kastonia to meet with his own king?

There was light ahead – a soft yellow glow that illuminated the tunnel and cast long shadows of herself and Hark against the stone. The low rumble of voices increased as they strode closer, and for every step they took she had to steady her breathing.

The tunnel opened out into a circular chamber with a firepit in the middle, and wooden chairs and tables peppered throughout the space. Half a dozen tunnels branched off the chamber, each of them covered with a dark sheet nailed above the archway. Her eyes followed the strings of torches burning gently around the edge of the chamber. It was warm in here, and it smelled heavily of smoke and sweat.

She had purposely kept her eyes from landing on the four bodies lounging on wooden pallets by the fire, as if her refusal to acknowledge them immediately would make her the most important being in here. But eventually, once she was satisfied that the chamber was not about to collapse on top of them, she greeted Hark's crew.

'I'm surprised a group daring enough to steal slaves from the king hasn't found anywhere better to base itself than an underground lair where you huddle like rats.'

'I'm surprised the King's Assassin looks so ... twig-like.' The voice had come from the silver-haired girl now standing with her arms crossed over her chest. Arla smothered a grin. It had been a long time since she'd had the opportunity to enjoy the sting of female bitterness.

'Funny, I thought Hark was into red, not silver.' It was a sly move, and one that delivered her the reaction she'd wanted. The silver-haired bitch's eyes widened slightly, and her fists curled. This had to be the girl she'd seen Hark sneak away with in Larkire. Arla didn't know Hark's preferences in women – he'd brought all manner of girls back to Castle Grey in the past – but *she* didn't need to know that. Something in the centre of Arla's chest twisted, a churning, irrational emotion that made her instantly hate the silver-haired girl. The thought of her touching Hark, of Hark touching *her*—

'Do you ever keep your mouth shut, Reinhart?' Hark grumbled, shoving past her to clap each of the men on the back before dropping into one of the wooden chairs. It snapped Arla out of that spiralling emotion that was too close to jealousy.

She pasted on a smirk, calling forth the swagger she so often flaunted in her own kingdom and began the act of circling the room.

'Somebody'd better start speaking,' she said, twisting a blade between her fingers as each of them watched her with morbid curiosity.

'Is she serious?' the silver-haired girl spoke, spinning to face Hark with a look of utter disbelief and ... hatred for the hurricane that had blown into their lair.

'I'm afraid so.' Hark looked exhausted as he ran his fingers through his hair, and it amused Arla to know that he was fully anticipating her attitude and need to control the situation. Too bad he'd chosen to keep this information from her; now she would become intolerable.

'Good morning, Lady Reinhart.' She was greeted by a tall, muscular man, with hair the colour of rich chocolate and a soft smile, who stepped forwards from the flames and bowed exaggeratedly. It was enough to stop her pacing and bring her close enough to the firepit to feel its heat seeping into her skin.

'I like him,' she said, tossing her braid over her shoulder and staring directly at Hark.

He only rolled his eyes at her, sighing deeply and pinching the bridge of his nose. 'I thought you might.'

'Now, somebody's going to start explaining to me what's happening or—'

'Or what?' the silver-haired bitch interrupted. Arla's hands twisted, itching to throw something sharp at her.

'Or I will cut each one of those jewels out of your ears and shove them down your throat.' She smiled sweetly, surprised at how easily the words came. She watched the girl's lip curl, and she did not miss the hand that strayed to the dagger resting on the table.

'Easy, Kase,' one of the other men murmured, not yet introduced, and doing an excellent job of not looking Arla in the eyes. *Clever man.*

'And you are?'

'Jaz. And you are upsetting what was a very easy apple cart, Miss Reinhart.'

Oh, this was going to be fun. No wonder they were friends of Hark's; each of them seemed as self-important as he did. And none of it was getting her any answers. She squared her shoulders, rocking forwards on the balls of her feet as she took a deliberate step towards the dark-skinned man and his firm grip on the girl who'd now been identified as Kase.

'Oh, I think there are going to be quite a few apple carts that are going to find themselves very upset,' Arla said, her voice lethally quiet. 'As it stands, I have you down for treason and theft. I can add many more offences to this little ... outfit and have you strung up in front of the king before you can even *think.*' Her foot swung out, catching the leg of a discarded chair and spinning it behind her to knock the walking stick clutched in a scrawny hand she had noticed in the corner of her eye before its wielder could even think of daring to lift it from the floor and strike her.

A deadly silence fell, and Arla's eyes flickered between Hark and his four accomplices.

'Glad to know you weren't lying, Stappen.' The man who had bowed to her chuckled, leaning against the wall of the chamber and flashing a grin between her and Hark, who looked positively fed-up with the back and forth already begun between his friends and the assassin he had brought along with him.

'No, Sebastian, I wasn't lying. And neither is she,' he snapped, slamming a hand down on the table. The group immediately turned to face him and Arla fought the urge to laugh. Hark so rarely revealed any loss of composure. Maybe the closeness of the walls and the knowledge that these tunnels could collapse at any moment was getting to him. It certainly was her.

'This is Arla Reinhart,' he began, standing up and beginning to pace the room. 'She is assassin to the King of Hadalyn, and she will sooner kill you than hand you over to him, so I suggest we all start cooperating. The same goes for you.' He shot Arla a pointed look, and she feigned surprise. Something had worked him up and it had been enough for him to start lecturing them all on respecting *her*. Perhaps he was worried she would turn them in. She couldn't deny this little covert operation had her intrigued, but if it weren't for their clearly successful track record of freeing the slaves, she'd have dragged each and every one of them back to Hadalyn already.

But what if what Hark had said was true? That both Cyrus

and Elrod knew what was going on and were actively involved in trading slaves?

Gods, she needed Hark Stappen and his little band of thieves as much as they needed her not to blow this entire job out of the ground.

Hark looked at her directly. 'This is Kase, Sebastian, Jaz, and Jack – my crew. Under my command, they've been rescuing the slaves, though it has admittedly become harder since the kings found out the slaves have been going missing. What began as smuggling a few people out in the middle of the night is now turning into deadly combat with soldiers. It's why Cyrus sent you up here – to neutralise the threat. Little does he know that the person behind his *shipments* going missing has been living under his roof all this time.'

How had she missed all of this? How had Cyrus kept something so … substantial from her? None of it made any sense. Why was her king even trading slaves in the first place? And when had the two kings decided to put aside their differences and work together in such a despicable – not to mention, illegal – trade?

'What exactly do you expect to happen now? The security on the camp at the northern border is tighter than anything I've ever seen, and they are obviously aware that slaves are being stolen – which I will come to in a moment – but what do you think happens now, Stappen? You surely can't be planning on extracting more people from a camp as secure as that?'

'That's exactly what we're planning.'

Gods help her, he wasn't joking.

'Right. And where do these slaves go? You set them free and expect them to survive only to be dragged back here in chains?'

'Don't be so—'

'Kase!' Hark warned, cutting the girl off before she could throw what was surely an insult in Arla's direction 'They are ... safe.'

'Excuse me?' Everything about Hark Stappen was so gods-damned cryptic, and she was sick of it.

'They are safe, and that's all you need to know. Right now, we need to focus on getting the rest of them out and figuring out what to tell the kings,' Hark said, every inch of him the commander of an army, not the Kastonian ambassador who read letters out at court meetings.

'We have a problem,' Kase said, green eyes glittering like emeralds.

'What?' both Arla and Hark said in unison, and Arla cursed herself for becoming so invested so quickly. She didn't trust these people, yet somehow it seemed she had been made an accomplice and traitor in more than one kingdom.

'The winter festival is tonight and it's the perfect opportunity for Elrod's soldiers to fill their slave quota. There'll be people going missing on their way back home to replace the ones we've been freeing.'

'Then we kill them before they have the chance,' Arla vowed.

There was a beat of silence before Jack spoke. 'It's not as easy as that, Arla.' Her name sounded strange on his tongue. Too ... casual. 'They'll be undercover, quiet. They'll keep their plans in hushed tones between themselves. You likely won't know they're there until it's too late.'

'You forget it's my job to spy on people,' she said, her voice filled with a certainty that bolstered the nerve she had felt herself losing on her way down here. 'It won't be difficult to discover who's planning on causing trouble.'

Each of Hark's crew was staring at her as though she was

mad. As if spying was the most preposterous idea anyone had ever suggested.

'I suppose it could work,' Jack mused, smiling at Arla as if she'd passed some unknown test. 'The minute the music starts and the ale flows, their disorganisation and loose tongues will reveal all we need to know—'

'If we can get close enough to listen, Jack!' Kase snapped, spinning to face the hunched man, silver braid flying behind her. 'They'll sooner cut their tongues *out* than speak of anything important if they see any of us sniffing around.'

'Leave that to me,' Hark began, a smile creeping across his mouth to reveal a dimple tugging the corner of one cheek. She hadn't noticed it before. 'I brought you the King's Assassin, didn't I?'

'I think you put too much faith in the King's *Assassin*,' Kase chirped, the venom around Arla's title a wicked, burning thing.

'I don't think you put *enough*,' Arla replied. Yes, it was refreshing to have a female opponent; she had forgotten just how sharp her claws could be. 'Now, if you don't mind,' she continued, turning on her heel and marching for the narrow tunnel by which they had entered. 'I don't wish to spend the remainder of my day in this ... *pit* you've chosen as a meeting house. Some of us have work to do.' She plunged on into the darkness, not allowing her fear of the tight space to touch the mask she was slipping back into place.

Good.

She didn't miss the low chuckle as she melted into the tunnel, nor did she miss Kase's shrill voice spewing a string of curses after her. And though she was now too far away to make out what was being said in the chamber, she didn't think she missed the *'Told you'* that came from Sebastian's lips.

CHAPTER 25
HARK

The urge to grab her had been all consuming. He hadn't expected her to leave – didn't like the fact that she was unsupervised and that nothing good had come of leaving Arla Reinhart to her own devices.

But she had been terrified.

Hark didn't know how she had mastered her fear so quickly, how she had pulled herself together and rendered Kase and his crew speechless. But she had left quickly and he knew there was no amount of talking and distracting her that would have persuaded her to spend another moment under the ground in those tight, narrow tunnels.

So he didn't reach for her as he watched her saunter out of the chamber his friends had made their own. He didn't force her to spend another second choking down her terror. He wished he didn't care.

'No wonder she drives you to drink,' Sebastian said with a chuckle, hauling Hark out of his thoughts and averting his eyes from following the ghost of a golden braid down the pitch-black tunnel.

'She'd drive me to cut my own throat,' Kase spat, and Hark smothered the smirk widening across his cheeks. It would do Kase good to have someone equally matched to her fiery temper and lack of compassion. He'd had to work hard not to explode into a fit of laughter when Seb had caught his eye during the girls' back and forth.

'She's beyond difficult,' he said on a sigh, dragging a hand through his hair as he made his way to a chair and accepted the glass sloshing with amber liquid that Jack handed him.

Gods, it was too early in the day to be drinking but he couldn't deny the temptation to knock it back and welcome the fiery burn in his throat.

'But she's deadly, and careful, and the fact Elrod holds some of Hadalyn's citizens in his camp means Reinhart is more determined than any of us to get the slaves out.' He didn't know if that was a good or bad thing yet.

'She's unpredictable, and she'll blow this entire operation.'

Hark had expected some resistance, but he hadn't expected it to come from Jaz.

His friend looked ... concerned as he leant against a table marked by knife slashes, his arms crossed firmly over his chest as he eyed Hark in the low light. Hark couldn't help the flare of irritation.

Fuck. Arla was getting under his skin.

It had almost been easier to hate her than to feel this ... *thing* that was growing between them. Was it friendship, or something far more dangerous?

Enough. Last night was a mistake. She'd said so herself.

'And what would you have me do, Jaz? Her King sent her out here, and she discovered the truth more quickly than even a cautious estimate could have accounted for. If we don't include her, we're as good as dead – in both kingdoms.'

'So kill her—'

'I think,' Jack interrupted, his cane scraping the floor which made Hark wince at the sight of it. It was his fault that Jack had ended up this way. If he hadn't goaded this band of criminals into helping him, his friends would still be fine.

'I think,' Jack continued, 'Reinhart might be of use to us. If her reputation is justified, the soldiers on the northern border can begin counting their hours rather than days.'

'Are you serious?' Kase slammed a hand down.

'Enough.' Sebastian's voice cut through the simmering argument. 'If Hark trusts her, I trust her. If he says she's an asset, we treat her as one. This is about the slaves, not about Arla's attitude or Hark's growing fondness of her.'

Hark shot him a vulgar gesture, earning a wink back from his friend. He was glad he was here; he could count on Sebastian to back him in anything, be it stupid or reckless. If it involved Arla Reinhart, it would likely be both.

A silence settled upon his crew and Hark was sad to realise that ice had formed between him and his companions in his absence.

Get a grip.

Too much time away at Castle Grey. The dynamic had changed since he'd last been in their company, and he was conscious of the gazes that held for a split second too long between Jack and Kase, and how Jaz gritted his teeth each time.

'I'm not growing fond of her,' Hark muttered, stretching his legs and stifling a yawn.

'Believe what you like, my friend,' Seb said. He sighed then pulled a map from beneath the table and spread the yellowing paper across the wood. 'But the Hark I know would have cut her throat long before he could ever write a letter about her.'

CHAPTER 26

'Where have you been all day?' Hark demanded as he entered her room at the inn, clad in a dark green shirt and gleaming leather boots.

'None of your business,' she snapped, forcing an earring through the hole in her earlobe. It had taken a long time to find jewellery in such a town, and in the end, she'd swiped them from a merchant's stall as she flirted with him. She doubted they were real gold – they were too shiny and the metal felt light in her fingers – but she pushed them through her ears anyway, biting her lip at the familiar sting of breaking the skin. Too many months without fine jewellery meant the holes had begun to close, thanks to the endless *jobs* Cyrus kept sending her on. If there was one thing she hated more than not wearing nice jewellery, it was losing it in a tavern brawl.

She'd not done too badly in finding a dress. In fact, it seemed dressmakers and tailors were just about the only skilled tradespeople in this lowly town. It had taken her most of the morning to hunt through the shops and stalls, but she'd come away with a white, silky garment with green vines stitched into the fabric to create something that might have been pretty had it been crafted from real silk by Hadalyn artisans.

She had washed her hair, too, and though the water had been cold and unpleasant, she'd made sure to pack her jasmine soap in her saddle bags so she could at least smell like she hadn't spent days on the back of a horse.

'It *is* my concern when you're supposed to be working *with* me and you're taking any opportunity you can to disappear from sight,' Hark snapped. When she finally turned to face him, his eyes widened slightly before returning to that pissed-off stare he saved just for her.

Arla laughed, crossing her arms over her chest. 'You're mistaken, Stappen. I don't work *with* you. I work for myself and for the King of Hadalyn. Don't mistake my willingness to aid in rescuing these people as a surrendering of my freedoms to you.'

A muscle flexed in his jaw. 'I don't believe for one moment you're surrendering your freedoms to anyone – your king included,' he began. 'But whilst our interests are aligned, I think it would be ... *appropriate* that you don't disappear.'

He didn't trust her, then.

Clever man.

She didn't trust herself most of the time; she wasn't sure even now what she was doing. She wanted to stop any scheme Elrod's soldiers had planned for tonight. She wanted to rescue the slaves and get back to Hadalyn to confront Cyrus and find out whether he had been lying to her. And for the moment, she needed Hark Stappen and his crew to do that. They would stop the soldiers taking anyone tonight and then they would free the rest of the slaves in the morning. Simple.

But she didn't know where that left her. Was she supposed

to go home to Castle Grey and pretend there wasn't a booming slave trade in Kastonia? Of course she couldn't.

And that meant war.

Enough, Arla.

All she had to do was save the slaves and go home. Cyrus could be manipulated, and if he had any involvement in this, she would find a way to turn him against Kastonia and shut down the entire trading system. Cyrus would not have done this without persuasion, or perhaps coercion, and she would need to work harder to persuade – or coerce – him that Kastonia and its king needed to fall.

Hark was watching her again; watching the battle she fought between her head and her heart. Hadalyn came first. She'd sworn on her sword to serve Cyrus and his kingdom, but her heart would not let her tolerate the trading of slaves – of her people. She couldn't explain the feeling. It was like a primal tugging in her very core that felt ancient, and had continued to grow until all she could think about was protecting them. Getting. Them. Out.

But she couldn't tell Hark that. He'd think she was mad.

'It all seems a little ... dramatic, getting so dressed up.'

'Because your parties in Hadalyn are nothing like this,' Hark said as he leant against the door frame. 'The festivals here are beautiful. They don't happen often, Reinhart, so it will be filled with thieves, and soldiers, and slave traders waiting to snatch people on their way back into Vorstrum.'

'We're leaving Vorstrum?'

'The market's just outside the town. We'll need the horses to get there.'

'And you let me stand here in a white dress?'

Hark laughed. It was a warm, lovely sound, the kind she so

rarely had the privilege of hearing. 'If you hadn't walked away this morning, sweetheart, I could have explained how this evening would go without you having to eavesdrop in the streets.'

She smiled, and for a few fleeting seconds forgot that this was Hark Stappen, the Kastonian prick she had been forced to bring with her. Since being promoted to the position of King's Assassin, she'd worked entirely alone. For those few fleeting seconds, she wondered if all the time by herself had made her hard and cruel. She dismissed the thought immediately, knocking Hark with her shoulder as she squeezed through the door beside him.

'You cut your face,' she said, and watched him out of the corner of her eye as he reached up to rub at his freshly shaven jaw.

~

The people of Vorstrum, it seemed, were well-rehearsed in their festivals, and Arla immediately understood Hark's praise for them. Her eyes were alight with the colour, and music, and sheer volume of people that swarmed before her, far more than could possibly fit into the simple town itself.

'People travel from all over Kastonia to come to Vorstrum's festivals,' Hark murmured in Arla's ear, leading her between makeshift barriers of ribbons and hay bales signalling an entrance to the hustle and vibrancy of the evening's festivities.

'They are well known, then?'

'Very. Even you might find a smile tonight.'

She shoved her elbow into his side in response and tried to hide the smirk that was born of his low chuckle. He hadn't moved an inch, and the memory of him shirtless with his hands on her sprung to the front of her mind.

Gods, she needed to stop. She *hated* him.

'You think the soldiers will be here?'

'Definitely,' he replied, a grim line setting his mouth into something sharp and worrying. Arla caught herself before her hand could reach for the blade strapped to her thigh. She couldn't give them away tonight; they were here to observe and, if need be, intercept those who would try to snatch vulnerable villagers on their way home.

No matter if all she wanted to do was gut each and every man that had been responsible for capturing the people chained at the northern border.

Hark led her through the mass of people, his tall frame forging a path through the rabble, and brought them out into a square of wooden, market stalls and people playing instruments.

It was ... beautiful – the first true flash of colour she'd seen since the inside of Kastonia's palace.

Children danced to the music, each of them twirling coloured ribbons in their wake to form a twisting, writhing picture of joy and laughter. People pushed their way through to the fronts of the stalls, haggling for the best jewellery or hand-carved wooden trinkets. Hogs were being roasted over open flames, and ale and hot wines were being consumed by the gallon. The sun was retreating slowly, bathing them in a golden light and, for now, keeping the cold at bay. Not that it would be a concern once the sun descended fully; men were hauling branches and wooden pallets to form a huge pyre which was surely to be lit as soon as the sun bid its farewell. There was chatter, and laughter, and *life,* and it was more than she had seen in years, more than she had known was still possible in the struggling kingdoms of Hadalyn and Kastonia. No wonder people flocked here. The joy was … infectious. She hated that he was right, but a smile was causing her cheeks to ache and there was an uncomfortable pricking sensation behind her eyes. It was beautiful. *This* was what was keeping people from giving up and from storming Hadalyn again in search of the gods and their dragons.

'So what now?' she said. She felt slightly in awe of such a place and irritated that she couldn't enjoy it.

'That's up to you, assassin,' Hark muttered in her ear. 'You're the one who spies on people for a living.'

She wound her way through the crowds, twirling with children that tugged at her dress and smiling at those who grinned openly at her. No, working alone hadn't made her hard and cruel; it had made her clever.

They settled in the shadows of the makeshift tent, commandeering a pair of high wooden stools placed behind a rickety table. Though the amount of people drinking under the cover of the canopy blocked them from view of the market square, Arla could clearly see the stalls and surrounding areas. A sweet scent met her nose and she moaned at the warm glass being pressed into her palms. Hark's own hands gripped a much cooler tankard of ale, though he didn't seem to mind as he took a deep swig of the alcohol.

'As grateful as I am for the wine, I don't drink when I'm on a job,' she murmured over the noise of chatter and bets being placed by the players of a rather complicated-looking card game on the table beside them. Hark scoffed, nudging her with his shoulder as he took another deep gulp of ale.

'Horseshit. Your most honest work seems to happen under the influence of alcohol, Reinhart.'

'Meaning?'

'That bar brawls seem to be your speciality,' he said wryly, and she couldn't help but snort at his words.

'You have your fun, and I have mine,' she murmured, and cursed at how easily she'd fallen into the easy banter of being with him again. She should hate him – she *did* hate him.

He had seen her almost breaking herself this morning, and the thought of it curdled in her stomach. She'd packed her saddlebag with rubble and sprinted up and down that hill until she could taste blood. Anything to stop her feeling that sour, burning rage. Anything to stop her feeling the utter despair and heartache at what had happened to her family – and now to these slaves. Anything to stop her feeling how alone she was in this world. She hadn't meant to cry in front of him – and she hadn't, really. The tears that had clawed at their watery prison hadn't been given permission to fall, but she knew he'd seen them all the same. She wished she could take the tears back; that she could have run one more length of that hill to stop any and all feeling. She wished she hadn't felt relief when he'd come to find her...

'I only kept it from you to keep them safe,' Hark said in a low voice, dragging her from the misery to which she had let her mind wander. 'I couldn't risk telling you in case you went straight to Cyrus and demanded an army. I needed time to rescue as many as I could.'

She could understand it, almost. But it didn't ease the sting. The fact that she hadn't known *any* of it.

'I know,' she said. 'But I'd have given everything to help

them if you'd told me the truth. The gods know I owe them that.'

Hark nudged her gently. 'It's not your fault, Reinhart. You don't owe anybody anything. You were a child when my kingdom came for yours. There was nothing you could do.'

There was nothing you could do.

Didn't she know it.

'It's easier to bear now, but there are still days where I think I won't be able to draw a breath without feeling like I'm drowning. I lost everything, Hark. I had no other family. I still wake up in the night aching for them. I'd have given *everything* to help you rescue the slaves if I had known.'

Silence filled the space between them, and for half a second her chest felt tight at what she'd revealed to him.

But then it passed, and she was glad he'd stayed silent. That he'd listened to the things that plagued her so deeply. Perhaps if the world weren't so cruel, they could have grown to be friends.

Hours passed, and the festival lit up in hundreds of orange lights strung together with thin electric wires, bathing the scene in a warm colour that reminded her of egg yolks. She bit back the comment, aware that Hark was not Perry, or Halos. She had sipped steadily on the wine Hark had bought her – so steadily that it had gone cold and now she longed for another steaming glass of it to chase the numbness from her bones. They hadn't moved in hours. They'd watched the dancing, and singing, and movement of people as they waited for the slave traders to show. There were plenty of young women here – men, too – who would make ideal targets on their way back to Vorstrum or whatever far-flung corner of Kastonia they had come from, but not one trace of trouble had arisen. The lack of any sort of danger made her anxious, kindled the flame in her chest that begged to go and help the slaves at the border.

Just when she'd about given up on anything amiss occurring at this spritely little festival, a shadow flickered in the corner of Arla's vision – the brief curl of a cloak at the very back of the tent. So quietly and smoothly that no one would detect her, she slid a hand under the hem of her dress, creeping her hand up her thigh to free her blade of its sheath. The sharpness of the steel whispered against her flesh, and she winced as it nicked the soft skin on the side of her leg.

'I could have cut a gap in the side of the dress, you know,' Hark murmured softly in her ear, mimicking her move by reaching inside his jacket to retrieve his own dagger.

'You certainly will not.'

'Hmm ... you've never been afraid to show a little flesh before, Reinhart. What makes tonight any different?' he whispered back, not caring to hide the amusement in his tone despite the looming threat gathering at the rear of the festival. She resisted the urge to elbow him. Of course, it was true, she had worn daringly low-cut dresses to state dances and dinners, and she was no stranger to what so much exposed flesh could buy her, but none of that had been for *him* to see.

'Because tonight, Stappen,' she said, lowering herself from the stool and edging slowly backwards into the darkness, 'I don't intend to charm anybody.'

She spun just as a hand reached for her.

Hark was there in an instant, his blade flush against Arla's where they pointed at the throat of a figure shrouded in black.

'Good evening, Miss Reinhart.'

CHAPTER 27

Arla barrelled through the side of the tent, her blade pressed tightly against the stranger's throat.

'Now, let's start talking, shall we?' She was met with an empty silence, and it only worked to enrage her. Pressing the tip of her blade so hard now against the stranger's neck that a bead of crimson bloomed in the darkness, she took a step closer, silently hoping that Hark would have her back if the figure pulled their own weapon against her.

'I mean you no harm, Miss Reinhart. I only wish to speak.' The voice was that of a woman, though it was raspy and hoarse. Sick or old, then. Or both.

'Then I suggest that you start speaking.' The worst part was that Arla enjoyed this side of her job. She found pleasure in the utter power she had over her victims, and how thoroughly helpless they became at her hand.

'You've done your job well tonight, whether you meant to be known or not,' the woman rasped, and Arla felt her patience fraying at the cryptic strangeness of it all.

'For the gods' sake,' she growled, pulling the hood of the woman's cloak down to reveal her face, which was aged with deep lines. Grey strands of hair were threaded through the black that hung below the woman's shoulders and she had deathly pale skin. It was the woman's eyes, though, that caused Arla to step back and remove the blade from her throat. Eyes that watched her with an intent that pricked the hairs on Arla's neck. The woman narrowed them, and it was as though Arla's soul was being laid bare, as if this person could see inside her and unravel her with nothing more than a thought. She couldn't describe it, the feeling that came over her, the feeling that her life was held in the palm of this stranger's hands. The irony was not lost on Arla that perhaps this was how her victims felt when she descended upon them. Arla's skin felt hot, and her heart raced as she stared at the woman; she felt as if something was now controlling her.

'Start speaking,' a voice cut in. Thank the gods for Hark Stappen.

He stepped between them, his frame blocking Arla's eye contact with the woman and allowing her to take a deep breath. She'd never felt that way before, and she'd looked into the eyes of hundreds of people before she killed them. What had made her hesitate?

'Your presence tonight, Miss Reinhart, has saved more than you would think.'

'And what's that supposed to mean?' Arla snapped, surging past Hark to stand before the stranger again. She kept her eyes averted though, not ready to risk the feeling of mortality that had gripped her so suddenly.

You're tired. It was nothing.

The stranger smiled, pulling her lips back over blackened teeth. 'Don't be so naïve, Miss Reinhart. Your reputation reaches even the furthest corners of the kingdoms. The merest glimpse of your face has held off those who wish to harvest the magic-wielders.'

Magic-wielders.

Arla's blood stopped pumping. A rushing noise filled her ears as she repeated the words in her head. Magic ... was ... an impossibility. It didn't exist. It had never existed.

And yet there was no doubt in the eyes of the stranger as she looked back at Arla. There was only a sincerity that had Arla's knees threatening to buckle beneath her.

Hark was impossibly still – barely breathing, Arla thought.

Magic...

Her fingers trembled as she met the eyes of the stranger again. 'What do you mean?'

'Ah, you don't believe the resurgence of slavery is for just the sake of slavery, do you?' The words came coated in sour breath and confusion, and Arla hated the way her feet moved even closer to the woman.

Hark's frustration boiled over, his arm flailing as he ground out. 'This is—'

'The king thinks they have blood magic?' Arla whispered, the pieces beginning to fit together in something that was ... absurd. Could it truly be real? Could all of this, this strange new alliance between Cyrus and Elrod, be because of *magic*?

'He doesn't think, Miss Reinhart. He knows they do.'

She didn't even know if she believed the words that burst from her lips. 'That's ridiculous! There is no magic—!'

'Like there are no dragons beneath Grey Hill, Miss Reinhart?'

A low, guttural noise escaped Hark's throat, and Arla's own temper flared at the mention of the dragons and what that false belief had meant for Hadalyn.

But ... but if magic *was* real, what did that mean for the dragons? Was there truth to that myth, too?

Her heart fluttered uneasily. There was something in her chest that reared at the thought of the dragons.

She shut it down in a heartbeat.

'Save them, Miss Reinhart. Not even the gods can reach them now.'

'We've heard enough,' Hark snapped, turning quickly and striding away from the two women. Arla watched him go, her heart thundering against her ribcage. The trembling in her fingers spread throughout her body because one by one she could feel the threads of everything she believed in coming undone.

'The soldiers won't come tonight, Miss Reinhart. I wasn't lying when I spoke of your reputation.'

Arla didn't know why she believed the words the woman spoke, but she knew them to be true. Had there been any intention of trouble tonight, it would have presented itself by now. She turned to look towards where Hark had stormed off to, and only saw the flick of canvas as he slipped back inside the tent. He'd known. She'd seen it in the way his face had paled slightly as the stranger had spoken. But it was all nonsense, wasn't it? Magic didn't exist and that was the end of it. Elrod was keeping slaves and trading them illegally because it was clearly filling the royal coffers whilst the rest of his kingdom suffered. Magic and dragons were a lie. They had to be.

The music was calling her to join Hark back at the festival. So with a nod to the stranger that she could only put down to the fact she hadn't needed to kill her, Arla turned towards the tent.

'Power lies beneath Castle Grey, Miss Reinhart. I suggest you wield it wisely...' The woman grasped Arla's wrist and pressed something cool and hard into the palm of her hand. Arla resisted the urge to hit her for the unwarranted touch, but she closed her fist around the object in her hand and pulled away harshly from the woman. By the time she'd made it back to the tent and looked over her shoulder, the woman had disappeared. Arla opened her fist to reveal a gold brooch. Her entire body lurched as she took it in, something in her very soul recognising it and drawing her to the piece of metal. A golden flame caged in a metal heart.

A dragonhart.

~

She found Hark just as she had expected to – with a scowl on his face and a drink in his hand.

'Are all of your people as mind-addled as her?' Arla said crossly, snatching the cold glass of wine from him and downing the contents. It burned her throat in a comforting, addictive way that made her ache for more of the rich liquid. It had been a long day, made longer by the nonsense the woman had spouted at her. Arla couldn't deny that Kastonian soldiers did not seem to be occupying the market square, and even though it was dark, and her eyes strained with the labour of too many days travelling, she had taken the time to observe the tops of trees and the narrow strips between stalls for anybody lurking there. Everything had come up empty.

Hark was ignoring her again.

Kastonian prick.

She thought about mentioning the woman's claim that magic lay within the blood of the slaves, but what was the point? She'd vehemently denied any existence of magic or associated dragons, and she'd have laughed in Hark's face had he tried to tell her otherwise, so what did it matter that he'd never mentioned it?

She twisted the brooch the woman had given her between her fingers. A dragonhart. A symbol of the old religion – for luck, the people said. Of course, Arla didn't believe in any of it, but she couldn't help the intrigue that perked up as she toyed with the object. It was weighty – solid gold she suspected – and it felt … sentient, almost, as if it were as drawn to her as she was to it.

It was all nonsense, though. It had to be. Perhaps she'd spent too long surrounded by these gullible fools who believed in magic and its tales.

She couldn't voice any of that to Hark and so she said nothing. She sat in silence and watched Vorstrum's festival until she could stand it no longer. She needed alcohol, or to go and dance, if only as a way to deal with Hark, with what the woman had insisted was true, with everything that was happening. There was an urgency in her blood. A call to go *now* and rescue the slaves. She had all but fought Hark on the journey here to ditch this ridiculous festival and go and storm the border *now*. Damn the soldiers that would be trying to fill their slave quotas tonight, the slave trade would be no more by the morning if Arla had her way.

Hark had denied her pleas, of course.

He'd told her that it was a foolish thing to do. That they

needed to wait and be prepared to go to the border tomorrow. And tonight wasn't a waste, he'd said. Tonight was a chance to make sure no other men, women or children were going to be caught in the crossfire of what would surely come when they crept into the slave encampment on the border and got to work freeing them in the morning.

It seemed to Arla that Hark's crew didn't have an ounce of urgency in them and it made her want to hit something.

Swiping another glass – this one hot and filled with fruit – from a grey-haired woman carrying wooden trays of the beverage, she dropped a coin into the leather pouch at the woman's hip and drank deeply from the glass. If he wouldn't let her go charging into the camp, she needed *something* to calm her agitated nerves. Forget the deadly focus she was supposed to wield like a sword, the stranger had told her tonight would be safe, she could afford to allow her mind to slip into somewhere a little more pleasant than what the world currently had to offer.

Besides, she could deal with the consequences in the morning.

'Steady, Reinhart. I have no intention of carrying you home,' Hark said, his eyes fixed straight ahead.

Arla scoffed. 'Don't flatter yourself. There are plenty of men here better suited to carry me to bed than you.'

'Meaning?' he ground out. She bit the inside of her cheek to hide the snigger at his annoyance.

'Meaning you're the last person I would allow to take me home,' she replied, licking her lips free of the sweet wine.

'Not what you were saying last night.'

Impossible prick!

'I suggest you stop drinking,' he added.

She swallowed the remaining liquid and beckoned for the woman who had served her to return. She took a larger glass than she had before, making a point to drop two coins loudly onto the woman's tray and throw a wicked smile Hark's way.

'Nobody tells me what to do.'

CHAPTER 28
HARK

It had taken her no time at all to ditch him in the tent and join the children and other women who were dancing. It had bothered him initially that she had abandoned the job so she could *dance*, but after that strange hag's words, he had to admit he had relaxed just a fraction, had been less inclined to stop her drinking the sweet wine she kept accepting from strangers who laughed as they twirled with her.

Besides, he couldn't very well scold her for it when she had been insistent they go storming into the northern border encampment tonight to rescue the slaves. He'd thought she might ignore him. Thought he might turn towards her at some point during the evening only to find that she had disappeared – that her patience had worn too thin and she'd disappeared to go and rescue those who had been captured.

So, no. He wouldn't stop Arla drinking. Not when he knew she needed something to help her relax, to begin to process what had happened and why she hadn't known a thing.

Tomorrow ... tomorrow they would utilise that burning

anger in her blood and silently slip into the camp and begin freeing the slaves, just as his crew had been doing for months now. Slowly. That was the only way they would manage this without finding themselves hung or with an arrow through the chest.

He couldn't take his eyes off Arla. Once or twice she had looked over at him, her eyes suggesting he join in. And, truthfully, he wasn't sure why he had declined. Except that at least one of them needed to stay alert to any threats on his people? And that he wouldn't degrade himself by being draped in coloured ribbons and dancing hand in hand with children? But mostly because he couldn't stand the thought of being so close to her, of becoming wrapped in that honey and jasmine scent she left wherever she went; of dancing with her and not being able to show her just how exquisitely *he* could dance? What other exquisite things he could do with her had he the courage...?

He had made her laugh, and even if he could somehow draw the sound from her again and again, he didn't think he could ever get enough of that lilting, childish laugher. She didn't do it half enough. He watched her sway and twirl, and couldn't believe that this unbound, happy person was the same girl he'd known for the last two years. He had seen her deadly, sarcastic, angry – gods, she was always angry – charming, plotting, but he had never seen her carefree and unrestrained as now. She carried burdens he wished she didn't blame him for – blame his *people* for – and they weighed heavily on her. After all she had been through, it was no surprise she looked older than her eighteen years; her face had aged into something more mature and ... beautiful. But there she was, barely an adult and with too much blood on her hands. He'd seen how ... violent she could be when she wanted. He'd seen some of the victims she'd been instructed to dispose of by her king, leaving some so mangled that he wondered what in the gods possessed the girl to butcher people like she did. In another life he would have believed her to have blood magic, because to be able to throw her knives the way she did was otherworldly. Maybe she'd worked herself to the point of breaking to become so talented.

Hark sighed as he watched her accept another drink, and after the next round of dancing had finished, he saw her feet falter for the first time in the two years he had known her. He was up and marching towards her in an instant. Arla Reinhart was as surefooted as they came, and now, after consuming half her bodyweight in hot wine, she had staggered.

It was time to go.

His legs were stiff from sitting so long and he was glad of the opportunity to stretch them as he strode towards her. 'As much as I'm enjoying watching you make an absolute fool of yourself,' he murmured in her ear, 'it's time to go, sweetheart.'

Her body stiffened, losing all the freedom it had exhibited only minutes before he had come to spoil her fun. Gods, she really was going to make him drag her away from here.

Surprisingly, however, she pulled away from the circle, laughing lightly as a child draped a blue ribbon around her shoulders. She walked silently beside him, and it was so strange for her to be compliant that he wondered if something was wrong.

It became clear soon enough. Her left foot stumbled on seemingly flat ground as they made their way back to where their horses were tied, and he was not blind to the fact she was drifting with every step she took. He kept his eyes alert and focused, mindful that although the palace soldiers had not tried anything at the festival, it didn't mean they weren't waiting to dispose of Hadalyn's most notorious killer on her way home, especially now that she was drunk enough to stab herself with her own blades.

'You're angry with me,' Arla commented, hauling herself onto Vetta's back with decidedly less grace than she usually did. He wondered why the mare put up with it, but Arla had sulked for so long when they had initially ridden out from Hadalyn on opposite horses that he had decided she and Vetta had been through more than she was letting on. He preferred Eros, anyway.

'No, I just think you're irresponsible,' he replied, nudging Eros's sides to catch up to Vetta.

It was only when they were half a mile from Vorstrum, and he could see the soft glow of its lights that he began to relax fully, and consequently notice how close she was to falling off Vetta's back.

'Fuck,' he cursed, digging his heels into Eros, and trotting up beside Arla's slumping body.

She shot upright, her fingers tightening on the reins as she adjusted herself in the saddle. Had she actually fallen asleep?

'I'm fine, Stappen...' she mumbled, blinking her eyes.

'Sure. You can hardly sit up.'

'I can.'

He smirked. She was quite amusing when she was drunk, or at least when she wasn't trying to attack him with words or swords, so it made for a refreshing change.

She slid from Vetta's back the minute they arrived at the inn, and he questioned how she had even managed to stay upright as she stumbled backwards. Maybe her time as an assassin had aided her intoxicated feet. He would tell her tomorrow just how reckless she had been, but now he wanted to get inside and lock her somewhere safe.

'Come on,' he said with a sigh, heading for the door.

Nothing. Not one shuffle of movement.

'Reinhart, come on.'

Silence.

He moved towards her, eyes scanning her body for where she had concealed blades, because it was entirely typical of her to do so and he couldn't be sure she wouldn't use them on him in this state.

'Hey, we're going in,' he said gently, waving a hand in front of her. She blinked quickly, turning her head to face him.

'Mm-hmm, I'm coming,' she said before tripping over... What? *Gods*.

He reached for her, pulling her close, and for the first time she didn't resist. He had been cautious, too well versed in her violence and dangerously short temper to risk grabbing her without warning. But she allowed the touch and with whatever patience he had left, he hooked an arm around her and coaxed her up the stairs of the inn.

'Go to bed,' he grumbled, pushing her door open with one arm, and encouraging her through the doorway. She didn't say a word, and he would have continued walking and left her there had he not heard the telltale thud of her stumbling.

He caught her by an elbow before her knees could hit the floor, and he cursed under his breath. He couldn't leave her like this. Not only was she more than capable of choking on her own vomit, but there were people who would happily see Arla Reinhart dead – people who had probably observed how thoroughly ruined she was on her way back from the festival and may believe her to be an easy target. They'd be right. The windows were not impenetrable and though he'd never been concerned with Arla's ability to be half asleep and still drive a dagger through a man's throat, he didn't expect the same sort of sense of self-preservation from her in this state.

'Come on,' he said, hauling her to her feet and dragging her towards his room. It was the right thing to do. He needed her help to complete the job, and he didn't fancy explaining to the king that he had allowed his assassin to be murdered in her sleep. Not that he expected to be in Cyrus's presence ever again. He'd seen the betrayal and confusion in Arla's eyes when he'd told her of Cyrus's involvement in the slave trading, and she didn't yet know the half of it. He could still feel that burning anger in the pit of his stomach when Elrod had told him of the slaves and how he'd manipulated Cyrus into investing his own royal coffers into the scheme, too. It wouldn't surprise Hark if Arla never returned to Castle Grey again, other than to abolish its monarchy.

'Brave of you to let me in here, Stappen,' she slurred, swaying as she walked the perimeter of the room, her fingers grazing the few objects he'd brought with him on the trip.

'And why would that be?'

She turned to face him, laughter bursting from her lips before she spoke. 'Because you couldn't keep your hands off me last time.'

His heart stuttered in his chest, his skin suddenly too hot. 'Well I can promise you, *Reinhart,* that it won't be happening again. A mistake, as you so eloquently reminded me this morning.'

She raised a brow, flopping onto the bed with such a lack of grace he couldn't help but sigh. He shouldn't have let her in here. She needed to leave. Now.

But ... she was drunk and already lying on the bed, the white dress fanning around her. And she was ... beautiful. He'd always known it of course, just hadn't let himself think it. But here, now, she looked soft. And lovely. And oh, he was so fucked.

They were both silent for a while, Hark removing the blades he had strapped to his body and discarding the jacket he had chosen, and Arla ... watching. He could feel her eyes on him, and it made him nervous in a way he wasn't familiar with.

The bed creaked as he joined her on it, and she turned her head to face him. The moonlight poured in from the window in the roof above them, illuminating her in a shade of soft silver.

'Could you take the pins out of my hair?' she asked quietly, batting her eyelids as they drooped against the darkness.

'Do I look like a maid?' he huffed, reaching for her anyway. He didn't know what he was doing – gods, he had never tended to a woman's hair unless he was running his hands through it during rather less innocent activities – but he found himself gently prising the silver pins from the golden crown she had woven. Of course she had packed silver pins; she couldn't have settled on a less expensive – and more practical – set of hair accessories for travel. He rolled his eyes at the thought.

After what seemed an age, he collected the pile of pins in his hands and placed them on the dresser, averting his eyes from the girl splayed out on the bed, her hair a wave of sunlight around her. She had always had pale, golden, silky coils for hair that were unruly when left loose, but now they were wavy and less sharp than usual—

Stop it.

For half a moment it all felt wrong. They should be out there, like she'd said, rescuing those the King of Kastonia had ordered to be imprisoned. They should be—

An odd noise – something between a squeak and a breath – escaped her, immediately capturing the gaze he had withheld seconds before. She hiccupped again, and he bit sharply on his lip to fight the laughter clawing its way up his throat.

'It's not funny,' she protested, turning on her side to face him.

Gods, she needed to stop looking at him like that.

'You're staring, Stappen.'

He was.

He didn't think he could stop.

It was why he had noticed how cold she was. She shook slightly and it pained him to watch her look so vulnerable.

'You're cold,' he said.

'Obviously.'

Don't you fucking dare.

'Come here.'

Fool.

She looked at him, her body becoming preternaturally still for a heartbeat. And then she was shuffling closer to him, turning so that her back was pressed against his chest. She was freezing. But the feel of her against him...

'Don't tell the others,' she whispered.

It dragged a smile from Hark. Arla Reinhart, who had never once given a single thought to the way others perceived her, asking him not to breathe a word of it to his friends.

Slim chance of that ever happening. Not when the feel of her pressed against him was sending him spiralling.

'I wouldn't dream of it,' he managed, groaning when she shifted even closer.

She turned slowly at the sound, until she was facing him and her lips were only inches away.

'This is a bad idea,' she whispered.

Hark swallowed. 'The worst.'

She huffed a laugh. 'I don't even like you.'

'You're the bane of my life.' He was sure their faces were closer now. 'Fuck it.'

They came together slowly and then all at once. Where the last time he had kissed her had been lust, desperation and revenge all tangled together, this was gentleness and patience. Their lips moved together as if they had been carved from the same mould, and in that moment there was nothing else that mattered besides the girl he held so desperately close.

She moved against him, pressing her body closer, *closer* than he thought was possible. He could feel every inch of her. Every curve and swell. And when she ran her hands down his torso, lower and lower until the hard ridge of him was beneath her palm, Hark thought she could kill him right then and he'd let her do it.

She kissed him harder, her hand a blessing and a curse as he struggled to hold on to the edge of sanity. He wanted her. Wanted her so much it *hurt*.

But no.

No, he couldn't.

Not when she'd drunk so much. Not when she'd barely been able to make it to this bed without him helping her.

He gripped her wrist gently, *so gently,* and held her hand in his. 'Not tonight, Reinhart,' he whispered softly.

The pained groan that came from her had him questioning his ability to keep his hands off her. 'Another night, when you're not so deep in your cups that you don't know what you're doing. When I touch you again, I want you to remember every second of it.'

Her chin dipped, everything about her softening as she smiled weakly.

He almost choked on the laughter in his throat when she hiccupped again. 'You'll hate yourself tomorrow,' he said, stretching his back against the wooden headboard.

'Yes,' she said, with too much surety for his liking.

He felt overcome with an unfamiliar emotion. Regret. For what had happened to her family and to her kingdom at the hands of his people. Regret for what it had made her into. The only thing that eased the ache was how soft she was in this moment, when the world had made her so unbreakably hard.

'Go to sleep, Reinhart,' he whispered.

He was met with silence, her chest already rising and falling deeply. He counted each breath she took until his eyes became blurry, and then he let the darkness swallow him, too.

CHAPTER 29

You'll hate yourself in the morning.

He was right.

Her head pounded in time with her heart, and her whole body ached as she came round to the world.

Gods, she was an idiot.

Hark Stappen had all but carried her to bed – *his* bed – last night, and she had been so far gone in her cups that she hadn't thought of the consequences of kissing him. She didn't dare breathe, aware that he would hear the change in rhythm and likely confront her about the state she had got herself into at the festival. Or worse, he would bring up what had happened between them.

She didn't often let herself go like that – or ever, really – but she had been so hurt by the possibility that Cyrus had kept something so enormous from her that the lure of the alcohol had been too much. She'd pay for it today. Hark would taunt her through whatever he and his crew had in store, and her body was already protesting at the strain she would put it under again. She was surprised her ankle withstood everything she put it through; she'd never let it heal properly after breaking it two years ago after falling from the side of the castle which she was climbing in order to prove a point, and it reminded her daily – often hourly – of that mistake.

She didn't want to face the day, no matter that she was more than ready to cut the heads off the soldiers guarding the slaves. She felt ... a little lost, if she was honest. She played close to the line, often dancing on it and taunting death with some of the risks she took. She couldn't do that now, not when other people were involved – though she didn't object to allowing the Kase girl to risk her own neck.

She couldn't allow herself to care though; it only ever got her hurt and often at the cost of those she cared about.

Sitting upright with the fluidity of a wraith, she turned her head sharply, ready to intercept whatever retort he had for her before he could voice it.

But he wasn't there.

Something in her chest tightened and—

Fuck.

She was beginning to care, wasn't she?

Her eyes scanned the room, taking in every notch in the wood of the panelled walls, the fingerprints pressed in dust on every surface. He had left her a note. Which meant she was late.

Without thinking, she sprinted down the hallway to her own room, ignoring the puzzled look another guest at the inn shot her as she flew past them in a blur of white and gold. Halos would kill her for letting her hair end up in such a state.

Flinging the door open, she was surprised to find her saddlebags already packed and her cloak lying on the bed beside the gloves she had stolen back in Irelliad.

Gods, he was going to love this.

~

Eros was saddled and Hark was in the process of getting Vetta ready, too, when Arla entered the barn, rather more dishevelled than she would have liked.

He'd told her yesterday that they would set off for the border again, and that they would be freeing more of the slaves that his crew had been responsible in rescuing in recent weeks. She had agreed immediately, her hands itching with violence to punish those responsible for such abhorrent practices, but she couldn't help thinking it wasn't enough.

They would free the slaves, send them to wherever it was that Hark's friends gave them safety, but then they'd have to do it again and again – an infinite cycle. She'd heard Sebastian telling Hark that the number of guards had increased, and that number would only rise the more times they broke slaves out of the camp. It needed to end, and it needed to end soon. There was only so much patience in her, and if Hark's crew didn't hand her a solid plan to abolish the trading for good and confirm that her king had nothing to do with it, she would take matters into her own hands.

'I'm surprised you can even stand this morning,' Hark said, trying to contain the smirk threatening to break free of his lips.

'Please don't,' she said, mounting Vetta.

There was no room in her agenda for Hark's taunting. Especially when she remembered the way she'd kissed him last night and was praying on any gods that would listen that he wouldn't bring it up. It had been a mistake. She'd been drunk and he'd been ... *there*. It meant nothing – *he* meant nothing.

'It'll take more than last night to stop me,' Arla tossed over her shoulder.

'You're not invincible, you know,' he called, and she swallowed thickly at the thought. She knew she wasn't. She'd seen just how vulnerable people became at the wrong end of a blade.

She ran her fingers over the gold brooch she'd pinned to her cloak this morning – not for luck, but because it was pretty, of course. 'I don't need to be invincible. Nobody gets close enough to me for that to be necessary.'

The chill of the air on her face soon brought her out of the alcohol-induced fog and blessed her with a scowl and a need for blood that had her fingers brushing over the hilt of the blade at her waist.

Hark's crew were each mounted on horses and wore hooded black cloaks similar to her own. Arla could make out the silhouettes of knives, swords, and bows strapped to their bodies and was glad she'd packed her own. They'd come prepared for battle, and she wasn't sure why that concerned her.

'Would it kill any of you to break a smile?' she called as she approached the group. Beside her, Hark sighed, running a hand through his hair, and Arla inwardly smirked at her own ability to elicit such exasperation from him.

'Here we go,' Kase muttered, the silver-grey horse she sat atop the same colour as her hair.

'Good morning to you, too, *Kase,*' Arla said sarcastically, baring her teeth at the girl.

'If we're quite ready, ladies,' Sebastian interrupted, tossing a grin at Arla who inclined her head at the only one of Hark's friends who'd showed her even a fraction of the respect she deserved.

The world was quiet outside the confines of Vorstrum, the

meadows wild and untended, the sun warm where it managed to push its way through the bite of cold air. She hated winter, but in the wild, where everything was green and free of the stench that riddled the towns, she thought she might like it. The only sound was the footfall of the horses, and Arla was content to focus on the sway of the mare beneath her.

'We go in quietly, just as before,' Jaz said, disrupting the careful quiet and setting her jaw tight as the looming task ahead of them was brought back to her attention. 'We take as many as we can without engaging with the soldiers.'

'And what are you doing with the people we rescue?'

'Jack will take them over the border to safety,' Jaz replied.

'Which border?' she questioned. 'Hadalyn?'

'Over the northern border. They'll make their way to safety once they're out of Kastonia. Hadalyn's not safe.'

Beyond the northern border were mountain ranges so hostile that no one had ever come back from them alive. Arla could only hope there was a route the slaves could take to the sea. Perhaps they were catching boats to the continent.

'What—?'

'We'll explain later. Let's focus on getting them out without dying,' Jack interrupted.

They were quiet for long moments, the movement of the horses carrying them further towards the camp with every hoof that marked the earth.

'Stay out of my way,' Arla said sternly. 'I work better on my own and I won't be held responsible for hurting anyone that gets in my way.'

It sounded ridiculous when she listened to herself, but she'd felt the unhinging that came with the violence: how she didn't know when to stop; how the anger sang to her and turned her into a ... a whirlwind that was entirely unstoppable until everything around her was dead. Her fingers moved to stroke that damned brooch at the thought, the action having become a comfort in the short time she'd owned the thing.

'Absolutely not. Hark stays with her—'

'We work as a team. We—'

'Are you serious—?'

Her head spun as each of them objected to her statement, even though she'd said it to keep them safe.

'You leave her alone,' Hark's voice cut through them all, a hard, stony sentence that left no room for argument. 'Are we clear?'

'Crystal.'

'Kase,' Hark warned, and Arla felt a warmth bloom in her chest.

They rode in silence after that, the seriousness of their job settling over the group like a leaden blanket. She didn't hear Jack ride up next to her until his soft voice found her ears. 'I'm glad you're here, you know.'

It took her so by surprise she could barely form the words. 'I'm not here for your gratitude. I just want those people freed.'

'I know,' Jack said. 'I've given everything trying to help them. And I'd do it all again.'

Arla glanced at him. She saw how his back stooped despite his position atop the horse. There was tiredness in his eyes, but there was kindness, too – which he had extended to her no matter how many furious glances Kase threw their way.

'You haven't seen a healer?' she asked.

Jack smiled softly, shifting his weight awkwardly in the saddle. 'I will when we have the time. Right now, there's too many people at risk to worry about myself. I can't abandon the crew, especially— I just ... I owe them that.'

'You all care about each other. A lot. I can't say it's something I've had much experience with.'

It was true that she had never felt the camaraderie others experienced within the King's Guard, nor had she ever had friends outside of Halos. Seeing them now, she thought she'd like to have a team ready to lay their lives down for each other.

'How did you end up with this lot?' Arla asked.

Jack chuckled, patting the horse as he shifted his weight again. 'I caught them trying to break into the tunnels beneath the docks – I worked the boats, you see – and I don't know what stopped me reporting them but I'm glad I didn't. They invited me down there, told me what they were doing, and asked whether I wanted to be a part of it. Don't know why they trusted me so quickly. Perhaps because they could tell I knew they'd kill me if I breathed a word of it. We've been a family ever since.'

Jack was a kind soul. Arla knew it with a certainty. She saw it in the way he stroked Vetta's face when the mare was close enough. She saw it in the way he routinely checked if any of them needed water or food. Yes, Jack was too kind for the hand he'd been dealt and way his body struggled to keep up with the rest of them.

Jack was worth protecting.

The northern border towered on the horizon, a grey mass of hastily thrown-together buildings, tents, and cages set in a valley surrounded by sheer cliff faces. There seemed to be no end to it. It was a sprawling cold place that stretched as far as she could see – to the mountains in the distance and probably beyond them, Arla imagined. There were more soldiers than she could have ever expected, dozens upon dozens of black-uniformed guards that filled her chest with an adrenalin she couldn't be sure wasn't fear. And then there were the slaves. Too many to count. Too many filling the barren camp, the grey tattered rags they wore blending in with the landscape. This place was... well, it was enormous. It stretched for miles, the cliffs surrounding it reminding her too vividly of sentinels – strong and overwhelmingly large.

Arla swallowed the bile rising in her throat as they dismounted and crawled to the edge of the ledge. She wouldn't forget the shock or disgust she'd felt when she'd first peered over it with Hark at her side. The years of anger, hatred, and despair bubbled up inside her and threatened to boil over at the sight of slaves in chains.

It was busier than before. Soldiers stood at regular intervals every hundred yards for what must be miles – miles and miles of land with hundreds and hundreds of slaves. Thousands. Frequent raids of the camp had made the Kastonian soldiers careful, they hadn't dared leave a single body unchained in some way – either wrist or ankle – meaning that they would be more difficult to move quickly. There would be blood drawn, then, and Arla's fingers twitched at her side. That she could do.

'In and out, offload the slaves to Jack, and meet at the bloodstone.'

How had Hark become so good at leading rescue missions and ordering his ... acquaintances?

She didn't want to think about it too deeply. She only wanted to rescue the wretched souls, and then she would burn this kingdom to the ground and Elrod along with it.

CHAPTER 30

The northern border was a barren place, all rocky outcrops and angry cliff faces. The small amount of vegetation there was had been hardened by frost and covered the ground in thorny shrubs. It was at odds to Vorstrum and the rest of Kastonia – a world away from Hadalyn, too. There had never been anything much up here – a handful of buildings used as soldiers' outposts and only inhabited a couple of times a year. There were small villages that cropped up from time to time, the buildings all wooden and temporary and usually arranged around a firepit some poor soul had likely spent hours trying to coax into a flame. The villages never lasted very long – rarely more than a year.

Overall it was a miserable, soul-sucking place.

Arla's heart pounded against her ribs, the adrenaline bubbling in her veins at what they were about to do. Or maybe she missed how close Hark had been pressed against her side just a few moments before?

They crouched a short way from the camp behind barrels

filled with something that smelled sour and metallic. She didn't want to know what was in the wretched things, but they provided a shadowed corner where she could sit and wait out of the way.

The crew had split up, following Hark's orders with no complaint. Arla wondered how this operation functioned when he wasn't around.

Arla could make out the slaves slowly and quietly disappearing into the shadows of the cliffs that formed the perimeter of the camp. More importantly, she saw that nobody seemed to notice. The crew were discreet, and they were pulling men, women, and *fucking children* out of the grip of Kastonia, and sending them in Jack's direction. Where they would go next she didn't know.

She didn't like being kept out of the plotting and planning; the lack of control was making her twitchy.

She watched more slaves disappear, and now that the edges of the camp were thinning out, revealing gaps in the rows and rows of slaves being counted and moved, Arla saw that the soldiers were beginning to talk.

'Didn't have you down as the superstitious sort,' Hark murmured from beside her behind the barrels, glancing at the brooch on Arla's cloak.

'Perhaps your gods will spare us some luck if I wear it. Besides, it's pretty.'

A smile tugged in the corner of Hark's lips. 'Vain as ever.'

A crack cleaved the air, slicing through to her heart and rocking her on her heels. A yelp followed the noise, and Arla felt her blood run cold at the terrible sound, a sound she hadn't thought she would ever hear again following the days after the storming of Castle Grey. She narrowed her eyes, barely containing the tears of anguish that clawed at her eyelids.

'Easy,' Hark murmured.

'They're whipping them,' she choked out.

A warmth spread through her fingers as Hark's hand covered her own. His skin was more tanned than hers, and she was surprised at the softness of it. She had seen how he wielded a blade so the smoothness, the lack of callouses, surprised her.

'I know,' he said softly, his ice-blue eyes becoming the colour of steel in the low light. He was as pained as her and somehow that made this whole thing worse. She made as if to move and found him tightening his grip around her fingers.

'You can't,' he hissed.

'I will not stand here and watch them be tortured. I won't do it.'

'Just wait. Please, wait.' Gods, she didn't want to listen to this, but he was *pleading* with her.

'I won't leave them,' she said gently, her fingers going slack in his.

'I'm not asking you to, Reinhart. But not today. You can't save everyone. You can't save them all.'

Gods, didn't she know it. Had she been good enough she would have been able to do *something* to save her parents that day, to save Hadalyn's people from the terror and destruction that had swarmed their kingdom. To save them all.

You were a child.

Her eyes locked with his. She didn't like the *thing* that was passing between the two of them. It was too similar to understanding, to kindness, to friendship. She hated Hark Stappen.

But now he was so close, his lips parted so perfectly she could lay her own against them—

Enough.

She made herself look away; made herself look towards what was happening in the camp as more and more slaves disappeared, until all of the group they had discussed on the way here had been removed from captivity and were hopefully on their way to safety. Arla felt her shoulders visibly relax, the tension easing out of her now that they'd succeeded without being caught. She had wanted to be involved, of course, had wanted to make her mark, but Hark had told her no, and looking now at how seamlessly his crew worked together she acknowledged that he'd been right. She had needed to sit back and observe.

Kase, Seb, and Jaz would be coming back any moment now, today's mission complete, and they could go back and plan for another raid tomorrow. They'd keep going until Kastonia didn't have a single slave in their possession.

Sudden shouting ripped her attention back to the camp and a commotion that was unravelling down there. Hark tensed at her side, his eyes wide as he scanned the scene with her, trying to unpick what exactly was happening.

Kase was visibly upset, her arms waving, her feet shuffling with no clear purpose as Kastonia's soldiers began to move through the crowds of slaves, right towards the heart of their crew's operation.

'Fuck,' Hark whispered, shifting beside her.

'What's happening?' she murmured, though Hark could have no better answer than she herself as they watched the carefully constructed plan come undone.

Soldiers moved through the crowd, approaching Jaz and Kase, the swords they now unsheathed reflecting the weak sunlight; Sebastian was isolated from them by the crowd but no less at risk. This ... this wasn't supposed to happen. The group was supposed to stay close to one another. Tight. Careful.

But Sebastian was shoving slaves behind him in the direction of the extraction crew, not caring how many he dragged.

None of the slaves he reached for were today's intended targets.

Arla could only watch. And wait. And chew her nails short as the soldiers moved closer, their bodies swallowed up by the mass of slaves, becoming a writhing, invisible wave amidst the crowd so that she could hardly tell the soldiers were embedded within it at all. Kase stilled, the proximity of the soldiers too dangerous to risk drawing attention to herself and Jaz.

But Sebastian didn't falter for a moment. He shoved every man, woman, and child he could reach back through the crowd towards the rockface. Jack would be hiding there somewhere, ready to direct the slaves where they needed to go.

Yet Arla couldn't take her eyes off Sebastian and the determined strides he took through the crowds; couldn't take her eyes off the soldiers closing in. They had to have realised what was happening now, had to have guessed that the same crew that had been responsible for stealing their slaves had infiltrated the camp.

'Fucking leave them,' Hark chuntered under his breath, the muscles in his jaw tense as the commotion surrounding Sebastian grew and ... then the soldiers broke through the crowd.

There was a heartbeat during which Arla thought she might be forced to watch Sebastian's head be cleaved from his shoulders, but then the soldiers came to a halt before him.

That heartbeat was over as quickly as it had arrived, because when Sebastian began hauling slaves behind him, the soldiers launched for them with a waspish vigour, their fingers wrapping around the wrists of any flesh they could.

And then they disappeared.

The slaves winked out of existence, as if the world had swallowed them whole.

Arla didn't have time to consider what in the gods-damned hell had just happened because chaos consumed the landscape.

Kase hurtled towards them, silver braid flailing and a wicked grin splitting her lips.

'Kase,' Hark growled, already tugging on Arla's hand to make their escape.

'Little problem,' Kase called, no longer caring how loudly she was shouting or how visible they were to the soldiers now shouting orders behind her.

'It doesn't look little to me,' Hark grumbled, his grip on Arla's hand never wavering as they careened through the valley and up the steep slope towards the top of the cliffs. Her legs burned with the strain of the ascent, but she pushed through the pain to keep pace with Hark. She was King's Assassin; he'd never let her live it down if she revealed her rigorous training programme had not prepared her for sprinting up steep rockfaces.

'We got them! All the ones we wanted!' Kase shouted over the pounding of their feet and the hollering of the soldiers now giving chase. 'But Seb wanted to get the next group—'

'Of course he did,' Hark growled, tugging harder on Arla's hand. Gods, she hated running.

'And then they had to do that fancy, light-flicker thing and that was it, they were on to us,' Kase continued.

'What are you talking about?' Arla bit out, trying to keep her breathing even despite the strain her body was under and the loose gravel under her feet. She'd seen those people disappear; she wanted answers *now*.

'It doesn't matter,' Hark shot back. 'Where are the others?'

'Meeting us at the Bloodstone. Or dead.'

Questions pulsed on the end of Arla's tongue, but before she could voice them, Hark gave a sharp tug to her hand, yanking her to the right as they reached the top of the slope.

She didn't know how she had missed it before – the rolling woodland spanning out before them. Some assassin she was. Still they kept running, drowning out the distant shouts of the soldiers. She hadn't seen where Jack had taken the freed slaves, and she couldn't shake the annoyance that they'd left him to get all those people to safety on his own. Unless…

She and Hark were a distraction.

The irritation at being used as bait pushed her legs forwards, her feet flying over roots, and dips, and something that snapped with a sound, too, like bones breaking.

It had all taken her by surprise, and she couldn't help wondering, as their feet pounded the packed earth, what that said about her and about her suitability for her job. She'd lost control of this quest, and she was being kept in the dark about things she should have seen before they unfolded. Was Hark right? Was she too confident in her own abilities? She'd gone unchecked for so long in Hadalyn that she hadn't truly thought it possible that someone might be able to catch her out.

Trees blurred past them in a smudge of green and brown, and her lungs burned. Her ankle screamed at her for the strain she was subjecting it to with every footfall. There wouldn't be any lavender oil or hot baths to soak it in later.

Just as she began to think the trees were an endless, rolling prison called up by the gods, Hark pulled her into a clearing, coming to a stop that had her almost barrelling into him.

The clearing was an odd shape, with awkward angles and trees jutting into it at irregular intervals, but the thing that had drawn her eye immediately and on which Kase now rested an arm as she bent double, gulping in huge gasps of air – *ha! Not as fit as you think you are, then* – was a large rock, about the size of a small child, protruding out of the ground. Its surface was worn smooth from what she guessed were thousands upon thousands of hands gliding over it, though a brown, rust-like stain marred the top. Arla had dealt with enough of those stains to recognise blood and therefore to conclude that the rock against which Kase leant was the aforementioned bloodstone.

'Anybody care to explain what the *fuck* that was all about?' Arla snapped, throwing the blade she had strapped across her back to the dusty, leaf-strewn ground. She whirled on Hark. 'If you think for one *minute* that I'll stand to be used as bait in your little schemes without being informed first, gods help you I will walk away from this right now and bring the might of Hadalyn down upon you!'

Kase, thankfully, remained quiet as Hark stepped up to Arla, his eyes shining with a threat in which she was all too ready to engage.

'If you wish to blame anyone, blame me and me alone. You do not speak to them that way, and you certainly do not threaten them with an army. They have done more for our kingdoms than most, Reinhart.'

It was ... regal, the way he spoke; a voice that commanded respect and obedience that she would be stupid to challenge. It didn't stop her trying.

Hark must have seen the challenge in her eyes, because

without breaking their gaze he said to his three friends, 'Kase, go with Seb and make sure there are no surprises waiting in the trees. Jaz, firewood. We're stopping here tonight.'

She heard each of them move, not a question or challenge from any of them as she held Hark's stare.

Only when they could no longer hear footsteps did the cord between them snap.

His hands were on the front of her shirt, pulling her up so she had to stand on her toes to keep any sort of contact with the ground.

'You ever threaten me or my friends with an army again, I will cut that pretty little throat and leave you bleeding on the ground of another kingdom,' he seethed, his breath hot on her face.

She summoned every hour of training, every minute of foot-work, every second of fine-tuned deadliness and wrapped it around her so that even she couldn't identify the seam between herself and the king's most lethal weapon, ready to go to war with Hark Stappen and let him know exactly how it would feel to bleed.

But in that moment, something inside her broke.

She sagged against his grip, wrenching her eyes from his to stare at the toes on which she was balancing so precariously.

'Okay,' she whispered.

'Okay?'

'Okay.' She shrugged, pulling herself free and turning her back on him.

She didn't want to do this anymore.

CHAPTER 31
HARK

No way. Absolutely no fucking way.

'Pick up your sword,' he said.

Something had changed behind her eyes; he'd seen the fight go out of her. He'd *felt* her stop caring. He wouldn't let her walk away now, not when he was beginning to find comfort in someone so deadly having his back – having his friends' backs. She would fit in well with them if she managed to pull her head out of her own arse for ten minutes. Even Kase liked her – though she would never admit it. He'd seen the girl he'd come to love like a sister cover a smirk at some of Arla's better comebacks.

He hated that he didn't hate her.

'Pick. Up. Your. Sword.'

Her shoulders slumped as she said, 'What?'

'Pick up your sword.'

Fight me for the gods' sakes.

'I know you're going through something right now, but you're not going to walk away from your emotions, and you're definitely not going to walk away from me.' Her fingers flexed. 'Pick up. Your sword.'

Before he could blink, she had spun, the leaves under her feet scattering as if she had magicked them away. Fire flared in her eyes, but he didn't even see her fingers curl around the hilt of her blade and arc it through the air.

He met her with a clang loud enough to wake the dead.

The force of her blade striking his reverberated through his bones. Again.

Again.

Again.

Gods.

He couldn't begin to untangle what she was feeling, what might be going through her head, but he would bet on it having something to do with her dead people and how the slave trade had been going on underneath her nose for years.

He was sweating, and yet she kept coming. Lunge, strike, block. She kept up an unwavering assault on him, sweat beading on her own forehead as she forced whatever she was feeling through that solid piece of metal.

He saw a gap and took it. The aim of her sword was slightly off so that it left her open. He slid his blade into the space, forcing her to take a step back and then the tip of his blade was resting at her throat, pressing into the creamy column of skin exposed only to him.

'Done?'

She nodded, stepping away slowly and shaking her head, as though the act could dislodge the thing that had made her turn away; the thoughts that had made her believe that it was somehow her fault; the idea that she could have done anything to stop what had happened to her people. What was still happening now.

He closed the gap between them, lifting her chin between his fingers so her eyes met his.

'We'll save them, okay? It won't happen again.'

'You're right, you know.' He'd never heard her sound so ... fragile. 'I don't know what I'm doing. I didn't have any idea this was happening. Fucking hell, I don't know when you're following me through Hadalyn half the time. I'm a fraud, aren't I? I throw a few knives, kill a few thieves, and stab a blade through my hand and somehow that makes me King's Assassin? Gods, it's tragic.' She sobbed a laugh.

She was going to break him with nothing but her words.

'Stop it. You're deadly with a blade – even with your arrows, when they fly the way you want them to.' She didn't laugh at his joke. 'You spot things most people would miss. You spare the lives of people like Brik because you think there's something worth saving inside them. You're willing to storm a camp full of Kastonian soldiers on your own to save slaves that may or may not be your own people. You are a good person. Now get a grip. We *will* save them.'

Her lip rolled between her teeth and, fucking *gods*, she was tearing him to pieces. It took everything in him not to kiss her right then; to take her to the floor in this gods-forsaken clearing and distract her in the only way he knew now.

'I do hope you've packed something alcoholic, Stappen. Gods help you tomorrow if I'm being made to sleep on the floor.'

There you are.

CHAPTER 32

She had needed that. And he was right; she *had* been running away from everything, because she couldn't bear to confront how she felt or come to terms with where that left her. But the sight of him so close to her, his fingers on her face, his lips right there...

He was carving away at the stone around her heart and she hated the way she was allowing it. She wished she'd never known what it felt like to have his skin beneath her fingers because now ... now she couldn't get the craving out of her head.

It wasn't surprising that Kase, Jaz, and Sebastian returned almost immediately after her spar with Hark; she had sensed them lurking in the treeline the entire time. She hoped Kase didn't realise how close she had come to falling apart completely; she'd hate to have to cancel out that little flash of vulnerability with something wicked to prove she wasn't weak.

Hark was right. She would save the slaves – every single one. There was no other option.

The flames of Jaz's hastily built fire brought Arla to the very edge of consciousness. Her eyelids heavy and drooping as the first warmth in hours licked at her skin. Whisky and leather wrapped around her, the scent comforting and familiar and ... Hark.

'Tea,' he said, handing her a steaming cup of the sweet-smelling liquid. His kindness was another chink in the armour of her heart.

What was happening to her? She couldn't be softening at the edges, could she? Though it wouldn't come as a complete shock, she had felt, in one way or another, not herself since leaving Castle Grey. Her hand strayed to the brooch on her cloak as she watched Hark's crew.

Something was cooking over the flames – rabbit, if she was not mistaken – skewered so crudely on a branch that she looked away. Hark and the others were speaking in quick, raised voices, so overlapped that she couldn't decipher what was being said. They were in disagreement, or at least, Hark was in disagreement with his friends.

Kase's silvery voice had become grating and high-pitched and Sebastian looked positively flustered as Hark asserted whatever power he wielded over the group.

Stretching her legs and ignoring the throb of her ankle, Arla levered herself off the ground and slotted herself into the circle of Kastonians.

'As much as I thoroughly enjoy telling Stappen where to stick his horseshit ideas, I'm sick to the gods of listening to you all squabble like children. So, if *one* of you could explain whatever it is that's going on, you'd be doing my head a favour.'

They turned to face her, and she didn't miss how each of them flicked their eyes between her face and the bloodstained stone against which she leant. Once the dispute had been resolved, she would ask.

'Waiting.'

'Hark thinks we should get them out. All of them. Tomorrow,' Sebastian said, pinching the bridge of his nose as Hark raised a brow.

'The slaves?' Arla asked, though they could hardly have been referring to anyone else.

'All of them. We storm the camp and destroy it. No more slaves, no more trading, no more almost killing ourselves in these raids,' Hark stated, his voice gravelly and full of something she couldn't quite place.

'Are you fucking serious?' Kase snarled, tossing the tea she had been sipping onto the floor and flinging her braid over her shoulder.

'Kase, those people could have been killed today because of our fuck-up—'

'*Our* fuck-up? Again, are you serious?' she snapped, her blue eyes staring him down. 'They never listen! I told them to keep quiet and move slowly, then one of them has to fucking flicker in and out of existence, drawing the attention of the entire camp of soldiers. So please, Hark, explain to me where *we* fucked up?' She was ... intense. The very air seemed to become heavy as she challenged him, and the muscle ticking in his jaw told Arla everything she needed to know. Kase was yanking too hard on whatever tether he used to leash his temper – a tether Arla knew all too well how to snap. But—

'Explain this *flicker*. I watched them disappear with my own eyes, but there must be an explanation. It's not possible,' Arla interrupted.

'Ma—'

'Leave it, Kase. She won't believe it anyway,' Hark said with a sigh.

'Leave what?' Arla demanded.

Kase smirked, sticking her tongue out at Hark in such a childish way that Arla almost laughed. 'The slaves are magic-wielders,' she said. 'They crossed through whatever boundaries apply to everyone else and back again. They flicker in and out of existence.'

Not again. The stranger in Vorstrum had said the same thing. That the slaves they were trying to rescue bore blood magic.

The words felt useless as she spoke them. 'There's no such thing as magic.'

'One point to Stappen. You truly don't believe me, do you?'

'I— Magic is—'

'Real,' Sebastian interrupted, 'and it's why they're being rounded up. The King wants the magic.'

The truth settled on her like a lead blanket and she was sure the golden brooch felt warm through her cloak.

'It's true, Reinhart,' Hark said. 'Those rumours about the magic healers living in the mountains? Here they are, rounded up and being traded. Elrod is trying to harvest that power for himself.'

She didn't know if she fully believed it, but clearly Elrod did. And if he did, then what...?

'How is he harvesting this so-called power?'

'Bloodletting. Sacrifices. He does horrible things to them, and he's getting worse the longer it takes for any sort of magic to present itself within him,' Sebastian explained, and she was glad it hadn't been Hark. She'd barely forgiven him for keeping the slave trading from her in the first place, so to keep something as abhorrent as this from her... Gods, she felt sick.

'We're getting them out. Now,' she said, her exhaustion melting into red-hot, burning anger. Something in her was desperate now, urging her to save them all.

'Not at night, Miss Reinhart,' Jaz said gently, his first words to her all day. 'They double the patrols at night and the slaves are kept under strict supervision. We've taken too many under the cover of darkness, and it has become our enemy, rather than our friend.'

Gods, gods, gods!

They'd been taking these slaves from under the king's nose for how long? How had he retaliated? she wondered. More slaves? More blood? More sacrifices?

'Does Cyrus know?' She whirled on Hark again, a small part of her hoping against all hope that Cyrus didn't have a hand to play in this. He was a good king. He protected her people. He had protected *her*.

'I don't know what Cyrus believes, Reinhart, and I don't know how completely Elrod has manipulated him – if at all – but he knows of the slaves, and he knows of the sacrifices. He sent you here to ensure the slaves make it into Elrod's hands. He sent you here to stop *us*.'

Something small and delicate cleaved in her chest.

'So what's the plan?'

CHAPTER 33

She'd always been a light sleeper, but even for her this was ridiculous.

The ground dug into her back like miniature mountains, and the bedroll she'd packed was worn and bearing the strain of over two weeks of travel. She wished for a blanket, not this useless scrap of a cloak she had picked for fashion and stealth rather than as a practical garment for sleeping on forest floors beside a bloodstained rock. She'd laid out her bedroll as far from the group as she could, but now she gave up trying to sleep and scrambled off the floor, dragging the useless bedroll behind her.

The dark humps of bodies slept soundly, their silhouettes rising and falling with each breath. At least none of them had died.

She threw the scrap of fabric down beside the fire, a body she reluctantly identified as Hark on her other side.

Now that she was warm, sleep danced at the edge of her mind, teasing her with the oblivion she so needed after the day

240

she'd had. She lay there, arms crossed over her chest, listening to the soft breathing of Hark's crew. There was nothing to light this dark corner of the world besides the stars blinking their protest against the night, and the softly glowing embers of the fire. Arla smothered a scoff at the thought that Kase's hair was perhaps its own light source. But her amusement was short-lived, and she didn't know how long she lay there, staring at the sky, twisting the dragonhart brooch in her fingers before a rough, smoky voice spoke.

'People once believed they could use those to communicate with the dragons.'

She didn't turn to face him, unsettled by the feeling in her stomach after hearing his voice thick with sleep. She didn't think she could stomach looking at him, his hair tousled, his eyes that searing blue, the colour that reminded her—

Stop it, Arla!

'Another fiction,' she whispered, ignoring the pulse of warmth she swore she could feel radiating through the brooch as she held it against her chest.

'Is it? You didn't believe in magic until recently.'

She sighed. 'I'm still not sure I do.'

'Aren't you?'

Silence settled, thick and heavy, with the reality of what they were going to do.

She was edging closer to him before she could stop herself. 'I just want them to be safe. Even knowing that I'll lose every-thing I've worked for is worth it if I know they're safe. If my people don't have to go through it all again...' She paused. For Halos, who feared the resurgence of slavery, for her children, and for the rest of Hadalyn's people who were at risk... 'It's worth it.'

Hark was silent for long seconds, and the quiet that stretched between them was far easier than it had ever been.

'What's the bloodstone?' she asked then.

Hark chuckled softly. 'People used to use it to honour the gods. They'd cut their palms and place them on the rock in some sort of payment or a thank-you, I guess.'

'Is that how he's trying to take their power? By using a bloodstone?' She didn't know why she said it. She hadn't really given any real thought to *how* Elrod was attempting to access their magic. The thought of it made her sick.

Hark's voice had a faraway tone when he finally spoke. 'He's been trying to infuse their blood with his. It's dark magic, forbidden even in ancient times. There are dozens of books in the royal library detailing how dangerous it is and how it goes against everything the gods stood for. Some think that to try and infuse one's blood with that of a magic draws on the power of a fallen god – one who was banished for his cruelty and need for power.'

Oh, none of it was sounding good. The worst part was she was finding herself starting to believe it.

'I think someone's helping him. Orson's been mightily interested in Elrod's rituals and sacrifices. It wouldn't surprise me if he'd been researching it to try and help him.'

The thought of it brought bile to the back of her throat.

Orson. Hadalyn's ambassador.

If he was involved then...

Gods, she didn't have the capacity to imagine Cyrus being involved in something as abhorrent as this.

Her chest was getting tighter. And the trembling in her fingers was becoming downright uncontrollable as she thought on it.

She'd been so fucking *blind*.

Hark reached across, his hand bruising hers gently and sending sparks skittering down her spine.

'I know I've been cruel, but you're an excellent assassin, and your heart is bigger than it should be. Kastonia nearly broke you and you've found it in yourself to save these people, not knowing if their blood runs grey or scarlet. I think that's enough to tell you that everything will be okay. The gods won't abandon you, Reinhart.'

For the first time, she didn't object to the mention of the gods. And had the world not been so cruel, she might have believed in them.

～

Perry had told her he would take her into the town today. It had been too many weeks since she'd seen another child, and she was bored of wandering empty halls, looking at the same portraits, playing the same notes on the piano that Cyrus had taught her.

It hadn't taken her long to stray back down to the lower levels of the castle when Perry hadn't shown at her rooms. She had positively stomped down here when a grey uniformed soldier had appeared to tell her that Perry was occupied with the king, and that there wouldn't be time to go into the town today.

Arla missed her parents.

She missed their little cottage by the river and she missed them all swimming together.

She missed the feeling of never being alone, of always having someone to nag her to brush her hair.

The air smelt funny down here, like sulphur and secrets, and the walls were made of a rough stone that felt nice on her fingertips.

There was a huge wooden door, too, and Arla knew she should turn back towards the upper levels of the castle or even the kitchens. But she heaved her tiny body against it anyway, hissing between her teeth when the door didn't budge and her shoulder ached enough to tell her it was bruised.

Sighing, she bit her lip against tears as she dragged herself back up the steps towards the comfort of her rooms.

A gentle light was turning the inside of her eyelids a soft orange. It was a soft, warming thing that encouraged her to wake properly. There was a heavy cloak draped over her, trapping the little heat there was against her skin.

Hark must have been frozen last night, but he had given up his cloak anyway, and she had slept well for it. Her head was clear, and the job she would have to do today seemed straight-forward and uncomplicated compared to how she had felt last night.

Despite the pale, dawn light breaking through the boughs of intricately woven branches above her, the air felt damp and smelled of rain. It would be a miserable day, but she would endure it to save the people who had been shackled and chained together like livestock at an auction. It ended today. All of it.

'Good morning,' a low, smoky voice came from behind her. She tipped her head up to see Hark Stappen leering over her with a steaming mug of tea. How they'd managed to fit the leaves inside their packs and keep them dry, she didn't know, especially when half those bags were still attached to the horses Jack had led with him when they'd freed the slaves yesterday.

She wondered where they were now, and if they'd made it

without being hunted and killed. Hark hadn't divulged where exactly it was he was sending them, but she hoped the slaves weren't exchanging one prison for another.

'It's going to rain,' she grumbled, pulling herself up off the floor and stamping some feeling back into her toes.

'It is, and with the temperature so low it's likely to freeze before it hits the ground. If it rains too hard, the border will be too difficult to pass and we'll have to hide them in the mountains,' Hark said, running a hand through his hair and twisting his lip between his teeth.

'Then let's get them out before it snows.'

She hated working as part of a team, but for something like this, she might appreciate the extra eyes at her back.

CHAPTER 34

The rain lashed down, and her fingers had gone numb around the hilt of the blade where she gripped it. Arla could hardly see Kase and Jaz pressed against the side of the rock face a hundred metres from her, and she didn't even know where Sebastian was anymore.

Hark, at least, was pressed tightly at her side, their shoulders so close together they were almost fused. The rain hadn't relented for the hour they had stood in cover of the rockface, waiting for the moment to drop into the camp and destroy what Elrod had worked so hard to build.

'How does Elrod know they're magics? Some of these people are from Hadalyn and I'd never have known they had a single drop of magic in their blood,' she said quietly.

Hark leaned closer to her and she hated that she was beginning to enjoy the feel of his body against hers.

'Some have ink tattooed on their skin – usually the dragonhart symbol on the inside of their wrists. The others – and the children – well, Elrod has spies all over the kingdoms waiting for one of them to slip up so he can take them. Most have limited control over their power. When they slip it's... Well, people notice.'

She didn't want to know what that meant or what Elrod did when he captured them after a *slip*.

She took in a shuddering breath and turned her attention back to the scene below. Kase had already leapt down onto the back of an unsuspecting soldier brandishing a whip, and he hadn't uttered a sound as her blade had sliced across his throat. It had taken her mere moments to drag his body beyond the sight of the camp and scale the rockface. Arla couldn't help but be impressed by the girl. She was ruthless, and strong, and knew how to handle herself. Kase was someone Arla could come to like, if she could temper that mouth of hers.

A low, rumbling sound began in the distance, the noise of hundreds of feet being forced to march from one end of the camp to the other, where huge metal cages mounted on the back of wagons waited to carry the next batch of slaves to their death, or whatever else Elrod had in store for them. It was the signal the crew had all waited for, the moment they hoped to infiltrate the crowd and turn them against the guards.

Arla wasn't fully sold on the plan – not when too much of it relied on rumours and *magic* she still didn't fully believe in. She was far more confident in what a blade could do, and was glad she'd strapped so many to her so that she could pass them off to slaves. Arla Reinhart would not rely on some made-up magic tricks to slaughter a camp full of Kastonian soldiers.

It's real, you fool.

The blur of women, and men, and children began to take form in the distance, and with it, came the thundering of heavy, sharp hailstones that pelted her so harshly she had no other option than to lean into Hark for some sort of protection.

His body was a solid comfort against the rock that was becoming quickly slippery beneath their feet. She found herself pressing as closely into him as she could, and instead of shrugging her off or making some jibe like, *how could she ever be an assassin if she couldn't handle a little rain*, she was surprised to find his arm link with hers and hold her tightly against him.

'This storm's going to get worse, you know. We need to get moving,' he said, his jaw rigid with what she thought was worry.

'A little longer,' she said in a low voice, eyes scanning the approaching group of slaves and uniformed soldiers.

'Reinhart, as much as I admire your lack of enthusiasm for bloodshed this morning, I don't think we can hold out much longer. Kase and Jaz are going to be difficult to reach as it is.'

It *was* worry. His gaze was a rapid, everchanging thing as it crossed between the slaves, to Kase and Jaz, and then back to her. She'd been wrong to ever doubt him as an ambassador; he filled the role beautifully. He cared for the people more than anyone else.

'A few more minutes, please,' she urged, shuddering against the thick flakes of snow now beginning to fall from the sky.

'Because you said please.' He smirked, and she realised she'd missed that from him in recent days. Everything had been too serious, too dangerous, too scary to warrant the usual bickering between them. When exactly had the snide remarks morphed into playful banter?

'Don't get used to it,' she murmured.

'I don't think I'll ever get used to you saying please. Especially when the next time I expect to hear that word is when you're begging me to touch you.'

Gods.

He wasn't even looking at her, which was good because she was certain there was a red bloom spreading over her cheeks. She sucked in cool air and cleared her throat.

'Why can't they escape the chains if they have magic?'

'The cuffs are made of iron,' Hark replied quietly, his eyes never straying from those who marched below them. 'It nullifies the magic. No one knows why.'

Iron.

The iron her king had lied to her about.

The slaves marched closer, their feet a drumbeat for a war that was about to be rained upon the soldiers flanking them. A crack echoed over the noise of the wind, a chilling, sickening sound that turned Arla's stomach. Hark's arm squeezed hers, as if to anchor her against the blind rage into which she was about to descend.

But rather than that red-hot, boiling anger she felt in her heart, an eerie calm settled over her, focusing her attention on the bloodied, exposed backs of slaves and the whips shredding the flesh there. Sound became a faraway thing, only her own breath gracing her ears and sharpening her into a lethal killing machine. Her fingers twitched, aching to feel the smooth wood of the bow on her back as she rained down arrows upon the soldiers.

Through the storm she saw two shadows drop into the crowd, Kase and Jaz merging with the slaves and becoming unidentifiable within the sea of heads. Just a few minutes longer, a few metres closer before she and Hark would follow their lead and lower themselves into the throng, knives drawn, hands deadly before they would split open this camp and destroy those who ran it.

'You know, if we die—' Hark began, and had she not become so used to the way he spoke, to the way she could identify the amusement in his voice, she might have mistaken it for worry.

'Stop right there. *I'm* not going to die.'

'Smartass.' He elbowed her lightly.

The ground beneath them became a writhing mass of bodies as the first line of slaves passed under the cliff. Arla unclasped her cloak, her fingers lingering on the soft material as she pushed down the regret at abandoning such a lovely item at the northern border.

'Ready?' Hark asked, letting go of her arm and rolling his shoulders.

They were silent as they fell through the air.

～

For half a second, she was caught up in the knot of people fleeing the swords and death of Kastonia as their soldiers invaded Hadalyn.

A heartbeat later, she was reassuring the people around her that she was not going to hurt them, but that they needed to do as instructed when the time came. Her knives were a comfort at her sides, her bow fastened tightly against her spine in the hopes no solider would notice her or it. Hark's dark head of wavy hair two rows in front of her was a comfort, too.

Onwards they marched, the dull outline of the mounted cages close enough that she could see the shackles chained to the bars. Cyrus hadn't sent her on many northern-border jobs, but it had never been as cold or stormy as this.

Another crack shuddered through the valley, setting Arla's jaw rigid and causing her to grind her teeth together. Those gods-damned whips.

A tiny, soft hand crawled into her own. Arla's heart squeezed at the sight of the head of tight, brown ringlets and the cold face that stared up at her. Gods, the children were so young. Children walking in this dreadful cold, chained ankle to wrist. Children about to be carted to whatever hell Elrod had in mind, whatever *sacrifices* he was ready to demand of them. Arla couldn't shake the image of it being Ettie or Neb who walked beside her.

'Are you here to save us?' the tiny voice whispered, barely audible over the crunch of marching meet and the endless clinking of chains.

'I'm going to try.' Arla offered a weak smile. She would make no promises. Never any promises, but something in her very core was screaming at her to save them.

'HALLLLTTTT!'

Almost instantly the mass of slaves stopped, most stumbling into the backs of those in front of them.

Arla flexed her fingers, squeezing the little girl's hand lightly before finding the hilt of one of her knives. One chance. She had once chance to end this.

A tremor ran through the crowd – a shivering, wicked thing. Arla stood her ground, twisting the knife in her palm, waiting, waiting, waiting. It would be this part of their stupid, unreliable plan with too many people involved that would cause them to stumble – would take away the element of surprise they had gained by striking at this time of the day, in the middle of a snowstorm.

A murmur reached her ears, a barely audible sound but it

was the one she had been waiting for. Kase and Jaz were moving then, preparing the slaves, ready for a quick getaway when the time came.

Arla had spent enough hours within the bosom of crowds to know when things were about to turn dangerous. She could feel the prickle of anticipation in the air, the throbbing heart of violence about to be unleashed.

The people were shifting, changing the internal structure of the rows and rows of slaves, shuffling to put Arla, Hark, and his crew in positions where they were sure to be unexpected.

A body slammed into the back of her, and as she spun to see the commotion and its cause, a scrawny, barely clothed woman was dragged from the crowd and hauled by her skinny arms to the front of the group.

The commander's eyes were cruel – even from a distance Arla could see the disdain and violence simmering there, waiting for an excuse to be unleashed. Maybe he didn't need one. Maybe he'd be violent without reason. It wouldn't be out of character for a Kastonian, would it?

Not a sound left the slave's lips as the solider that had hauled her to the front struck her behind the knees, dropping her to the freezing ground at the feet of the commander. White-hot, blinding fury coursed through Arla, her hands trembling with the effort to keep her knife in her grip instead of planting it in the chest of the sadistic Kastonian guard.

The woman was still *alive*, though Arla didn't know how. Even from eight rows back, she could see the woman's collar-bones jutting out at awkward angles, the greasy, knotted hair lying limp across her bare shoulders. The thin scrap of fabric hardly covered her decency. Arla couldn't fathom how the woman hadn't died from the cold alone. This place... Gods, it was evil. The devastating, faraway look in the hollowed-out faces of these slaves told her everything she needed to know about the things they had endured. *Not anymore.*

Her fingers reached instinctively for the dragonhart brooch she had tucked into the pocket of her trousers for safekeeping. When her fingers brushed the metal, she was certain something in the centre of her chest awoke, and it was a raging, wild thing that protested against what it saw. Arla's hand lingered there on the brooch, for some reason unwilling to let it go.

The commander spat at the kneeling woman, and the sneer on his face was plain to see. The woman, to her credit, didn't balk under him. Didn't shake. Didn't look away as he undoubtedly told her all the things he would do to her. All the things this kingdom would do to her.

The hand that swung for the woman's face was suddenly blood red, and only now did the slave cry out.

Arla never missed with a blade.

CHAPTER 35

The second between her knife burying itself between the commander's eyes and the chaos that ensued amongst the slaves immediately after was the longest second of Arla's life. She had expected Hark, or his crew, or one of the slaves even, to be the cog in the machine that faltered and put everything in jeopardy. In the end, it had been her.

And she didn't regret it.

She'd seen what he was about to do and something in her chest had roared against it. Never again would Kastonian brutes make vulnerable people suffer at their hands. Never again.

Women and children were screaming, men were... Gods, men were fighting with the soldiers! Where the fuck was Hark?

Kase's hair was like woven moonlight against the storm, her silver braid catching the miniscule rays of light glinting off blades and swords. She was hauling people with her, rounding up any that would go and leading them to the safety of where Sebastian was waiting. Jaz had all but abandoned the plan they had thrown together around the campfire at the bloodstone last night, but she couldn't be angry with him because she had caused this bloodshed.

A yelp dragged her into motion, and she pulled one of her knives free of its strap and plunged it into the neck of a solider.

Hark swept in like an angel, swiping a child from the path of a solider and throwing the girl to Arla, but Arla's side was no place for a child too sickly to fight. Crouching to the child's level, Arla pointed at Kase and where the group of slaves were now being reassembled, each of them steely eyed and ready to protect the new resistance.

Arla could only pray to gods she didn't believe in that the child could run quickly enough across the open space to make it to safety.

Hark was a dark blur, downing soldier after soldier as he fought his way through them to get the slaves into Kase's blockade beside the rocks. Seb would protect them there, would keep them as solid as a wall, whilst it gave the others the chance to kill every Kastonian that had dared raise a hand to them. Arla swung her sword with unprecedented ferocity and fired her bow, too, when she was granted an extra second to nock an arrow.

Soldiers poured in from every angle and Hark seemed to not notice the ones coming from behind. The sight was enough to turn Arla feral – every hour she'd spent training, every target she had ever hit with her knives flooding back to her – as she charged across the space, blades swinging, fire burning deep within her. She would not fail them. She would not let this happen again.

Blood rained wherever she went. They were falling at her feet, falling like they never had before. Kase was there, dragging anyone who could not fight to the safety of the cliff face.

The sudden twang of a bowstring caused her heart to falter, and Arla felt her blood run cold. She watched the arrow fly towards Hark's back, poised to land directly between his shoulder blades – to pierce his fierce, unyielding heart.

It happened so slowly.

So very slowly.

Her feet carried her over the fallen bodies around her, her scream threatening to tear her vocal cords as she begged Hark to move. She'd never felt fear like this. Not when Kastonia had come to Hadalyn. Not when she'd been locked inside the dresser. Not when she'd watched her parents die. But this... The thought of that arrow burying itself in his heart made her want to die. It made her want to put her own body into the path of that arrow if it stopped it striking him.

There was a word for that kind of feeling.

She didn't allow herself time to dwell on that word, because Sebastian was there, slamming into Hark, sending the pair of them rolling through snow, and ice, and blood. Relief flooded her as that silver-tipped arrow hit the chest of one of the soldiers instead.

She didn't allow herself the time to watch Hark right himself and begin swinging his sword again, because the Kastonians were upon her. She knew the slaves fought – the strongest of the men, at least – using the chains that had bound their hands, slamming the iron into skulls and any open bit of flesh they could find on their oppressors. Jaz and Kase continued ferrying the rest of the slaves to their position against the cliff, forming an impenetrable wall of what she could only guess – in her fevered state – was magic. It was the only explanation her brain could come up with, because the wall seemed to deter any soldier who moved in that direction.

The soldiers would run towards the slaves but then slam into something invisible yet solid enough that they fell flat on their backs. Arla was sure she could see the air ripple, as if the slaves held fast a barrier of wind with their hands, which they held out in front of them, palms facing outwards, while snowflakes and loose gravel were whipped into a violent frenzy around the edge of the shield.

They were doing it.

Slowly, so bloody slowly that she hardly noticed it at first, the Kastonian soldiers were depleting, becoming piles of black smudges against the landscape. They were doing it.

But then her stomach tumbled when she saw a group of children huddled on the other side of the field, eight soldiers running towards them with swords drawn and fury in their eyes.

She'd never make it.

No matter how many miles she ran before breakfast, no matter how many hours she trained in the company of the King's Guard, it was impossible to cross such a vast distance – nearly half a mile – and get to the children before the soldiers reached them.

It wouldn't stop her trying.

Her feet were nimble across the hardened ground, bounding over bodies as she charged after the soldiers.

The children – not one of whom could be older than thirteen – didn't balk in the face of imminent death. They didn't shudder, or shout, or even attempt to escape. They simply … smiled, as if that ray of innocence would be enough to prevent a blade running through them.

She could hear the grunts of soldiers fighting with Jaz and Hark behind her, the shouts of fury from the slave men who had joined the fight. She almost didn't hear Kase screaming her name.

'REINHART, NO!'

Was she fucking serious?

Arla kept running, kept pounding across the earth. She wouldn't let the children die.

'Reinhart, leave them!' Kase screamed, her voice desperate and shrill.

When they got out of here she was going to kill that silver-haired bitch. Arla wouldn't leave the little ones to die. She couldn't.

'Leave them!' it was a different voice this time – masculine and low and full of terror. Hark.

Gods, even Hark was telling her to leave them.

She would not.

The soldiers were nearly upon the group, their swords just feet away from the children, who still did not move. And just when she thought her feet couldn't carry her any further, the last twenty metres seemingly an impossible distance, she was forced to accept that she would watch the children be slaughtered. She would unleash hell upon those soldiers and leave not one alive. Not one.

Before her very eyes, the children vanished.

They were there, and then they were just ... gone.

Arla stumbled at the shock of it, her feet tripping over themselves to leave her face down in the mud. It wasn't possible. What had just happened was simply *not possible*. Her mouth was suddenly too dry as she kept blinking at the place where the children had been only seconds ago, as though if she concentrated hard enough it wouldn't be real. She'd been in denial about what she'd seen yesterday – perhaps tiredness or an overactive imagination – but there was no denying it now.

She didn't have time to consider it, though, because the soldiers that had been aiming for the children suddenly found themselves impaled on the ends of a row of glinting spears belonging to another wave of their own army.

Arla had been so focused on saving the children that she hadn't noticed the emergence of another group of Kastonian soldiers from the eye of the storm.

Someone was swearing – Hark, maybe – but there was no time for her to turn and see because in that moment an entire army descended upon her.

It was so rare these days that Arla needed to tap into that violent, unfeeling level within herself where she became death incarnate, where nothing could reach her, or stop her, or break the lethal spell she had woven.

In the face of her astonishment, she found that place to be a welcome friend as the Kastonian army swarmed her.

With a scream that could have stopped the world from turning, she swung her sword quicker than ever, her feet dancing on the line between life and death. Her knives found themselves free of the straps in which she had confined them and were flung from her fingers, downing any who strayed in their path. Her blood sang to her, a song of vengeance and wrath and fury. She would not let it happen again.

Distantly, she was aware of Hark, Jaz, Kase, and even Seb fighting beside her, each of them grunting at the effort as they followed her lead through the rows and rows of soldiers. Arla knew they were there because she could hear the shouts of agony from those who slipped past her blades and met their ends upon the blades of the others.

She didn't know what was happening with the slaves and didn't have room to think about it, not when every minute action and reaction was the difference between life and death. Either they were fighting or they were hiding. Either they were alive or they were dead. What else was there?

Magic, her heart seemed to say. *There's magic.*

But she couldn't afford any distractions now because ... because...

Because Hark was on his knees.

She hadn't seen him fall; hadn't seen anyone even near him when she turned her head for a split second between killing soldiers.

But he was there, kneeling on the ground, and there was a soldier aiming for him.

Gods, she was beginning to loathe worrying like this about someone else, especially him. Because she did, didn't she? She worried for him. She worried and she cared and she knew there was no way back from the place they had arrived at. If they made it out of here she might have to tell him so. Especially now that Seb wasn't there to save him, to haul him free of the swinging blade, because Seb was at *her* side, cutting down those who came at *her*.

But her attention was fixed on Hark and the sword about to strike him. She couldn't draw her bow or her arrows quickly enough to save him.

He caught her eyes across the vast space, and in his look she saw resignation, acceptance, surrender.

She began screaming—

Something heavy knocked her on the head, and then darkness swept in and carried her into its oblivion.

CHAPTER 36

There weren't any other children in the castle.

It had been hours since she'd seen an adult, actually. Cyrus had left her with one of the maids, but the girl had quickly returned to work in the kitchens. So here Arla was, wandering the huge corridors of Castle Grey again with nothing but her own thoughts for company.

She tried not to think of her mother and father – of what she'd seen from that crack in the dresser – so she spent hours and hours wandering the many levels of the palace, wishing she could wear the same pretty dresses that the ladies in the court wore, or have a nice horse like the men in the paintings that hung on almost every wall she passed.

It was cold down at this level; probably because it was close to the dungeons, she imagined with morbid delight. It had taken her all morning to make it this far beneath; she'd had to avoid the tight servants' staircases and the corridors that were so narrow they made her heart race.

It took all her strength to push open the heavy wooden door, her *hands pressing into the metal bands running across it. It creaked open on loud hinges, and a gust of cool, strange-smelling air hit her head-on.*

She thought for a minute that perhaps she should be scared, walking into a dark corridor this far from the inhabited levels of the palace, but they'd left her in that room with the books and piano for so long that she didn't care to head back up there. So she crept forwards into the smoky, sulphurous tunnel, dragging her soft fingertips over the rough edges of the wall. She must be a long way underground here, she thought, because she'd never seen walls made of this sort of rock before, as though they'd been carved out of a cliff.

She kept walking, her feet echoing in the empty space.

Something whispered to her. Something whispered constantly in this castle. Not that anybody else ever believed her when she spoke of it. They all thought she was mad, probably. But Arla had never felt alone here. There were always strange whispers that she couldn't understand, and there were always invisible eyes on her.

'Arla!' a worried voice called, and she turned to find Perry hurrying towards her. 'You shouldn't be down here,' he panted, wrapping a gentle hand around her arm and guiding her back towards the light.

'I was bored.'

'I know, sweetheart, but you can't be down here on your own.'

She let him lead her away, smirking to herself in the low light as she slipped one of Perry's gold buttons into her pocket.

~

Someone was banging.

And ... shouting.

'We do as we always do. He's not exactly in danger, is he?'

'He's a fucking *prisoner,* Kase,' a male voice replied, followed by another bang, this one quieter.

Arla had lain silent and still before on other jobs, and it was a skill she'd taught herself so she could obtain information under the guise of sleep.

This was different.

Everything came flooding back to her in a rush: the slaves, the camp, *Hark*...

She bolted upright, wincing at the pain in her head and the black spots merging in front of her eyes as she took in where she was.

Shadowy light curved around her, and there was nothing but pressing walls and a round windowless chamber to give away that they were back in Vorstrum. She lay on a cot by the fire, blankets piled on her but her clothes... Gods, where were her clothes?

'I wouldn't move too quickly,' a soft voice said, and Arla turned her head slowly to see Sebastian leaning against one of the tunnel openings that led from the chamber. Kase stood across from him, a scowl pinching her pretty face into something wicked.

'What happened?' Arla demanded, trying to stand before a wave of dizziness overcame her and she lowered herself back onto the blankets.

'Easy, Reinhart.' Jaz sat on the other side of the fire on a similar cot, a bandage wrapped around the upper half of his arm. 'You're safe. You took a blow to the head.'

'How long have I been asleep?'

Jaz's face was grim. 'Three days.'

Three days.

'No, that's— That's not possible, I can't—'

'Easy,' Jaz said, reaching for her. 'You're lucky you're not dead. Took quite the battering. It was chance that we had a healer there to tend to you. You might not've woken if he hadn't got to you so quickly—'

'I don't care about me,' she snapped, slamming her hands into the side of the cot just to channel her confusion and frustration somewhere. 'What happened at the camp? Are the slaves safe? Did anyone get hurt? Hark, I saw him go down, I saw him—'

'Hey, hey,' Sebastian started, reaching across to place his hand on hers. 'It's okay. Everything's going to be okay.'

It wasn't. Gods, it wasn't, because where was Hark?

Kase stepped forwards, her expression grim and her hair marred with streaks of red and something darker. 'Hark went down and you got struck with the pommel of a sword. I got to you, but by the time I'd checked you were still breathing, Hark—'

'What happened to him?' Arla shouted, kicking her heel into the ground, and welcoming the dull bite of pain that came with it.

'He's alive, but the soldiers took him back to Kastonia. The latest information we have suggests he's being kept in his rooms in the palace.'

'And the slaves?'

'We got them all,' Sebastian smiled softly.

'All of them?' Disbelief clouded Arla's voice because she'd seen how outnumbered they were; she had seen the four of them overwhelmed with the number of blades coming their way. So to get out of that alive, let alone with every single slave, and to get them to safety...

'Jack arrived at the last minute to help move the slaves. They were out in minutes, and they took us with them,' Kase said, and then it all began to become very clear to Arla what had happened.

'Magic,' she whispered, finally believing in it after a lifetime of swearing against it. But she'd seen it with her own eyes, and there was no other way they could have escaped without something ... otherworldly aiding them, be it the gods or the blood magic Elrod wanted. She reached for the dragonhart brooch still safe in the pocket of her trousers. It warmed beneath her fingers, a comfort and a bolstering presence at once.

'That's why I told you to leave the children,' Kase said, sitting down beside Jaz and pulling a blanket over her damp clothes. 'They were there as bait, as a distraction for the soldiers so the soldiers would kill each other. The children were safely behind the wall no more than a second after you saw them disappear.'

'What wall?' Arla asked, her hands trembling at everything she was trying to comprehend.

'I did try to tell you it was real, Reinhart. The magic-wielders moved to the mountains years ago, but it's no secret that it runs thick in the Kastonian mountains.'

Burning fucking gods.

Later. Later she would let shock course through her. But now...

'We're getting Hark out.' She was sure she heard Sebastian mutter a *Told you*. 'And Elrod will be made to step down as king. The bastard can burn for what he's done.'

Her voice didn't falter as Arla squared her shoulders and stood.

'You might be King's Assassin, Reinhart, but you're crazy, or stupid, if you think there's even a chance you're getting into that castle and removing Hark Stappen from it. They'll gut you before you enter Larkire – and Elrod would sooner die than give up his throne.' There wasn't anything mocking or cruel in Kase's words, just raw certainty.

'I won't be breaking into the castle,' Arla began, and each of Hark's friends looked back at her as if she'd gone mad. 'I'll retrieve Hark *without* your help. And when I bring him back, we'll storm that city and burn its king to ash.'

A promise. One that wouldn't be broken.

CHAPTER 37

Her head pounded as she galloped across miles and miles of open land. Her sore body ached for the familiar comfort of Vetta, not the horse she had stolen from outside a tavern in Vorstrum. Vetta was safe with Eros in the care of Jack, Sebastian had told her. None of Hark's crew had revealed to her yet where exactly the safe haven was, and there was no way in this gods-damned world she would admit her curiosity by asking.

Hours and hours passed, the sun dropping to leave behind a clear night with only the stars to light her way back to Hadalyn. Her mount, a stallion the colour of autumn, did not fail her. His legs pounded against the earth, giving her everything he had, for hours, until even her well-accustomed body screamed in protest. She wouldn't stop now. She would keep going if it meant bringing vengeance to every man, woman, and child Elrod had captured. It went beyond politics, beyond faith. This was personal, and it had been festering since the moment the first Kastonian dared to breach Hadalyn's borders.

The rest Arla allowed herself was brief, and the sleep her stallion fell into did not come so easily to her. She kept seeing Hark over and over, his knees buried in the bloody snow and that blade flying at him. She needed to get him out of the palace. She needed to tell him how it had made her feel to watch him almost die before her. She couldn't lose another person she cared about.

The shuffle of hooves dragged her out of her daydream and into the dawn of another day. She would return to Hadalyn, and she couldn't look back even if she wished. Hark was a prisoner, and his crew wouldn't act, not with him at risk of being killed should they attempt to steal slaves again.

But she could.

Something had grown inside her – something she was terrified of, something she didn't understand. But she would not turn her back on them. Not now.

As the wind flowed through her hair, she vowed to get Hark out and end the slave trade. And if Cyrus had known, had really *known* what was happening, she would take both kingdoms, and damn the consequences.

~

Arla breathed a little easier as she rode into Hadalyn. She'd been gone three weeks but it felt like half a lifetime.

Her feet sang as they landed on familiar, worn cobbles. She didn't need to look at her reflection in the windows of shops to know how hideous she looked. She knew blood still stained her hair, and her clothes were filthy and torn from the fighting. She would not walk into Castle Grey like this. She needed to play the part of King's Assassin once more; she needed to be Lady Rein-hart; she needed to be in control of every single moment that would take place between her and Cyrus.

Because there could only be two outcomes: he kept his throne, or he didn't.

She patted the empty sheath at her side and sighed. She hated being without a knife, but there weren't many places that stocked the razor-sharp blades she favoured.

At least her bow had made it out of the battle and still hung at her back.

A flash of silver in Madam Touse's shop window caught her eye as she strolled the familiar route back to the castle, wondering if this would be the last time she did so.

She couldn't help herself. The jewels glittered so delicately, and she could almost feel the silk of the dress in the window. It was actually a gold so pale it passed for silver. It would do nicely, and she would look every bit the threat to the throne she needed to be.

Madam Touse, regrettably, was not working, so Arla hastily handed over the coins for the dress to a young girl she hadn't seen before. Touse's runner boy was there, though, and he offered to take her new dress directly to her rooms at the castle, probably eager for an extra coin. Arla declined, carefully putting the garment now wrapped in paper into the bottom of the saddlebag slung over her shoulder and handed the boy a coin anyway. It was all for nothing if she couldn't be kind. She wouldn't let being an assassin harden her into something cruel and deluded.

Arla slipped out of the shop into the busy street, eyeing Halos's shop across the way. Something tight twisted in her stomach at the thought of seeing her friend. What would she think of her now? Halos had hated what Arla did for a living, and that had been before she'd slaughtered soldier after soldier in that camp...

Bells twinkled above her as she entered the shop, her hair loose around her shoulders to hide the worst of the blood in it. Arla strode towards the back of the room where Halos was tending to a woman with greying hair.

'Be with you in a second,' Halos called cheerfully, not looking up to see who had entered the shop.

'Oh, I'm sure I can wash my own hair. I was mainly looking for the soap I like.'

The young woman broke into a delightful smile, her teeth a dazzling white against the deep brown of her skin. Arla loved her. That smile had been a salve to more than one type of wound in the past.

'Why am I not surprised to find you looking like ... that?' Halos asked, waving Arla to a chair. 'How did it go? Did you bed Mr Stappen in the end?'

Something in Arla's chest clenched at Hark's name, a clench that meant too many things at once for her to focus on. She realised now just how close they'd become since they'd left Hadalyn, and that without his shadow she felt cold and vulnerable. She felt like she could burst into tears at any second and she wouldn't have the strength to stop.

'What's wrong, Arla?' Halos asked, suddenly serious as she worked the soap into Arla's hair, cursing as her fingers ran over the egg-shaped lump on the back of Arla's head and the crusted blood coating it.

'Things didn't go well,' Arla said gently, not afraid to tell Halos everything. And, truthfully, she really needed to speak to someone, if only so they could convince her she wasn't completely crazy.

'Hark's in trouble, and I'm going to do something dangerous to get him back. It's going to save a lot of people but ... is that bad?' she whispered, scared of the words that had been looping in her head for hours. It occurred to Arla that she never really gave much thought to how old she was. How *young* she was. She felt like a child now, more than she ever had.

'You're a good person that terrible things have happened to. So, if you need to do something stupid, if it means people get hurt because you're trying to save others ... it doesn't make you bad. You're the one person I'd want at my back, and if you need something, Arla, you only have to ask.'

Her friend really was too sweet. Arla couldn't tell her about the slaves; she wouldn't incite that fear in her friend. Besides, she was going to stop it all. She was going to remove that Kastonian bastard from the throne and set free every man, woman, and child under his imprisonment.

Arla cleared her throat. 'The only thing I need from you, Halos, is to make my hair smell beautiful and look even better.'

'Consider it done.'

'Where are the twins?'

'Asleep, finally. They've been terrorising my customers all day,' she chuckled, and Arla felt her heart swell with love for the two toddlers.

'Magic's real,' she whispered, the sound barely reaching her own ears. She didn't know why she said it, but she needed Halos to know. She needed her to understand what she'd seen so that her friend wouldn't think her mad when she inevitably found out what Arla had done.

'I know,' Halos whispered back, and Arla didn't know if she

was shocked or not to hear her friend say it. They'd never spoken about it at great length, but Arla had always assumed Halos held the same view as she did about magic, and dragons, and the whole lot of it being made up.

'Crazy, isn't it? That some people are born with that in their blood?' Arla said softly, for the first time really marvelling at such a possibility, at the sheer beauty of it.

'Don't you think everybody has a little piece of magic in them, Miss Reinhart?'

Arla's body went cold. That voice. Raspy, full of phlegm. The greying hair she had seen on the way into the shop. She turned her head to meet the eyes of the stranger she had spoken to at the market outside Vorstrum, the night she'd drunk far too much and ended up in Hark's bed.

'What?' Arla gaped in disbelief at the woman staring back at her.

'Do you wonder how your friend can work wonders with hair and skin when others can't? Or how your knives have never missed a mark? How Mr Stappen's way of avoiding death confused even you at the border? Everybody has a little bit of magic inside them, Miss Reinhart, if only you know where to look.'

Arla didn't know what to say, and the unwelcome prick of tears behind her eyes came on so suddenly she couldn't stop the lone tear that rolled down her face.

'I don't know what to do,' she whispered, her voice breaking.

Blood magic must run through the woman's veins. How else could she know everything that had happened to Arla? The dragonhart brooch was still in the pocket of her trousers, a symbol of the old religion and everything she had spent her life disbelieving. She was certain, now, that it held its own sort of sentient magic. It was always warm beneath her touch and she'd felt drawn to it in a way that made sense now.

'I already told you where the power lies, girl. Use your head, Arla Reinhart. It has not failed you so far.'

CHAPTER 38

Arla drew deep breaths of cool air into her lungs as she stepped outside Halos's shop. She had hugged her friend tight when she left, and Halos had made her promise to be careful. It wasn't a promise she could keep, but she knew she would try.

Get a grip.

Right. She looked like herself again. She was ready to take on the might of Kastonia – and Hadalyn, too, if they would not lend her an army.

The woman's words had shaken her, but she could not afford to falter on this path.

'I already told you where the power lies...'

It came to her so shockingly that Arla's entire body jolted.

Heaving the bag containing the silk dress onto her shoulder, Arla Reinhart set off into the slums of Hadalyn to find Brik Novan.

～

The thief was as dirty and sneaky as usual.

Arla watched him from the roof of a printing shop down a dark alley, his hands slipping into the pockets of unsuspecting passers-by.

Only when he turned to retreat down the passageway, his own pockets now filled with the riches of those unfortunate enough to cross paths with the scrounging wretch of a man, did Arla swing from the roof to land neatly in front of him.

'Shitting gods, you have to stop doing that,' he snapped, unconsciously tightening his fingers around his scruffy jacket and the undoubtedly expensive loot tucked inside. He'd been busy, then.

'Let's take a walk,' Arla said sweetly, and Brik was right to gulp as she looped her arm through his, scrunching her nose at the stench rolling off him.

The thieves walked arm in arm towards the slums of Hadalyn, a fitting destination for the conversation they were about to have. It wouldn't matter if Arla's vultures heard what she had to say, they respected – or feared – her well enough not to breathe a word of what came from her lips. She had been all too clear in the past on what would happen if they did.

'Heard you've been running with that boy from the palace, Reinhart,' Brik tattled, chuckling to himself.

'You heard correctly, and that's why I'm here.'

His feet slowed on the cobbles, forcing Arla to tug him forwards. This action unfortunately sent a spray of a suspicious-looking liquid up her booted ankles.

'I ain't in the business of stealing anythin' from the Kastonian lot. His king'll have my guts if 'e finds out,' he protested, and Arla suppressed the urge to snap his wrist at the outright lie.

'Lucky for you, then, that I'm not asking you to steal anything. I'm asking you to get me in.'

His feet really did stop then, and Arla tightened her arm around his as he tried to rid himself of her.

'What you askin', Reinhart?' Brik eyed her, and she admired him in a way. She'd believed the thief would do anything for a coin or two, and it only confirmed her suspicions about him. She'd been right not to kill him all those times.

'I need you to get me beneath the castle.'

A heartbeat of silence.

'You don't mean the sewers, do ya?'

'Good. We're learning.' She smiled, wrenching his arm so violently he nearly tripped over his own feet.

She could feel dozens of eyes watching her from the shadows and busted-in doorways of the hovels that passed for houses. She missed the knives whose presence was so familiar to her that being without them was like losing a limb.

'I ain't getting you in nowhere, 'specially under Castle Grey. You're mad, woman,' he objected, fraying Arla's line of patience with every word he spoke through his blackened teeth.

'Tell me, Brik,' she began softly, using the tone she reserved for people like him – people she was instructed to dispose of as part of her job.

She felt him tense. *Good.*

'How did those cuts I gave you the last time we had a little *chat* heal so completely, leaving your miserable body delightfully unscarred?' she said.

He gulped, and the burst of satisfaction she got from that telltale spot of fear fed the nasty, wicked side of her heart. 'Did you steal silver from a rich man on Grey Hill to pay a healer? Or did you forgo the money and just rob the healing remedy yourself?'

The threat was clear, and she saw the exact moment he gave in. How his shoulders sagged, and his eyes rolled with disdain for the blonde girl fused to his arm.

'What makes you think I can get you below Castle Grey, Reinhart?'

Seriousness didn't suit Brik Novan. Arla hated it on him, actually.

'Because I've seen you do it before.'

~

Sneaking into Castle Grey was not an easy feat – not least because Arla herself had ensured it wouldn't be so – but it was made harder by the vagabond who would no doubt be cursing her name because of how long it was taking her to retrieve the knives from her rooms.

All thoughts of winning Cyrus over in her lovely new dress were banished.

Her bedchamber was exactly as she'd left it three weeks ago – her books piled high beside the bed and the space free of clutter and trinkets. A thin layer of dust had settled on the surfaces, and Arla ran a finger through the grey fluff on the mantelpiece.

Arla was glad the maids had heeded her warning and left her rooms alone. Too many secrets lay hidden between the pages of novels and under loose floorboards. No one was allowed into this corner of the castle when she was out of the city.

Her knives were where she had left them – one beneath her pillow, one behind the bookshelf, one secured under the bottom of the dresser. She went from place to place, finding the hidden blades as well as a few jewels and a necklace of her mother's she'd kept concealed all these years.

She strapped the knives to her body quickly, like old friends reuniting once more. Only when she had her armour in place did her mind steady enough for what she had to do.

Arguments had rarely broken out between her and Cyrus, and when they did, they were quickly resolved and Arla would laugh it off and make some joke about who *really* ran the palace.

Her hands shook at the thought of confronting the man who had helped raise her alongside Perry. The man who had given her a home and somewhere safe for nine years.

Gods, she hoped Cyrus would tell her the truth and that she wouldn't have to become the cold-blooded killer he had made her into.

'It's not worth it, Arla. You don't understand.'

She spun, heart thundering at the familiar voice. He was leaning against the entrance to the suite of rooms.

Perry looked older, somehow, as if the weight of the world had crushed him in the weeks she had been away. He'd always been kind to her – there to wipe her tears in the middle of the night, and there to listen to her complain about how Cyrus had pissed her off. It didn't matter that she had caught them tangled together in bed more times than she dared to count.

'What are you talking about?' she asked sweetly, hoping he would buy her innocent act when it was obvious from the clinking as she moved and the fresh sheath of arrows on her back, just how well armed she was.

'Arla Reinhart, you have commanded the attention of this

palace for nine years with your outrageous antics, yet now you've snuck in here unnoticed, armed to the teeth and with murder in your eyes. Don't insult us both by pretending you don't want to tear into Cyrus after what you've seen.'

Something in Arla's chest ached at the words. This man, he knew her – really knew her.

'I have no idea what you're talking about,' she said, turning her back on him again under the guise of rummaging through a set of drawers.

'Arla. You failed to return after the messenger said you would. You have sent no letters, and I understand you must be angry at what you've seen at the border but you don't und—'

She whirled on him. 'Tell me, then. What do I not understand?'

'The gods are angry, Arla. The balance of magic is off. The magic-wielders are using their abilities for their own gain whilst the rest of the kingdoms suffer. The gods are punishing us for it, and if those responsible aren't dealt with...'

'And you think killing them is the right thing to do?' she whispered, understanding cracking and splintering her heart. 'He really has got you fooled, hasn't he?'

'No, Arla. Elrod is doing what's right for the kingdoms—'

'He's doing what's right for *him*!' she snapped, slamming her hand on the top of the dresser. She didn't want to be hurt, to be upset, to be ... confused or redirected from the path she had chosen.

'I thought I heard your voice.' The King of Hadalyn appeared beside his advisor and lover. He looked weary, too, as if Arla's time away had drained the life from him. For a minute she almost wished it had.

'You know,' she began softly, stalking towards Cyrus and

Perry with lethal grace, 'I don't even know anymore why you sent me to the border. At first I thought it was to catch Hark in his betrayal and kill him for knowing about the slaves. And then he told me that you knew. That you *all* knew. I didn't believe him, but it's true, isn't it. What did you think I would do, Cyrus? You thought I would accept it? You thought my loyalty to you would lead me to kill anyone who tried to free the slaves? For someone who raised me from a child, you don't know me very well at all.'

Cyrus didn't move an inch – a statue poised to defend his kingdom. Arla had never expected to become his enemy. A hardness came over him, and as she watched it settle into the familiar lines of his face, she mourned the loss of the man she had known.

The loss of them. Whatever they had been. Whatever *he* had been to her. A saviour? A father? A leader? Her king? Something else?

In the end, none of it would matter, because when he spoke, everything Arla had known shattered into a thousand crystal pieces. Castle Grey would never be home to her again.

'If you move against my kingdom, those who housed you and cared for you, and those who trained you, will march at my command and put your severed head at my feet. You might think you have grown beyond my command, Arla Reinhart, but I will always remember the orphan I rescued. You are nothing against the might of my kingdom.'

She could feel her heart splintering, her chest constricting around the cracks.

Could she do this? Did she want to? Could she really leave it all behind? Let go of everything she'd worked so hard for?

Perry took half a step towards her, his hands reaching out for her. 'Arla.'

'Don't,' she said, resignation lining her throat as she pulled herself together. It was done. There was no use fighting her king when his mind had already been made up. His actions and choices were confirmed by the words he threatened her with. 'Don't come calling for me when your kingdom bleeds.'

She slipped out of the window and was down the side of her tower before they had crossed her bedchamber.

CHAPTER 39

The grates over the openings of the castle sewers that spewed filth into the Canus River were rusted with age. The air smelt damp and unclean, and it took everything in Arla not to gag at the colour and odour of the water flowing through the grates, which acted like filters, catching bits of muck and filth.

'Told you it ain't pretty,' Brik muttered as his quick hands ran across the railings, searching for a way in.

Arla had never forgotten the time she'd watched Brik open the grates and disappear into the foul sewers. It was two years after the storming of Hadalyn, and she'd had no idea why he wanted to sneak into the palace via such a revolting entrance. She'd been eleven and thoroughly furious with her tutor for making her read some strange language when she wanted to be running laps of the castle grounds with the soldiers, and she'd taken herself off to sit on a window ledge that looked out over the river.

She had seen him then – a mere slip of a teenager – pry open the iron grates and scurry inside. She hadn't understood it back then, but Brik had always been a thief and she had assumed he'd been after a silver goblet or a fork from the kitchens, which lay on the lower levels of the palace.

She'd listened out for talk about the sewers being a route into the palace and had heard a few rumours, but they had been exactly that – rumours. There was no access into the castle via the sewers, only tiny grates opening into tiny tunnels barely wider than a body. Arla herself had tried. Numerous times. She'd held her nose and spent hours searching for a way into the castle but all she'd achieved was wasted days and a scolding from her maids about the foul state of her clothes and hair.

She shuddered at the memory, concentrating on Brik's nimble fingers and the latch with which he was fiddling.

The iron creaked open, and then they were inside the tunnels and it was exactly as she remembered: the bottom four inches of liquid and filth saw her feet and ankles ploughing through a thick sludge that had her almost retching.

'Be careful. There's a tunnel on the right that drops thirty feet. Nearly died last time I came in 'ere,' Brik said, pulling closed the grate behind Arla. He described again the route she must take to find the way in she'd never managed to discover when she was a child.

'Thank you, Brik,' she said in the semi-darkness, suddenly feeling sick at what she was about to do. 'No one ever understood why I spared you but ... I'm glad I did. You were worth saving.' She saw his face soften, and for a few fleeting seconds she was looking at the face of the boy he had once been instead of the man he had been forced into becoming.

'Thieves look out for thieves, Miss Reinhart.' He winked at

her, a sad smile growing steadily across his features, as if he knew he wouldn't see her again.

'Maybe,' she whispered, watching him turn and begin the long walk back up to Grey Hill.

'Brik!' she called, her heart clenching as he spun to face her. 'Leave Hadalyn. Go to the continent where it's safe. They'll look after you. You could have a new life, get a job—'

'Be safe, Arla.'

His final words to her as he dragged his too-thin body back towards the town.

~

She had counted twelve openings, never straying from her course or her purpose. Lucky number thirteen, Brik had said. As if. She turned into it, easing her body into the sludge as she crawled through the maze of tunnels that lay beneath Castle Grey.

Onwards. Always onwards.

To the legend and myth she had doubted all her life. To the dragons and their magic that she could no longer deny.

She hoped she didn't end up dead.

Her tunnel began to dry up, until she was free of the foul stench entirely. She could breathe again, yet she reached into her pocket to rub the dragonhart brooch for comfort. Touching it, she felt an increasingly familiar call to something ancient and powerful that seemed to linger in the back of her mind. She kept going, looking around her for ... some sign to tell her where to go next. Behind the column of rock, Brik had said. She ran her fingers along the wall afraid she would miss it in the darkness, but then suddenly there it was – the hidden grate.

A creeping sensation trickled down Arla's spine. She felt watched. She felt opened up, laid bare, as if she were at the mercy of something greater than her.

When she turned to look about her, she saw nothing. She held still for a second, two, three, but all she could hear was the beating of her heart in her ears. She was alone in the darkness.

She found the latch of the grate with her fingers, and was able to open it too easily for what should have been rusted metal embedded in rock, untouched for so many years. Bile rose in her throat as she contemplated the bottomless void into which she now had to climb.

'Come on, come on, come on,' she whispered to herself, as she crawled into that tiny space and felt the tunnel walls scratch at her body.

This wasn't a fight she could tackle with knives, or wit, or finely curated aggression. This was a battle she had to fight in her own mind, just her and the darkness, and the years of nightmares filled with blood and screaming.

Arla dragged her stomach across the stone, gritting her teeth against the heavy press of thousands of feet of age-old stone. She pulled the grate closed behind her and crawled on.

Forwards. Forwards. Forwards she dragged herself along the tunnel, ignoring the quiver in her lip and the fear in her heart. The air was cool down here – just like it had been all those years ago when she'd escaped her minders and wandered the corridors and hallways beneath the populated parts of the castle.

A horrible, squeaky sound escaped her as the walls of the tunnel scraped her arms, tearing at the thin black tunic she wore. Was it getting narrower? Arla bit her lip, resisting the urge to cry out as she tried to scramble backwards in panic and found that she couldn't.

Her chest heaved and the walls pressed in. Stars bloomed behind her eyes and her heart pounded in her chest.

Gods, oh gods!

Get a grip, Reinhart.

She choked on the breath in her throat and repeated the words her father had once said the first time she had sat on a horse.

You can do anything.

She pulled herself forwards, loose stones rolling away from under her palms.

You can do anything.

In and out her breaths came, through her nose this time, and with each inhale she crept forwards along that tunnel, towards what she knew must lie ahead; towards what she knew she had almost discovered all those years ago.

You can do anything.

A pinprick of light appeared ahead, growing as she edged closer, a soft glow that began to light her way as she pulled herself along on her stomach. An odd smell reached her that was also strangely familiar – a sulphurous scent that had piqued her curiosity nine years ago in the corridors beyond the dungeons of Castle Grey.

Arla didn't know how many minutes passed as she crawled through the darkness, the spot of light a reward for her perseverance and self-control. Eventually, the tunnel came to an end at a sharp edge of rock with a ten-foot drop, past which was a labyrinth of cavernous chambers and tunnels so enormous she could not imagine how Castle Grey was not swallowed by them.

The open space was a salve to her trembling heart – the downright *fear* that had almost consumed her in that tight space still hammered at the edges of her consciousness. It was quickly smothered by a new fear, one she had never once had to deal with because she'd never once thought it a possibility. But she would do this. She would do it for the people Kastonia was enslaving. She would do it for the people of Hadalyn who'd had their lives destroyed. She would do it for Hark, who had captured her attention in ways she didn't dare begin unpicking. She would do it for Halos, her grandmother and her ancestors before her who had been slaves under the old regime. She would do this, and she would do it scared.

She dropped off the edge of the ledge, wincing at the pain in her ankle as she took one step into the strangely lit chamber. Torches adorned the walls so high up that they couldn't have been lit by any human. Arla passed under a stone arch – an arch that had been perfectly carved and assembled by skilled crafts-man, the gods knew how long ago – and her eyes settled on a thing of legend.

It took everything in her not to scream.

The dragon was a magnificent, hulking beast of iridescent scales in such a pale silver they looked almost translucent in the soft light. The creature was easily the size of three full-grown stallions, its tail twice as long again. The dragon did indeed slumber beneath Castle Grey, exactly as legend had it, not yet alerted to the presence of the young assassin and her fire-filled heart.

Arla wondered in disbelief if everything she had been told really was true – that the dragons truly slept so deeply not even the gods could wake them. If that were true, she had no chance of managing it.

She crept forwards, her steps soundless and light, the way she had been practising for years. Her fingers twitched, aching to reach out and touch the layers and layers of scales so intricately designed and interlocking, like personal armour, decorating the dragon's body. She lifted her hand slowly, gliding her fingertips softly over the hardened plates.

It was so ... smooth, and warm. Entirely the opposite to what she had imagined upon seeing the giant frame of the beast, her own body seemed so insignificant in comparison.

'It has been a while, Arla Reinhart. I was beginning to wonder if you had forgotten us entirely.'

She snatched her hand away, clutching it to her chest as she leapt back from the rumbling mass before her. Its voice was both inside her head and also echoing around the vast chamber that surrounded them. The dragon turned its head, and its eyes ... gods, its eyes were like nothing she had ever seen before.

They swirled like mist, like spun moonlight, like something magical, powerful, and *ancient.*

Words stuck in her throat, a lifetime of wonder and astonishment lodging them there.

'Or perhaps, you did not think of us at all?' the dragon rumbled, its voice soothing and deep.

'I—'

'You did not doubt for one second that I would be here, did you, Arla Reinhart?'

No, she hadn't. The second she accepted that magic was real, she had known the dragons were, too. She had known that they did indeed sleep beneath the palace, and that she had been a hairsbreadth from finding them all those years ago.

'How has no one else found you?' she whispered, easing forwards on her toes to close the distance she had somehow formed between them. 'The Kastonians stormed Hadalyn. They searched the tunnels. I just walked right in here...'

'Your stories are true. We sleep too deeply to be woken. There is a

special sort of magic that guards us. A magic granted to us only by those we serve,' the dragon said, its voice everywhere and nowhere all at once.

'Gods, magic,' she said on a breath, recalling the teachings drilled into her as a child. Her parents had never cared much for it – perhaps that was where her own scepticism came from – but at school, in pretty sandstone buildings close to the palace, Arla and her classmates had been lectured with teachings of the gods and their magic. And then her parents died and she never entered those classrooms again.

Once she'd been taken under the protection of the king, Perry had arranged for her to have private tutors and she had vehemently protested against the teaching of anything to do with magic. If the gods were real, they hadn't deemed her parents worthy of life. She'd be damned if she'd worship them for even one second.

But those lessons she'd had before her parents died, when she was very young, they were suddenly so important. There had truly been gods that walked the earth, their dragons, too, and all of it came flooding back; an avalanche of knowledge she had packed away and never examined.

'We cannot be found by those who wish to use our strength. But for you, Arla Reinhart, for you who has crossed mountains to save the people, to save the kingdoms, we may just lower the veil.'

She usually hated cryptic shit, but she was so transfixed by the sheer realness of it all that she took in every word.

'I know what to do, but I can't do it alone,' she said softly, edging closer to the dragon.

'Ah yes, the Kastonian ... boy.' The dragon tilted its head slightly.

'Hark, is he ... alive?' she voiced the words that had haunted her every moment since she had woken under the scrutiny of Kase. She hadn't dared speak them into existence; hadn't dared think too hard about what that meant.

'*He is alive, Arla Reinhart. Unlike so many of those who carry blood magic. How many more will King Elrod march to their deaths?*'

'None.' Not one more.

'*I suspected you would carry a fierce heart when the gods first spoke their prophecy, though it would have been a first for one of your kind to be meek.*'

She didn't understand. Her mouth was suddenly too dry. 'What prophecy? The gods spoke of … *me*?'

'*The gods have always spoken of those whom they have chosen to stand beside their dragons. Dragonharts, they are known as. Those who are blessed to be bonded to me and my kin, to protect any who have magic in their blood. Dragonharts were once worshipped like gods themselves – you have seen the symbols, worn in one fashion or another by the most devout. Some would set your importance higher than a king, Arla Reinhart.*'

A wave of nausea swept through her, her fingers trembling uncontrollably as she reached into her pocket for the golden brooch.

Dragonhart.

She'd never cared about what the word meant before, but … they couldn't be speaking of her, could they?

To be more important than a king…

The dragon closed its eyes, a sigh heaving from its chest. When it opened them again, the jet-black of its pupils bore into her, the shimmer of its irises forgotten against the intensity of the dragon's gaze.

'*You haven't changed, Arla Reinhart.*'

'I've never met you before,' she whispered, remembering the

darkness and strange scent of that tunnel in Castle Grey nine years ago.

'I saw your heart back then, and I see it now. It beats for the people. For Hadalyn. For those who cannot save themselves.'

Tears pricked at her eyes, and she blinked them away. She had vowed never to let it happen again but here she was, breaking it.

'I see you ... Arla Dragonhart.'

CHAPTER 40
HARK

H is hands bled.

He'd hardly slept since the Kastonian soldiers had taken him, though he supposed he couldn't complain since they'd locked him in his bedchamber rather than the dungeons below the palace.

But they had answered no questions – had given him nothing as his fists pounded the wall, hammering and hammering until the skin on his knuckles was cracked and bleeding.

If they'd hurt her...

Gods, why did he care?

Because she had jumped headfirst into this fool's mission of freeing slaves, and hadn't questioned her part in it? Because she had a heart of fire and it burned for those who had been wronged? Because she'd begun to look at him with something other than hatred – with something fierce and dangerous and alive?

At least the slaves would be safe with Jack by now. And he

didn't doubt for a moment that his friends would have fought to the death to keep Arla safe. He knew that no matter how much rivalry simmered between her and Kase, they would not leave her. He knew Seb had caught him watching her when he didn't think anyone was looking...

But he couldn't get the image of her falling out of his mind. How the hilt of that Kastonian sword had struck her temple because she'd been concentrating on *him*. She had focused only on him as his own soldiers came and she—

Fuck, she'd fallen like *dead* people fell.

She couldn't be, though. He would have heard, prisoner though he was, if Hadalyn's prized assassin had fallen at Kastonian hands.

He'd never been so grateful for his crew.

He wondered what would have happened had he not got involved. If he hadn't argued with the king over it all. If he hadn't been banished to Hadalyn under the guise of an ambassador and tried to keep it up from there. He wondered what would have happened had he not deprived his body of sleep to keep in contact with his friends and build a safe haven for these people. He wondered what would have happened had he not listened to his heart, which cared too much, which knew the king was wrong and his actions were an affront to the gods. He wondered what would have happened if he had grown up in Castle Grey and refused to believe in the old religion, like the girl he knew had stolen his heart.

He didn't need to wonder because he already knew. Elrod would have killed many more of the magic-wielders. He'd have brought ruin upon the kingdoms and spilled every drop of magical blood. The gods would have punished them already.

But maybe if he hadn't got involved, Arla would be safe.

It wasn't so bad, was it? To spend an age locked in this tower with only soldiers walking the battlements to break the monotony of it, if it meant *they* were safe. If it meant the slaves were safe with Jack. If it meant his friends were alive. If it meant Arla was safe. He would spend a lifetime locked in his rooms for that.

Fuck.

CHAPTER 41

Dragonhart? She liked the name. It sounded so ... impressive? And for what it meant. To be bonded to the dragons; to have a connection to the gods.

She'd felt the pull, though, hadn't she? She'd felt that strange connection to the magic-wielders and the instinctual need to protect them. It all made sense – that very need was in her blood.

And now she was going to ride a dragon.

A gods-damned *dragon*.

'I never asked your name,' Arla said, moving close to the tunnel wall as the dragon shifted its huge body, its tail dragging in a movement she had seen grass snakes make.

'Abredus. Though it has been many centuries since that name has been uttered.'

Centuries.

Gods, how old was he?

'When did you last fly?'

'It doesn't matter; I will not be making the trip with you.'

She had expected as much, though she had thought— For a minute she had thought he would help and she wouldn't have to take down Kastonia by herself. Not that she was scared – she harboured enough confidence and swagger to feed an army – but she wasn't stupid. No, not even she could hope to tackle an entire army unaided.

'Oh, well,' Arla stuttered, 'sorry to have wasted your time.' She turned on her heel, shielding her disappointment with the respect that a creature of the gods commanded.

'*You misunderstand me.*'

She turned again to find shimmery, glazed eyes staring back at her.

'*My daughter will be your guide, Arla Dragonhart. Thara has missed the wind on her back for too many moons now.*'

A shiver ran over her skin, and she tried to ignore the Dragonhart namesake – whatever the hell it meant.

'There are more of you?'

'*There is more than one god, is there not?*' Abredus answered, his eyes twinkling in the dull light of the tunnels.

'I can't say I believe in them,' Arla replied, shame suddenly coating her tongue in a thick, oily taste that couldn't hide her regret. How foolish she had been.

'*Then you'd best hope they believe in you.*'

Arla jumped at the rich voice echoing through the stone – through her bones – as she beheld a second body, this one slightly smaller, though no less impressive.

The dragon was the colour of the reeds that grew in the ponds surrounding Castle Grey, a deep, darkest green, almost black in the muted light. Her eyes were glittering, oval-cut emeralds boring further into Arla's soul than even Abredus had.

Her heart raced, her mind unable to think clearly as she felt herself at the mercy of another, as she felt her own decisions hang in the grasp of another being. Something grander and more majestic than she was.

Gods, magic, and dragons. Well.

'Thara will accompany you on your journey, Arla Dragonhart, while the rest of us ride in your heart. The gods' prophecy has long spoken of one with a heart of flame to unite this world, who will end the torture of those who bear magic in their blood. That it would be the last Dragonhart that would take on the task of ending the evil that has leaked into the world.'

Arla didn't think she could be any more shocked.

'Your kings speak of the imbalance of power, Arla Dragonhart, but the man who wears the Kastonian crown was the one who disrupted that balance in the first place.'

She'd been right, then. Elrod had started it because he wanted *more*.

'Go and save those people, Arla Dragonhart. The gods ride with you.'

~

'You've been able to leave this entire time?' Arla asked in disbelief.

She had to shield her eyes from the stark contrast of near darkness to bright sunlight as she followed Thara's body which snaked through tunnel after tunnel and out to the mouth of a cave so enormous she couldn't fathom how anybody, including herself, had missed it. More magic, perhaps.

The dragon huffed a sound that sounded suspiciously like laughter. Arla's fingers tightened into a fist.

'Even dragons can't sleep forever. We have awaited your arrival

for almost a century. So long that the veil over our resting place has become indistinguishable even to those who carry magic. Before we went to sleep, the gods spoke of a prophecy that said there would be one who would come to unite the kingdoms. The last dragonhart. We slept deeply after that... Until some of us began to feel you. The day you were born, eighteen years ago, was the beginning of our waking. My father woke first and I was not long behind. We have felt your presence in Hadalyn from the moment you took your first breath.'

Thara's voice rumbled inside Arla's head. There was a tugging in her core, too, something that felt old and primal. Something that told her this was where she was supposed to be, side by side with this creature whose existence she had denied all her life.

'The gods' message kept us clinging to the hope that humans are worth saving, that they don't all deserve to die for the mindless slaughter of those who bear magic. We have waited all these years for you and you alone.'

Arla was finding it harder to breathe, and yet she couldn't deny the peace that had settled over her the moment she had heard Thara's voice inside her head.

'Why me? Why was I chosen out of everyone else?'

'We dragons do not know the factors that influence the fates, nor why the gods deemed you worthy of carrying the burden of such a task. You are of an old bloodline, Dragonhart, one that was passed down through generations. But you are the first in almost a century to feel it. Your parents and your ancestors before them carried the blood, but it is you the fates have chosen. It is not for us to question it.'

Her parents. They had been born of this strange bloodline too? Had they known it? Had they known she would be the last one?

'Your parents would not have known what blood ran in their

veins, or that their daughter would be the one spoken of in the prophecy.'

Had Arla spoken out loud? Had the dragon somehow read her thoughts? Could she speak to dragons the way they seemed to speak into her head?

'*It is a bond as old as time,*' Thara continued. '*Many have sought to explain how the bond between dragons and the gods' chosen works, and still have come no closer to understanding it. Just know that we are connected now until death. You will learn to tune me out, eventually, but I will always be a presence in the back of your mind. As you are now in mine.*'

Arla's mouth was dry. This was too much at once. Too much she hadn't expected.

And yet the thought of Thara being with her until her death didn't fill her with the terror she had expected. There was something that felt inherently *right* about the bond between them.

'*So I'll be able to talk to you whenever I like?*' She tried out thinking rather than speaking her question. It was a strange thing to comprehend. That they would exist with one another until the end. Thara's steadying presence soothed Arla's fears about what was to come, and what she must do. They were hers to deal with another day.

The dragon made a noise that was either frustration or a huff of laughter. Arla hoped for the latter.

'*I suspect you will have trouble speaking to me through the bond at first, and find it almost impossible when we are apart, but you will find your way, Dragonheart. Like those before you.*'

'What do you mean, those before me?'

'*Another day,*' Thara said. '*For now we have a pair of kingdoms to unite.*'

And a pair of kings to punish, too.

'*I don't imagine you've ever flown before?*' Thara questioned. Arla shook her head. '*Then please do be careful not to poke me with the obscene number of blades that are strapped to your body.*'

Arla smiled, the first kernel of humour she had found in hours. Thara lowered her enormous body as close to the ground as she could manage, and with a fluidity she couldn't explain, Arla pulled herself onto the dragon's back. Her thoughts strayed briefly to Hark, and to what he would think if he could see her atop a dragon. She hoped she wouldn't have to wait too long to find out.

The creature beneath her was deadly, and old, and entirely capable of killing her. Arla couldn't describe the feeling that came over her as her thighs gripped the smooth scales beneath her. Couldn't describe how she'd managed to climb aboard and not have a panic attack.

But it felt *right*. Like something long hidden within her was finally singing.

It felt like finally feeling the warmth of the sun after years of only knowing darkness.

Thara moved, the dragon's muscles rippling as she stepped out beyond the mouth of the cave, feeling the open sky on her scales for the first time in a century.

The dragon shook her huge head, the movement purely feral as she breathed deeply, her body expanding underneath Arla as she sucked in fresh, cool air.

'Can you remember how to fly?' Arla asked tentatively. It had been a hundred years, after all.

Thara's body shook beneath her, the voice filling Arla's head filled with a tone she couldn't quite unpick.

'*Do you forget how to breathe, Dragonhart?*'

Point taken.

'What about the others? Aren't there more of you down here?'

'They will sleep a while longer. Don't fear; they will come when you call.'

'How many of you are there?'

'There have always been twelve that serve the gods, Dragonhart. You have woken two of us.'

Twelve.

Twelve dragons sleeping beneath Castle Grey for longer than anyone she knew had been alive.

She desperately wanted to tell Hark all about it.

'Where do we fly to, Arla Dragonhart?'

Gods, it sent shivers over her skin. She didn't think she'd ever get used to hearing that name.

'To Kastonia. This ends today.'

Thara beat her wings, the leathery mass of them cutting through the air with ease until the ground began to sway and ... and they were no longer on the ground. Arla gripped with her knees, her hands digging into the horned spikes that decorated Thara's shoulders.

Thara beat her wings again, the movement rocking Arla gently on the beast's back, and then they were up. Up, up, up above the Canus, above Grey Hill, above Hadalyn. She was flying. She was really flying.

It was both horrifying and invigorating at once, the rising altitude stealing her breath as Thara climbed higher and higher, the rush of wind against Arla's face was exhilarating in a way she had never experienced before. She gripped tightly as the dragon lurched beneath her, twisting her body before righting herself.

Arla was sure the dragon was toying with her.

'*It has been a long time since I've had the pleasure of open air across my back. You'd do well to hold on.*'

It was the only warning the dragon gave before she picked up speed, her wings beating rapidly, brushing against Arla's legs in a way that made her certain she'd go tumbling to the blur of earth below.

'*I won't allow it.*'

Arla's face split into a grin. This was ... this was something beyond her wildest dreams.

She wondered if magic kept them shielded from the view of the people, or if all of Hadalyn could see the enormous dragon in the sky above them. She didn't care. Let them see her. Let them know that help had come for Hadalyn.

Laughter erupted from her throat, a childish, howling thing that seemed to heal all her wounds. Tears streamed down her cheeks as they cut through the sky, the sun steadily descending and spilling oranges, pinks, and reds in its wake. She told herself it was the wind, and not that the tears were of joy. Of fear. Of *hope*.

She had fought her entire life to get to where she was, and all it had done for her was grant her a position close to a king so brainwashed he was supporting the downfall of his own kingdom. And worse, its people.

Thara let out a sound that trembled through her body and through Arla's, too, a roar into the steadily darkening sky. A promise of vengeance, of wrath, of fury. Arla laughed. It was a pitiful sound, but a promise of her own.

Never again would she be alone.

Never again would she kill in the name of the Crown.

Never again would she tell Hark how much she loathed him.

CHAPTER 42

They flew for hours with the stars their only guide. Arla's legs ached in a way that was unfamiliar to her, and she found herself missing the comforting strides of Vetta. She hoped the mare was okay, and that Jack and the slaves had managed to make it to their safe place. She hoped Hark hadn't given up believing that she would come for him.

Thara was a majestic creature, and the awe that rolled through Arla was like nothing she had ever felt before. The dragons had revealed themselves to her, and they had given her their aid when no one else would. She would carry the Dragonhart namesake with pride. If the gods had chosen her to free the people, they had chosen well. She was King's Assassin, and now she had a dragon.

The voice in her head jolted her to attention – it was still such a foreign thing.

'There will be a plan for this, I hope,' Thara challenged. 'I have fought against those who have not been prepared over the centuries, *and they have succumbed to their disorganisation. It is not the way of dragons.'*

Arla had been waiting for the dragon to question her – had been eager for it, actually. Maybe she sought the reassurance that her plans were well prepared.

Perhaps she was too vain and just wished for the praise.

'I shall be the judge of whether your mortal plans are worthy of acclaim.'

Warmth spread across Arla's cheeks. She really would have to get used to someone listening in on her thoughts all the time.

She cleared her throat, flexing her hands around the horns on Thara's shoulders. 'I will enter Larkire Palace and request an audience with the king. I will give him no choice but to abdicate after what he's done. The act of keeping slaves is forbidden amongst our people—'

'As it should be in every world. An abhorrent practice,' Thara growled.

'If he doesn't comply, he will die.'

This was her promise. Her oath.

The dragon sighed, her body expanding beneath Arla's thighs. *'Then you will end up dead if you decide to kill a king, Dragonhart.'*

'Not if you can lure the guards away.' Arla swallowed.

It was a gamble. She was confident in her ability to take out the soldiers that would guard the King if she needed to, but what of everybody else inside the castle? The barracks full of soldiers? No, she needed a dragon on her side for that.

'Lure them into the city. Create whatever distraction you must. The people will be tripping over themselves to get a glimpse of you. Make sure the guards are drawn into the chaos, too. Just long enough so that I can kill the king and get Hark out safely, if it comes to it.'

A noise of approval escaped Thara's throat. *'That I can do.'*

It wasn't a solid plan, but Arla hoped it wouldn't come to that, anyway. She would make Elrod see the error of his ways and he would give up his throne in favour of Prince Reuben. She hoped it wouldn't come to her taking the king's life.

Silence stretched between them for long minutes before Arla plucked up the courage to ask, 'You say you've fought other battles. What is it like?'

'Nothing like what you will face here, Dragonhart. Don't worry about that,' the dragon said softly through the bond. *'The wars dragons have fought have always been in the hands of the gods. The last time we fought, before we went to sleep, it was enough to bring the world to ruin. It is a blessing no human from that time is alive today to remember the destruction that followed that wretched war.'*

'What happened?' Arla asked gently, inhaling cool air as they soared through fluffy clouds.

'It is a story for another time, but know that not all gods have been good. And neither are those who have served them. The repercussions of a deep hunger for power led to a war that pitched dragons against one god in particular. It left us without the energy to take to the skies. That is why we have slept beneath your palace for so long, Dragonhart.'

Arla couldn't imagine the scale of something so terrible. She couldn't imagine what a war between such creatures would feel like or how devastating the consequences would be.

Both she and her dragon were silent for the remainder of their journey.

~

Larkire Palace was a bruise on the horizon as Thara carried Arla into Kastonia. They had flown all night, and now a pale dawn was settling on the kingdom. As sure of herself as Arla was, she wouldn't risk revealing her hand just yet.

They landed in a meadow outside the city. Thara's huge, clawed talons sank into the lush grass and her tail beat the earth. Arla slid down from the dragon's back and rested a palm against her scaled neck. All of this felt so natural, as if it was indeed in her blood that she should have an affinity for the creature before her. It shocked Arla beyond words.

'Be careful, Dragonhart. It has long been known that those who forcefully take magic do not give it up without a fight,' Thara's voice warned. She knew it wouldn't be easy, confronting Elrod, but she had trained for this her whole life.

'I need you to take Hark somewhere safe once I get him out,' Arla said. 'Don't wait for me.'

Not a question, not a request.

A low rumble sounded from Thara's throat, setting the hairs on Arla's neck standing tall. It would go against Thara's nature to abandon the one she served, but it was not negotiable. Hark was to be kept safe. He had shown her the truth, even when she refused to see what was right in front of her, and she would repay him with her life, if she had to.

'The dragons call for you, not the boy—'

'I am not asking, Thara.'

The dragon sighed, a puff of smoke releasing from her nostrils. Arla wasn't sure if it was in resignation or disappointment.

Without looking back, Arla placed one foot in front of the

other and set off towards Larkire Palace. She ignored the cleaving of her heart as she tried to push the thought away of what she would do if Hark ... if Hark ... wasn't safe. She needed him for her own selfish heart, yes, but this mission ... this wasn't about Hark.

This was about vengeance against a king who had broken the unwritten laws of humanity as well as the actual laws in the treaties that had been signed following the war. This was about holding him to account for his actions. This was about justice.

⁓

Kastonia was eerily quiet.

Not a soul walked its streets. Not even the birds sang. Nobody crossed Arla's path as she approached the gates to the castle. Had this been a different job she might have scaled the side of the palace and slipped in unseen.

As it happened, she was sick of being invisible. She demanded to be seen – to be felt. She rolled her shoulders as she approached the guards standing inside the gates, unconsciously counting and checking her blades.

'Tell His Majesty that Arla Reinhart is here to see him,' she said, standing flush against the metal bars, and eyeing the solider who stood on the other side. She observed the flicker of acknowledgement between the guards; she didn't miss the shuffle of feet as they realised who she was. Her reputation had served her well – too well, sometimes – and she was so very glad that she had let people believe in her penchant for stabbing first and asking questions later.

The gates creaked open, and a guard dressed in a highly decorated tunic approached her, his throat bobbing before he slid his own impenetrable mask across his face. Too late. She'd already seen the fear behind those green eyes. There were not enough vacant expressions and tight lips in the world to keep that from her.

Good, let them fear me.

It would be easy. And if not easy, simple.

Elrod would listen to her, and if he didn't renounce his claim to the throne and release all slaves he still had in his possession, she would kill him. She'd mentally prepared herself to kill him so that if the moment came she wouldn't flinch or hesitate. She'd also prepared herself for how fast she'd have to flee in order to outrun the repercussions of killing the King of Kastonia. This was for the people who deserved better. This was for her father's friend who she hoped was safe. This was for Halos's grandmother.

This was for the people she knew it was her responsibility to protect.

'Weapons first,' the guard said, his hand straying to his own blade sheathed at his waist.

'Absolutely not,' she hissed back. There was no way in this world she was about to walk into that palace without her weapons. Thara had told her to be prepared; she wouldn't let her dragon down now.

'If you don't hand over your weapons, Miss Reinhart, you won't be coming in.'

Quicker than blinking, her left hand shot through the bars of the gate to snatch the front of the guard's tunic, tugging him towards her so his chest pressed hard against the gates. Her right hand held a thin knife to his neck, the bob of his throat brushing the gleaming silver as he eyed her nervously.

'If you don't let me inside I will kill you and every single one of Kastonia's soldiers before a warning bell can even be rung.'

She watched the fight leave his eyes and released him, shoving him back roughly.

'Follow me, Miss Reinhart,' the guard stuttered, trying to keep at least a few feet between them as they walked. Arla enjoyed the shudder that ran through his body.

She hated that she loved this castle.

From the moment she'd first stepped inside she had enjoyed the colour that blessed the halls of Larkire Palace, so unlike Castle Grey. What a shame all she could see now was blood painting its walls.

The guard led her to a drawing room of red-velvet couches with colourful cushions and golden drapes decorating the windows. A fire roared beneath the mantlepiece and Arla had to physically restrain her hands from roaming over the rows of books crammed neatly into dark oak shelves. How rude, to leave her waiting. At least she hadn't come across Orson.

She had been left sitting for close to ten minutes before she could no longer contain the thief within her. Her feet carried her across the room, her hands brushing over ornaments and gold buckles lying on top of desks, and shelves. If they left her here any longer—

'Did your mother never teach you it was rude to steal?' a honeyed, familiar voice cooed from the doorway.

'No, Prince Reuben, she didn't.' She turned to face him, craftily slipping a gold pin into her pocket. 'Your people killed her before I had a chance to be taught good manners.'

'Hello to you, too, Lady Reinhart.' He was smiling at her, a twisted, defiant sort of smile that reminded her fleetingly of Hark.

Gods, just the thought of Hark sent a spear of ice through her heart.

'As much as I enjoy looking at you, Your Highness, it is your father I have come to see,' she crooned, crossing her arms over her chest and leaning against the mantlepiece. Gone was the friendship they had developed a few short weeks ago. She could see it in the way Reuben eyed her as if she were a firework about to explode. She could see it in the way that not a shred of decency lined his face.

Fine. He could die, too, then.

'Hmm, I thought we might hit this little snag,' he said, a cold smile still on his face as he pushed off the doorframe and approached her.

She didn't know why she didn't move her hand to one of the many knives hidden on her body, but Reuben intrigued her in ways she wished he didn't. He wouldn't hurt her.

'And what snag would that be?'

'That you are not welcome here. His Majesty wants your head. It's only out of respect for the King of Hadalyn that he has not ordered you dead on arrival.'

Arla swallowed the laugh so desperately ready to come barking out. 'Oh, he can have my head, Your Highness.' Reuben tilted his head slightly at her words, as if he couldn't believe they were coming from her tongue. 'But he has to come and get it himself.'

She tossed him one of her best courtly smiles and glided past him, through the doorway he leant against, as she followed the path she had mentally plotted the first time she had stepped foot inside Larkire Palace.

The throne room was easy to find and the guards standing with their blades crossed in front of the huge doors not unexpected. The thought of a confrontation sent a thrill through her blood.

'Do you ever listen?' Reuben called after her, his voice breathy and strained.

'Not usually,' she chirped back, finding far too much amusement in teasing the Prince of Kastonia. She ignored the writhing, sharp feeling in her stomach at the thought of killing his father in front of him. Would Prince Reuben balk at the sight of blood?

His father certainly hadn't.

'Then I suppose it is no use keeping the wolf from the door, is it? Weapons first,' Reuben ordered, and for the first time since meeting him, Arla saw a sliver of the royal blood he bore. The authority and command in his voice left no room for even her attitude.

'Don't you dare,' Thara growled through the bond.

She didn't have a choice, though, did she? She had come here to avenge all those who had been affected by Elrod's abhorrent practices, and to make sure Halos never had to worry that her children would face the same atrocities their ancestors had.

She needed to face Elrod today and the only way to gain access to the king was without her weapons.

One by one she unstrapped what she had concealed on her. Blades slid from inside her sleeves, pressed securely against her wrists. Knives at her hips dropped in their scabbards onto the polished stone floor. Her bow was laid carefully on the ground as she pulled more blades out of her long boots, and even brutally sharp silver pins slid from their place in her hair.

Reuben looked at her in mild amusement, bewilderment

smudging his features as if he couldn't quite fathom the number of weapons such a small woman could mask on herself.

'Finished?'

She nodded, her tongue curling over her teeth as he scanned the length of her body.

'All of them, Reinhart.'

She sighed, pulling the final item from inside the waistband of her leather trousers and allowing it to fall to the floor with a thud. She was careful to leave the dragonhart brooch pinned to her jacket.

'All done. Now that I've promised to be a good girl will you *please* let me speak to your father?'

Even Cyrus wouldn't let her get away with the mockery and sarcasm she stitched into her voice. *Lady Reinhart indeed.*

'Gentlemen.' Reuben gestured to the soldiers guarding the entrance to the throne room, nodding as they sheathed their blades and pushed firmly on the doors. Without a glance towards her, he strode through the doors, leaving a clear path for Arla to follow.

CHAPTER 43

King Elrod tracked her through unyielding eyes as she sauntered down the red velvet carpet to the foot of the dais. The air was still, as if the room held its breath for what Arla was about to unleash on the world.

'No need to look so serious, Your Majesty. I've only come to talk,' she said sweetly, mentally plotting the position of each soldier around the perimeter of the throne room.

'The problem, Miss Reinhart,' Elrod began in a voice bitter and cold, 'is that I don't believe you. Don't pretend you're here for anything other than violence.'

A vein bulged in his forehead as he spoke down to her. She bit her lip between her teeth, tasting the metallic twang of red bursting on her tongue as she held back words she had sharpened in long hours of training.

Every soldier in the room held a sword, and she wasn't foolish enough to ignore the potential for crossbows to be hidden somewhere in the labyrinth of wooden beams and arches crisscrossing off the ceiling. She was the most lethal weapon of them all, though, and they knew it.

'You know,' she started, beginning to pace in front of the dais with an inhuman gracefulness. 'I've thought over, and over, and over again about what I want to say to the man on whose orders my parents were murdered and my kingdom ransacked. Ironically, now that I stand before you, I don't think you deserve a word of it.'

Arla Reinhart was known for her lack of mercy. For her ability to chill the blood of her victims before unleashing a wrath of violence reserved only for them. As Arla Dragonhart, she would be no different. She wanted the king begging before she decided what to do with him.

'Shall we skip the niceties, bitch,' he spat, and she smiled at the clear riling of his temper.

'Gladly,' she continued. 'This will be very, *very* simple for you, Elrod.' His eyes widened at her blatant disrespect, and Arla felt more than saw the tensing of the soldiers who were positioned around the room.

'You will remove yourself from the throne. You will free any slave you still have in your possession, and you will *beg me* to show you the mercy you have not shown the human beings you have captured and slaughtered for being born differently to you.'

Something flickered in his icy eyes before he said with the same dangerous quiet she had offered him, 'No wonder my son has grown fond of you.'

'Reuben doesn't know me well enough to grow fond of me.'

'I'm not speaking of that useless specimen.'

Her body stilled.

'Ah, so he didn't tell you, then. I wondered.' A sly smirk twisted the corners of Elrod's mouth into something grotesque.

'What—?'

'It's a shame, isn't it, that you've lived under the same roof for the last two years and kept so many, *many* secrets from each other. Some assassin you are, Miss Reinhart.'

Gods no.

No, no, no, no.

But ... it made sense. The icy-blue eyes that stared down at her resembled a set of eyes so ingrained in her mind that she had trouble sleeping without them as the last thing she saw before she closed her eyes.

The secrets, the half-finished sentences, the—

'Hark,' she breathed.

'Does it make you hate him, Miss Reinhart? Does it make you want to cut his throat as you do mine? Come now, we all know you despise Kastonia and its people. Why not its prince?'

She didn't think she'd ever draw breath again.

'If you've hurt him—'

'Hurt him?' Elrod scoffed. 'My dear, you're the one who's going to hurt him. Do you know the punishment for threatening to kill a king? I'm certain Cyrus hasn't sanctioned this little escapade, but if he has then it is an act of *war*.'

Her hands trembled at his words. This was not how she had imagined their conversation going.

'So no, I have not hurt him. I will leave that to you when he's forced to watch you hang by your neck.'

'Where's Orson?' She didn't know why she asked it – didn't think the ambassador would help her, anyway. She'd seen the way he trailed after the king, desperate for the approval he hadn't won from Cyrus. But if there was a chance he was still on Hadalyn's side, it was worth taking.

Elrod looked blankly at her. 'Not that it's any of your business, Miss Reinhart, but young Orson is currently preoccupied with a … personal project of mine.'

She could see it for what it was: an admission that Orson had been helping him with the slaves and the sacrifices; that Orson had betrayed his king and his country.

'Tell me, *Elrod*,' Arla sneered. 'Tell me why.'

'Why?'

'Why have you been killing them? You can't do anything with their magic, so why? Slavery is a relic of the *past*. You want to be seen as a strong, modern king and yet all you've done is wind the clock back to how things were before.'

He scoffed, leaning forwards on his throne – a dark, wooden thing as hard and cold as the man who sat upon it.

'I can't do anything with it? Oh dear. You really are letting yourself down today, Miss Reinhart.'

'What are you talking about?' she snapped.

'Arla, Arla, Arla,' he tutted, and she hated how his mockery made her feel. 'That's where you're wrong, *assassin*. I *have* found a way to harvest their magic. You see, blood is easy enough to store in the right conditions, especially when there is magic inside it to keep it stable. I have more than enough to last me until I find a way to use it. And when I do, well, the other kingdoms won't know what's hit them.'

Gods. It was true.

What Elrod had done to Hadalyn before … it would be annihilation if he had access to magic. There would be no collection of kingdoms. There would be only brutal Kastonia and its treacherous reach across the world.

And he was keeping their blood. No matter that he was sacrificing them, *killing* them, he was storing the blood until he could figure out how to use it. And ... and she'd seen that locked door in the palace. She'd seen the number of guards positioned in that hallway and figured perhaps it was where he kept the most valuable of his jewels.

But diamonds weren't important to Elrod, were they? Not when he had something that was worth far more than a rock. There was not a doubt in her mind that he was keeping the blood of magic-wielders in that room...

She couldn't stop her hands from shaking.

The king leant forwards on his throne. 'And as for turning the clock back, have you actually asked yourself how things were back then? The kingdom was prosperous. Thriving. Look at it now. Perhaps backwards is the way forwards, Miss Reinhart.'

She couldn't believe the words coming from his mouth – couldn't fathom that he *believed* it.

'Does he know?' she asked, teeth bared and eyes blazing with an anger she couldn't put out. 'Does Cyrus know what you're doing with the blood?'

'Cyrus doesn't have any business knowing *anything*, Miss Reinhart. But seeing the company he keeps'— a pointed look at her—'it's best he's kept in the dark, don't you agree? It's easier that way. He's a fool because he wants to believe that he's helping his kingdom even when deep down he knows it's all a lie.'

'You—'

'Lied? Yes. Your king and that little lapdog of his ate up the lies I gave them because that way they don't have to face the harsh reality. I'd have to be blind not to see that Hadalyn is beginning to fail the same way Kastonia did. People are dying because the kingdoms are failing, Miss Reinhart. So when I sent my *son*'—a scalding fist gripped her heart at the mention of Hark—'with a message for Cyrus explaining that a priestess had come to me from Malarye, bearing a message that the gods were angry that so many people were wielding magic for personal gain instead of for the benefit of all, he agreed to turn a blind eye to my purging of them to appease the gods and restore harmony to our lands. What a shame that he's so trusting.'

Hark had come to Hadalyn two years ago, which meant...

'You've been hunting them down and killing them for two years?' She could hardly believe what he was telling her.

'Double it.'

Four years.

Bile rose in her throat.

'Regrettably, it took eighteen months of bloodletting and sacrifice before we found a way to store the blood, but now that we've perfected the art of it, we need only learn how to *use* it.'

He had gone mad. She truly couldn't believe what he was telling her.

'Hark knew what you were doing and asked you to stop, didn't he?'

He had to have. There was no way he would have risked his own life as well as his friends' to begin extracting slaves if he hadn't already exhausted every other option.

'He begged me, actually.' Elrod was ... *smiling,* as if the memory of his own son, his *heir*, begging him not to take the lives of innocent men, women, and children was something to be laughed at. It made her sick.

'The gods will curse you. You think they'll accept this—?'

He laughed – a brittle, wicked sound. 'The gods will *bless* me.'

She couldn't believe the delusion of it, of what Elrod *believed.*

'You're not worth trying to save. Your reign has been all terror and death. You deserve the same fate,' Arla sneered.

'As do you, Miss Reinhart. I have thought of many things I'd like to do to you.'

'Elrod—'

Arla hadn't given a single thought to the queen, who stood behind Elrod's throne, though she was so unremarkable it wasn't hard to miss her. Arabelle reached for Elrod, as if she could temper the violence and wickedness exuding from his every pore.

Arla winced as the king's hand collided with Arabelle's cheek.

'Touch her again...' Arla growled menacingly as a red mark appeared on Arabelle's pale skin.

'You dare threaten me in my own palace?' Elrod seethed, his knuckles draining of colour where they gripped the throne.

Arla felt the soldiers creep forwards; could almost see them run their fingers over the weapons they kept sheathed at their waists.

She'd been in plenty of situations in which she was outnumbered, but it was rare for Arla not to have multiple escape routes. She couldn't very well throw herself through a window, and the doors through which she had been escorted were sealed shut and blocked by the scarlet-clad Kastonian soldiers she could feel were itching to lay into her.

'Careful, Dragonhart. You mortals are breakable and I can't save you from out here.' Thara's voice rumbled softly in Arla's mind.

It went against everything Arla had become to take half a step backwards, edging her body closer to the doors. Elrod would not give up – that much had been clear from the very moment she had stepped foot in the room – and if she wanted him dead, she needed a clear escape route, preferably with Hark in tow.

She didn't know where Reuben had run off to. She hadn't even noticed him disappear after he'd led her into the hall. But then, why would he stick around after the way his own father had spoken of him?

'If you have any self-respect, Arabelle,' Arla began, frowning at the look of sheer surprise on the queen's face at being addressed, as if it were such an unimaginable thing to happen in her own court, 'you'll take the next carriage to Hadalyn and ask for shelter in Cyrus's court. We don't *hit* women in my kingdom.'

Arabelle stupidly stepped towards Arla, as though her body yearned to be free of this gods-damned place and already on the road to Hadalyn.

Arla watched undiluted rage spread across the king's face, like ink blotting silk. She saw the movement in his shoulder before he had fully lifted his hand to strike the woman he claimed to love.

Before she'd thought through any sort of plan or consequence, Arla's hand was sliding the blade disguised as a hair accessory from its hold and with a flick of a well-practised wrist, sending it hurtling towards the King of Kastonia.

Time stopped.

The soldiers lining the room paused with swords half-drawn, and not a single eye blinked as the blade flew through the air, spinning wildly, as it was supposed to, and pinned the

King's black velvet tunic sleeve to the solid ebony of his throne.

'You little bitch!'

And then the chaos that had been simmering since the moment she had stepped foot in Larkire Palace boiled over.

There would be no mercy for her – not now that she'd let her temper fly. The best she could hope for was to get out of here alive, with Hark, and hope to come back at a later date and deliver the fate the King deserved.

Elrod tugged at his pinned sleeve, bellowing at being restrained as his soldiers descended upon the assassin from Hadalyn.

Arla moved with expert grace, ducking beneath blades, and kicking out at the ankles of those who aimed for her, dropping them where they stood so she could leap over them and make her escape. She had no weapons, but nothing would stop her now.

Arla used the body she had spent years crafting to knock guards off balance, to shove her way through the heaving mass of red and gold. She twisted, spun, and ducked until the huge double doors were two strides away. If only she had thought to make sure they were open...

As if blessed by the gods, at that moment the doors swung open so that a dozen soldiers could rush in. As they trampled through the entryway, confusion smeared their features as they tried to locate the threat to the king.

But Arla was already winding her lithe body through the chaos, slipping behind the guards swarming the throne room and sprinting to where her knives lay discarded when Reuben had stripped her of them. She had no idea where the prince had gone.

She swiped the array of blades as she passed them, ignoring the irritation at having to leave her bow behind. There was no time to secure it to her body and there would certainly be no room to fire it inside the castle walls. Her feet carried her forwards, the map of the palace laid out in her head as she sprinted on and on, through the winding corridors and vast expanse of open halls. She knew they would follow her as soon as they discovered the threat had slipped away amidst the chaos, and they would be on her like bloodhounds.

But her years lurking in shadows allowed to her to slip away unseen, and as she sped through the palace, one destination a flaming beacon in her mind, she was wrath, and fury, and vengeance. She was blood, and fire, and truth, and she would never again be useless. She would never again be that child locked in a dresser, watching her kingdom fall before her.

CHAPTER 44

HARK

His brother was here.

Hark's hearing had sharpened in the days since they had locked him in his rooms. Any sound, no matter how small, had him lunging for the door, desperate for a way out.

So the sound of his brother's footsteps on the other side of the door reminded him of a war drum, tugging at his weary mind. He was exhausted. He had pounded these walls with bloodied fists for hours and had contemplated more than once leaping from the window.

Reinhart would have done it.

He'd seen her scale the tallest of towers with her bare hands and no safety net to catch her, and he knew she would find a way to scramble down the sheer drop had she been the one locked in this room.

'I know you're there, Reuben,' Hark said gruffly, running his fingers through his hair. He wondered often why Reuben hadn't been formally declared his father's heir. The gods knew Hark didn't want it and he could surely be passed over if Elrod wished it. Hark wouldn't rule with a fist of iron like his father did, and they would walk all over him for it. At least Reuben, a natural joker, displayed a nasty temper from time to time so that everyone inside Larkire bent to his will.

'I ... I'm sorry, Hark.'

He stilled at his brother's words, so sullen and distant. If something had happened to Arla—

'He's a bastard, I know. And if I had a backbone I'd march down there and demand he let you out but...'

'But you don't, Reuben. You never have, have you?' Hark snapped, slamming his fist into a wall already decorated with the results of his earlier outbursts.

'It was always you. *You* were always the special one, *you* were always fawned over, *you* were always given the already divided fucking attention of Father—'

'Oh, and you think I wanted that? Fuck, Reuben, you don't get it, do you? I don't want the fucking throne. I don't want the kingdom, or the castle, or *any* of it!'

'Because you love her?'

His blood stopped moving.

'What did you just say?' The words were lethally soft.

'You love her, you stupid prick. I saw the way you stared at her over dinner. Don't think I didn't realise you got yourself so thoroughly pissed beforehand because you couldn't stomach the thought of Father going head-to-head with the girl whilst you were still fucking sober.'

His own heart pounding was the only sound filling his ears.

Reuben scoffed. 'I thought so. You'd throw it all away for her. Shame you couldn't have done it for me, or Mother.'

Rage boiled in Hark's veins with a force violent enough that nothing would stand in the way of him wrapping his hands around his little brother's neck.

'You think I don't *hate* what goes on behind these walls! I stayed *for* you and Mother. I went to Hadalyn under his orders to keep *you* safe! I could have gone far away. I could have left you and escaped this hell and I didn't!' He was trembling now, sweat beading on his forehead as a furious, pounding anger brought an unwelcome stinging to his eyes. 'He told me he'd hurt her if I didn't go! Told me he would *kill* our mother if I didn't go to Hadalyn and become the fucking ambassador. I didn't want *any* of it.'

There was a click so soft he barely heard it.

His brother sounded weary when he spoke, as though his very soul had left him.

'Go get her, Hark. Just don't forget those who never forgot you...'

His feet were moving before his brother had finished speaking.

CHAPTER 45

Her blood sang with the violence of it all.

Bodies fell without their owners seeing what had been unleashed upon them. Wherever a soldier stood in her path, he died. Her knives flew through the air as if they were gods-blessed. The King's Assassin had never missed a mark. Today was no different.

There was a roaring in the distance, the call of a dragon finally awoken. Arla could only imagine the chaos that would follow in the streets of Larkire. Kastonia's people had all believed in magic, had all been loyal to the old religion, and for a dragon to be summoned here, for her...

What if Thara got hurt?

'I have won greater skirmishes, Dragonhart.'

Arla's heart stuttered at the dragon's voice in her head. How had she managed to communicate even from so far away?

'Concentrate.'

Her breath was torn from her as she slammed into a solid

figure, her feet sliding as she was pulled roughly into what had seemed to her to be another section of castle wall.

Darkness swelled in, pushing her closer to the body that had dragged her into this tight space as the hidden door closed softly behind them. She spun, eyes widening in the dark to try and make out whoever it was.

She had hoped for one silly moment in her pathetic heart that it was Hark. That he had found her, and they would fight their way out together. But it wasn't Hark. This scent was spicier, like cinnamon and ... ginger.

'Go straight to the end and keep your sword drawn. You'll find him—'

'Reuben, stop. What—?'

'You don't have much time. The castle's swarming with soldiers and if you two don't get out now...'

She couldn't think quickly enough to argue with him, not when the sound of dozens of pairs of military boots pounded on the other side of the secret passage, shouts of confusion reaching her even through the solid stone.

She gripped Reuben's wrists, searching in the dark for his eyes.

'Come with us,' she urged, tugging the bony wrists beneath his velvet sleeves. He was Hark's brother. And, prince or not – Kastonian or not – if Hark had changed, so could his brother. She wouldn't let him feel the same loss she had endured.

'I can't.'

'Hark—'

'Will be fine. Look after him, Arla. He loves you.'

And then he was pushing her away from him, shoving her down the passage towards what she could only trust was not a trap. She didn't let her mind dwell on what he'd said – on what he'd somehow concluded about her relationship with his brother.

Later.

Gods there *had* to be a later, didn't there?

There were too many things she needed to say. So much she needed to explain and apologise for.

She wanted to look him in the eye and tell him she didn't hate him.

Get a grip, Reinhart.

Her feet carried what her heart could not decipher yet, and she pushed past the throb of her ankle as it protested at the complete hammering she had subjected it to over the past few weeks. Later she could stop. Later she could rest her ankle on a stool as she sipped wine and watched Larkire Palace burn.

But first she needed Hark. She needed to know he was alive, and then there would be vengeance. She had a dragon in her service, after all.

The passageway was shorter than she had expected, and when she reached the heavy stone door at the end, she pressed her ear against it and waited.

Nothing.

It could be a trap – gods, Reuben didn't owe her anything. He and Hark could hate each other for all she knew; it had been a stupid idea to trust the young man. But she wouldn't know if she didn't open the gods-damned door.

Both ends of the corridor lay empty, and it took her a minute to pull up that mental map of the palace and pinpoint exactly where she was amidst the chaos. The door just a few strides to the right was the sign she had needed – the very bedchamber to which she had been assigned when they stayed here. Which meant ... Hark was on the other side of the palace, if they were confining him in his rooms.

Somewhere in the distance she could hear her dragon and knew there would be fires cropping up around the city to lure both innocents and soldiers from the castle.

'*They will pay for ever daring to enslave those who carry blood magic.*'

The promise spurred her on ... until she ran directly into the path of an oncoming army.

'Fucking gods,' she murmured. Adrenaline would keep her going for only so long – hopefully until she stumbled across Hark – but she needed the strength to actually escape these walls.

She met the first two with a swing of her sword that had their heads rolling back – all the way back. She could see the fires now through the arched windows, buildings alight and ... there were flames engulfing one of the towers. Gods, if Thara was this close to the palace they'd shoot her down. Arla had no idea how scales would hold up against crossbows and ballistics from the tower's defence system.

'*Concentrate,*' Thara growled. Despite the bond that she shared with her dragon, Arla knew it would take a while to get used to the new voice in her mind. It lay there, heavy and sentient in the back of her head as though she no longer belonged to just herself.

'*You are mine as I am yours. You will get used to the bond eventually.*'

She didn't mind it so much as she had initially, now the shock had worn off. She could feel the weight of it settle with every thought and movement, a reassuring presence that bolstered her and made her feel less ... alone.

'*This isn't the time for emotions, Dragonhart. You're about to be impaled.*'

Arla spun, ducking as a blade jabbed towards her. She had no idea how Thara had known – she couldn't see the dragon save for the glimpses of scales flying past the window.

'*Some magic cannot be explained.*'

'Maybe not,' Arla said out loud. 'But shouldn't you be focusing on your own task?'

Thara huffed an amused snort down the bond, its friendly fingers caressing the back of Arla's mind. '*Some of us are able to do two things at once. Maybe once you're reunited with the boy you'll stop being so ill-tempered.*'

'Imagine a *dragon* calling *me* ill-tempered,' Arla muttered as she veered left to avoid the sharp point of a sword.

Thara laughed then – or at least, the noise she made in Arla's head sounded too similar to laughter to be mistaken for anything else. '*My point exactly. On your right.*'

So absorbed was she in her task and in the growing connection between her and Thara, Arla hadn't spotted the three soldiers waiting for her in the shadows. She didn't notice how they surrounded her, blocking any escape route and pinning her between them.

It was rare that Arla danced on the line between life and death, but with three blades creeping closer to her, she could sense the dark figure looming, waiting to snatch her soul and present it for judgement. Not that the gods would send her soul to the eternal gates; she was a terrible, wicked person and she didn't deserve anything but hell once her life was taken from her.

Everything she was and had been flashed before her: from

the gangly child on whom a king had taken pity, to the lethally sharp assassin she was now. Would this be it?

A voice that set the world trembling cut through the fog clouding her mind, and her heart faltered at the sound of it.

'If you're dying at anyone's blade, sweetheart, it'll be mine.'

~

Her eyes filled with useless tears at the sight of him, black hair tousled and wild, his eyes gleaming with violence as he mouthed something at her.

Duck.

A memory flickered before her for a fleeting second, a flash of forest, horses, and raiders.

Her body dropped to the floor on instinct as Hark's blades flew, piercing the chest of the soldier behind her. The other two whirled, only to meet his wrath and fall with a spray of scarlet that warmed her cheeks.

And then Hark's hands were there, ironically soft and warm as they gripped her hands and hauled her up.

'You came,' he said, something Arla couldn't quite place smearing the edges of his voice.

'Of course I bloody came!'

His lips slammed into hers, a desperation there that had her stomach swooping low as he claimed her with the kiss. She didn't try to hide her response to him, how he lit her on fire with his touch. He looked weary, angry, and *dangerous.*

'Reinhart, I—'

'Whatever it is you have to say, please don't say it whilst we're being hunted. You'll only ruin it,' she grunted, grabbing his hand and setting off at a run.

'I hope you've got a plan.'

'I would if everything was actually going to plan, *Your Highness*.' She smirked, looking over her shoulder to gauge his reaction at the revelation of what she now knew. He shot her a vulgar gesture that had her grinning.

They careered around a corner, having made it to the floors above the royal suites now, the grandeur of expensive carpets and artwork forgotten in these higher levels of the castle. All that lay before them now was bare stone hallways so unremarkable there was no telling them apart as they met a junction of corridors that left Arla feeling uncomfortably disorientated.

'Which way?'

'Not left?' Hark ground out.

'Why not left?'

Thara roared in the distance, the sound reverberating through the chilly stone halls. Every window Arla passed glowed with flames as smoke began to fill the palace. An urgency crept over her, slowly and then all at once, until her heart was pounding in time with the sound of feet.

Arla turned to see Hark bracing himself, sword in hand as he stared down the length of the corridor.

Arla peered around him, her eyes adjusting to the sight before her. An army marched towards them, their synchronicity an impenetrable wall.

'Fuck.'

CHAPTER 46

Hark's fingers threaded through hers as he gave her hand a tight squeeze.

His eyes didn't leave the approaching army as he said, 'Carry on straight and don't stop. It'll bring you out onto the battlements and you can escape from there.'

Self-sacrificing *bastard*!

'And you?'

'I'll keep this lot distracted.' His eyes didn't leave the approaching army – dozens upon dozens of soldiers, filling the hallways. Too many for them both to take on, let alone just him. It was more than she had ever expected Kastonia to have, a wall of red and gold marching towards them, swords at the ready.

Arla could hear Thara's roars, the sound both outside the castle and inside Arla's head.

Gods, what had she done by coming here?

'Absolutely not,' she snapped in response to Hark's ludicrous plan.

'For once in your life, Reinhart, just do as you're fucking told.'

'No, Hark. I almost lost you before. I'm not going to do it again.'

His eyes softened then, his fingers smearing the splatter of blood on her cheek. 'Show them exactly who you are, then.'

Something grew in her chest and crawled higher to lodge in her throat. 'Together.'

He gripped her hand. 'Together.'

The first wave of soldiers was upon them in seconds, their cries echoing off the stone, merging with the harsh noise of swords clanging. Hark and Arla moved together as one, an unwavering wall of violence that cut down any who stood before them.

Where her blade missed, his was there to strike true; where his feet stumbled over the bloodied carpets, she was there to steady him. Their bodies moved as though they were two halves of a whole, destined to move with a synchronicity she couldn't have imagined. Bodies fell in their wake, and when there was finally a moment of respite, they took it and ran towards the battlements.

Hark was there beside her, his bloody fingers entwined with hers. It was perhaps the only thing holding her up at all as she tried to breathe past how heavy her sword was, how her arms ached, how her breaths weren't coming quick enough.

A shadow passed by the window, something big enough to block the sun for a few seconds as it passed.

'Don't you dare drop that sword. You'll make us look bad.'

Somehow Arla found it in her to smile. She didn't have a clue who'd be left for them to look bad in front of.

～

Arla thought she knew chaos; thought she had caused it, been it, fought through it.

But this was something else. Fires burned across the battlements, arrows were being fired at the dragon who was twisting through the sky above them, picking off any she could get close to and ripping them off the ledge. The dragon's huge, clawed talons rattled the very structure of the towers, showering Elrod's army in rubble large enough to kill them. Two dozen warriors waited for them, stationed equally across the parapet. Arla didn't know which corner of her mind had thought to slam the door behind her and snap one of her knives in the lock so that no one else could gain access to the battlements, but she was grateful that some semblance of the assassin was still in there.

'About time, Dragonhart,' Thara grumbled through the bond.

The soldiers were upon them immediately, not recognising or not caring that their prince fought them.

She wanted it to be over.

Arla didn't know for how long she kept swinging the blade, only that these soldiers were not falling. Then she saw Hark, his back to a guard armed to the teeth with blades so wicked she herself had never had the privilege of owning one. And he wasn't looking.

She moved as though the very gods had blessed her feet. Moved like fire, and water, and death as she ploughed through the soldiers, striking with her sword and screaming at Hark to *move.* A sharp pain registered in her side, but she was moving too quickly to care. Her feet flew over the battlements, a death waltz if ever there was one.

Arla whistled, a shrill sound that paused everyone on that gods-forsaken castle for a fleeting second before she struck down the sole remaining soldier between her and Hark.

She didn't stop, wrapping her hand around his free wrist and tugging him after her, closer to the edge, closer to a bloody death if they fell.

A ringing clang of metal lit up the sky, and then more soldiers were storming through the door she had shoved her blade into. It had only been a temporary hold.

She knew she held Hark's hand because he was squeezing hers tighter. Their hands joined but she couldn't see where because there was so much *red* – blood, uniforms, more blood.

Her chest was too tight, her ears rushing with her own heartbeat as she struggled to breathe in and out. They were going to die here. She'd caused all of this and they were going to die here. Her breaths came too quickly then, her fingers trembling around the hilt of her sword, its weight long forgotten.

But then there was a voice like deep night in her ear, sinking beneath her skin to rest just above her heart. 'I'm here, I've got you, I won't let anything happen to you.'

She didn't know how long she'd waited to hear that. To hear that she was safe; that someone cared. She didn't let herself think as she turned and pressed her lips against his cheek, revelling in the heat burning through her as he pulled her closer.

She smiled against his skin as she saw out the corner of her eye his sword had impaled a soldier through the chest. She couldn't help the thought that he was made of the same thing she was – that their souls already knew each other inside out.

'You're going to get killed if you keep succumbing to the boy's inability to keep his hands to himself.' Thara's voice rattled through her skull.

Right. Battle.

Arla blinked slowly, as if that single act could pause the world and the madness that had descended. A huge shadow crossed behind her shut eyelids, and when she found the strength to open them again, she stopped swinging her sword and called up the last ounce of her courage. She didn't know why her fingers closed around the golden symbol pinned to her jacket – perhaps a reminder that this was real and she was still here – and as she felt that metal beneath her touch, something in her chest ruptured.

A foreign strength coursed within her, power surging through the bond between her and Thara. She knew as she raised her sword again that anyone stupid enough to challenge her would fall at her feet.

Arla swung the blade as if something ancient guided her. Hark was at her side, barely keeping up, but he hadn't let her down yet and she knew he never would.

Thara was above them, setting light to any who emerged onto the battlements.

There was a strength in Arla's body she'd never known existed, as if she shared the dragon's power. It had been there for only a second, but it was enough for her to clear a path for her and Hark, for them to escape because this was a fight she couldn't win. Not today.

'Don't hesitate,' she called over the shouts of soldiers and the wind tearing through them, whipping her blonde curls into a matted knot she knew would take forever to comb out.

Hark looked at her as if she'd gone mad – she thought perhaps she had, because no one in their right mind would do what she was about to do. But he didn't hesitate. He didn't pull her back from the edge of the roof as they reached it and carried on.

Into the sky. Into an endless, open drop.

She squeezed her eyes shut as they fell, Hark's hand locked in hers.

Only when she met the solid mass of scales, did she finally open her eyes.

CHAPTER 47

'Reinhart, this—'

'Thara, my dragon.' Arla couldn't find the breath to be amused at Hark's disbelief, to chuckle at the stunned silence. She could barely suck a mouthful of air into her lungs as Thara's huge wings beat through the air, carrying them away from Larkire Palace. Arla wished for her bow because if there was one image she wanted to leave behind for all Kastonia to see, it was the sight of her firing arrows from the back of a dragon.

'There's no room for theatrics, Dragonhart.'

She didn't think she could describe the feeling she had for Thara. Wonder? Awe? Shock? Adoration? Too many to decipher.

She could still hear the chaos behind them, and she didn't think she imagined the booming voice of King Elrod himself as the burning castle began to fade into the distance. But rather than the relief she knew she should be feeling – at escaping with her life and with Hark – she couldn't help the anxiety that came with leaving a job unfinished.

She didn't think the king would be so stupid as to begin killing magic-wielders again – at least not so openly – but where was the vengeance? The *justice?*

Maybe it was just the exhaustion weighing in, but her limbs felt heavy and everything *hurt.*

'Are you out of your gods-damned mind?' Hark called above the roar of the wind, and she had never been more grateful for the warmth that burnt through Thara's body.

'Maybe,' she said, grinning against the tide of cold that swept through her. 'There's a lot you've missed, Stappen.'

'What, like you finding a gods-damned dragon?' he called back, and Arla turned her head slightly, finding Hark's eyes lit wildly and his hair flowing behind him. He looked *alive.* And brilliant. And powerful. And magic.

She laughed, wrapping her hands around the spikes on Thara's back to try and force some heat into them.

'What's the plan?' he asked into her ear, and something thick and oily settled in her stomach at the realisation she hadn't thought beyond this moment.

'I ... I don't know,' she admitted, confusion blurring the edges of her thoughts.

The dragon rumbled beneath her, and Thara's voice filled her head. She knew from Hark's silence that Thara had chosen to speak only to Arla.

'*Where to, Dragonhart?*' the steadying, ancient voice asked.

'Somewhere safe. Somewhere I can rest,' Arla replied.

The dragon banked to the south, as if to head back to Hadalyn. Arla didn't know if that was good or bad, considering the declaration of war she had essentially announced in Kastonia. Did an assassin of Hadalyn represent the king? Had her actions sparked war between the two kingdoms?

She didn't care; she was too exhausted, both hot and cold at once. And as Thara straightened herself, Arla didn't. Her body began to slip sideways, the world becoming a blur. She tried to open her mouth to speak, but her lips felt heavy and she was unable to form words.

Firm hands caught her from sliding off Thara's back to an ending she probably deserved, but there was...

Gods that was *painful*...

She cried out, a whimpering, hurting sound.

Pain lanced through her side, snatching her breath away and turning her limp, melting her into something useless in Hark's grip.

His hand came away from her side, and she closed her eyes against the sticky, scarlet smear coating his fingers.

The world turned dark and heavy, the exhaustion of the last weeks pounding her from every direction and dragging her beyond words or comprehension. She sagged against him, no longer caring that she looked weak, that she was now struggling to draw a breath against the pain as she leant against Hark's chest.

'Fuck, Arla.'

Arla.

He hadn't called her that before. Only ever *Reinhart* or *assassin*, or——

Gods, it *hurt*.

Hark adjusted his grip on her, sending another streak of blinding white pain through her side.

She cried out again, and she thought she felt a question appear in her head before merging with the throbbing agony.

'Dragonhart?'

Her lip bled from where she had bit it, and she couldn't help the whimper that escaped her tongue as she pressed her own hand to her side and watched it come away a bright ruby colour.

'It's okay. You're okay,' Hark said to her, and she knew he was panicking because his voice shook and damn, if that didn't scare her.

She felt his hand at her waist again, and the sight of her own blood on his hands made her feel sick. This was bad. This was bad because she was bleeding, and she hadn't known, and she didn't know how long it had been like this, only that she was exhausted and she...

She'd felt it, on the battlements. She'd been so transfixed on making it to Hark that she'd ignored the splinter of hot pain that had registered so flickeringly briefly.

She'd been hurt before. She'd been kicked and hit around the head and suffered bruises and broken fingers on other jobs. She'd gone through brutal training and she'd withstood the torture of that test. She'd driven a knife through her own hand to make a point and she'd kept running on a broken ankle but never, *never*, had Arla felt so close to the line between life and death.

'Hark,' she whimpered, no longer finding any reserve of strength to support her own weight. But he held her unfalteringly still so she didn't hurt.

'It's okay. You're going to be okay.' Did he know his voice was shaking? Or that his hand trembled where he pressed it against her wound?

'I'm cold,' she whispered, suddenly understanding why even atop a dragon her body was succumbing to a chill. That was death, breathing down her neck. Waiting. Calling.

'I know, but I'm going to fix it. I-I'm going to fix it all,' he stuttered, a promise she knew couldn't be kept. Not this far from home, not in the sky on top of a fucking dragon.

'I'm sorry,' she whispered, gulping as another bout of pain shot through her.

The pain had come on so quickly after the adrenalin had settled, but now, now the shoots of blinding agony were becoming further apart, not as sharp as they had been...

'Hey, hey, you don't need to apologise for anything,' he urged, his voice sounding stronger than it had since he had noticed she was bleeding. 'You did great. You saved the slaves, and you found me, and you found the dragons, Arla.'

Arla. She liked her name on his lips. So much nicer than on anybody else's.

'Open your eyes.'

What?

'Arla open your eyes.'

Had she closed them?

'There you are,' he said, as she found the energy to open eyes that were too heavy.

The sky was growing dark. And when had she lain far enough back to look up and see Hark's eyes?

She didn't want to. She didn't want to see that worry and pity there. That was a look reserved for the family members of the people she killed. Wretched, evil people. Perhaps she wasn't any better? Perhaps she deserved this?

Never.

Was that Thara or her?

'It doesn't hurt so much now,' she managed to say. It wasn't a lie. The pain was ebbing into something soft and dark. Something comforting and all too easy to want to slip into. Something held her back, tethered her here to prevent her from wandering into that darkness.

She would go willingly, she thought. She had struggled for so long, fought so hard. She was *tired*.

'That's good,' Hark said, gifting her a smile she so rarely saw. Never a smile for her, not like this one.

But it broke her failing heart because Hark was trembling where her body rested against his. Hark who was solid, and steady, and not prone to emotion, and he was shaking.

'I'm dying, aren't I?' she asked, her lip wobbling because as much as she deserved it, as much as she would go willingly, she didn't *want* to die.

There had been a time when she did. Gods, she had once been so close to stepping off her balcony at Castle Grey. She hadn't had the strength to carry on after she'd survived the torture that promoted a soldier to the King's Guard. She had felt wrong – like she'd broken something in her soul to go through that and feel … nothing.

But now, now she wanted to see things. She wanted to see the stars in the mountains of the northern border. She wanted to swim with Halos and the twins in the Canus, when the sun finally returned. She wanted to explore Hark without the nastiness and hostility they had thrown at each other. She wanted to love him. *She didn't want to die.*

'Don't say stupid things. You're not dying.' But even Hark's reassurance didn't reach his eyes. She could see, even with her blurring vision, that he didn't believe what he was telling her.

'I'm so tired, Hark.'

He swallowed, raising his free hand to brush her curls from her face.

'Just a little longer. I've got you, all right? But I need you to stay with me. I need you to keep your eyes open.'

I need you.

How many people had needed her in their lives? Cyrus had *needed* her to kill people. But that wasn't the same, was it?

Nobody needed her. Gods, Hark had told her once that no one would ever even like her, let alone love her.

'Hey, hey, open your eyes.' He shook her gently, sending another wave of pain – this one duller than the previous ones – through her side until she was staring into those icy-blue eyes again.

'Talk to me,' she whispered, and she could have sworn that silver lined his eyes. Oh, gods, this was bad.

'You know, I've watched you every day for two years,' he began, his voice rougher than usual as he kept one hand pressed to her side and the other gently brushing over the hair across her forehead. 'But I met you before, you know. I didn't know if you ever remembered.'

'When?' she whispered, glad to listen if his voice was to be the last thing she would ever hear. She couldn't have coped with silence.

'When you were thirteen,' he continued. 'It was my birthday and my father had sent me to Hadalyn with the ambassador at the time to deliver a message to King Cyrus. We stayed there for three nights, and I remember watching you from the window of the bedchamber I was in, watching you sprint laps of the castle grounds every evening before it got dark.'

He was truly shaking now, the movement jarring her, but she didn't have the strength to complain.

'And when you weren't running, I watched you follow the exercises of the soldiers with their blades, and you had hold of this stick'—he laughed, a harsh, croaky sound that shouldn't have come from his soft mouth—'and you trained at the back of their drills every day. And that's not even the best part— Arla, open your eyes!'

It was an effort to do so this time, and she knew that if they closed again, she wouldn't find the strength to open them.

'Hey, you're all right. Stay with me.' She thought she nodded. 'But one morning I hadn't pulled the drapes over the window, and I remember opening my eyes to see you climbing past the window. Up the tower. No ropes, no guard helping you, nothing. I knew then that you were utterly insane. But I also knew that I'd never seen anybody so serious about their train-ing, and that if Cyrus didn't have you as head of his King's Guard one day that I'd beg my father to bring you to Kastonia. That was before I knew you despised us, mind—'

'I wish I'd never hated you,' she managed to say, her heart splintering as she witnessed the pain that crossed his face.

'Arla, open your eyes.' There was an urgency in his voice that cracked her splintering heart, and she hadn't realised that they'd closed again. Thara had gone silent and she couldn't feel the bond between them anymore either. Everything was dark now, too, but behind her eyelids there was Hark, and the memory of his icy-blue eyes tunnelling into her, and it was enough to stop her panicking as her body turned numb and her chest rattled as she tried to breathe in. She thought something roared then, but all she could hear was the beat of her slowing heart and the quick breaths Hark was taking as he cradled her to him.

'Arla,' he choked. 'Come on, sweetheart. You're stronger than this.'

Was she? Had she ever truly been strong at all?

346

Some might say she was, that she had fought against the odds to win her king's favour and that it wasn't a task someone weak could have managed. She hoped they remembered her that way – strong, a warrior who'd gone down fighting for a better kingdom. A better world.

In the end, she wasn't strong enough, and she waltzed into the darkness.

CHAPTER 48
HARK

Fuck, fuck, fuck, *fuck*.

'Open your gods-damned eyes!' he shouted, tapping her cheek which was now the colour of snow. Her eyes didn't so much as flutter as she lay in his arms.

He was shaking, but not with the cold, because she'd found them a gods-damned *dragon* and the fire burning in its belly was heating his bones despite the bite of the wind tearing through them. He was shaking because she wasn't opening her eyes and she wasn't talking to him anymore.

But her chest still rose and fell, and he could feel the faint beat of her heart where his hand rested against the wound in her side. He didn't dare look at the red liquid coating his palm. He didn't think he could stand to see her blood, so sticky and warm between his fingers. So he kept his eyes fixed on the golden brooch on the front of her jacket, a symbol that had been a constant in his life because he had always believed and now ... now she did too and it was too late.

She had come back for him.

He still didn't know why. He had been vile to her for years, and it was delusional to think that those years of animosity and resentment could be undone in a few short weeks. Though, if he thought on it hard enough, that resentment had been unravelling faster than either of them could have imagined. He'd felt the softness of her skin beneath his fingers, had learned of the things that plagued her mind, had begun to understand that they co-existed quite comfortably when they weren't fighting.

And it wasn't actually so strange at all that she would come back for him, was it? Because in every fibre of himself he knew he'd have done the same. He'd have moved the very mountains to come back for her if it had been *her* as his father's prisoner.

His heart eased slightly at the fury that had taken hold of his father at the discovery of what they'd done. How, after every last slave had been rescued, the rest of the magic-wielders had gone underground where they would be undetectable. He would not spill another drop of magical blood, and the inability to use the magic he had been so desperate to harvest had wound his father so tight that Hark had thought the vein in his head might burst as his father had struck him.

And Arla... She'd come back for him.

Had he ever known such a loyalty? Was that the right word for it? He knew his crew would defend him to his death, but he had explicitly ordered them not to come after him if he was taken.

But Arla had.

And now she wasn't opening her fucking eyes and it was going to be all his fault. She had fought like ... like something he'd never seen before. Like she was made of fire, and flame, and stars. Like she was wrath, and bloodshed, and death's own companion. And she had taken a sword in the side for him.

He couldn't even smell the jasmine on her anymore.

He choked back a sob, a wretched, broken sound as he pulled her closer to him.

Had she always been this tiny?

He could feel each of the perfectly defined muscles on a body that was thin, and in places, bony. When had she last eaten a proper meal? Had she stopped in Hadalyn to rest and gather her strength?

He doubted it. She had been at his side quicker than he thought physically possible, and she had managed to find a dragon!

A dragon that had roared into the clouds that masked them. A dragon that had flown her from Hadalyn to Kastonia. A dragon that had been waiting for her to jump off the battlements of Larkire Palace like a madwoman. If ... if anything could help her, if Arla Reinhart was going to open those coffee-coloured eyes and call him a name that definitely shouldn't come from a lady's mouth, he had to try, didn't he?

Clearing his throat, he called out to the beast, not knowing if it could hear or understand him, 'Take us over the northern border. I know somewhere she will be safe.'

He could have sworn the dragon rumbled in reply.

CHAPTER 49

S he hadn't expected death to be like this, but then again, she'd thought her soul would burn upon arrival at the eternal gates. Clearly there was something of her left if she could still think, wasn't there?

She couldn't see, and her mind was foggy but ... there was sound – murmurs and something more... Panic, maybe? The sound came and went in waves, dragging her from the darkness to some sort of semi-consciousness before submerging her once more in the oblivion where there was nothing and where she didn't dream. She might have been dead then, in those long, uninterrupted episodes of nothingness where she wasn't sure there was anything left of her.

She should have craved those brief moments of sound, should have clung to them with every morsel of herself but she found it all too exhausting. Those sounds hurt her head and her body, and whatever else she was made up of. The darkness was a reprieve when it swept her back under.

She had been in that darkness for hours and hours – or was

it days? Was there such a thing as time in this place? Then she was wrenched from her peace by something sharp and burning in her side. It was gone as quickly as it had come, but that pain had left her suspended in this strange half-state.

And then she was ... dreaming? Perhaps. There were flashes of pictures – memories, maybe.

She was somewhere dark and restricted, and she knew she couldn't speak or move. There was shouting and banging, and through the crack of light streaming into the darkness she saw two bodies slump heavily. One of them had pale blonde curls that stretched down beyond the swell of the woman's breasts.

The darkness pulled her under once more, and then there was nothing.

~

'*Dragonhart?*'

A lapse in the nothingness, but she didn't know what, or why, or if she was dreaming...

'*It's time to come back, Dragonhart.*'

She ... she didn't care to come back. She could lie in this darkness forever, floating in a painless, sleep-filled sanctuary of emptiness. She couldn't remember a before or what it even meant to *come back*.

'*You've fought so hard, Dragonhart, but it's time to come back.*'

A phantom arm of warmth licked down her spine, and it was as though flames coursed beneath her skin in answer. There was light, somewhere, getting stronger as the flames in her blood roared louder and louder. Was this death? Where she was heading now, into this increasing tunnel of light?

More light.

More warmth.

More sounds, low and gentle this time, not the hurried, panicked noises from before.

She wished the darkness would come back. She wished it would swoop in and drag her back into the oblivion, where there was no colour and no noise, and where her body felt rested for the first time in forever.

But a low light was becoming clearer – or was it simply that this darkness was not as absolute as it had been before?

Her hands were a thing, now, and she could feel something soft and warm beneath them – not silk, but a cotton so soft it could have been the familiar sheets in her bed at Castle Grey.

Was that where she was now?

There was something illuminating the space she was in, and when her eyes became real, living things again, she blinked them slowly.

She was indeed lying on top of cotton sheets, a fur blanket draped over her. And it was dark in here, save for the open, night sky, peppered with millions of bright, silver stars. It was so beautiful that she thought the gods must have stitched diamonds into the darkness.

Her eyes moved slowly, exploring the sky above her but ... but it couldn't be open sky because it was so warm in here. It had been winter when she'd been running through Larkire Palace...

Not knowing if her body had returned with her hands and eyes yet, she launched herself upright, glad to find that her most prized possession responded with lethal grace.

'Whoa, please, milady, be still.'

Arla's head snapped to her right, where a pair of pale grey eyes looked back at her with a worrying amount of concern. A scar on her jaw reflected the starlight from her face, and Arla felt her heart clench as Lilith – one of the maids that had served her during the days she had spent at Larkire – finished filling the glass of water she had been pouring from a jug so beautiful Arla wondered if, like the stars, it had been made from diamonds.

'Lilith?' she asked, her voice quiet and uncertain. She didn't know where she was, but if Lilith was here, it meant Larkire, didn't it?

'Be still, milady. You don't want to pull a stitch,' the young woman said softly, closing the space between her and Arla and offering a gentle smile.

'You're safe. You lost a lot of blood, but you'll be fine.' Arla could only imagine the shock and confusion on her face as the maid smiled meekly at her.

'What happened? Are we still in Kastonia?' she asked, wincing slightly at the tight pull in her side. Lilith moved slowly, as though she didn't dare make any sudden movements. Arla felt as though she'd been run through with a blade and every breath was exhausting.

'We are ... somewhere safe.'

Okay, then.

Arla pulled herself back against the headboard, exposing more of her body from underneath the blanket.

'Who dressed me?' she asked, the words too forceful for her battered state. She gritted her teeth against the ache of *every-thing*, and looked down at the silk slip covering her skin.

'I did,' a gentle voice said from the doorway, and Arla couldn't believe it as Rheia entered the dark room, the glow of torches beyond the doorway illuminating her figure as she carried a basin and linen.

The twins looked at her with a respect she didn't deserve,

and Arla couldn't form words to begin to question what was happening.

'Hark, is he—?'

'Unharmed. He asked for you to be well tended. We figured you would be more comfortable in this.' Rheia gestured to the midnight-blue fabric barely covering Arla, and her heart squeezed at the notion.

'I need to see him,' she said, gingerly attempting to swing her legs over the edge of the bed and stand. The action sent the twins into a flurry of panic as they both attempted to assist her.

Arla knew she should be resting. She could feel the strain on her body as she asked her legs to hold her for the first time in ... how long? The twins clearly thought the same, not bothering to hide the tight smiles they exchanged when Arla finally let them support a fraction of her weight. Was she so feared that nobody dared question her, even when she put the health and healing of her body in jeopardy?

'I need my clothes,' she ground out between clenched teeth, acclimatising to the strange feeling in her body and the alteration of balance required to accommodate the stitches she could feel pulling at her side.

'Ah,' Lilith began.

Oh gods, what now?

'They, regrettably, were quite ruined by the time you arrived here.' Why did her stomach ache at that? It was only a uniform.

Hadalyn's uniform. King's Assassin. Unique only to her.

'The blood, and the rips, and—'

'It's fine, Lilith,' Arla interrupted, trying to keep the bite from her voice as she pried herself from the maids' arms whilst they fussed about the room finding her a cardigan and dark leggings that were so soft and warm that she felt sleep press into the edges of her consciousness again. Had it not been for the gnawing need to find Hark and have him explain what had happened and where they were, she might have succumbed to the darkness where there was comforting emptiness.

Rheia combed through Arla's hair, gently teasing the knots from the mane of curls so they lay around her shoulders like a golden cape. Arla didn't know how the maid was managing to get a comb through what she imagined had been a matted, bloody mess, but her hair *smelt* clean, so she imagined that somebody had taken the trouble to wash it.

In fact, everything in this starlit room was clean and lovely. What she had thought was the open night sky was in fact panes of glass supported by thick, pale stone pillars and beautiful wooden beams. She'd never seen architecture like it. Such an incredible marriage of stone, wood, and glass. She felt free, and safe, and at peace in such a beautiful room that she was reluctant to leave it when Rheia combed the last knot from her head.

Straightening her weary body and wrapping the cardigan around her so that it nestled against her jaw, Arla breathed deeply, taking in the new smells of ... wherever they were.

'He won't mind if you wish to rest a little longer,' Rheia said softly, standing by her twin's side so that Arla could only tell them apart by the scar on Lilith's face.

Lilith held out a hand to Arla, a golden brooch in her palm.

Arla swallowed the tears threatening her as she accepted the dragonhart gently.

'I can rest when I'm dead.'

CHAPTER 50

The stitches in her side pulled tight as Arla took halting, unsteady steps behind Rheia, Lilith hovering behind like an overbearing mother. The maid led her from the beautiful, starry room in which she had woken, out into the hallway of pale stone and softly glowing torches. Their progress was slow and not helped by Arla's insistence that she would walk unaided, but she used the time to soak in the atmosphere. It was airy, with gently waving gossamer-thin, lilac-coloured curtains, the scent of vanilla and spices lingering on a light breeze that stroked the curls of her hair.

She tried to take it all in, tried to focus on the beauty of the place, but there was something missing, some integral part of her that felt out of balance. Arla reached for the bond between her and her dragon, urging her mind to latch on to that thread between them.

The answering call sent her to her knees.

'There you are,' came a familiar voice inside her head. *'I was*

wondering when you might decide I was important enough to acknowledge.'

Rheia and Lilith were speaking to her, she thought, the twins trying to lift her from the ground as if she might disappear into it.

She didn't care. There was only the bond and her dragon on the other side of it.

'You are important. I didn't think I'd ever see you again—' Arla didn't know if the dragon could hear her spoken thought, but that concern floated away as Thara's reply rumbled down the bond.

'I'm glad to see a brush with death hasn't stoppered your emotions. Perhaps two swords to the side might help you to control yourself next time?'

Laughter spilt over Arla's lips, mixing with the tears leaking from the corners of her eyes. She didn't know how much it had meant to her, this *thing* she shared with Thara. How deep that bond had managed to run in such a short period of time.

'Are you safe? Where are we? What about Hark? Is—?'

'Later, Dragonhart,' Thara said down the bond. *'Everything will be explained later. For now, get off the floor before you make the two of us look weak.'*

Arla smiled again, blinking rapidly as she became aware of the panicked expressions on the maids' faces. She allowed them to help her to her feet then, the creases between their brows deepening as she insisted she was fine. She had no idea how her being reduced to a weeping mess on the floor affected anyone's perception of the dragon, but she squared her soldiers and tried to make herself look a little less like she was about to collapse. Thara was right in that respect; Arla didn't want to look weak.

Rheia led her through another hallway, the glow of the stars a constant and steadying companion as Arla felt everything she knew slipping away from her and ... didn't care. She was so lost in the shock and bewilderment of it all that she almost didn't see the people now moving through these hallways, crossing between wooden doors buried in the stonework and ... and they were all looking at her.

That was Jaz, she thought, who had paused halfway through the door to turn back to face her, and there were others she had passed whom she now knew stood still behind her, undoubtedly staring at the utter state she was.

And then, ahead of her, standing with her back pressed against the wall, was Kase – silver hair braided tightly over her shoulder, blue eyes unblinking through the parted fringe framing her face.

A fist curled in Arla's stomach and a wave of heat spread through her at the sight of Hark's right-hand crewmate. Arla registered an irritating lack of energy inside her body, and the thought of going head-to-head with the silver-haired battleaxe exhausted the thin sliver of energy there was.

But ... Kase didn't curl her lips into the telltale sign that she was about to launch an attack on Arla. Instead, gods, she ... what *was* she doing?

Kase lifted her fist with a firmness Arla didn't know how to interpret and crossed it over her body to lay it on her heart. She tilted her head at Arla, a mark of respect she was sure she didn't deserve. What had happened to bring this about? If something had happened to Hark—

Arla turned, her side complaining at the sudden movement as she witnessed the rest of the hall mirroring Kase's gesture. Fists crossed over hearts and eyes dipped as Arla's gaze roved over faces unfamiliar to her. This was... What in the gods' names was going on?

But Hark couldn't be dead. Thara would have said something—

'Enough!' Thara's message came clearly now, and Arla was almost certain she heard roaring on the outside of this magnificent building. *'You will not fall to panic now. Your patience is a fickle thing. Wait, and all will become clear.'*

A strong hand rested gently on her elbow, demanding she turn to identify its owner, and when she did she saw silver hair and blue eyes blinking back at her.

'I'll take her, Rheia. I imagine there are a few questions it's best I answer while Hark is ... busy.'

Kase slowly led her to a circular room, the roof and walls a picture of night and starlight as the glass let the sky pour in. A fire burned beneath a mantel of wood and stone, and Arla sighed in relief as the heat embraced her. Kase helped her to a couch of white fabric and a mountain of cushions and blankets. Arla winced as she lowered herself onto it.

'Are you in pain? I can call for a healer?' She did not recognise the delicate, twinkly voice that belonged to Kase, but now she was speaking to her, Arla's eyes prickled unwelcomingly.

'I'll send for one now—'

'No, Kase, it's fine. I'm fine,' Arla said, her mind scrambling to make sense of Kase's new kindness.

'You are not fine. Must I coddle you like an infant? Tell the girl to send for the healer. I won't see you injured for longer than necessary. You humans are far too breakable.' Thara's voice held the command only a creature of the gods could possess.

Not that it made Arla want to heed her advice.

'Would that be a concern? I think you're getting soft since you left Castle Grey.'

A huff washed through the bond but the dragon didn't object.

'Tea, then?' Kase spoke, pulling Arla's attention back to her and the curious worry in Kase's eyes.

'Tea would be good,' Arla said softly, the weariness setting in quickly in this warm, comfortable room. How had her body become this useless? She'd been training for years and had been so sure that her body would never fail her in its strength or reliability. Now she was out of breath and wanted to sleep after a short shuffle down a hallway.

'Hark will be annoyed you're awake, you know,' Kase said as she stood by a cabinet close to the fire and poured tea into two cups.

'He's here?'

'He was. He's out dealing with something right now and assumed you would still be asleep, but I see that you're not one for resting.' Kase handed Arla the tea with such carefulness she might have believed herself about to fall apart.

'Where are we?'

'I'll leave that for Hark to explain, but you're safe. We're past the northern border. No one can reach us here.'

Beyond the northern border was *nothing*. It was mountains blanketed in mists too dense to navigate, and any time a soul had been brave enough to risk the journey beyond that icy, miserable border, they'd returned a shell of their former self, or not returned at all.

But Kase had no reason to lie about that, so until Hark returned from whatever it was he was *dealing with,* she would have to accept the vagueness of it all.

'It's beautiful,' she said, mustering the energy to sip from the cup. The second the liquid touched her lips she sighed, the sweet, earthiness of it washing over her senses with something so comforting and reminiscent of home that she found herself fighting a knot in her throat. What was *wrong* with her?

'It is.' Kase paused before continuing. 'Arla, when Hark arrived with you and ... and the dragon I ... I didn't have the words. I didn't expect him back here for a long while and the dragon ... I was surprised Hark brought you here.'

Arla didn't know if that was a good or bad thing, but when she looked at Kase, sitting opposite her on a couch identical to the one on which she lounged, she did not see accusation or dislike in her eyes.

'What happened?'

'I ... I've never seen anything like it. And I don't think I ever will again in this lifetime,' Kase began, a seriousness weighing heavily in her voice and her eyes, so much so that Arla found herself tensing, as if her body listened to that tone and expected danger or the need to defend herself. Thara grumbled in her head.

'You both arrived with the dragon, and I thought we were being attacked. I thought Kastonia had pulled off some fucked-up scheme and had sent the dragons to slaughter us. But that's not—' Kase's eyes refocused, snagging away from where they had settled on the flames of the fireplace and moving to look at Arla.

'It *has a name*,' Thara growled. Arla bit her lip to hide the grin that tried to spread across her face.

'It landed outside and before we knew what was happening, let alone launch a defence, Hark was dismounting with you in his arms and... Oh, Arla, I've never seen so much blood.'

'*Tell the silver girl I'll burn her bones to ash if—*'

'*Perhaps stop listening in on private conversations,*' Arla teased back down the bond.

'*Never.*'

Silver lined the bottom of Kase's eyes, and it unnerved Arla to see her so rattled.

'You lost so much blood. *So much.* And Hark was hysterical. He couldn't speak or do anything but barrel through all of us, screaming for a healer.' Something cold gripped Arla's heart, a sickening, horrid feeling in response to what Kase was telling her.

Had she come *that* close?

'*More than you know.*'

A shiver trailed down Arla's spine.

'The healer came, and she worked on you for a while. She stitched the wound in your side and then she said you needed to rest and that you weren't to be disturbed. That was five days ago, which is the last time any of us saw you – save for Rheia and Lilith. Hark carried you to your room and spent the day pacing and swearing at all of us. Arla—'

She started at the direct use of her name.

'I have *never* seen him like that. He went somewhere else, and no matter how many hours I spent talking to him, I couldn't get through to him. He visited you, I think, but then he left this afternoon and said he would return later. He said you weren't to leave your room, actually.'

Arla stared. And sipped her tea. And stared again at Kase. Hark cared, then. More than she thought he ever would. Her heart swelled with warmth and with the realisation that she hadn't imagined it – that there was something raw and burning between them. She'd felt it – gods, she'd felt it too much at times, no matter that she'd tried to deny it. But for Hark... She could never have dreamed he felt the same way. There were no words for the sort of feeling that bloomed in her chest, and yet if it could be bottled she was certain to get drunk on it.

Because in the past month she had come to care for him more than she ever should have, and maybe, without her knowing, it had even begun before that. She'd found him a constant, steadying partner, and the longer they'd worked together, the more she'd found herself longing for him to look at her. For him to laugh at whatever wicked thing would come out of her mouth next. For his hand to brush hers. For him to be there. Constantly. Forever.

She didn't know what it was supposed to feel like, that sacred, burning thing she had always been too scared to admit to wanting, but she thought it must feel something like this.

'*Your human heart feels too much. Stop it.*' And yet there was nothing mocking in her dragon's voice.

Kase cleared her throat, and when Arla was sure she could look at her without crying, she held Kase's gaze.

The woman swallowed. 'What?'

'Why the ... gesture in the hallway? Why have you suddenly decided I'm worthy of your kindness?' She might be sore and weak, but she wasn't a coward. A flicker of the assassin shone through in the bite of her words. The flash of shame flickering in Kase's eyes confirmed to her that she'd not imagined the animosity between them.

'You know what it means, for a dragon to serve you, do you not?' The air seemed to halt, as though the entire world held its breath. The bond suddenly felt too taut between her and Thara, as if the dragon daren't breathe for what came next.

'I asked them for help. They answered.'

Kase scoffed as if she couldn't believe what Arla was saying. As if she was being entirely stupid. 'Arla, you're the last dragonhart.'

Well, yes, she'd gathered that back in the tunnels beneath Castle Grey when Abredus had told her of the prophecy. She hadn't had much time to unpick what that all meant. She certainly didn't know how she'd managed to unite the kingdoms and was deserving of Kase's admiration. All she'd done was take on a king and almost die.

'I haven't united anything.'

'You helped free the slaves, and all those who have magic running in their blood have flocked here. Elrod can't touch them anymore. Is that not enough to unite kingdoms, Arla? If the gods are willing, the kingdoms should start to flourish again,' Kase challenged, crossing one leg over the other as she drank deeply from her own tea.

Arla remembered that Abredus had told her that the gods were angry with what was happening to the magic-wielders, that to spill their blood to use it for yourself would upset the balance of magic, and that was why the gods had punished the kingdoms. Maybe now that they had stopped Elrod's cruelty, those who carried magic were safe and everything would be okay.

She hoped so. She wished Halos and her children could find safe passage to this stronghold over the norther border. She hated to think of them trapped in the town if Hadalyn began to fall in the same way Kastonia had.

'So you're being nice to me now because I'm gods-blessed? Classy, Kase.'

Why was she like this?

Arla watched hurt shoot across the girl's face and Arla

immediately regretted her comment. She only had the one friend and she didn't know how Halos put up with her.

Kase squinted slightly, and Arla could see the internal battle taking place in the girl's mind about how much she dared say to Arla. How much she dared challenge a dragonhart. Arla hoped she wouldn't hold back.

'I won't pretend I wouldn't love to go up against you in battle, *Reinhart*,' she said finally, 'but I'll have you know that my opinion of you changed when you woke up after Hark had been taken and you decided to gallop back to Hadalyn with a concussion in order to save him. I was on your team then; don't make me regret it now.'

How odd that Arla respected the girl now more than she ever had before. Perhaps it was the brutal honesty that had not dimmed just because Arla now commanded dragons.

'What happens now?' Arla asked, an overwhelming flood of emotion now battering her because ... she hadn't felt like this in so long. She'd fought with everything she had to become King's Assassin, to feel like she belonged somewhere and that she had a purpose in life.

Now ... now she had effectively declared a war on Kastonia. She couldn't return to Hadalyn for fear that Kastonia would use that as an excuse to invade, so she was ... she was lost. Lost and drifting with nowhere to go.

'Now we move on,' Kase said, leaning forwards and reaching a hand out to rest on Arla's knee at the sight of a tear escaping her eye. That one tear was the crack in a dam that had been too close to bursting for too long, and suddenly she was sobbing.

Heavy, salty tears splashed on her hands, and her shoulders shook. She was broken, and lost, and worthless. She *knew* nothing and she *had* nothing.

'*Never.*'

'Why are you crying?' Kase asked gently, pulling herself off the couch to crouch by Arla's hunched figure.

'Because I'm lost, and I have nowhere to go.' Arla wept, the vastness of her situation crashing down on her.

And then there was a voice in the doorway, a low, soft voice that sent her heart pounding and drowned out the rest of the world.

'You have me.'

CHAPTER 51

Arla knew she would regret the suddenness of her movement as she launched herself off the couch and crossed the room to where Hark Stappen stood. She didn't think at all as she hurled herself at him, not caring if his arms opened to catch her or not, because *he was here*.

She couldn't hide the noise that squeaked out of her as he pulled her tightly against him, burying his head in her hair.

'You're okay,' she sobbed into his chest, gripping the front of his shirt in her fists.

'I'm here,' he murmured softly so that only she could hear it, and just the sound of his voice made her weep harder.

He held her through it all, unyielding as she poured years' worth of hurt into him. Never again would she let herself deny what she felt for him. Never again would she allow them to be apart.

'I've got you. It's okay.' So softly, so unlike them. How had she survived without him before?

He pushed lightly on her shoulders, creating a gap between

them so she could see his face: the strong curve of his jaw; the dimple he only ever blessed others with, never her, but there it was, peaking from the corner of his cheek; the soft sweep of his hair, tousled and bouncy on his forehead; and his eyes, a different blue today. Not the icy coolness of his father's, but lighter, warmer than they usually were. And he was looking at her.

'Hark—'

'Don't you ever do that again,' he interrupted, his voice desperate and pained as he held her by the shoulders, fixing their gazes and sending bolts of electricity through her.

'What?' she whispered. Words were not coming easily, which was rare for Arla – talking was a trademark of her personality. She shifted her weight, wincing at the pull of the stitches in her side and their protest at her insistence on moving.

Concern marred Hark's face, and he turned her gently by the shoulders, his hands burning hot embers through the wool of the cardigan.

'Sit. You're still weak,' he said softly, throwing a glance at Kase who swiftly moved to the tea cabinet and began pouring fresh cups for each of them.

'Weak indeed. Tell the boy to get his hands off you—'

'Jealous?'

Thara growled. *'You were far more tolerable when you were asleep.'*

Hark was fussing again, moving cushions for her as though she were a second away from breaking.

'I'm fine,' Arla protested, unused to being so cared for.

'I know. But you— Arla, you nearly *died*.' There it was again. Her name. On his lips. The second time in her life he had ever used it. Did it take a sword to the side to earn your own name?

'Well, if I was going to die, at least it was riding a dragon.' She chuckled through her tears and Hark looked at her like she was insane – she probably was, because it really wasn't the right time to find humour in something that could have so easily gone the other way. Thara's own amusement flowed down the bond.

His hands found her cheeks and she had to resist the urge to reach for a non-existent blade at her waist at the sudden, unexpected contact. She was glad, at least, that her reflexes hadn't fled her along with her energy and her ability to stand without gasping for breath.

'Do you know how fucked up that was? Damn, Arla.' He ran a hand through his hair, a gesture so familiar and heart-wrenching that Arla had to swallow the tears climbing in her throat. 'You were dying. You were dying and you jumped off the castle onto a bloody dragon with your fucking eyes closed! Do you know how that felt?' He was ... borderline hysterical, actually, and she knew she was looking at him with wide eyes.

'Yes,' she said softly, watching as he opened his lips to question her. 'I know how it feels to lose someone. And I know how it feels to believe that you'll never see someone again. I went into Larkire knowing I probably wouldn't walk out alive. But as long as you got out and I knew you were safe, I was okay with dying. I told Thara to save you, not me.'

'A fool's request,' Thara huffed. *'And yet for you, Dragonhart, I would have saved the boy.'*

Her heart ached at the dragon's words and the promise that went against the oath she had sworn to Arla.

'Never do that again,' Hark demanded.

Was he angry that she had saved him if the price was her life? She didn't know. But she knew that had it been the other way around, she would have sooner died than go back to a life without him at her side. There had been too many nights during which she'd wished it had been her that had been killed rather than her parents. Nights during which she knew it would have been easier for her to die because it would mean she wouldn't have to live with the pain of being without them. Was that what Hark had experienced in that moment? Had he wondered how he was going to continue without her?

She wasn't brave enough to ask.

'Is it done now? Are all of the magic-wielders safe? Are there any that we couldn't rescue?' Arla asked, letting her eyes drift around the room and up to the stars witnessing the reunion.

Hark smiled softly. 'Elrod can't touch them anymore. Anybody known to have magic is safe and out of Kastonia. It's done.'

'Where are we – exactly, I mean?' she asked, not knowing if they would trust her enough to answer. And for a moment she didn't think they would. Hark eyed Kase, her mouth a thin line against her pale face. But then her chin dipped slightly in a movement Arla might not have clocked had she not been used to studying people and anticipating their movements.

Hark inhaled deeply, as though preparing himself for something difficult, something he knew he couldn't take back once he'd voiced it into the world.

'Welcome to Claret Hall, Dragonhart.'

'I think you ought to begin explaining, Hark.' Her voice was stronger than she'd expected, some of the fire within her trying breaking through.

'I think it might be easier if I show you,' he replied, smiling as he offered her his hand.

She took it, again surprised at his warmth as he helped her

stand. Her breath immediately became strained, and the ache and exhaustion of her body had her steadying herself against the couch.

'On second thoughts, I'm taking you back to bed,' he said.

Not a chance in hell!

Her hand was free of his grip and around his throat in a second, daring him to continue with what she knew he was about to do.

'*So violent, Dragonhart,*' Thara purred in her head.

'If you even *think* of manhandling me, Stappen, you will very quickly find out how thoroughly uninjured I can make myself,' she said in a lethally soft voice, channelling the pain and exhaustion as she dug her nails into the soft flesh of his throat. She ignored the wave of encouragement Thara sent her way through the bond and watched his eyes flicker with some-thing ... before amusement danced back at her.

'Understood,' he said, eyes twinkling.

'Gods spare me,' Kase muttered, tossing her braid over her shoulder, and swallowing the remainder of her tea.

'You can hardly stand, Arla,' Hark said. 'Walking the distance to what I want to show you is likely to take you all night.'

'Good job I'm not in a rush, then,' she replied sweetly, sticking her tongue out at him before pulling the cardigan tightly around her shoulders.

～

She'd be damned if she ever admitted that Hark was right and that, yes, it would have been quicker for her to be carried. Or that, yes, now she was walking she wished instead to be in that comfortable bed in that beautiful room and explanations could wait.

But she'd said she was going to walk and not even the gods could stop her from shuffling alongside him. She knew he knew she was regretting it, but surprisingly, he kept his undoubtedly irritating comments to himself, instead opting to hover too closely by her side, his arm never far away should she stumble.

She didn't.

Kase trailed behind them with silent feet that Arla appreciated with an expert ear. Perhaps one day she could go head-to-head with the girl and Arla might finally have someone skilled to practise against.

'Go, Kase. You've been here long enough,' Hark said lightly, not looking back at his friend as he dismissed her.

Arla had been expecting it, and she didn't know how she felt at being left alone with him – glad, yes, because she was fed up with feeling smothered and was too tired to keep up a pretence of feeling better than she did. But there was a part of her that was flapping wildly in her stomach at the idea of them being alone. It was ... different now. All of it. They'd gone from outright dislike to this understanding that they couldn't bear to be apart. Where did it leave them?

'*Where are you?*' she asked her dragon, a pathetic excuse to try and avoid what was coming next. She'd been so eager to know everything, and now, well, now she felt a foreign nervousness she couldn't unpick.

Thara's reply was instant. '*Close by.*'

'Kase,' Hark reiterated at the girl's silence. Arla could almost feel Kase's reluctance at leaving them together, as if she didn't trust Arla – or perhaps Hark.

'I won't be far if you need me,' Kase said eventually, her

sparkling voice so timid and gentle in the silence of these perfect, cinnamon-scented hallways. Arla listened as the girl's feet sounded in the opposite direction, and she took a deep breath as the world settled around the King's Assassin and the Ambassador-Prince of Kastonia.

'She feels responsible, I think. She hasn't left the hall in days. Jack's been out of his mind pining for her,' Hark chuckled, though Arla could hear the guilt in his voice.

'Why?'

'Because it wasn't her that came to Kastonia—'

'Hark, it's not her f—'

'I know,' he interrupted, raising a hand to silence her. 'I never wished for Kase – or any of my friends – to come after me. To be honest, I couldn't quite believe it when *you* did. But Kase regrets that it was you who almost died for me. She'd rather it had been her.'

'What, so she could brag that she took a sword in the side for you? That she's perfect, and loyal, and—'

'Kase doesn't think that about herself,' Hark said suddenly, his voice too serious for Arla's liking and she immediately felt ashamed at her words. 'She sees you, Arla, and she respects you. You are the last dragonhart, you are the King's Assassin, and you have become ... you have become a part of us. She wishes it wasn't you for more respectable reasons than you give her credit for.'

'Tell the boy he speaks to one chosen by the gods and his disrespect will not be tolerated—'

'I've got it, Thara.'

Arla chewed on her lip, resisting the urge to argue with him. To fire back with something wholly unnecessary just to make herself feel better about what she'd said. But she didn't. She walked gingerly at his side, each step on a floor carpeted in the same creams and whites she'd seen elsewhere ... until she was hit with another wave of exhaustion and dizziness.

But before she could become too weary and reluctant to walk even one more step, Hark led her to a set of glass doors at the end of a hallway. Beyond it, through the glass framed by wood and stone, were stars, stars, and stars. A vast expanse of midnight and beauty. The freedom of it took her breath from her.

'It's beautiful,' she said, pausing as Hark rested his hands on the curved silver handles of the doors.

'Oh, it's about to get spectacular, sweetheart,' he murmured, smiling softly at her. Her heart fluttered at the sweep of his mouth, the tease of a dimple flirting with her. Their eyes locked, a thousand thoughts passing between them.

She was swallowed in an embrace of cold air, the shock of it drawing a gasp from her as the doors swung open and Hark stepped outside.

He was smiling at her, his hand outstretched and encouraging. She blinked, adjusting to the sudden chill, and placed one foot outside Claret Hall.

There was an utter stillness to the world beyond the doors. Everything had become cold, perfect, and quiet. She took Hark's hand in hers – still an unfamiliar sensation but one she was beginning to enjoy.

'I won't bite,' he said softly, beckoning her closer.

One step. And then another. And then another until she was in front of him.

A balcony stood proudly behind him, a tall, stone-columned structure that she desperately wanted to see beyond. But his gaze had captured her, and she didn't care what was beyond it at this moment.

'You asked me where we were. I hope this provides an explanation I cannot do justice by putting it into words,' he whispered.

And then he was leading her to the balcony and the world beyond it.

Her knees became weak, and a tiny sound squeaked from her at the sight of what had been forged in this tiny corner of the world.

For the stars appeared to have fallen from the sky, and hundreds upon hundreds of twinkling, perfect lights shone in the valley beyond Claret Hall. A whole kingdom of light, colours even in the dark cover of night blinked up at her, an entire kingdom of faraway music and ringing laughter that reached her even at this height.

A whole kingdom lay in a valley peppered with pine trees and bordered by snowcapped mountains – a steadfast protector against any intruder. Hundreds and hundreds of stone buildings and houses decorated the valley, smoke curling from the tops of them and lights shining proudly in the windows.

'Welcome to Flambriar.'

A great, winding river ran through it all, a snaking blot of midnight water to give life to a vibrant, magnificent kingdom. Half a dozen stone bridges arched over the water at regular intervals, twining the two sides of the valley together in a crescendo of life.

And then there were fireworks.

Huge, brilliant explosions of colour and sound, and she could hear the laughter of children even from so far above the valley.

She looked up at Claret Hall, a striking, magnificent edifice of glass, wood, and stone that clung to the side of a mountain overlooking the kingdom. Balconies jutted out above and below them, an acknowledgment of the sheer size of the building they stood in – a palace, rather than a hall.

'Why are you crying?' Hark asked gently. She hadn't been aware the tears had spilled but, sure enough, they were carving silent tracks down her cheeks, cool in the chill of winter air surrounding her.

'Because it's perfect.'

CHAPTER 52

'Walk with me,' Hark said, offering an arm for her to lean on. She didn't hesitate. He had seen her at her most vulnerable – in more ways than one – so there was no point trying to disguise the fact it was painful to move.

He kept the pace slow and provided a warmth against the chill of the air as he led her along the balcony. It seemed to work its way around the entire perimeter of the building, a connection to every chamber of this level of Claret Hall. It wasn't long before the brilliance of the kingdom faded and left them in soft torchlight along the balcony, the darkness a shroud of quiet and privacy. Arla tried not to notice how perfectly her arm fit in Hark's and how her body was the ideal height for her head to rest on his shoulder if she dared.

She wanted it all, she thought, but to admit it was to admit that she didn't know how to do this. She hadn't loved, or cared for, or been another half of a person before. Was her heart too wicked to be worthy of him?

'What are you thinking?' Hark asked her, drawing her attention away from the spiralling thoughts and into the stillness of the world around them.

'I'm wondering why— How Rheia and Lilith are here?' Not a complete lie – she had thought of it briefly when Kase was explaining to her that they were no longer in Kastonia, but she wasn't ready to voice her internal battles with him yet.

Hark chuckled – a lovely, brilliant sound. 'The twins were my maids, too, you know. They're loyal to those who show them kindness. It doesn't take much to understand that my father was the exact opposite of that to them.' Arla nodded her head slightly, imagining how the twins had been treated by Elrod. She'd seen the way he treated Arabelle, and her heart hurt at the realisation that they'd left her at his mercy in that castle. She wondered if that thought hurt Hark, too.

'And besides, it wouldn't take him long to realise they aren't like the rest of the staff inside Larkire.'

Arla turned her head sharply to face him, halting them where they stood.

'Magic?' she asked, disbelief working its way into her voice.

Hark nodded, a grin widening across his face. 'You don't think just anyone could tame all that hair of yours, do you?' He winked at her, and before she knew what she was doing she was elbowing him, bursting into a laugh when he didn't so much as move an inch.

'They came here with you to be safe?'

'Everyone here is here for that reason. All they've wanted for years is safety away from my father. It was hard work but between us we managed to get them out.'

'Explain it to me,' she said, reaching for his arm. She'd seen him slip away from Hadalyn for days at a time under the excuse of meeting with his king but ... it was all making sense now. Why he always returned looking so weary he could barely sit through dinner. Why he always disappeared into his rooms for days after he came back. She'd suspected he was meeting with a secret lover and had taunted him endlessly at Castle Grey whenever he returned looking so weary. Now it all made sense... 'How did you manage all of this?'

He was silent for a moment, his gaze roaming over the kingdom he had created below them. 'I'd never have done it on my own,' he said eventually, dragging a hand through his hair. 'But four years ago, when my father came up with his hare-brained scheme to steal magic, I knew I couldn't support what he was doing and I knew I had to find a way to keep the magics safe, even if it meant building somewhere new – somewhere hidden. I already knew Seb and Jaz from when we were younger, and Kase, too, for nearly a year by then – Jack, too. We became a crew, and between court meetings and the outings to Hadalyn we managed to start helping some of the magics flee beyond the mountains. After that we took it in turns, each of us spending days at a time helping build this kingdom.'

She could see the anger bridling the angles of his face and saw the promise in his eyes that he would kill his father if Arla didn't get there first.

'My father knew I hated what he was doing. The only thing that stopped me from killing him was the fact that the magics were safe in Flambriar and he knew nothing about it. He sent me to Hadalyn not long afterwards. I confronted him about taking their blood. I told him it was an affront to the gods to try and seek their magic.'

She couldn't believe he'd managed it. Perhaps she would have to thank Orson, the traitorous bastard, for not revealing that Hark had never returned to Kastonia during those trips he'd claimed to be travelling home to brief the king. She bit back a smile at the memory of the night she'd caught him fleeing and wondered if he'd been on his way to Flambriar then.

'But how did you build all of this? I thought nothing existed beyond the border. Anyone who's ever ventured this far north has never returned. The rest of the world believes it's desolate — a frozen wasteland.'

A soft smile parted Hark's lips. 'That's what I hope they'll continue to believe.' He dragged a hand through his hair. 'There were rumours of a town here long ago, before the dragons went to sleep. The magic-wielders whispered about it, though they kept it a secret for a long time before they had the courage to share it with me. We needed somewhere to hide them — somewhere they'd be safe so we took the risk and brought them here. There were a few half-collapsed buildings sagging beneath the weight of the snow and it was all but a forgotten place. I thought it was too much in the beginning, that it would be too hard to build anything so far away from the rest of civilisation, but the wielders felt a draw to this place; something magic, they said. And so we stayed. Stone by stone we built it together, day by day, year by year.'

'You have incredible friends,' she said, meaning every word. But his face was marred with a sort of ... sadness, and she hated to see it.

'They're more than I deserve,' he admitted, staring over her shoulder as if the world beyond it would swallow him and make him a better person. 'And they kept this going after I came to Hadalyn. And Jack... Gods, there isn't anything I could ever do to make up for what happened...'

'Could the healers fix him?' She had no knowledge of the

magic the healers bore – or any magic, actually. How she regretted her refusal to listen to the teachings and whatever stubbornness kept her from reading about it when she was older.

'The magics control *things*. They can manipulate objects and living things – this building and the materials it's made of, were created by magics manipulating wood, stone, and glass. The body is not so different. The healers manipulate what is already there. I should think they could help him in some way.'

Arla couldn't imagine the effects that magic had on the human body, though she thought now that she'd felt the fingers of it when she'd spoken to the strange woman at the festival in Vorstrum. It had made her feel vulnerable and out of her mind. She didn't know how Jack bore that every day, but it wasn't Hark's fault.

'Are Kase and Jack...?'

Hark smiled softly, a warmth filling his eyes. 'Who knows?'

She smiled back. If that was yet to be revealed, then so be it. She wished them a lifetime of happiness. It was more than she deserved.

'Will you stay?' he asked her, with hope shining in his eyes.

Her heart pounded against her chest. She hadn't thought about what would happen if she made it out of Larkire alive. It was all too much, too fast. Hark might have planned for this but she never had. And ... was he intending to stay here? To give up the throne of Kastonia and lead this new kingdom instead?

'I don't even know what you're planning,' she said softly, and she hated the ache in her throat as she tried to blink away the tears. 'What about your throne, Hark? Just because your father is an evil bastard doesn't mean you should give up on your kingdom.'

She certainly wouldn't if she were faced with abandoning Hadalyn.

Hark looked pained, as if she'd struck him in the heart and he didn't have the ability to stop bleeding. 'I don't want Kastonia or its throne. I want Flambriar to be somewhere free of my father's iron fist. I want to help these people, to *guide* them, not rule them like he does. You might not have believed in the gods or magic before, Arla, but for those of us who've followed the old religions, the magics represent something so precious that I have to help them. I have to lead Flambriar and keep them safe. Damn Kastonia and my father with it! We can build a new world, together, a world in which it doesn't matter where you're from or whether the gods blessed you with magic. We can start a new life here.'

Her heart was thundering, her mind spinning with the revelation that Hark had been living a whole secret life whilst keeping his cover in Hadalyn. It was all so much. Too much. She didn't think she would ever recover from the shock of it.

But there was another part of her, the weak, stupid part of her heart, that longed for it. It would be beautiful, she thought, to spend the rest of her life in these mountains, in this kingdom and ... with Hark. But could she?

Had she worked so hard for so long just to abandon Hadalyn in its hour of need and live in peace here?

Thara was quiet, the bond between them suddenly feeling like a faraway thing she didn't know how to access. Perhaps it was a good thing, because this decision had to be hers and hers alone.

'I can't leave them,' she whispered, lowering her eyes to avoid what she knew would be staring back at her.

'You've done enough for your people,' Hark countered, his voice becoming harder with each syllable.

'I won't leave them to fend for themselves. Do you know how long my people suffered after Kastonia swarmed my kingdom? I can't, Hark. Not when Elrod is still on the throne. He'll find a way to blame Cyrus for what *I* did and he'll wage war.'

Hark looked at her, his eyes steely when she met his gaze.

'It's not up to you to keep fighting. Let Kastonia come for you; they won't risk touching Hadalyn, not when they've seen you fly away on a fucking *dragon*.'

Thara growled low and long through the bond.

It was all so tempting. All of it. To live here. To forget. To never drag a knife across a thief's throat on the orders of a king. To never push herself to the point of passing out again.

'I need them to be safe.'

'They will be,' he urged, reaching for her hand. She didn't know why she let him take it. Perhaps she was becoming weaker the longer she stood on this balcony lit by stars and soft torches.

'Arla, Hadalyn is safe. The magic-wielders are safe. *You* are safe here.'

Something in her was shifting, and it scared her beyond anything she'd ever experienced before. Something hot and burning, and something she wanted for herself.

'Halos gets to come here – and her children,' she stated, her voice shaking as she lifted her chin and made her demand. Something flashed in Hark's eyes – the pleasure of being challenged, perhaps – but she saw the fight leave just as quickly as it had come.

'If Halos wishes to leave Hadalyn, she'll be more than welcome in Flambriar.'

A promise. A home. Perhaps, if she could force herself to let go.

A whinny sounded in the night and her legs threatened to buckle at the noise. *Vetta.*

'Where?' she choked out and Hark was already leading her by her shoulders to the far side of the balcony. From here she could see Vetta and Eros looking up at her from stalls in a courtyard delicately lit with tiny white lights. Vetta whickered again.

'She's safe,' Arla said on a sob, pressing her hands against the stone of the balcony to steady herself. She hadn't known emotion like this, and it felt like it had been battering her since she'd awoken.

'*I do hope I'm worthy of the same reaction, Dragonhart.*'

'I hear from Jack that your horse has been rather unruly since you've been parted. I didn't fail to mention that her disposition obviously matches yours.' Hark smiled, a blinding, lovely smile that had Arla spilling into her own grin.

'Ow, stop, it hurts,' she said, clutching her side. She didn't mind. When was the last time she'd laughed like this, so freely?

'Stay,' he said, his face softening into something pleading and solemn. Her laughter ceased immediately, and she felt her heart splintering because she didn't know what to do.

'Hark, they need me—'

'*We* need you, Arla. *I*—' He ran a hand through his hair. '*I* need you. Gods, I can't hope to lead this kingdom on my own.'

Gods.

Hark. Ruling Flambriar.

She'd never known he was the heir to the Kastonian throne, let alone a secret kingdom he'd kept hidden from the world. She'd believed him to be an ambassador. Just an ambassador. But, oh gods, she couldn't understand it. Hark! A king! She'd have laughed if someone had suggested it before they set out on this journey. She couldn't settle her thundering heart.

'I am no queen, Hark.'

'I'm not asking you to be one,' he countered. 'But I've seen you sit in court, I've seen you organise soldiers, I've seen you become a queen in your own right and if anybody can hope to lead Flambriar, to keep them safe, it's not me. Not without you.'

'You seemed to manage just fine until now,' she whispered, not sure she was really hearing him right.

'Arla, I'm twenty-two. It's taken everything I have to build this place. I'm exhausted. I've spent four years trying to do this, keeping it secret, working in the shadows and I cannot do it on my own anymore. So please, *stay*.'

Oh gods, she was going to break if he kept talking like this.

'If I stay,' she began, her voice trembling and tripping over every word. '*If* I stay,' she continued, 'I need your word that if anything happens to Hadalyn, we create an army and we go to their aid—'

'Done.' *Oh gods.*

'If your father makes a move against the ... *magics* again'—it was a strange word on her tongue, but she supposed she had to get used to it—'I will burn him and his kingdom to the ground.'

'*Yesss,*' Thara hissed.

'I'll help you do it.'

He couldn't truly mean any of it, could he?

'I can't promise to lead a kingdom, but I will keep them safe,' she offered, not understanding herself what any of this promise would mean, but Hark was grinning at her, his balance switching between his feet as though he couldn't wait to declare her to his kingdom.

'And Hark—' Gods, she was going to do this. She was going

to lay her heart bare and reap the consequences for it. Gods help her. 'I can't do this anymore. I can't pretend that my heart doesn't falter when I hear your voice. And I can't pretend that I don't feel my body soften every time I catch a scent of whisky. And I can't pretend that I don't search for myself in you, that I don't look to find something good in me because it comes so easily in you. And I know you don't feel the same way, but I can't do this without you knowing. And if it's too hard I will build my own place to stay down there.' She flung an arm out in the direction of Flambriar and its occupants, not realising how heavily tears were streaming down her cheeks until those same tears landed on her cold hands. 'I can't pretend with you anymore. I can't pretend that night in Irelliad meant nothing. I can't pretend I don't long for those touches and those smirks and the moments where I think I might come undone. And if you want me to stay here, I cannot be around you. I can't drive myself insane anymore.'

Silence.

Complete, all-consuming silence.

Her chin dipped to her chest, sending a cascade of salty tears dripping onto the floor.

Okay, then.

She had laid herself bare, and still it had not been enough.

But then his hands were on her cheeks, lifting her chin gently and she was meeting blue eyes through her tears.

'You are infuriating,' he whispered softly, a caress of breath on her face. 'I have loved you from the moment you drove a knife through your palm at dinner. I watched you train every day hoping you would find an excuse to argue with me – and you did – for two years. I haven't been able to breathe when I'm around you for a long time, Arla. And when I watched you close your eyes and felt your blood beneath my fingers, I thought that if you were going, I was going with you. Because for too long I have denied myself the privilege of navigating this thing between us, and I'll be damned if you make it to the eternal gates and inhabit another world without me getting the chance to tell you: I would have followed you to the next world. And the one after that, and anything else that comes after. I will not pretend either, *Dragonhart*, because I have loved you for too long to break our hearts any longer.'

CHAPTER 53

I have loved you.

She didn't think she was breathing.

He was looking at her in ways she had never allowed herself to dissect before. And she didn't know if any of it was real because she felt like she was dreaming, but she couldn't deny the longing ache in her heart as their eyes locked.

'Please say this is real,' she whispered, her hand closing over his where it cupped her cheek.

'It's the most real I've ever been.'

Arla blinked, and as easily as breathing their lips came together in a soft, delicate brush. Her heart soared as she clung to him, two souls combining in a bridge between bodies as they came together, the stars their only witness as Arla felt her carefully constructed walls tumble around her, making way for another. A partner. Someone from whom she didn't have to hide. Someone who had seen her at her worst and had still, against all odds, come to love her.

She breathed him in as his lips moved across hers, whisky and leather and something that felt like *home*.

She smiled against his lips, and she felt him pull her closer, taking care to be gentle with her injured body. She fit against him as though they'd been made from the same mould, the two of them separated and destined to find each other. How had her belief in the fates and the gods changed so drastically in such a short amount of time?

He pulled away slowly, and gods-damn her if she didn't miss the feeling of his lips against hers already. But she didn't think she would ever get used to the way he was looking at her or to the way she *knew* she was looking at him. As if they were seeing each other for the first time and it didn't matter what colour their blood ran. It didn't matter that his father had ordered her kingdom to be slaughtered, because she had come to learn that he was more than his father's faults and failings. She wished she could take back everything she'd ever said about the people of Kastonia. They didn't all deserve to burn, not if they were like Hark Stappen.

A roar that shook the glass windows in their frames echoed across the valley. Arla's blood rushed in her ears, her heart thundering as a great winged beast flew up from beneath the balcony and soared above them, fire streaming from her open jaws to light the star-studded sky.

A squeak slipped through Arla's lips. *'Thara...'*

'I told you I was close by, Dragonheart. Did you think I had abandoned you?'

Laughter spilled from her, the movement tugging the stitches at her side and it had her leaning against Hark to stay upright.

'You know,' he murmured in her ear, 'I get the impression your dragon doesn't like me very much.'

'The boy has sense, at least.'

'I think you'll have to charm her,' Arla replied, smiling as he tucked a loose curl away from her face.

'Like I did you?' Hark purred.

'You didn't charm me, Hark,' she said softly. 'You made me want to kill you. That's even better.'

He laughed then, unbridled and free, something Arla wished he'd do more. Would vow to make it so, actually.

Thara flew closer, landing heavily on the stone balustrades of the balcony. Arla was sure the whole building rattled.

A soft rumble sounded through the bond, tugging on something in Arla's core that drew her towards her dragon, hand outstretched to rest on Thara's scaled snout.

Her dragon breathed softly, hot air wafting across Arla. Hark hovered behind her, his hand reaching for her spare one.

'Can he?' she asked Thara, wary of what her dragon would answer.

'If he must,' she said with a sigh.

Arla turned to Hark, her fingers tightening in his as she pulled him closer. She could see the wariness in his eyes, in the way they widened and his feet were slow to move.

'It's okay. She won't hurt you,' Arla said as she lifted Hark's hand, inching closer to the dragon perched on the balcony.

'That is not a promise, Dragonhart.'

'It'd better be.'

Hark tensed as his palm settled on Thara's snout, the low rumble escaping her throat sending him pulling backwards.

Arla didn't allow it.

Whether it was Arla's own confidence or the fact she would

never let him live it down, she gradually felt Hark relax beside her, their breaths settling into sync with Thara's. It was ... healing, she thought. For just a moment it was the three of them, connected in ways she could have never foreseen.

She felt Thara's impatience through the bond before the dragon could make it known and do something unforgivable, like tear Hark's hand from his arm. Arla pulled her hand away quickly, taking Hark's with her as Thara launched herself off the balcony, disappearing into the night sky and leaving the two of them alone, watching the stars.

'What happens now?' she asked, unsure of what any of it meant for her future – their future.

'We build a better world. We begin with Flambriar, and all we can do is hope the rest of the world follows.'

It was a lovely dream, and her heart pined for it.

She didn't stop herself from reaching to kiss him, and her stomach fluttered as his lips met hers again, his touch so gentle and warm where his hands brushed her skin. She could stay there forever, suspended in this starlit dream, nothing able to break—

'Fucking finally.'

Arla's head snapped up, jerking to the side to see Sebastian leaning against the wall of Claret Hall. A grin greeted her, his eyes amused and hair gleaming like his own personal halo where the torchlight illuminated him.

Arla took half a step back, her tongue leaden and her words failing her for the first time in her life.

'Don't look so embarrassed, Dragonhart. I'd be lying if *I* said I hadn't dreamed about kissing Hark Stappen, too.' Seb winked, and Arla felt her cheeks warm as she stood blinking, as though she'd been caught in something far more sinister than admitting to herself – and to Hark – that she cared. Desperately. Deeply.

'I sincerely hope you have a good reason for interrupting us, you prick,' Hark snapped, though Arla could tell the annoyance didn't reach his eyes. There was nothing but love and trust between Hark and his friend, and Arla didn't doubt Seb had been a steadying hand whilst she had lain unconscious and wounded.

'Fine, starve then,' Seb retorted, spinning on his heel and trying unsuccessfully to smother the smirk gracing his lips.

'I hope you're hungry,' Hark sighed, linking his arm through hers and holding her close.

$\sim$

They followed Sebastian into a surprisingly cosy dining room. A large but unremarkable wooden table occupied the centre of a room while a fire burned in the corner of the room, a splash of colour against the neutral palette making up the carpets and curtains. Though high-backed wooden chairs were arranged around the table, there were armchairs and settees positioned around the fire, and there was nothing to suggest this was a formal or courtly palace. The décor was simple and personal – blankets, tumblers of whisky, and half-read books with their spines cracked lay scattered throughout a room that was thoroughly *lived-in.* It was so unlike the rooms in Castle Grey and the few she'd seen at Larkire, all of them pristine and grand, and ready to entertain whichever guest would arrive through the doors next. She loved Claret Hall, and she loved this room most of all.

Her nose carried her to the spread of food on the table and

the people gathered around it. A roasted pheasant rested on a silver platter, and there were trays of potatoes and vegetables and all of it so hearty and so simple. Wine bottles littered the table, and the scent of everything combined had Arla's stomach clenching uncomfortably.

She didn't know whether the others had noticed her arrival or whether Kase and Jaz were so invested in arguing over who would carve the bird that they didn't care to greet her. She didn't mind. She had felt awkward under the gaze of so many, when the people had offered her the silent gesture of respect, and she was glad to be just Arla for a while.

'Evening, Arla,' Jack said from his seat beside Kase, raising a frail hand in welcome. She needed to thank Jack for taking such good care of Vetta. She smiled in return, beginning to pull a chair out for herself before Hark took over and removed her hands from the smooth wood.

'I'm not *dead*,' she snapped, ramming an elbow into Hark's side and shoving him out of the way. He raised his hands in defence, arching a brow at her as the rest of the room finally turned their attention to the pair of them.

'*You* might be, though, if you keep *coddling* her, Stappen,' Jaz chirped, sliding a bottle of wine across the table towards him.

Arla resisted the instinct to grab it before it could reach Hark but kept her hands where they were.

Hark uncorked it and poured a hearty glass each for himself and Arla.

'What took so long?' Jack asked, spooning golden potatoes onto his plate. Arla didn't miss the way his other hand rested on Kase's knee beneath the table. Would she ever stop noticing these things? Or was she doomed to have the keen mind of an assassin forever?

'I was showing Arla around and telling her a bit about how Flambriar came to be.' Movement at the table halted. Arla thought she could feel the room hold its breath.

'She's staying, then,' Jaz stated. Not a question, and Arla didn't miss the challenge in his voice.

'Of course she's bloody staying.' Kase's hand slammed down on the table, her eyes dark beneath her fringe. Arla tensed; she hadn't expected hostility at her arrival here.

Before she could open her mouth to – what? Defend herself? Or spit venom like she had done on countless occasions – Kase continued. 'She's a dragonhart. She's *the* dragonhart. She went into Larkire *alone* and got Hark out. You want to discuss it, Jaz, I'm sure I can schedule a portion of my evening outside—'

'Enough,' Hark growled, dangerously low so that even Arla's stomach coiled with something that felt a little like fear. 'It's Arla's choice. She has chosen for the moment to stay at Claret Hall and that's the end of the matter. She's more than capable of handling herself.'

Her heart fluttered. Had he always been so ... attractive?

'Forgive me, Dragonhart,' Jaz began, his eyes tunnelling into hers with a sincerity she didn't think she deserved. 'I have no objection. It's ... a surprise, is all.'

She didn't blame him. She had shocked herself at her decision to stay here with Hark. There were things that needed discussing, beginning with how in the gods' names Hark was planning on leading this kingdom instead of ruling the one he'd all but disowned. She supposed there was always Reuben to step into Elrod's shoes but the barrage of information she'd received tonight had made her head throb and she wasn't sure she'd properly thought anything through. 'Well, I hope it doesn't surprise you that rescuing His Highness'—she shot a pointed look at Hark—'has built up rather an appetite, and all I can think about is how long you and Kase have spent arguing over this bloody pheasant. So'—Arla leaned across the table, ignoring the tug at her stitches and swiping the carving knife before stabbing the bird with it—'I'll be more than happy to talk *after* dinner.'

Silence.

And then a chuckle escaped Jack's mouth, followed by Sebastian, and Hark before they were all laughing into their wine glasses.

～

Arla hadn't managed to eat half of what she'd thought she would. Her body had decided that she had gone for so long on so little food that to eat a second plate was beyond her, and she had collapsed into the couch by the fire not long after.

The wine tinged the edges of her mind, but she didn't care. Hark lounged next to her, his arm draping casually over the back of the couch as Arla rested against him under a thick woollen blanket.

'I'm glad you're staying, you know,' Sebastian said kindly as he perched on the arm of the couch.

'There are a lot of things to sort before I can settle here, Sebastian—'

'Kastonia's spun a story describing how you corrupted Hark and led him astray, but died in your feeble attempt to escape Larkire Palace.'

Fucking gods!

'So they've made themselves look strong by claiming to have killed the King's Assassin, and at the same time—'

'Prevented war with Hadalyn by suggesting you acted alone when you stormed the Palace. That *you* and you alone are to blame for this mess,' Sebastian explained.

Thara growled softly through the bond.

'And Cyrus?' He couldn't believe she had turned on Hadalyn. She never would.

'Has no choice but to believe you're dead. You never returned.'

Clever. So fucking clever.

'Then, I can't go back anyway, can I?' she said, sighing and leaning her head back against Hark. She didn't think she would ever get used to this.

'Not if you want to keep them safe.'

Was it so hard? To leave them? Her heart ached at it. All she had to do was leave. Now that the blood of the magics wasn't being spilled, the gods would stop punishing the mortals and the kingdoms could return to the prosperity they had once enjoyed.

All she had to do was leave them.

'I will be at your side wherever it is we are to settle.' Arla's heart swelled at Thara's promise.

'Excuse me, everyone, but you don't get to be this beautiful by going without sleep so I will be taking myself off to bed,' she said softly, carefully untangling herself from the blanket.

Hark was at her side immediately, his hand resting at the small of her back as they strolled back towards her room. From the moment she'd woken up, Arla had been mentally mapping the layout of this magnificent building, a skill she would never be without.

Something flipped in her stomach at the realisation that Hark was coming with her. It's not like they hadn't already slept together, but this was different somehow. There was too much between them. Too many years of animosity and now ... now too much of something *other* for her to treat this situation lightly. She'd taken a sword for Hark, and she would do it again.

Her bedchamber was as beautiful as it had been hours ago, the stars shining through and casting a gentle, delicate light over the space.

'Will you be all right in here?' Hark asked.

'Hark, for the gods' sakes, I've spent the night in far more disgusting places than this. I'll be fine.'

'I can't believe you're here,' he whispered as she climbed into the bed, taking care not to strain the stitches in her side more than she already had.

'Why?'

'Because I've dreamed of it for so long. From the moment I felt myself falling for you, I wanted to tell you everything. I wanted to share all of it with you. And now that you're here... Anything you want Arla'—he sat on the edge of the bed, taking her hands in his—'*anything* you want, it's yours. I would give you the stars if I could. Gods, I don't know how I found you, how I got so lucky. And the last dragonhart ... how did we manage that?'

Dragonhart...

'*What about the others? The other dragons under Castle Grey?*' The thought came to her out of nowhere – a question for Thara, though, not Hark.

'*Some still sleep, others are just waking. They watch over Hadalyn, ready to fly to your aid if needed.*'

She could feel it. In the bond. Some distant, aching thing that went beyond the connection she had with Thara. But for *all* of them to be willing to fly to her aid...

She still had no idea what being a dragonhart meant, how it connected her to the gods' creatures, and perhaps even to the gods themselves...

'We each swore an oath. Be assured, we all fly for you.'

Hark was watching her, his eyes full of something that made warmth bloom in her chest.

'Thank you, Hark,' Arla whispered, her throat clogging with tears she had sworn she would not shed. 'For everything.'

And then her lips were on his again, and again, until she didn't know how much time had passed, only that he had lain down beside her and she was melting at the feeling of his hands running through her hair as she rested her head on his chest, fighting the darkness threatening to swoop in and claim her.

She was so grateful. For him, for this life, and to still be a part of it.

Flambriar would bring her peace, and perhaps, one day, that peace would spread beyond these mountains to the rest of the kingdoms. One day the kingdoms could be unified again just like the dragons' prophecy claimed. She would think about what was expected of her as the last dragonhart tomorrow because the scale of their ambition was overwhelming.

But with a dragon at her side and Hark behind her, she would do it. For the people, for the magics, for the kingdoms.

And before sleep finally claimed her for its own, her last thought was of this. Of a better world.

Acknowledgments

I can't believe I am able to write these words, and that people want to read them. This is a dream, and one I will be forever grateful for. Seeing *Dragonhart* turn into something more than a story about a girl in my head has been the most wonderful journey and wouldn't be possible without such an incredible team behind me.

Firstly, a huge thank you to my agent Vicki, who told me we were going to hit the ground running, and wow, haven't we just? Thank you for your endless enthusiasm; I can't wait to keep knocking down these publishing doors together.

Thank you to my incredible editor, Jennie. This version of *Dragonhart* would not exist without you. The love for Arla and Hark from the very second I pitched you the book blew me away, and you have made my dreams come true. From the very bottom of my heart, thank you.

To the amazing team at One More Chapter, thank you for loving Arla as much as I do, and for transforming this story into something truly magical. Charlotte, Emma, Kara, Chloe, Grace, Lucy, Lydia and Emily, thank you so much.

Dad, thank you for buying me every book I ever wanted – and for reading them too.

Mum, for always saying 'I have a good feeling about this one,' no matter how many rejections I faced.

To Harry, who I could write a whole book for. Thank you.

Thank you to Holly and Alicia who were there when I started this dream and long before that.

Rhiannon, you're the best cheerleader for this story; thank you for telling everyone about it and for always talking to me about books, no matter how boring I can be.

Thank you to my in-laws for always being so excited about everything bookish I talk about, even if you don't really understand why, and when I haven't shut up for thirty minutes.

Thank you to Caitlin, my first writing friend who has helped me out of one too many plot holes. You're the best. I'm manifesting we get to go on tour together one day.

I am endlessly grateful for the authors who have shaped me into who I am today, and whose work holds pride of place on my bookshelves. Sarah J Maas, Olivie Blake, Kate Dramis, Victoria Aveyard, thank you for creating such incredible worlds to escape into.

Thank you to Sara and the Cheshire Novel Prize. I learnt so much from you and I will be forever grateful.

And Wilson, who isn't with us anymore. Thank you for sitting with me through hours of plot holes and of course reminding me when to take a break. I'm sure there are echoes of you between these pages. Love you, Winks.

And finally, and most importantly, to my readers. Hi guys, it's so nice to meet you! If you made it this far, thank you thank you thank you! It is a privilege to be able to write the stories of my heart, and I hope you'll stick around. This is just the beginning.